THE LAST GONDOLA

OTHER NOVELS OF VENICE BY EDWARD SKLEPOWICH

EDWARD SKLEPOWICH

THE LAST GONDOLA

THOMAS DUNNE BOOKS / ST. MARTIN'S MINOTAUR
NEW YORK

THOMAS DUNNE BOOKS.

An imprint of St. Martin's Press.

www.minotaurbooks.com

Library of Congress Cataloging-in-Publication Data
Sklepowich, Edward.
    The last gondola / Edward Sklepowich—1st ed.
        p. cm.
    ISBN 0-312-29049-7
    1. Macintyre, Urbino (Fictitious character)—Fiction. 2. Americans—Italy—Fiction. 3. Venice (Italy)—Fiction. 4. Biographers—Fiction. 5. Nobility—Fiction. I. Title.

PS3569.K574L375 2003
813'.54—dc21

                                                                            2003041268

First Edition: July 2003

10   9   8   7   6   5   4   3   2   1

To Nancy Lendved,
with love, admiration, and gratitude
for all she's done
for me and mine

I will go out this evening in my cloak and gondola—there are two good Mrs. Radcliffe words for you.

—LORD BYRON

THE LAST GONDOLA

PROLOGUE
Urbino Obsessed

O n this February afternoon the Caffè Florian whispered a
history of plots and intrigues into Urbino Macintyre's
receptive ear as he sat across from the Contessa da Capo-
Zendrini.

The maroon banquettes, the elegant portraits, the painted
mirror, the wood wainscots, the decorated arched vaults, and
the parquet floor—all of them surely had a tale to tell, each
from its own point of view.

"Murder, theft, betrayal, adultery, treason, revolution,"
Urbino recited. "All hatched here in the Chinese salon. From
the eighteenth century to this very minute, you can be sure."

His gaze swept the room for a likely culprit, but the three
Germans who had been sitting at a nearby table had left without his noticing it.

"No one here but the two of us, *caro*," the Contessa said.
"And the only thing I've been contemplating in this den of
duplicity is shaking you violently by the shoulders. You're
doing it again."

"Doing what?"

"Brooding about that dreadful man in his palazzo in San
Polo, Samuel Possle."

The Contessa was right. Dominating his thoughts this

afternoon, as so often lately, was the person she had named. Urbino could think of little else these days but an elderly American whom he had never seen in the flesh. The recluse had rejected all of his overtures. The success or failure of his next biography—in fact its very existence—depended on gaining access to the man.

"Obsession is a terrible thing," the Contessa observed. "Lost in your own world and not seeing the real one in front of you."

Urbino felt properly chastised. He smiled at his good friend. "But if you mean not seeing you, you're wrong. You look lovely."

Indeed, she did. With her stylishly coifed honey blonde hair and slanted gray eyes, she was in the full prime of her middle years and carried it with grace and elegance. Her deep purple dress of simple lines and her onyx necklace bestowed a subdued, even penitential air, that suited this time of the year after the festivities of *carnevale*. But yet, as his closer scrutiny now detected, beneath the surface of her repose ran a current of uneasiness.

And then in a rush, like birds coming home to roost, overlooked clues that had been accumulating this afternoon descended on him. Her almost imperceptible sighs, her fleeting frowns, and perhaps, most telling of all, the untouched petits fours. No mood of any kind had ever interfered with her enjoyment of them. He refrained from articulating any of these perceptions, however, knowing that the Contessa, like himself, liked to play a game of hide-and-seek with her own emotions.

"Samuel Possle would be a real feather in my cap," he said, succumbing to the gravitational pull of his own problems as he waited for the appropriate time to bring up hers. "Venice's oldest expatriate. Think of it."

"Its most ancient reprobate," the Contessa corrected with a barely discernible edge to her voice. "Isolated in that house of his like that disreputable marquis you're so fond of."

"Good old Des Esseintes. He's a duke," Urbino said with a smile. "You haven't brought him up in a long time."

"Because I don't want to contribute to your confusion between art and life—if you can call that decadent book art, that is."

The Contessa was referring to Huysmans's *Against Nature,* a French novel about a reclusive bachelor. Urbino, purging the book of its many excesses, had patterned his own secluded life in Venice after it. It had been a bone of contention between them ever since they had first met twenty years ago at a reception for the Biennale.

"Well," the Contessa said, with an air of resignation, "you've always had an obsessive personality as long as I've known you. I should have taken warning from the way you would always talk about the mad duke as if he were a living, breathing person instead of some outdated character in a novel."

"But Samuel Possle *is* living and breathing," Urbino pointed out, "at least at the moment. You'll have to admit that my obsession is more justified in his case."

"I'll admit nothing," the Contessa replied.

Urbino took a consolatory sip of sherry and looked out into the square.

What Napoleon had called the finest drawing room of Europe looked more suited to aquatic engagements than social ones. Deep pools of water mirrored a leaden sky, a slice of gold-and-blue clock tower, and jagged ribbons of narrow arches and rounded windows. Elevated planks marched past the Basilica to provide dry passage. The Piazza was almost empty, and the people strolling beneath the arcades and looking in the shop windows were mainly Venetians. This was one of the blessedly dead times of the year for the city. Mardi Gras had brought *carnevale* to its wild end two weeks ago. Tourists and student groups wouldn't begin to descend for another month.

"These gray days are seeping into my soul," the Contessa lamented. "And it's still only February!"

She gave a little shiver despite the overheated room and glanced down at the petits fours. "You've noticed that I haven't eaten one," she said.

She might just as well have said that she had no patience with their tacit game of concealment.

"I've noticed more than I've let on, Barbara. Either you're going to tell me what's troubling you or I'll have to resort to some form of torture," Urbino replied.

"As if you've been so eager to know! And speaking of torture, hasn't it been just that to listen to you go on and on about Samuel Possle? You've barely given me a chance to say anything. Before you bring up his name again, let me just tell you in no uncertain terms that I may be losing my mind. There!"

Melodrama was one of the notes that the Contessa often liked to strike, but this afternoon there was more appeal than provocation in her words. Her eyes seemed suddenly glazed with fatigue.

"Didn't I say the gondola was madness?" Urbino teased in the hope of dispelling her mood. The Contessa had recently given him nothing less extravagant than a gondola in commemoration of their friendship.

"I wish that were the extent of it," she responded, with a rueful smile. "I'm all too serious. We need to talk. You keep hinting that you need my help with Possle. Well, *caro*, I need yours with something much more serious. But I'd like a fresh pot of tea before I say anything more."

After this was supplied, along with a sherry for Urbino, she began to explain.

"I have to go back to about three weeks before the beginning of *carnevale*. You and Habib were so involved in getting the Palazzo Uccello ready for the celebration that I kept quiet."

Habib was Habib Laroussi, a young Moroccan artist who

was living at the Palazzo Uccello with Urbino. He had left for Morocco a few days after *carnevale* to arrange for the shipment of his work to be exhibited at the Biennale in June.

"It all began with the silver cascade you gave me. You haven't seen me wear it recently, have you?"

Urbino gave an involuntary start when she mentioned the necklace of beaten silver ovals from Marrakech. The necklace, as well as the Contessa herself, had a connection to a recurring dream that had been disturbing his sleep during the past few weeks. The dream also involved Samuel Possle, the object of his desires. More and more often he was sleeping through the seven o'clock and seven-thirty bells that pealed over the city every morning. The Contessa had become aware of his changed routine, but not the disquieting reason behind it, for he had been accustomed to calling her at an early hour, but seldom did so these days.

"No," he said, averting his eyes, "but I didn't think anything of it."

"Well, you should have! I'm sorry," she apologized, although Urbino had hardly registered her vehemence; he had been too concerned that she might notice his own reaction of surprise. At the moment he did not want to explain why her reference to the necklace had disconcerted him.

"You know how much I love that necklace. I wanted to wear it for the reception at the Casa Goldoni. But it wasn't in my jewelry box. I put it there after I wore it at the Feast of the Salute in November—or I think I did. And now it can't be found. We've turned the house upside down."

"Surely you've mislaid it."

"If it were that simple! It's so confusing. I don't know what's going on. There have been other things."

"Other things? Other pieces of jewelry?"

"No. Items of clothing. One of my favorite dresses, for one thing. The mauve-and-blue tea dress. I don't think I've seen it since we went to the film festival. And my Regency scarf is gone, too! And of all things, my old slouch hat with the flowers." She stared blankly at him. "And it was so strange, *caro*. As soon as I missed the silver cascade, I noticed that I was missing these other things. I went through my whole wardrobe to see if anything else was gone, but how could I tell? What I put Silvia through! She was mumbling under her breath for days afterward." Silvia was her personal maid. "I just know that I'm going to miss something else, probably a lot more, any one of these days."

"I hate to say it, Barbara, but someone in the house must have taken them. But why that particular necklace? You have so many other pieces of jewelry that are obviously much more valuable. It's a bit of a puzzle. And why take your used clothes, exquisite though they are? Strange, but we know all too well the kind of things that can happen, even at the Ca' da Capo."

This was Urbino's way of reminding her of the violence associated with a member of her staff, which had been his most personally troubling case to date.

She shook her head.

"Not this time. I almost wish that were the case. If it were only the necklace or some other piece of jewelry, I could accept the possibility that someone had stolen them, even someone in the house. But as you say, why would anyone in his right mind take used clothing? Don't you see what this means? I'm sailing into the darkness! I'm losing my mind!"

"I would say, my dear friend," Urbino replied, restraining an involuntary smile at her exaggeration, "that you're losing items of your clothing and one piece of jewelry. If they haven't been stolen, it could be a hoax of some kind, a peculiar one, I admit. I'd advise you to reconsider what I said about your staff."

"But how do I know that I haven't taken these things myself and—and put them somewhere?" she asked, ignoring the thrust of his comment.

"Mislaid them. But of course."

"Not mislaid them, no! Taken them, I said, and put them somewhere or tossed them away, deliberately but—but unconsciously," she finished more feebly than she had begun. "My mind has been getting a little clouded lately. I forgot an appointment with my dressmaker last month, and Vitale tells me that I never asked him to see that the door knocker was repaired, and I was so sure that I had."

"You're reading too much into everything. We're all absentminded from time to time, and as far as your clothes are concerned—"

"And sometimes," she interrupted, "I'm afraid I'm going to forget somebody's name, someone I know as well as myself. On top of everything I have these *conversazioni* beginning next week."

Urbino now understood why his friend had become needlessly fixated on her memory. She was delivering three informal talks at the Venice music conservatory where she had studied before marrying the late Conte. At the Contessa's request, however, Urbino would be attending only the last one, when she would give a musical concert. It would distract her, she said, to have him in the audience for the other occasions. Her fear that her memory was weakening was surely just one more example of her anxiety about her ability to perform.

"You'll be splendid," Urbino reassured her. "You'll remember things about those days that most people want to forget. There's nothing to worry about. I would have noticed something long before you."

"In usual circumstances, yes, that's what they say; but the way that you've been so engrossed with Samuel Possle, as if there's nothing else under the sun? Samuel Possle this and Samuel Possle that? Probably creeping around outside the Ca' Pozza at night with your elegant pencil flashlight and haunting it in the daytime as well? No, don't be so sure that you would have noticed anything."

Urbino retreated into a sip of his sherry. Fortunately, the

Contessa didn't realize that, in a fashion, Possle was a ghost sitting next to them even here in Florian's. Urbino felt he could almost reach out and touch the old expatriate.

He raised his eyes and saw his own reflection in the mirror opposite.

"And don't forget," he said, turning his attention back to the Contessa, who had been staring at him with expectation, "that your doctors in Geneva gave you a clean bill of health. That was right before Christmas."

"A clean bill of physical health," she emphasized. "These things creep up on you. Then—then they leap! And don't tell me I'm too young," she added, raising her voice. "I'm not!"

She looked bewildered, caught as she was between her vanity and her need for sympathy. "I don't mean that I'm old, you understand. What I mean is—is—" She broke off.

"That it can begin at a relatively young age" was Urbino's offering. "Yes, even as young or as old as mine."

The Contessa had always shrouded the actual, incriminating number of her age in mystery, but according to Urbino's computations, it was almost two decades more than his own. If she had already reached sixty, as he strongly suspected, she had carried it off without any obvious celebration or depression.

"Ah, you give and you take away, but, yes, you're right. You understand how I feel then, and why you have to help me. You have to find out what's happening!"

"I'll help in whatever way I can, but it won't be a challenge to my detecting abilities, I'm sure. Whatever answer we find will have nothing to do with this nonsense about your memory. Let it be. Your *conversazioni* are going to be a great success, I tell you."

A tentative smile brightened her face. "And you're going to get your interviews with Samuel Possle," she matched him. "I'll think of something. I'll take down that Turkish scimitar in the gallery, the one handed down in Alvise's family, and cut through the Gordian knot for you. Just you see!"

"A scissors might be all you need! Or a few strings pulled here and there."

"If they haven't disintegrated after all these years." She punctuated this with a nervous laugh. "You'll help me, and I'll help you. Isn't that what we've always done? What we'll always do? One for all and all for one!"

"You make a most attractive Musketeer."

"But we're not three, are we? Habib isn't here. Are you going to be all right with him gone for a while? I'm afraid you might sink deeper into the waters of your own obsession without him around."

"But I have the mystery of your disappearing wardrobe to exercise my mind. My thread of sanity," he joked. "I'll get to the bottom of it." He raised his sherry glass. "And with or without Habib, we're inseparable. Never doubt that."

It was what the Contessa wanted to hear.

"Like Venice and water!" she threw out.

"Like masks and *carnevale!*" Urbino countered.

"Like gondolas and—and—"

The Contessa faltered. The almost inevitable word "death" washed over Urbino.

"And gondoliers," she offered.

"Like gondoliers and '*O Sole Mio*'!"

A smile of satisfaction and relief lit the Contessa's face. Urbino took her hand. Quietly he sang in his uneven tenor, " '*Che bella cosa na jurnata è sole, n'aria serena dopo na tempesta!*' "

The two friends looked out into the square.

But the scene seemed about to betray the optimistic words of the song. If they were to judge from the dark, menacing clouds being driven in from the lagoon, another storm would soon batter their frail, serene city.

PART ONE
IN HIS CLOAK AND GONDOLA

I must get in," Urbino said to himself at two o'clock in the morning. He stood on a narrow, humpbacked bridge in a remote corner of the San Polo district.

The full moon broke through the clouds and splayed a solemn brightness over the scene.

The Ca' Pozza was wrapped in silence, and completely dark behind its windows. Urbino felt a thrill of fear and a wave of melancholy. Even if he had not known who was within its walls, hidden from public view all these years and filled with so many memories that time would soon snatch away, the building would have stirred in him the same mixture of feelings.

Urbino closed his umbrella. Surrounded by puddles of water and the reek of moldering stone and vegetation, he was far removed from the civilized comforts of Florian's, where he had sat with the Contessa yesterday afternoon.

He peered down at the black waters of the canal. Scraps of vegetables drifted in the direction of the Grand Canal. Mesmerized by their slow motion, he watched them until they passed from view under the bridge. He was now staring at the faint, masklike reflection of his face.

Vaguely uneasy, he jerked his head up. His unexpected

image in any reflecting surface invariably disconcerted him as it had at Florian's. It always left him feeling, for many confusing moments afterward, that he wasn't the person he thought he was but someone else who only looked the same.

He focused his attention on the silent and secretive Ca' Pozza to dispel the wave of anxiety coursing through him.

The building with its crumbling broad front, eroded stone loggia, and rows of curtained windows frowned down at him from above the small canal as if it disapproved of his intrusive gaze.

Urbino had always found the San Polo district, choked by a loop of the Grand Canal, to be filled with more of a sense of death and decay than anywhere else in Venice. Since his preoccupation with Samuel Possle and his dilapidated palazzo, this feeling had deepened and darkened.

If the bridges and alleys seemed more twisted, the covered walkways danker, and the Rialto farther away, it was because of the baleful influence cast by the Ca' Pozza. Even the nearby Fondamenta delle Tette, where women once bared their breasts to entice customers away from homosexual prostitutes, somehow thickened with more sensual associations.

Whether penetrating the Ca' Pozza's secrets would dispel the building's peculiar influence or increase it, Urbino had no way of knowing; but he wouldn't be at peace until he gained access. Since Possle never came out, Urbino would have to get in. It was as simple—and as complicated—as that.

How far he was prepared to go to achieve this end seemed ominously foreshadowed by the urgency of the phrase he kept repeating to himself in an almost audible voice. "I must get in. I must get in."

He was unable to pull his gaze away from the building. He let his imagination wander through rooms he had never seen, seeking out the old man as he might be sleeping and dreaming of days gone by or sitting with a pile of yellowed letters.

Urbino knew as much or as little about Samuel Possle as

everyone else seemed to know or had been allowed to. His background was wealthy but otherwise undistinguished. His family had made a fortune in the shrimp industry in South Carolina. Since he was an only child, it had all come into his hands with the sudden deaths of his parents in the forties. The larger world beyond Venice had heard of him, not for anything he had accomplished, but rather for his former glittering entourage and for what he had always seemed to promise. Time was running out on the promise as he approached his ninetieth year.

Possle, a frequent guest of the rich and famous, and the indefatigable host of sensational gatherings at the Ca' Pozza, appeared briefly, but memorably, in the memoirs and biographies of many people now long dead. His marriage to a German poet had ended in divorce decades ago, and he had never remarried. After all his years of high society, he had gone into seclusion.

He was supposedly working on a book he had once made the mistake of saying was a "meditation on time and the human emotions" intentionally evoking Proust's *Remembrance of Things Past*. However, his version, he had said, would be more sensational and even longer.

Suddenly the Ca' Pozza jolted Urbino out of these thoughts. With an almost blinding flash, the tall loggia doors on the *piano nobile* were illuminated from within. A few moments later a silhouette appeared behind the curtains of one of the unshuttered doors that was closest to Urbino. The figure seemed to be staring out, although positioned as it was behind the curtains and standing in a lighted room, it was doubtful whether it could see anything.

Urbino assumed the figure was a man because the hair seemed closely cropped. It stood motionless behind the panes of the door, almost as if it were posing, and then turned slowly and presented itself in full profile.

The sex of the figure didn't become clarified, but as Urbino stared one detail drew all his attention. The figure held up to its face an object that gave every appearance of being a severed head. The nose of the head was sharp and the chin prominent; its skull was remarkably smooth, and Urbino assumed it must be completely bald.

The figure remained at the door as if to give Urbino time to take in the disturbing scene and then moved to the side and out of sight. The light was extinguished a few moments later.

Yet Urbino waited, standing on the bridge as motionless as the figure had stood at the door earlier. It was as if Urbino knew that something else would happen tonight on this visit to the Ca' Pozza. He was not proved wrong.

Suddenly shrill, high-pitched laughter assaulted his ears. Distorted though it was, it sounded more like a woman's laughter than a man's. It continued for a few moments, subsided into sobs, and then silence.

Because these disturbing sounds broke the stillness so soon after the mysterious figure at the door, the Ca' Pozza was their likely source. But as they faded, leaving behind an even more deathly silence, he realized that they could have come from the building next door that shared a wall with the Ca' Pozza and whose entrance was up the dark, narrow alley that wound its way from the bridge.

All alone in the night and with a nature that had recently become slightly superstitious under the influence of the fatalistic Habib, Urbino couldn't shake the feeling that he had been drawn here tonight to see the figure and to hear the laughter.

He drew his cloak around him against the chill and began to pick his way over the slick, uneven stones of the alley. After a few oblique turns, it would take him to the next bridge. He cast a quick glance up at the building next to the Ca' Pozza from where the laughter and sobs might have come. Not one window was lit.

He broke into a regular rhythm of walking. If he were lucky, he should now be able to get to sleep when he returned to the Palazzo Uccello. If he did, he hoped that it would be without having the dream that had been brushing its dark wings against him for so many nights and that had even cast its shadows over his rendezvous at Florian's with the Contessa.

He had not gone far when a pool of water blocked his passage. After a moment's hesitation as he considered retracing his steps, he waded through it. Water seeped over the tops of his rain shoes.

Clouds obscured the moon again, and a damp, penetrating wind from the direction of the lagoon, funneled by the narrow alleys, whined in his ears. More rain would fall before the night was over.

The *calle* ended at a canal bordered by a portico and crossed by a crooked, stone bridge. Boats moored by the mossy water steps were covered with tarpaulin and plastic. On a bright sunny day this spot was full of charm. Tourists would often congratulate themselves on having discovered the area all on their own, but at this hour of the night they would have been less enthusiastic. There were too many places for someone to be hiding, too many slippery stones that could have you falling into the canal, and too little reassurance that anyone was inside the closed old houses to come to your aid.

He entered the portico. Most of the buildings were in a poor condition and were vacant. Stucco facing had fallen off to reveal the bricks beneath. Doors and windows were boarded over, with CHIUSO painted in red letters on the doors. Narrow openings between the buildings led into a labyrinth of alleys.

As Urbino went along the passageway, being careful to watch his step in the darkness, Possle and the Ca' Pozza crept back into his mind. They had tormented him all evening at the Palazzo Uccello until, at midnight, he had ventured through the rain to San Polo.

These almost compulsive visits were his substitute for passing through the front door of the so-far impregnable building. He had done his best to keep his obsession a secret from the Contessa even though it had been a strain. He had told himself that this was only because of his concern for her peace of mind as she prepared for her upcoming *conversazioni,* but the truth was that he was both jealous of his fascination with Possle and embarrassed by it.

Ever since having taken her into his confidence, he had had to endure the kind of well-meaning banter that he had gotten a good sample of this afternoon. He felt comforted that he had her golden promise to help him in his pocket. She could very well be his last chance.

All his own attempts had failed. He had sent letters, which had been promptly returned. On one occasion he had tried a gift of flowers, on the assumption that since Possle had bought a palazzo with a garden, he must have a fondness for them. But the urn of flowers, accompanied by a note, that Urbino left at the entrance one morning, after no one had acknowledged the bell, had remained there, apparently untouched, for two subsequent days. Urbino and his gondolier had removed it.

The Contessa's efforts might not prove to be so abortive. Not only did she have contacts that she could marshal on his behalf, but she also had enjoyed a brief acquaintance with Possle. She might be able to exploit it if she were willing. After her arrival in Venice to study at the conservatory, her path had crossed with Possle's, although never at the Ca' Pozza. The Conte Alvise had put an end to the acquaintance when they became engaged. By then Possle had already made a reputation for himself as one of the city's glamorous, but morally questionable, figures, along with his friends Peggy Guggenheim and a well-known composer who had murdered his family and then killed himself. The Conte had once—

Urbino's thoughts broke off. He was not alone. Someone had been stealthily approaching the covered passageway. Part of his mind had registered a scrape against the stones of one of the alleys to his left. It sounded like a fumbled footstep and was followed by the clank, albeit muted, of something metallic.

He came to a dead halt and listened. The wind moaned. Water lapped against stone. But the other sounds weren't repeated. If they had been, he would have been less wary, but he had the impression that someone was trying not to make any further noise.

It was completely possible, given the disorienting acoustics of the city, that the sounds had come from a distance, even from over the roofs of the buildings.

Urbino, however, saw no reason not to be cautious. He was all alone at an hour of the night when his cry for help, echoing from stone and water, would have more chance of sending someone in the opposite direction than of leading him to where Urbino was in distress.

He therefore didn't remain rooted to where he was under the dark, damp passageway but strode at a brisk pace toward the bridge. He paused on the parapet, watched, and listened. He saw and heard nothing that settled his mind one way or another.

If he didn't get inside the Ca' Pozza soon, he feared he would have little relief from his own overactive imagination and his growing sense of inadequacy. Once he was inside, logic and reason would surely prevail.

With this reassuring thought, Urbino broke into an even stride that soon had him crossing the Rialto Bridge.

2

B ack at the Palazzo Uccello half an hour later, Urbino sat in the library with his cat, Serena, on his lap, and read a passage in a late nineteenth-century guidebook that he had practically memorized:

> *Upon emerging from the* sottoportico *we turn left along the* fondamenta *until we reach the Ponte Cammello. On the other side of the bridge is the Ca' Pozza (XVII cent.), built by one of the followers of Longhena and once the home of the Sanguinetti family and the Bombicci family. It possesses one of the most ample and magnificent gardens of Venice, which, on occasion, used to be open to the public. The Ca' Pozza has a broad front dominated by a heavily pilastered and arched balcony on the* piano nobile. *One explanation for its name is that the Ca' Pozza is built on the site of a pool, or* pozza, *of miraculous fresh water that flowed from the marshes when Venice was founded.*

Urbino closed the book and stroked Serena as he reflected about the passage.

Despite his search through not only his own library but also the Biblioteca Marciana and the State Archives, he hadn't found anything that added much more than this to the description and history of the Ca' Pozza, at least not anything that would be of much use to him.

In any case, it was not its distant past he was interested in uncovering, but the period since the 1950s when Possle had acquired it. Urbino believed in the close, almost uncanny similarity that could develop between a house and its owner. If this belief had been formed in childhood when he had read Poe's *Fall of the House of Usher*, it had been reinforced by his experience over the past twenty years with his own Palazzo Uccello and the Contessa's Ca' da Capo-Zendrini.

In fact, the Palazzo Uccello had its secrets along these lines. The Contessa had touched on one of them at Florian's when she had chided him about the character of the decadent duke he admired so much from the French novel. The story of the neurotic aristocrat who retires to his mansion outside of Paris to lead a self-contained, eccentric life of the mind and senses had influenced Urbino at a young age.

When he inherited the Palazzo Uccello, he realized that to live in a palazzo in this museum city would be to go the character of Des Esseintes one better. Behind its walls he was far above the crowds yet close enough to the flow of life to make him feel snug in his solitude.

Things had changed since Habib had moved to the Palazzo Uccello, but he still felt that he inhabited a delightful ark within the greater one of Venice, and he remained indebted to the book.

He had even devoted part of his library to various editions of the novel and to critical and biographical studies of its notorious author. His eyes moved to the far corner where the books gleamed behind their glass case. On the wall next to the shelves were several illustrations of scenes from the book. One of them was a watercolor Urbino had executed himself many years ago.

Yes, he said to himself, to know more about the Ca' Pozza

would be to know more about Possle, just as the same could be said about the Palazzo Uccello and himself. To gain access to the old building would be to become privy to the very personality and character of the man.

Trying not to disturb Serena, who had fallen asleep, Urbino reached for several pages of a magazine article. He had clipped them from an old magazine he had found at the Ca' da Capo-Zendrini. It was typical of a few other articles written about Possle over thirty years ago.

It was filled with photographs of Possle and his friends and acquaintances socializing in various places in Venice and at the Ca' Pozza. Most of the revelers were now dead from either suicide or natural causes or, in one much publicized case, murder when thieves broke into her apartment by the Park Monceau in Paris.

One photograph showed a smiling Possle, surrounded by friends, walking across the bridge of boats that connected the Zattere Embankment and the island of the Giudecca every July in celebration of the Feast of the Redeemer.

Another showed a house party at the Ca' Pozza. Men and women were ranged on two sofas in a room hung with paintings and tapestries. A young woman, whom Urbino recognized as an Italian actress who had enjoyed a brief fame many decades ago, stood facing one of the groups with her face contorted and her arms thrown in the air. The photograph was captioned "Possle's Apostles Play Charades at the Ca' Pozza."

Urbino's favorite, however, captured Possle and Peggy Guggenheim on the terrace of Guggenheim's palazzo on the Canalazzo, as the Venetians referred to the Grand Canal. Possle had his hand resting on Marino Marini's tumescent bronze horseman while Guggenheim looked at him, laughing, her eyes hidden by her Max Ernst sunglasses.

The magazine was a slick one, and the article itself was a mere accompaniment to the photographs. It provided no insight, but like all the other things Urbino had been able to find out about Possle, it whetted his appetite.

He was in sore need of a project. The ones he had recently turned his hand to had collapsed or evaporated after a month or two. He had been drifting while Habib, fortunately, had been making advances in his career and establishing a reputation for himself. Urbino had started to question his own ability to make the right choices. And then Possle, who had been there all along, right there under his nose, had captured his imagination with his possibilities one evening when Urbino was considering his own life as an expatriate in Venice. Possle would give him a chance to paint a picture of one expatriate's life so different from his own and yet with points of similarity.

It would be a departure for him. His previous biographies had been, for the most part, about well-known figures who had accomplished something with their lives. They had made a degree of difference in the world. Possle, instead, was important only for the people he had known and for the lifestyle he had led. He was, in a strange way, both trivial and significant. Urbino was determined to see what he could make of him. Anything else he might do with his time and energies paled in comparison.

He would need to fill in the gaps, to sort out fact from fiction, to reconstruct the man from all the fragments, from ruins where mainly ghosts walked. And what he might learn, from Possle or anyone else, would only be a version of the truth. Urbino would have to add his own to it.

It would be a challenge, and he needed to start with the man himself.

Somehow Possle had managed, in an age of high publicity, to remain enigmatic and elusive, and therefore all the more intriguing to Urbino.

Most of Urbino's other work had been excavations of the distant past, but with this project he would be visiting a much more recent and palpable one. The man and the house; the house and the man. Urbino wanted entry to both.

In a few days he would see someone who should be able to tell him more current things about the Ca' Pozza. As for the man himself, Urbino was putting a lot of faith in the Contessa. If she could set things in motion, his own form of boldness, often underestimated by others, and his mastery of the diplomatic arts, if not duplicity itself, would gain him the prize.

And he would do his best to find out what had happened to the Contessa's items. The more he thought about it, the more it puzzled him that clothing was missing. Someone might have coveted the cascade necklace on the mistaken assumption that it would bring him a lot of money, but why would anyone have gone to the risk of stealing used clothing, even if it did include a Regency scarf?

Yes, there was a bit of a mystery here, but Urbino had no doubt that the Contessa's mind was not the problem. It was as sharp as ever.

When Urbino went to bed, it was not to have a restful night. He suffered his dream again.

He was in a room whose proportions were irregular, a room crowded with furniture, books, and tapestries. On angular chairs sat two figures, immobile like royalty in a Byzantine mosaic and dressed in flowing white clothes. One was a small man with the features of Samuel Possle in his prime. The other was veiled. Urbino assumed it was a woman because the Contessa's silver cascade was unmistakable against her chest.

The Contessa, dressed in a gold-sequined, embroidered silk vest he had brought back for her from Morocco, approached the two figures. Before she reached them the tapestries caught fire. Smoke filled the room. The Contessa collapsed to the floor.

Urbino always awoke at this point, covered in sweat and with his heart pounding. It was no different tonight.

4

The next morning Natalia, Urbino's housekeeper and cook, had a woebegone expression on her round face. She held out a small piece of metal in her palm. "I broke the key in the front door again, Signor Urbino. I don't know what's the matter with me."

"Don't worry about it. That lock's difficult to turn. It's almost happened to me. Call Demetrio Emo," he said, as he was about to walk away.

"Oh, I don't like that man!" Natalia cried out. "He makes me uncomfortable."

"He's Gildo's uncle," Urbino said, knowing how fond Natalia was of his young gondolier.

"Like night and day, those two," she grumbled. "Very well, but please try to be here. I don't want to be alone with him."

"Have him come at noon. I should be back from the Contessa's before then."

She gave him a doubtful look and went back to the kitchen.

On his way to the Ca' da Capo-Zendrini on the Grand Canal,
Urbino felt alternately warmed and chilled, depending on
whether he was walking in the sunshine or through the shadows of the damp alleys. Even on the hottest days of summer,
they never seemed to relinquish their dankness.

The streets were busy, especially when he reached the Rio
Terrà Maddalena on the main route to the train station. He
greeted friends and acquaintances, and stopped in a bar for a
quick glass of Cynar. This brown liqueur brewed from artichokes, with its medicinal taste, was particularly effective in
restoring the warmth stolen from him by the narrow Venetian
streets.

He paused afterward on a bridge and looked toward the
Grand Canal. A gondola, making its way from the large waterway deeper into the Cannaregio district, passed beneath the
bridge. It took a few moments to recognize the gondola as his
own and the gondolier as Gildo, with an abstracted expression
clouding his handsome face. Urbino called out to him, but he
couldn't attract the young man's attention. Urbino went to the
other side of the bridge and called again, but the self-absorbed
gondolier kept staring straight ahead from the poop.

Then Urbino noticed a large, curved piece of wood lying

against the cushions of the gondola. It was a *forcola* or the oar-lock of a gondola. Another *forcola* was properly attached to the gunwale of Urbino's gondola, and Gildo was maneuvering the oar in the waters of the canal with the help of its surfaces.

Urbino watched the gondola until it passed out of sight in the direction of the Palazzo Uccello. He left the bridge and turned down an alley that would bring him to the Ca' da Capo-Zendrini more quickly than the broad street of shops and hotels.

He wondered what Gildo was doing with the *forcola*. Could it be a replacement for the one already on the gondola? If so, why hadn't he mentioned it? And why did the young man look so melancholy these days? He had caught the same expression on his face several times recently when the gondolier had been doing work around the Palazzo Uccello or guiding the boat.

He made a reminder to himself to look into the situation.

Urbino found the Contessa in the sun-washed morning room staring blankly at a folio-sized maroon leather volume. It was no time to trouble her with his concerns about Possle and the Ca' Pozza.

"Have you noticed that anything else has gone missing?" he asked. "Any jewelry?"

"No, but I'm waiting to discover that something else has. I've become nervous every time I go to look for something to wear."

She put the book down on a table.

"Your days of waiting and worrying will soon be over," Urbino said in as cheery a voice as he could muster. "We're going to find an answer that will clear away all your ridiculous doubts and fears. I'm going to start right now."

The Contessa gave a tentative smile. "You are?"

"Right here at the Ca' da Capo. But you have to give me free rein to ask your staff whatever questions I want. Your staff might be reluctant to speak. Why don't you have a few words with them first."

As Urbino waited for her to return, he walked around the cozy room. He was tempted to pour himself a drink, but he had already indulged in the Cynar and had corrected his morning coffee with some anisette, although he had become enough of an Italian over the years to consider it as almost a property of coffee itself.

He played scattered notes on a fin de siècle Viennese piano, set the antique metronome going for a few seconds, and glanced through the music sheets, all yellowed with age. One of them was his favorite Bach sonata. He assumed the Contessa was putting together her musical program that would end her series of *conversazioni* at the conservatory.

He examined the watercolors on one wall. They were mainly landscapes of the English countryside, the Venetian lagoon, and the Dolomites. Two, however, depicted the Ca' da Capo-Zendrini and the Palazzo Uccello, and like the others were captured in morning light to suit the morning room. These paintings of the Contessa's and Urbino's residences, as well as many of the others, had been done by the Contessa's friends who descended on Venice every year with their collapsible easels, paint boxes, and amateurism. But the Contessa displayed them here as proudly as she did the Girtins, Cotmans, and one splendid Turner that adorned the wall.

He picked up the maroon volume that the Contessa had set down on the table. It was a scrapbook of her days at the conservatory. He dropped into an armchair to look at it.

The book was filled with her acceptance letter from the conservatory, evaluations from tutors and coaches, photographs with friends and conservatory members, tickets and program notes from theaters in Venice, Milan, and Florence, a review of her première student performance from the local newspaper, congratulatory letters, pages of musical notation, and, on the last page, a faded, gilt-edged calling card engraved with the name of the Conte Alvise Severino Falier da Capo-Zendrini.

The young Barbara Spencer's talents at the conservatory had drawn the attention of the count, and their marriage had ended her days there.

Urbino turned back to a photograph of the young Contessa. It showed a patrician-featured girl, who had not so much changed since those days as gradually aged into the mature look already present in the otherwise fresh face.

"Contemplating what I used to be?" came the Contessa's voice from the door.

"Don't fish for compliments. You know how little you've changed, considering."

"Ah yes, *caro*, we mustn't forget the qualification. A great many things must be taken into account." She took the album from his hands and clasped it against her chest. "I've been going through all my memorabilia from those days. It's my attempt to be as sure as I can be that I'll remember enough to talk about."

"As if that was ever a problem," Urbino replied.

"Ah, the old days. 'The hand moves over the face every ten years,' Garbo said. But other changes are far less dignified. No, don't say anything," she protested, although Urbino had given no indication that he was about to agree or disagree. "I'm determined to be as strong as possible in the face of the inevitable."

"As if you really believe such nonsense! *Mens sana in corpore sano*. That's you, my dear Barbara. I know it and so do you."

A pleased smile curved her mouth.

"It leaves us with a bit of a mystery though, doesn't it? So begin to put your talents to work. You can hold your interviews in the *salotto blu*. I've made it clear to everyone that they're to tell you whatever you want to know. And don't worry about me listening outside the door. Even if I wanted to, I have a dress fitting in the Dorsoduro in half an hour. I'll take a water taxi so that you won't have to wait for Pasquale to speak with him."

7

If the Contessa's personal maid gave Urbino one more evasive answer, he was afraid he was going to say, like some superintendent in a nineteenth-century novel, "Now, young woman, listen to me—and mind you speak the truth!"

Instead he asked in an even tone, "Exactly what do you mean when you say that things haven't been the same around the house lately?"

"Did I say that, Signor Urbino?"

Urbino gave an inward sigh. "Excuse me, Silvia. Sometimes my Italian isn't as good as it needs to be. You see," he went on, realizing at last the tack that he should take with her, "I've noticed that the Contessa hasn't been herself. I wonder what your impression has been. You seem to be a perceptive girl."

The girl perked up at this and gave him a bright smile. "Thank you, signore. Since you speak about the Contessa in that way, I confess I can agree with you. I'm worried about her these days."

"We both want to help her however we can. Why are you worried?"

"I did say that I was worried, yes," she reaffirmed to Urbino's relief. "She's very nervous. I'm with her early in the morning and late at night, and many hours in between. The

Contessa is like an actress. Oh, I mean it in the best sense. She always tries to be good and brave when she's in company, not that you are company, signore, but you understand what I mean."

Urbino nodded at what sounded like a maid's version of the saying that a mistress was never a heroine to her maid.

"As I was saying, the Contessa is a nervous type, and I mean it only in the best sense. She's sensitive, too sensitive. And it's been doing her harm. She wakes up with a sad expression on her face and goes to sleep the same way. And she becomes upset when she can't find something. I haven't known her long, not like you and my cousin Lucia, but I can see the difference, yes."

Silvia was relatively new in the Contessa's employ, having replaced Lucia when Urbino was in Morocco. Vitale, the majordomo, and Pasquale, the boatman, had also joined the Ca' da Capo-Zendrini household recently.

"The Contessa tells me that she's been missing items of her clothing and a piece of jewelry, the necklace with the silver ovals. You know the one I mean, don't you? It's not valuable at all, but it's quite lovely."

Silvia stiffened and stared back at him.

"Of course no one believes that you're in any way responsible for what's missing," Urbino added.

This was less than the truth, however, and Urbino hoped that such a simple explanation could be found. It was conceivable that an envious and malicious maid would take her employer's personal items, but his instincts told him that this wasn't what had happened at the Ca' da Capo-Zendrini.

"I hope not, signore," Silvia said curtly.

"What do you think has happened to these things?"

"We've been looking everywhere. The Contessa is the kind of person who would turn the house upside down to search for a pin. I mean it only in the best sense, of course. These days she's always asking where did I put this, where did I put that. I put everything in its correct place, I tell her, just as she wants. But I don't think she believes me."

"But some things have gone missing. Do you think some-one could be playing a trick on the Contessa?"

"A trick, signore?" Silvia seemed genuinely perplexed.

"Taking her things and hiding them, making her think they're gone, and then putting them all back again sometime later?"

Silvia looked at him with surprise. "Why would someone do that to our Contessa?"

"As a little game. So that everyone would laugh afterward, including the Contessa."

"You know the Contessa very well, Signor Urbino. She wouldn't find it amusing. She's almost sick with worry. It would be very cruel. No, perhaps the Contessa gave her things to some charity or a friend, and she doesn't remember. I mean it only in the best sense, for her kind acts are too many for her to remember every one. And her memory isn't the sharpest these days. She forgot her dressmaker's appointment last month, and she's never done that. Today I reminded her that she had another one, but she didn't seem pleased. She remem-bered quite well for herself, she said."

8

U rbino next spoke with Vitale, the majordomo. His name
could not have been more appropriate with all his evident vigor and good health.

"You can be sure I wish to help, signore," he began before
Urbino asked him anything, "but I know nothing about these
lost objects. I learned about them only a few minutes ago from
Silvia."

"The Contessa never mentioned them to you?"

Vitale shook his imposing head with its graying hair. "It
isn't something that directly concerns me. Such things are the
responsibility of Silvia."

"In some ways you're responsible for the security of the
house."

"That's true, signore, but this isn't a matter of security in
the way that you mean. The Ca' da Capo-Zendrini hasn't been
entered by any, how shall I say, *unknown* undesirable person,"
he emphasized.

His implication was clear. In his opinion the loss of the
Contessa's objects was to be explained from within the house
itself.

"But the Contessa has no electronic system to protect the
house."

This was one of the Contessa's many peculiarities when it came to the eighteenth-century building. She tried to keep it as close as possible to what it had been when the Conte had died more than twenty years ago.

"Nor is one needed, signore, even here with what is a much larger building than your own."

Urbino allowed himself an amused smile at Vitale's condescension to the Palazzo Uccello.

"Nonetheless isn't it possible for someone unknown—undesirable or otherwise—to enter the house?" Urbino persisted.

Urbino could think of some ways to get into the building, the two most obvious being through the garden or the water entrance.

"Vigilance, signor. We are most vigilant."

Urbino wondered whether the imperious Vitale was indulging in the 'royal we,' or whether he was referring to all the staff members and the Contessa as well.

"I have no doubt about that."

Urbino then asked Vitale the same question he had asked Silvia, whether someone in the house might be playing a trick on the Contessa. The majordomo's response was similar to Silvia's.

"It would be a strange thing to do, signore. We all care about the Contessa too much to play cruel games with her. And we are not children. If you will excuse me, I have something I must attend to."

"One more question. The Contessa mentioned something about a door knocker."

"A misunderstanding. The Contessa wished the old one to be replaced but forgot to tell me. It's been attended to, as you must have noticed. Good day."

9

Urbino learned nothing more of interest from any of the other staff members until he spoke with Pasquale, the boatman and chauffeur.

The young man had been hired shortly after Urbino's return from Morocco when the position had become vacant with the death of his predecessor.

Pasquale stood at attention, his white cap in his hand. He was a small, muscular man with dark eyes and crisp, black hair.

"I don't know what happens in the house," he said.

On the face of it, this comment was borne out by Pasquale's position and its circumstances. Like Gildo at the Palazzo Uccello, Pasquale had rooms on the ground floor with immediate access to the motorboat and the water; and almost all his duties, by their very nature, took him away from the Ca' da Capo-Zendrini. Yet during all the in-between hours he was free as long as he remained in the house or within close call. From time to time he took his meals with the others, if he wished.

"I understand that," Urbino said, "but you have opportunities to observe things that people like Silvia and Vitale, for example, don't."

"The view from the water, yes, it's a different view." A smile lit up Pasquale's rugged face. "As signore sees from his gondola."

Urbino nodded. He wasn't to be distracted, however. "So has this different view allowed you to observe anything that might be of help to the Contessa? Anything out of the ordinary perhaps? You know how troubled she is about her missing items."

The humor faded from the boatman's face. "Some of the others have told me. But the Contessa lost nothing from the boat," he added. "She lost nothing when she was with me."

"That appears to be the case, yes. Have you seen anyone suspicious around the water steps? That door is often unlocked. It wouldn't be impossible for someone to enter that way."

"But the doors up to the first floor are locked, signore. At least, most of the time. I have a set of keys to use, as I require. So does Vitale. But I haven't seen anything that could be of help." He paused. "Unless—but no, that was nothing."

"What were you going to say?"

"I suppose it was out of the ordinary, as you said before. Three or four months ago I brought the Contessa back from the Palazzo Uccello. It was almost midnight. A rowboat had become unmoored from the water steps of our *calle*. It had drifted near the Ca' da Capo-Zendrini. I made sure it was properly tied up for the night and went to bed."

"Was that the first time it happened?"

"To my knowledge. It's always tied up in the same place, from what I've seen. It's just an old rowboat, signore. I suppose whoever owns it doesn't think anyone would want to take it."

Before Urbino left the Ca' da Capo-Zendrini, he sought out the *androne* of the building. This was the entrance hall from the water, which in the old days used to be the main entrance of the building. It was flanked by rooms, which, in previous centuries had been warehouses, but today were storage rooms and Pasquale's apartment. A formal staircase led up to the *piano nobile*. The *androne* was decorated in a sea motif with portraits of sea captains and a frieze of a Venetian ship with the Da Capo-Zendrini coat of arms.

Urbino opened one panel of a double door ornamented with gilded sea horses. Immediately beyond were the waters of the Grand Canal and the blue-and-white-striped *pali* of the Contessa's boat landing, where the Contessa's sleek motorboat was moored to the broad steps.

The Contessa used this entrance whenever she went out in the motorboat. On the occasion of her parties, it was the point of entry into the palazzo for those of her guests who arrived by boat.

Urbino closed the door. A massive armoire carved with dolphins and seashells caught his attention. He went over to it. Inside were umbrellas, boots, and a waterproof. If so inclined, he could easily have climbed inside and, though slightly cramped, closed the door behind him.

10

Urbino hurried back to the Palazzo Uccello to keep his promise to Natalia, but as he walked over the bridge in front of the building, he saw that he was too late. The locksmith had already arrived and he was bent over the front door lock, surrounded by his tools and kit.

Demetrio Emo was an obese, baldheaded man in his early sixties with unusually pale skin and small features lost in the vast expanse of his face. But it was not his grotesque appearance that disturbed Natalia. It was his reputation. Emo had once been a priest attached to the nearby parish of San Gabriele until scandal had hounded him. Ten years ago, affairs with two women parishioners had led to censure from the bishop. Emo had left the priesthood rather than allow himself to be sent to Sicily as the bishop had ordered. Rumors had circulated for a while after he left. Some claimed he would marry one of the women, others that he still said mass in his apartment for a small group of devotees. But Emo had remained a bachelor, if not a celibate one; and whether he was conducting rites, no one had ever been able to verify.

Urbino wasn't judgmental about Emo. The locksmith was better out of the priesthood and leading the kind of life he was more suited for, although Urbino often wondered if he was proving to be as successful with women now, denuded as he was of his vestments and the allure of forbidden fruit. Urbino gave him his commerce for Emo's sake as well as for Gildo's, his nephew, who had fallen under his care since the death of both parents shortly after Emo had left San Gabriele. From what Urbino had seen, he had done a good job with Gildo, and the young man spoke well of him. Gildo bore no scars of an immoral influence.

But devout Natalia had never become reconciled to the man. She referred to him as a devil and kept her distance.

One corner of Emo's mouth twisted upward in a smile when he saw Urbino. "It seems that Natalia has more strength than you have, Signor Macintyre, maybe too much for a woman her age." Emo's voice was low and smooth. It forced Urbino to listen carefully.

"It's beyond repair this time," Emo said. "I'm putting in a new lock. The very best."

"Good."

Urbino left him to his work and went to the kitchen. At the counter Natalia was measuring out hazelnuts and dried fruits.

"He did it on purpose, Signor Urbino! He came half an hour early! He knows I don't like him! He probably knew you weren't here. You should have stayed," she said, in a wounded tone.

"But you don't seem to be punishing me, Natalia. Isn't that *panforte* you're making?"

"Go away and take care of that devil," she replied, not able to restrain a smile. "You'll have lunch whenever he decides to leave. *Sarde in saor* and *polenta* unless I change my mind and just give you a tin of tuna fish!"

Urbino returned to the ground floor and went to Gildo's quarters. They were small and wedged in beside Urbino's studio for art restoration. It was a hobby of his, but he hadn't pursued it recently. If he couldn't find more time for it by the end of the summer, he would expand Gildo's cramped living space.

The door of Gildo's apartment was wide open. Urbino called his name. There was no response. Magazines and catalogues about boats and sailing were scattered across the floor of the parlor. Several atlases weighed down a shelf, and one wall displayed a large, detailed map of the Venetian lagoon, which showed all the channels, islands, and mudbanks.

On a table beside the door was a mobile phone. Urbino had given it to Gildo as a convenience for them both.

In the middle of the floor was a *forcola*. Urbino assumed it must be the same one he had seen in the gondola with Gildo a few hours before.

Not wanting to intrude any farther into Gildo's private space, he looked at the oarlock from the doorway. When installed it would be affixed to the starboard gunwale. By deft positioning of an oar in its notches and curves, the oarsman steered the gondola in various directions. With its liquid double curves and smooth, polished surface, the *forcola,* carved from walnut wood, resembled a piece of modern sculpture. This one, however, had some flaws in its carving. Urbino was able to note them even from a distance.

"Good day, Signor Urbino."

Urbino turned around. Gildo stood a few feet away holding one of the cloths used to polish the brass and steelwork of the gondola.

He was slim with curly, reddish blond hair cut short. His face was open, handsome, and ingenuous, and touched with a melancholy that made it more appealing.

"I was just admiring the *forcola.*"

"It's not so perfect, but I like it. Please come in."

The two of them stood looking at the *forcola.* Gildo gave a barely audible sigh.

"Is there something wrong with the one on my gondola?"

"This is not for your gondola."

"Oh." Urbino paused. "Where did you get it?"

"A friend made it. He was a *remero* apprentice in the Castello district."

A *remero* was the skilled craftsman who made the oarlocks. Urbino nodded.

"But your friend should continue as an apprentice. He has a good chance of being one of the best if he sticks to it."

Gildo did not respond right away.

"It's kind of you to say that, Signor Urbino, but my friend is dead." He moved his hand over the smooth surface of the *forcola*. "No one wants it. I'll keep it here if that's all right with you."

"Of course. I was thinking before you came in about how a *forcola* wouldn't be out of place in a modern museum. I've seen things that aren't half as lovely and interesting. It has a fine form."

The melancholy expression lifted momentarily from Gildo's face. He seemed about to say something.

"Ah, here you are, Signor Macintyre," Demetrio Emo said in his soft but insistent voice. The large man had somehow crept upon them unheard. He cast a quick glance at the *forcola* and then at his nephew. "The new lock is installed. Here are the keys. Let's hope that Natalia uses less force with it."

"What do I owe you?" Urbino asked, as he pocketed the keys.

"Don't worry about it now. I'll send you a bill. Gildo and I will have a little visit before I go back to the shop." He squeezed into the room. "I haven't seen much of him lately." He threw his arm around the young man.

Urbino said good-bye and left. Before he was out of earshot, Emo said to Gildo in a tone of disapproval, "Do you think it's a good idea to have this here to look at all the time, my boy?"

The gondolier's response was lost on Urbino.

11

Two mornings later on the last day of February, a Thursday, Urbino was sitting at one of the cafés in the Campo Santa Margherita with the person he hoped would give him more information about the Ca' Pozza. She was his friend Rebecca Mondador, an architect who had helped him with the original renovations of the Palazzo Uccello.

It was a brisk day. Clouds moved quickly above the broad open space in the direction of the Madonna on the tall, red campanile of the Church of the Carmine across the rooftops. Residents of the area, most of them either elderly men and women or young mothers with children, gossiped and shopped among the stalls of the fish and vegetable markets set up beneath bright awnings. Two children with a broom and a rowboat oar were trying to dislodge a soccer ball from the bare branches of the tree outside the window of the café. From a building at the far end of the square, statues of Santa Margherita and the devil that devoured her looked down on the lively local scene.

"The Ca' Pozza and the building next door were owned by the Ruspoli family from Rome until the fifties," Rebecca was saying, her raised voice doing its best to compete with the music blasting over the café's radio. She was an attractive woman with a small, pointed face. "The Ruspolis bought them for almost nothing after the war. They completely renovated them on the inside. You know how it is. You can do anything to the interior as long as you maintain the integrity of the facade."

Rebecca, who had earned her degrees in the States, spoke excellent idiomatic English.

"I hoped to get plans and photographs, maybe before and after shots," she explained, "but there's nothing in the archives. The architect is dead, and the contractors have gone out of business."

She looked out into the square with a puzzled frown.

"In fact, it's unusual how little information there is on the renovations of either of those two buildings," she went on. "If I search around more, maybe I'll find something, but you shouldn't get your hopes up too high. This is Italy, not America. But to keep to what I know, Samuel Possle bought the Ca' Pozza back in fifty-six at a real bargain."

She named the figure. It was low, even allowing for inflation over the years.

"Maybe he gave them double that in dollars under the table," she said. "And it gets stranger. Once Possle moved in, he had most of the interior restored to what it had been before—or close to it from what I've been told. He used the same architect and contractors."

"What about the records from that renovation?"

She shook her head.

"Nothing. But I'm surprised that you didn't learn some of these things from Benedetta Razzi."

"What has she got to do with the Ca' Pozza?" Benedetta Razzi was a widow who had helped Urbino in one of his cases.

"Not with the Ca' Pozza. The building next to it. You mean you don't know? She bought it after Possle bought the Ca' Pozza."

Rebecca was referring to the building that might have been the source of the laughter and sobs the other night.

"She's not too happy with the building these days, I hear,"

Rebecca was saying. "There're been a series of break-ins in the neighborhood over the past few months and one or two muggings." Rebecca lived in San Polo but not near the Ca' Pozza. "They say it's a gang of kids. Drug related, it seems, and a teenager fell to his death from Razzi's building. She claims it's all bringing down the value of her property."

"I was in San Polo late the other night," Urbino said. "I had the feeling that someone might be following me."

"Be careful! I certainly am. These kids have mugged people even in the middle of the day. I know how you like to take your long walks, but you're not invulnerable. You've been mugged before, remember, and it was near San Giacomo dell'-Orio, wasn't it?"

Urbino nodded. San Giacomo dell'Orio was on the edge of the Santa Croce district near San Polo. This had been in the summer, in the middle of one of his investigations.

"I'll try to be careful. Benedetta Razzi, you say? Looks as if I'll pay her a visit."

"Don't forget your charm and a little gift for her children."

Rebecca was being ironic when she mentioned Razzi's children. Razzi was childless, but she had a vast collection of dolls she pampered.

One of the boys outside the café had finally managed to get the ball down, and he was kicking it around with his friend. It collided with a man in his sixties wearing a long, gray coat. He was walking from the direction of San Bàrnaba. He had a full head of snow white hair. The man smiled good-humoredly and kicked the ball back at the boys. He was carrying a large black portfolio and a small wooden box with a handle.

"Oh, it's Lino Cipri," Rebecca said.

Cipri was a painter who spent most of his time and made most of his money copying the work of other painters. He was excellent at it, and it was all very legal as long as he signed his own name to the canvas.

"Cipri's overdue on a painting for one of my clients,"

Rebecca said, as she stood up. "It's all your fault, your fault and Eugene's, that is."

During a visit at Christmas, Urbino's former brother-in-law, Eugene Hennepin, had commissioned Cipri to make a large number of copies of paintings in the Accademia Gallery and the Ca' Rezzonico. He was still working on them. Urbino was the middleman.

"I think I'll walk with him and see what's going on, if you don't mind being left alone. I'm afraid that all he can think about these days is Eugene's money. I need to impress him with his other responsibilities."

Rebecca pulled on her coat.

"By the way," she said, "how is Habib doing? I thought he would send me a postcard."

She and Habib had become close during the past year and a half.

"Give him a chance! He's fine, but busy. He'll be back in early April."

"Good. Plenty of time before the installation."

Habib was exhibiting at the Aperto, devoted to up-and-coming artists. It was mounted every Biennale at the old naval rope works near the Arsenale.

"Habib at the Biennale! Who would have thought it!" Rebecca enthused. "Give him one of these for me as soon as you see him."

She bent down and kissed him on each cheek. As she straightened up, she put her hand under his chin and lifted his face.

"You look tired, Urbino dear. Burning the midnight oil at the Palazzo Uccello?"

"Something like that," he said. Urbino had been suffering from the same dream for the past two nights.

Rebecca dashed across the square toward Lino Cipri. The painter had caught sight of her and was waiting for her to join him.

12

At three o'clock the next morning, Urbino made an attempt to loosen Possle's grip on him. Even sleep provided no relief because of his troubling dream. He had awakened from it a few minutes ago, and the faces of Possle and the Contessa were still swimming toward him, encircled by bright flames. He would not be able to get back to sleep easily. He needed to chase Possle away.

Fortified with a glass of the bourbon he saved for special occasions, he went to the library. He put Elgar's Symphony Number One on the player and sank into an old leather armchair that had once stood in his New Orleans house. Serena settled herself in his lap a few moments later.

Encouraged by the noble theme introduced in Elgar's first movement, he devoted himself to considering the Contessa's problem. He reviewed what he had learned from her staff and from the Contessa herself. The more he went over the details, few as they were, the more he realized that he needed to know several essential things before he could even hope to make any progress.

He put a time frame around the Contessa's loss of her items. She had worn the mauve-and-blue tea dress on the afternoon they had gone to the film festival on the Lido. If he remembered correctly, she had also had her slouch hat with her. It was a bit battered, but it was a personal favorite of hers. The film festival had been in early September. She had decided on the silver cascade necklace for the Feast of the Salute. That had been on November 21.

She had noticed the necklace missing in the middle of January, and in quick succession she had discovered that the other items were gone. There seemed to be a period of four and a half months. Anytime during that period her things could have been taken. He now had a rough framework to work with. In one way or another, the previous autumn was the crucial period.

As the *allegro molto* movement of the symphony began, Urbino reviewed the Contessa's schedule the past autumn. From what he could remember, she had been at the Ca' da Capo-Zendrini all that time, except for day trips to Florence and Milan, three days in Rome in late October, and a week in Geneva in early December for her medical tests. Whenever she was away for extended periods of time, Vitale gave extra vigilance to the house, or he was supposed to. Urbino had no doubt that the majordomo would emphatically inform him that he had done just that.

Urbino tried to recall the Contessa's houseguests during this period. Two young English cousins had spent several days at the Ca' da Capo-Zendrini at the time of the Regata Storica. That had been in September after the film festival. Between Christmas and New Year's the Conte's grandniece and grandnephew had stayed with her.

All these visits had fallen during the period when the objects had disappeared. He didn't think that any of the Contessa's guests had taken them, but their presence in the house would have meant less attention to security with their comings and goings.

The lyrical *adagio* movement began. Urbino leaned back and closed his eyes, stroking Serena. It was the most perfect thing Elgar had ever done, and Urbino found encouragement in the fact that he had done it in his middle years.

When the movement was over, Urbino returned his thoughts to the Contessa's items and ran through the tentative time scheme that he had put together. There would have been many opportunities for an enterprising and lucky thief to have got into the less-than-secure Ca' da Capo-Zendrini and taken the dress, scarf, hat, and necklace. But there was some comfort in having established some points of reference that could prove to be useful as he continued to look into the matter.

After awaking Serena, he got up and straightened the scattered books as the fourth movement played. Then he searched through some old newspapers and magazines. After a few minutes he found what he was looking for. They were photographs of the Contessa that had appeared that fall. They had both joked about how she had been getting a lot of positive media exposure during a relatively short period of time.

He examined the color photograph of the Contessa with some friends from Nice. It had been taken on the afternoon she had gone to the Palazzo del Cinema on the Lido. She looked fresh and pretty in her mauve-and-blue tea dress. She was carrying her slouch hat with the flowers. Another photograph, this one in black and white, caught her at Santa Maria del Giglio. The snowy domes of the Salute were in the background on the other side of the Grand Canal. Around her neck was the silver cascade necklace. She somehow made it look appropriate for the celebration of health and good fortune. In a third photograph, in color, she wore her pashmina and silk Regency scarf on the loggia of the Ca' da Capo-Zendrini. It had been taken the Sunday of the Regata Storica. Urbino and Habib were standing beside her.

All the photographs had appeared in the local newspaper and supplements.

13

E *ccolo!"* came a woman's voice as the long, black body and bright steel beak of Urbino's gondola slid past the embankment the next morning. *"L'americano!"*

If Urbino had been regarded as an eccentric in all the years he had been living in Venice, to his own secret amusement he had become even more of one recently because of his gondola. The only people who rode in style in gondolas these days were tourists for their requisite forty-five minutes and a photograph by the Bridge of Sighs. Even wealthy residents had long since abandoned their private ones. Collective gondolas might ferry Venetians across the Grand Canal at strategic points, but such hurried, utilitarian passage hardly counted as a gondola ride, not in the old-fashioned sense.

And it was precisely its old-fashioned associations that had inspired the Contessa to make her gift.

"You'll seem like someone from another world," she had said, during the gondola's maiden voyage. "Gliding out into the canals like a spirit from the past, just the way you entered my life. *Where has this young man come from?* I thought. And here we are now. Two lovers of Venice, and one gondola between us. But beware, *caro,"* she had said, touching his arm beneath the cloak. "The gondola is yours and so will be most of the talk. No matter how often I go out with you, people will know you for what you are. But you'll find it all delightful."

It hadn't been delightful at first, not for someone as temperamentally shy as Urbino. He had only gradually become accustomed to the smiles, stares, and comments like the one the woman had just made. Even so, he knew he would never feel completely at ease. For if riding around in a gondola was romantic and graceful, it was also more than a little proud and self-indulgent, especially when the gondola was your own and you had the services of your private gondolier.

The only thing that might have made it worse was if the gondola was any color but the customary dead black and if Gildo, like the gondoliers in a Carpaccio painting, wore a red jacket, checkered tights, and a plumed cap, and broke out into spontaneous song.

But despite the unwelcome attention and jokes, Urbino had taken to this new, or rather old, mode of transport. Although it could never take the place in his heart of his rambling walks, its vague air of invalidism suited that part of him that was not so much passive as receptive and observant. His mind, which by its nature was always seeking connections and making metaphors, often imaged the craft as a kind of drifting palanquin, with a lone gondolier instead of two bearers and with a *forcola* and an oar instead of poles. Yet on other days, even ones less dark and gloomy than this one, Lord Byron's description of "a coffin clapt in a canoe" seemed much more apt although much less consoling.

Most of the times he had ventured out in the gondola so far, it had been with the *felze* attached, as it was on this gray day on the first of March. Although the small, covered cabin was designed as a protection against bad weather, it had additional attractions for Urbino. It encouraged his musings. From behind its shutters, he had the luxury of seeing without being seen.

It was not hard for Urbino to feel, for long delicious moments afloat in his gondola, like a pasha reclining against plump Oriental cushions. He would fantasize about being rowed to some secluded unfamiliar canal unmarked on any maps or to somewhere far away in the lagoon where he could reconstruct the absent city in his imagination.

Urbino straightened up against the dark blue cushions. He peered through the slats to try to glimpse the woman who had drawn attention to his passage, but all he saw was a piece of crumbling wall, mossy water steps, a tarpaulin-covered row-boat, and the low-hanging branches of a tree, all slowly and dreamily sliding by.

Ever since he had taken to the water in this fashion, Venice had become wrapped again in the same delicious confusion as it had been for him once. Familiarity had stolen some of the city's mystery, and now he was regaining it through the Contessa's unpredictable and extravagant gift.

Pasquale's comment about the different view from the water came back to him as Gildo gave a sharp, warning cry and brought the gondola around the corner of a canal. Weathered, rose-colored brick moved past. Exactly where they were, he didn't know, except that they were *di là del Canale*, on the other side, as the Venetians referred to the one that didn't include San Marco.

As he continued to watch the scene, or what the narrow apertures of his womblike space permitted him to see, he fell into a languorous mood. He was soon almost asleep, fatigued as he was by his recurring dream of Possle and the veiled woman and the Contessa in a room that blazed into flames.

His mind now inevitably drifted toward Possle and all the things that he might learn if the doors of the Ca' Pozza were ever opened to him.

The shouts of children playing football in a square startled Urbino into fuller awareness. He stared through the cabin opening to the gondola's prow where the steel *ferro*, with its curved blade and seven blunt prongs, sliced through the morning air. In an exercise that entertained him from time to time, he idly speculated about the possible meaning of its unusual shape. But whether the baroque-looking *ferro* was merely a counterweight to the gondolier on the poop, a device to measure the height of bridges, or, more exotically, a vestige of Egyptian funeral barques was fortunately unresolvable. Although Urbino's mind was one that preferred answers, this little mystery of the *ferro* didn't trouble him. Even if he were able to reach an answer, it would not be a disturbing one. And nothing was at stake. If only the mystery of the Contessa's lost items were the same, he thought as he rearranged a cushion behind his back.

He had not yet given her the details of what he had learned from her staff. The Contessa, absorbed in her preparations for her first *conversazione* the coming Friday, a week from today, hadn't pressed him. But he was determined to speak with her tomorrow.

He was ashamed to admit it, but he was grateful for the Contessa's problem. It gave his mind something to exercise itself on other than Possle. For months now, almost everything he did, everything he picked up to read, every painting he saw, every walk he took, had seemed to lead him in some way to the Ca' Pozza and its occupant. Yes, he said to himself in the dark little cabin, it was a welcome tonic to be involved in at least one thing that didn't relate to the old recluse.

A few seconds later, however, a glance through the shutters revealed how little he could escape his obsession. Looming up from the canal's edge and doubled in its waters were the crumbling walls of the Ca' Pozza.

When he had pulled away from the Palazzo Uccello, he had given Gildo no destination. Yet here they were, gliding past the coveted building. On previous occasions when he had directed Gildo to take them through San Polo, he had asked the gondolier to slow down as they approached the Ca' Pozza. Gildo, perhaps to please him, was slowing the gondola now. It rocked gently from side to side.

Urbino angled the shutters so that he could see the upper stories of Possle's building. The attic frustrated his scrutiny; it displayed a row of darkly curtained squares. The windows of the *piano nobile* were hardly more cooperative, but at least they were larger, arched, and draped, with one exception, in lighter material. He searched the row of tall doors of the stone loggia above the canal. At one of them the figure had appeared the other night, the figure that had seemed to be holding a severed head. It had been a ridiculous notion, he now reassured himself.

So much of his life was lived in the mind, in his imagination, that it sometimes colored even the barest of realities. He was all too frequently in a state of mild disappointment or fleeting confusion. So far he had always eventually returned to the proper balance, but he feared that someday the necessary efforts on his part would become much more strenuous than they had been so far and less capable of producing the desired results.

These thoughts, in their way, were not all that different from the Contessa's fears, unfounded in his opinion, about what the disappearance of her items might mean for her.

Urbino cast a last glance up at the Ca' Pozza as the gondola resumed its usual rhythm.

Suddenly a woman's cry broke the silence. It was like a howl of pain. A middle-aged woman in a tattered blue housedress stood on the embankment. She shook her fist and shouted in Italian. Only a word here and there could be made out, but no sense came through. She appeared to be venting her fury against the gondola and toward the poop where Gildo was making the required balleticlike movements as he maneuvered the vessel.

Or perhaps Urbino was deceived by his less than clear view of the woman, for the next moment it seemed indisputable that the Ca' Pozza was the object of her rage. She glowered up at the silent building. Curses faded in and out of coherence on the morning air, succeeded by deep sobs. This was surely the same voice that had broken out the other night into shrill laughter and sobs.

Who was the woman? What was her relationship to the Ca' Pozza? And why was she filled with such anger and sorrow?

These were the questions Urbino posed to himself as the gondola quit the area of the Ca' Pozza, moving more quickly, it seemed, than usual.

14

"I'm sure of one thing," Urbino told the Contessa the next afternoon in the *salotto blu*, "Silvia and Vitale don't hold a candle to their predecessors."

The Contessa stared back.

"Did I need you to put on your stalker's hat and polish your magnifying glass to find that out? I'm well aware that most things are in decline here."

"Your body, mind, and spirit, you mean. I don't believe it for a minute and neither do you. Vitale, however, is insufferably smug, and your Silvia is flighty and evasive."

"Now you're telling me that my staff are like characters from a Goldoni play! Before we know it, you'll be referring to them as servants."

"If they *are* like Goldoni characters, Barbara dear, don't forget that Goldoni shocked most people by showing that the serving class could have story lines and intrigues of their own."

"So now the fruit of all your investigation is to tell me that Vitale and Silvia have a life away from the house and from me? What a shock!"

She was aiming for levity, but the faint smile on her face soon faded. "But we've had our experience with the secret lives of my staff, haven't we?" she asked, alluding to the tragedy last year surrounding her previous boatman.

"We can't count it out," Urbino said. "It's not that I mistrust any of your staff, but we need to keep all possibilities open."

"You haven't mentioned Pasquale."

"The best of the lot, perhaps. I'll get to him. As for Vitale, he said that you didn't ask him to repair the door knocker, as far as he can remember," he added, although the majordomo had expressed no apparent doubt. "He doesn't seem the type to admit to a mistake easily. And he's adamant that no one got into the house. Not on his watch. And I advise you again, Barbara, you should install some kind of security system. As a first step why not at least have Demetrio Emo—"

A quiet knock on the door interrupted him. Silvia, with a nervous smile on her pretty face, entered with the steaming kettle.

Breaking into Italian, the Contessa said, "I've noticed, Urbino, that your sweet Gildo has been looking sad these days. Is he cross with you for some reason?"

She threw a glance at Silvia as the young woman placed the kettle above the silver lamp on the table. The maid lingered, making unnecessary adjustments to the kettle and the teacups.

"He's been abstracted," Urbino responded in Italian, wondering what little game the Contessa might be playing. "But he's as competent as ever. A friend of his died recently; someone in apprenticeship to be a *remero*."

"Poor boy. Yet it's given him a melancholy air that suits his profession, considering how handsome he is."

Silvia closed the door behind her.

"What was that all about?" Urbino asked.

"Silvia has the biggest crush on Gildo. An example of the private lives of my staff."

"And so you want to torture the poor girl?"

"You know I like playing Cupid, although I may have a

difficult job of it with Gildo. And besides, *caro*, since we were discussing my staff, Silvia included, we didn't need to have her blabbing it all over the house." She sliced into a trim loaf of cake on the table. "If you haven't noticed, I've made some Madeira cake."

They were the only cakes Urbino had ever known her to make, and she did them to perfection. But she never turned them out unless she was in an agitated state, and then she was likely to bake enough to furnish a small *pasticceria*.

"In that case," Urbino said, getting up, "I'll have some of your Madeira instead of tea."

He poured himself some of the wine, a dry variety, and reseated himself. The Contessa handed him a generous slice of cake.

"There's no need for Demetrio Emo or anyone from that security company you use," she said, deftly picking up where they had left off before Silvia had come in. "There are locks on all the doors. Stout ones. The camera at the land entrance is enough. Do I want electronic beams in every corner setting off lights and alarms? Men rushing to my rescue when all I'm trying to do is get a glass of milk in the middle of the night?"

"It works well at my place, and I don't have a tenth of what you have to worry about. Just look at what you have in this room alone."

He made a wide gesture. Almost every painting, print, bibelot, and piece of furniture crowded into the room came with a story—and, in most cases, a high price tag. He took a bite of the cake.

"But you have yourself to worry about," the Contessa countered. "Your sleuthing has made you unpopular with quite a few people."

It was true enough, and it was one of the main reasons he had installed his security system. But the Contessa, as his closest friend and confidant, was herself vulnerable from that direction.

"Is this a version of the lady or the tiger, *caro?* Do I have to choose between losing my mind or having had someone break into the house?"

"Or considering that someone in the house might be mischievous," he said, before taking a sip of Madeira.

"I like your choice of words. Anyone in particular?"

"The likely suspect would be your infatuated Silvia. She has immediate access to your personal objects. If only we could figure out if your things all went missing at the same time."

"Why is that important?"

"Someone in the house would be inclined to take them one at a time. A person who broke in would probably take everything at once."

"Yet a clever person attached to the house," she responded, "might take everything at once, wouldn't he—or she? It would appear to be a robbery. But I have no idea if they disappeared all at once or one at a time. As I've told you, once I noticed that the silver cascade was missing, I got anxious about what else might be gone. That's when I discovered the other things—or *didn't* discover them. The middle of January."

Urbino sketched out the time frame he had been considering the other night in the library.

"So let's go through this together," he said. "No one could have taken the tea dress and the hat before the beginning of September. Do you remember seeing them anytime between then and the middle of January?"

"I'm not sure, but I think they were in the closet in the middle of November before the Feast of the Salute."

"And the Regency scarf? You wore it at the regatta. Did you wear it after that?"

"In October when I went to Florence," she said after thinking for a few moments. "A German woman on the Ponte Vecchio commented on it. And it was in my armoire right before the Feast of the Salute, too! I remember!"

She smiled as if she had pulled off a great feat.

"That means that your things went missing sometime after the middle of November to the middle of January. It narrows the picture quite a bit. And there's something else that might help us. Are you aware that you wore the dress, the hat, the scarf, and the necklace in photographs? They were in *Il Gazzettino, La Nuova Venezia,* and *Marco Polo* from early September to the end of November." He paused. "All local."

"But what does it mean?"

"Maybe nothing, maybe everything. We may be on the trail of something. It's just that I don't know what."

He waited for her to take a sip of tea before he went on. He described how Pasquale had found the rowboat between its mooring and the water entrance of the Ca' da Capo-Zendrini.

"I didn't notice it," she said. "And he never mentioned it to me."

"No reason why he should have, really. Not at the time. Anyway, someone could have taken the boat to your landing, and from there got into the house. The door from the water entrance opens into that seldom-used area with the large armoire. The person could have slipped inside and stayed until it was safe to come out."

"And then have roamed through the house and taken my things."

"All at the same time or at different times, as we've said, but my guess is that it would have been at the same time. It's unlikely anyone treated your house as his or her own personal orchard."

"Him or her, you say, but it must be a woman. Remember what I'm missing."

"I take nothing for granted. If someone came into the house that way or some other way, my guess is that it was when you were up in Geneva. Or when you had Alvise's relatives as houseguests at the end of the year."

"But why then? You're not suggesting that they—"

"Not at all," he interrupted her. "It's just that it was one of the two times when no one was on the usual schedule, especially not at the end of the year with people who don't live here coming and going."

"But the staff know them very well!"

"True enough, but nonetheless there could have been opportunities for getting in that someone took good advantage of."

"Bad advantage is more like it."

"And there's an aspect of this whole thing that's stranger than anything else."

"What's that?"

His gaze swept around the richly furnished room. He put his plate down on the table and went to one of the cabinets. He opened the glass door and withdrew an exquisite cameo. In slow motion he put it in his pocket.

"And there are a dozen more of them, not to mention your rose Pompadour and bleu celeste Sèvres pieces. Any one of them is worth more than what you're missing put together, and they would be extremely easy to carry off. And why would anyone want your used clothing? The necklace I can almost understand, although why that particular piece of jewelry? If someone came into the house, he—or she—was running a great risk. It's the used clothing that keeps puzzling me. The situation would be a lot easier to explain if some of your small valuable items were missing. Do you think they could be?

"I'm beginning to think that anything is possible. Your cures are as bitter as the disease. Maybe more so."

"I'm administering no cures yet. But be on your guard. Why don't you hire a night watchman if you're not ready to install a security system? 'We are vigilant,' Vitale kept saying, but he and whoever else he was referring to don't stay up all night or have eyes in the backs of their head."

"I cringe at the thought of some man with a flashlight and stick patrolling the house, but I'll think about it."

She remained silent, sipping her tea and gazing at the glass-fronted cabinets.

"Well, *caro*, you're keeping your end of our promise," she said, after a few moments. "I wish I could say the same for myself. With the *conversazione* coming up on Friday, I haven't been doing a thing yet about your Samuel Possle. But I've got something planned for tomorrow. No, don't ask what it is. We might put a jinx on it. As soon as I have something to tell you, I will. Just go home and wait. And three Madeira cakes are all wrapped up for you to take with you. One each for you, Natalia, and Gildo."

15

For five days after his talk with the Contessa, Urbino was busy, but none of his activities involved Possle or the Contessa's lost items.

On a windy and rainy Monday morning he went with Rebecca to the Corderie dell'Arsenale to examine Habib's installation space. They lunched afterward in a nearby *trattoria* to discuss the things that they needed to do for Habib before he returned. But all through the meal, part of him was far away. He could tell that Rebecca noticed, but she didn't say anything.

The next day he took the train to Milan to see his translator. The hours spent with her, however, only served to increase his anxiety about Possle because she kept asking him what his next project might be.

When some friends came unexpectedly from Paris for a few days, he welcomed the diversion. He devoted himself to showing them around town and took them on an outing to Torcello in the gondola after Gildo had been able to arrange for an additional rower. It had been delightful, if rather chilly, but he had been unable to part company with Possle's ghost, who seemed to be one more passenger, albeit insubstantial, for the two young men to row across the lagoon.

Urbino restrained himself from contacting the Contessa, who was preparing for her opening *conversazione*. He had no doubt that she was doing what she could for his benefit, and he wondered what had come of the plans she had hinted at. Her own silence, unusual in itself and dispiriting, indicated that she had nothing encouraging to tell him yet.

Whenever he went for a walk, he kept himself clear of the Ca' Pozza, and Gildo didn't, by design or accident, guide the gondola in that direction either. His avoidance of the Ca' Pozza was perhaps harder than anything else Urbino had to endure during this period, for the old building seemed to be beckoning him from afar with what seemed a promise, at other times a threat.

To make matters worse, the dream of Possle and the fire haunted him with even greater intensity.

Urbino, who had tried whatever he could over the past month short of breaking into the Ca' Pozza, waited, and while he waited, he put his trust in the Contessa—in her and in something he sometimes called fate.

Then, at eight-fifteen in the morning on Thursday, March 7, the day before the Contessa's first *conversazione*, the doorbell of the Palazzo Uccello awoke Urbino from a fitful, troubled sleep and everything started to change.

16

It's a gentleman to see you, Signor Urbino," Natalia said through the closed door of his bedroom.

"Have him wait in the parlor."

Urbino pulled on his dressing gown and dashed water on his face. When he went down to the parlor it was empty. Natalia bustled in from the kitchen, wiping her hands on her apron.

"I asked him to come in, but he just stood where he was," she whispered. She looked toward the hallway with a puzzled frown on her round face. "He's a very strange-looking man. And he didn't speak one word. Not one. All he did was point at an envelope with your name on it. But he wouldn't give it to me."

She shook her gray head. She had seen a lot of strange things since she had been working for him, she seemed to be saying, but this was the strangest.

When he went into the hallway, he understood her reaction.

"I'll take care of it. Thank you."

Standing in front of the entrance was a long, lean man with a hard-featured and forbidding face. Black hair streaked with gray was combed back from his forehead. Urbino estimated his age to be in the early sixties. His eyes were large, black, and shining. Something in their look filled Urbino with a vague dread and discomfort. He was dressed from top to toe in black. It accentuated the extreme pallor of his skin and the small white envelope he held out to Urbino. His hand was gnarled with scar tissue as if from a severe burn many years ago. Urbino glanced at his other hand. It, too, was scarred. A stale, unwashed odor struck his nostrils as he moved closer to the man.

Urbino took the envelope with distaste. It did not go unnoticed.

His full name, Raphael Urbino Macintyre, was scrawled in dark purple ink on the envelope. He was surprised. Very few people knew that he went by his middle name or that he even had any other.

"Would you please come into the parlor?"

The man remained silent. A faint smile crept across his thin lips. It did nothing to dispel his gloomy and menacing air. Before Urbino could say or do anything else, the stranger, piercing him with one last look, opened the door, without having said a word, and left, closing it behind him.

Urbino wasted no time in opening the envelope. Inside was a sheet of white paper of good quality, but yellowed with age. His eyes raced to the signature.

"Samuel Possle"

The entire message consisted of the day's date and one sentence:

"Be at the Ca' Pozza at four-thirty this afternoon."

17

It was a summons, not an invitation. But this made little difference to Urbino at the moment. He was about to achieve his goal. And he had the Contessa to thank for it.

He was reaching for the telephone to dial her number when the doorbell rang. It was such an unusual circumstance to have one visitor, let alone two, at this early hour, that when he went down to open the door, he expected to find himself confronted by the same grave man in black.

Instead, the morning fog swirled around the painter Lino Cipri with his painter's kit and a black leather portfolio. He gave Urbino an apologetic look. It shaded into keen embarrassment when he took in Urbino's dressing gown.

"Excuse me, Signor Macintyre. I hope I didn't awake you," Cipri said in Italian. He was a good-looking man with a smooth face despite his close to seventy years. "I'm always forgetting how early it is." He looked down at his watch in a nervous gesture. "And I should have made an appointment."

"Not at all. Come in."

"Are you sure you don't mind? I have something to give you."

"Of course not."

Urbino glanced outside. Fog curled over the surface of the

canal and drifted across the quay and the bridge. Possle's dark messenger was nowhere in sight, but Gildo suddenly emerged from the side of the building near the water steps. He seemed surprised to see Urbino in the open doorway and gave him a silent nod before bending over to tie his shoe.

"I'm usually up before the seven o'clock bells," Urbino said, as he closed the door. "Would you like some coffee?"

"No thank you."

Cipri was sweating as if he had been walking quickly. Or perhaps he was ill. His eyes had a somewhat feverish sheen. Urbino took his coat.

Cipri's heavy woolen cardigan, unraveling at one sleeve, and his flowing tie made the appropriate artistic impression, aided by an impressive head of thick, white hair.

Urbino led him into the cramped parlor. Cipri put down his kit but held on to his portfolio. He looked at the Bronzino portrait of a pearled-and-brocaded Florentine lady over the fireplace.

"Lovely," he said. He went closer to the painting. "It's been repaired, I know, but you would never be able to tell."

When Urbino had been in Morocco, he had engaged an American couple to look after the Palazzo Uccello. They had managed to do a great deal of damage to the interior and to some of his most prized possessions. For some unknown reason they had removed the Bronzino from the wall and leaned it next to an open window, where it had become saturated during a storm.

"Unfortunately, I can tell you exactly where the damage is," Urbino said. "I can see it even now."

"It's not always good to be such a connoisseur if it interferes with your enjoyment of a painting as beautiful as this one. I assure you there's no trace of the damage, and that's a professional opinion."

Cipri balanced his portfolio on an ottoman in front of the sofa. He opened it. "I've finished the two Longhis for Signor

Hennepin. I thought it would be best to bring them here. My apartment gets smaller every week between my paintings and my wife's books and magazines."

Urbino and the Contessa had never met Cipri's wife. They had heard that she was ailing and kept to their apartment on the Lido.

Cipri withdrew two small, unframed paintings from the case. They were both copies of works from the Longhi Room at the Ca' Rezzonico on the Grand Canal. One depicted masked ladies and gentlemen peering at a black rhinoceros, and the other was a fortune-teller reading the palm of a masked woman.

"Excellent," Urbino said. "Eugene will be pleased. You remember how much he liked the originals."

Cipri smiled. He was probably as pleased at the prospect of soon receiving some more money from Eugene as he was by the praise. He was said to be often in need of money, possibly because of his wife's illness. He occasionally set up his easel in front of the Giardini Pubblici near the Piazza San Marco or on the Riva degli Schiavoni to do quick portraits of tourists or what were actually something closer to caricatures.

"The Molière of painters," Cipri said, referring not to himself but to Pietro Longhi. "That's what my wife says he's called."

"And you do him excellent justice. I'll see that they're sent off in the most secure way possible," Urbino assured him. He placed the two paintings side by side against the back cushions of the sofa. He made some more enthusiastic comments, not wanting Cipri to feel that he was eager to have him leave.

"I have the documents all ready," Cipri said.

He withdrew a large manila envelope from his case.

"You'll find the commission order, an invoice, and a verification that the paintings are copies. Everything is all filled out and stamped and certified."

Urbino took the envelope.

The two men stood looking at each other in an awkward silence.

"Are you sure you wouldn't like some coffee?" Urbino hoped that he sounded more hospitable than he felt. "Perhaps some breakfast?" his guilty conscience made him add. "I haven't had mine yet, and Natalia could have it ready in just a few minutes. It would give you time to take a closer look at the Bronzino and to see if your first opinion holds up."

"Oh, I'm sure it does! But thank you kindly. I must be on my way. As you Americans like to say, time is money, and I want to get to the Accademia to do some work for Signor Hennepin. If you're ever on the Lido, please feel free to stop by for a visit. I'm almost always home in the afternoon. My wife will be pleased to meet you. She's heard a lot about you."

He put on his coat and collected his kit and portfolio. Urbino accompanied him downstairs. Before he closed the front door, he watched the man until he vanished into the fog on the other side of the bridge. Gildo was no longer on the embankment.

18

Urbino drank down the tiny cup of espresso that Natalia pressed on him as if it were medicine and took a few bites of Madeira cake. He promised her that he would have a proper breakfast shortly. He had to make a telephone call first.

He dialed the Contessa's number from the library as he looked from the window down at the empty, fog-wreathed quay. He usually didn't call her before nine-thirty, but this was a special occasion.

The Contessa picked up after only two rings.

"Whatever's the matter, *caro?*" She sounded worried.

"As if you don't know, you wonder worker. If I hadn't found out today—in fact, it was only a few minutes ago—I was going to break down and beg you to tell me what you've been up to. I can't wait to give you a great big kiss and hug. It worked."

"What worked?"

"Whatever it was you did, whatever strings you pulled, whatever promises you made, whatever spell you cast. I love you and I love your Madeira cake! I'm in. I'm in the Ca' Pozza, or I will be at precisely four-thirty this afternoon!"

There was silence at the other end of the line.

"But I didn't do a thing, Urbino!" the Contessa cried out,

after a few moments. "Not one single solitary thing. I had to leave for Bologna on Saturday evening right after I saw you. Poor Clementina is desperately ill." Clementina was the Conte's elderly cousin. "I was afraid I would have to postpone my first *conversazione*. I was at her house until last night. She's out of danger now, thank God. I was going to call you later and apologize." The Contessa drew in her breath, then added, "So you see, you've done it all on your own, you clever boy."

"But how did I do that?"

PART TWO

THE GONDOLA ROOM

19

A t a few minutes before four-thirty that afternoon Urbino approached the Ca' Pozza on foot, as puzzled now as he had been this morning. No matter how he thought about the situation and whom he had contacted, the reason for his good luck eluded him. The fruit had fallen into his lap, it appeared, without anyone having had to shake the tree.

He had decided against arriving in the gondola. It would have compounded his uncomfortable passivity. Now, after his long, meandering walk from the Palazzo Uccello through a thickening fog, he could at least say that his own steps had carried him from his door to the one that now stood temptingly in front of him, ready to open for him at last.

As he paused on the narrow bridge, a warning thought insinuated itself. *More tears are shed because of answered prayers than unanswered ones.*

As a child, he had heard these words over and over again from his mother on various occasions. For years he had thought they were hers. By the time he had learned that their true source was Saint Theresa, he had also learned their truth. He feared learning this bitter lesson all over again in the Ca' Pozza.

He cast his eyes up at the silent building. The lower floors were wreathed in fog. The attic story seemed to float above them with a life of its own, its gray-and-pink stones glowing with a strange intensity as if they had absorbed all the available dying light.

The moment had come. If Urbino had been a smoker, it would have been the time to toss his cigarette into the canal and make his way to the building. What he did, instead, was to toss away or rather press down into the dark waters of his consciousness all his misgivings. Now was the time for positive thinking. He walked down the steps of the bridge and pushed the rusty bell.

20

T he door was opened almost as soon as he took his finger off the button.

The uncanny messenger of that morning stared at him with his piercing eyes. A stone staircase rose behind him. To one side a partly open door revealed the worn arm of a sofa.

"I've come to see Signor Possle," Urbino said in Italian.

All he got in return was stony silence.

"At his request," he added, although the man must already know this. The Ca' Pozza was all too obviously a house where no one was admitted unless invited and where a stranger at the door was spied out from some concealed perch.

The man moved to one side. Urbino stepped across the threshold. A faint smile crossed the man's stern face. He pushed the heavy door closed behind them.

Urbino breathed a sigh of relief. He was in. This would not be the only time, he swore to himself.

It was colder inside the house than outside, much colder than was usually the case for buildings, even in Venice. It was as if a pall had dropped over Urbino. This surely was nothing but a superstitious impression, he thought, but it was not any the weaker because he recognized it for what it was.

The valet—for this was the title that Urbino now ascribed

to the man as his mind, confused and irritated, searched for some aspect of normalcy about him—took Urbino's cloak and placed it on a mahogany clothes stand carved with gargoyles and lilies. Urbino was reluctant to relinquish it, given the chill in the building.

The man silently ushered him across the damp and musty lower hall. He had an almost stealthy step, and he held his scarred hands close to his sides. His stale and acrid odor was stronger than it had been this morning.

His form slashed by deep, dark shadows, he began to ascend the high stone staircase. Urbino stopped after taking a few steps. Perhaps it was a trick of perspective from where he was standing or his own heightened, almost painful state of awareness, but the staircase seemed tilted at a slight angle to one side. Urbino had a brief, disturbing moment of dizziness as the silent valet proceeded up the staircase. Everything, momentarily, became either black or white, without any color.

The valet stopped and turned his head. His hard features were set in disapproval. Urbino shook himself and followed him up the staircase. At the top a long *sala* opened out. There seemed a strange stillness over the room and, in fact, over the whole house itself. He halted a few feet beyond Urbino.

A Murano chandelier in a vaguely pagoda shape, with broken pieces of glass and missing beads, hung precariously from the ceiling. Faded full-length maroon drapes covered a bank of tall, glass-paned doors to the right of the staircase, that opened onto a loggia. Two windows with the same drapery faced the loggia from the far end. Heavy wooden chairs were lined up with their backs to the long sides of the room. Closed doors of impressive architectural design between the chairs led into more private chambers. One of these doors on the opposite side of the room was wider than the others, and contributed a sense of disharmony to the room.

Large portraits of centuries-dead men and women in chipped and broken frames and as dark as Tintorettos, but in no other way comparable to the great master, stared out at Urbino. Plaster peeled and flaked from the walls. An ormolu table with a cracked vase beneath one of the portraits completed the furnishings of the depressing room, which had once seen such legendary gatherings.

The man gestured roughly toward a chair. It was close to the doors that opened onto the loggia. Urbino understood that he was expected to seat himself and wait.

After proceeding with scarcely a sound over the bare *scagliola* floor, the man opened the wide door and entered the room beyond.

Urbino didn't seat himself. He went to one of the loggia doors. He calculated that the figure he had seen during his late night vigil had stood behind this one. He pulled the heavy drape to one side. Anyone standing here had an uncluttered view of the bridge.

He walked across the *sala* to one of the wide, high windows. One of its shutters was thrown open. Dust scattered through the air as he moved the drape blocking whatever air might come in. Down below was an overgrown garden enclosed with a high brick wall on two sides.

Urbino felt a prickling at the back of his neck. He turned around. The sinister valet stood only a few feet away, having traversed the hard, shining floor without a sound.

Urbino followed him to the wide door. It was now ajar. Warmth from the room beyond brushed against Urbino's face, but it somehow only made him feel more chilled. Keeping to his habitual silence, the valet turned away and vanished through a door at the far end of the *sala*.

21

Urbino stood in the doorway.

There were so many objects in the room to attract attention that at first he stared about him, almost without seeing anything at all. By degrees, however, the room resolved itself into a space much larger than Urbino would have expected it to be, familiar as he was with the plan of seventeenth-century palazzi. Usually the rooms off the *sala* were much smaller than this one was. Urbino, remembering what Rebecca had said about the interior renovations of the Ca' Pozza, suspected that two rooms had been combined into one.

Daylight had been banished. Shuttered windows opposite the door were covered in dark green drapery. Yet there was a deceptive form of illumination that came from a fire kindled in the grate to the right and from wax candles of different sizes and shapes and thickness, but all white, which were arranged on the floor, on scattered tables, and on the mantel. A large mirror in an elaborate carved and gilded frame danced with the reflections from the candles.

The heavy scent of the candles and the smoke in the warm room was threaded with another, more delicate one, which was reminiscent of a bouquet of flowers.

The walls, hung with portraits and still-life paintings, were a deep shade of orange. Books, bound richly in leather, were piled on the floor and stacked on a shelf beside the door. The ceiling, slightly domed, was covered in heavy Morocco leather and held an oval of royal blue silk resembling the sky. Silver angels floated against it. Suspended from the ceiling on a silver chain was a little cage of silver wire.

But all these details suddenly became inconsequential as he took in the startling and unpredictable object that dominated the far end of the room. It was a gondola. Not a replica of one, but a full-size vessel that, if it had been placed in the canal below rather than up here in this room, would have sailed as surely and truly as Urbino's own.

The black-painted gondola displayed before him in such an unlikely place had its curving *forcola*, ironwork *ferro*, and brass seahorses. It did not have a *felze* attached, however, and whatever sedan chairs it had once had, had been removed. In their place was a profusion of bright orange cushions that entirely filled the cavity of the boat from prow to stern.

The gondola was held steady with sawhorses and angled into the room prow first so as to accommodate all thirty-five feet. A block of small wooden steps stood in front of it to provide access. Hanging above was a scarlet silk canopy with festoons.

Two high-backed armchairs faced the gondola. A table with a carafe and two goblets of Murano glass stood between the chairs.

The gondola, so unexpected in a room, created a distinctly surrealistic effect along with the other décor and accoutrements. And to complete the picture, lying at full length in the gondola against the cushions, was the strangest person Urbino had ever seen.

The figure, dwarfed by the size of the gondola and surrounded by magazines and newspapers was still and unmoving. It seemed to be a part of the boat itself. Its garments were of red satin and purple silk and vaguely ceremonial in their cut. The small head was tightly swathed in purple silk, almost as far down as the wispy eyebrows, creating the effect of an Eastern turban. Around the thin neck hung a gold chain with a large odd-shaped talisman of some kind, embossed with a crescent. It weighed heavily against the silk shirtfront. The head reminded Urbino of the severed one he had seen held by the silhouetted person behind the door of the loggia.

The figure in the gondola resembled nothing so much as the preserved body of a saint dressed in fine clothes and displayed for some liturgical celebration. If Urbino had not been expecting to find a man—for surely this must be Samuel Possle—he would not have been able to swear absolutely, during these first confused moments, about its sex.

The dim, flickering light of the candles, some of which were on the poop of the gondola, revealed a frail body shrunken within its garments. Possle's face beneath the scarf was sharp and foxlike, dominated by small, dark eyes. One side of his face was much more wrinkled than the other.

Possle no longer looked anything like the photographs Urbino had seen of him or the young figure in his dream, but it was unrealistic to expect him to. The most recent photographs had shown a man in his fifties. And yet Urbino could not shake the feeling, strange though it seemed, that Possle had been the victim of an extraordinary and accelerated aging.

But something in the recluse's eyes, something keen and curious that flashed across the distance between the two men, told Urbino that the man was as hungry for life as he had been three, four, five decades ago.

Urbino had no idea how much time had passed since he had entered the room and begun to register all his impressions. It probably had been only as long or as short as a minute, but whatever it was, he sensed that Possle had remained silent in order to give him the chance to absorb all that he saw.

Possle's voice now broke in on his thoughts. "I bid you

welcome to my house, Mr. Macintyre!" Possle said in English. "Enter freely and of your own will!"

These words sounded somewhat forbidding to Urbino's ears and if they had been intended to put him at his ease, they did not have the desired effect.

"Please take the chair closest to me. My hearing is poor."

Possle's voice was thin and dry, with a strange intonation. It must have come from all the years of speaking and hearing another language. Urbino could detect no trace of Possle's southern origins in his voice, any more than, he was told, people could in his own.

Urbino allowed himself to be swallowed by one of the imposing armchairs, being careful not to disturb any of the candles ranged on the floor beside it.

"Look at me all you want, Mr. Macintyre. I'm a curious specimen, I know. All yellow skin and bones. So new to you, so old to me. So strange to you, so familiar to me. So melancholy to both." The words were like an echo of others that Urbino had heard or read somewhere. They contributed to Urbino's disorientation since entering the Ca' Pozza.

"Those are the words of a sad lady," Possle resumed. His small, dark eyes bore into Urbino. "Do you know who she is, Mr. Macintyre?"

"I seem to have heard the words before. A woman, you say?"

"Miss Havisham in *Great Expectations*. Which puts you in the position of poor little Pip."

"But I see no wedding cake with cobwebs, Mr. Possle," Urbino joked in an attempt to deflect the thrust of Possle's reference to Dickens's naïve and manipulated character.

Possle raised a hand, then let it fall back weakly against the cushions. "You are most welcome to the Ca' Pozza. May you come freely and go safely." Again uneasiness crept over Urbino.

"Thank you for your invitation," he said, in what he hoped was a hearty, sincere tone.

Possle's tongue darted out and moistened his lips. "I'm pleased that I was able to lure you out of your palazzo." He regarded Urbino with a little smile that puckered up the wrinkled side of his face even more. He seemed to be gauging Urbino's reaction. "Veneto-Byzantine, it is, your little palazzo. I'm familiar with it, but I haven't seen it since you moved in. I never go out anymore, you see. I haven't gone out more than six or seven times since your first fateful visit to Venice, when you came and never really left."

His voice seemed to gain more energy as he spoke, although it never lost its tremulous hesitation. "That was twenty years ago, I believe, add or take a few months, not very long after your divorce and the death of your parents in a car crash. You came home to your mother's native land, your beloved mother with her love for Raphael." It was almost a mechanical recitation. Possle's small eyes searched Urbino's face. Then, in a different tone of voice, less conversational and more formal, he said, "America is our country, and Venice is our hometown."

These words, like the others, sounded familiar, but Urbino couldn't place them either. At the moment, however, he was more concerned with how Possle knew things about him that few other people did.

"Perhaps you'll stay as long as I have," Possle said, his eyes searching Urbino's face, "and eventually look like me. Ah, here is Armando."

The valet, or whatever he was, stood in the doorway, his arms against his sides.

"C'est l'heure du thé," Possle went on, as Urbino felt more and more disinclined to speak, "but I'm not your Contessa even though it would be nice to offer you a flawless blend of Si-a-Fayoune, de Mo-you-tann, and de Khansky. Lovely names, don't you think? You can almost smell and taste the tea, can't you?"

Once again these words carried the trace of others with them. A smile, somehow both amused and disappointed, crossed the old man's face.

"I prefer something stronger," Possle said. "Armando's not the type to make tea, are you, Armando? I always have some Amontillado at this time. Would it suit you as well? Good. Before you leave, Armando," he said in Italian, "I need you to help me with my glasses. Our friend has the advantage of seeing me better than I can see him."

Armando climbed the steps in front of the gondola, bent over, and rummaged among the cushions. He extracted a pair of glasses with large, black frames, and put them on Possle's face. He then rearranged the cushions and left.

"I would have proposed bourbon, but I gave it up many years ago. Ah, bourbon! A pleasant memory. Bourbon for the two of us. Two sons of the South. You from New Orleans, and me from Charleston. But you know that. I think you know many things about me."

"And you, Mr. Possle, you seem to know some things about me."

"I might not go out, but I'm not unaware of the world beyond these walls."

Urbino shifted his position in the armchair, but all he succeeded in doing was sinking an inch or two more into it.

"You've lived in Venice a long time," Urbino said.

"Almost since the year you were born! And the last time I was home, if either of us can call it that anymore, was many, many decades ago."

If Urbino's memory was correct, this had been in the late fifties, shortly after Possle had bought the Ca' Pozza. He had gone by boat from Genoa, with so many valises that they had taken up an extra cabin, and according to—

"Yes, by boat in 1958, Mr. Macintyre," Possle said, startlingly mirroring Urbino's thoughts. "The only way to travel, if one is obliged to. But now this is my only way; my gondola that goes everywhere and nowhere."

He ran a hand against the black wood of the boat.

"You think you have the last private gondola in Venice, Mr. Macintyre. You can glide around all you want in the Contessa's gift, but it won't carry you as far as you really want to go. Not in these very, very different days of ours. No, Mr. Macintyre, this is the last private gondola in Venice. Forget about Peggy Guggenheim's. Mine was—*is*—the last."

"I wasn't aware of that."

"I saw to it, I tell you! I kept it in service three months after she retired hers. Peggy! A fascinating woman. She would let me unscrew the erect penis from the statue of the horseman on her terrace whenever she was expecting overly sensitive guests. One time I hid it under one of her bedroom pillows."

Urbino was reminded of the magazine photograph of Possle next to the bronze horseman.

"We used to argue about the art she spent her money on," Possle was saying with a shake of his head. "Not to my taste, but she had the last laugh. I took everything in my stride, even her insults. Ah, the tales I could tell!"

With this observation, which Urbino interpreted as not completely innocent or spontaneous, Possle closed his eyes. Urbino, who didn't want to break his reverie or risk distracting him from any revelations about the American art collector, remained silent and waited.

He let his gaze roam around the room and had an opportunity to take in more of its details. Clustered on the carpet in front of the gondola and on a long table to one side of Urbino's chair were small, squat pots of plants and flowers. Urbino didn't know much about horticulture, but he recognized the flowers as being exotic and of tropical origin. He wondered how they were able to thrive in this darkness and whether the scent in the air came from them.

Possle had now been silent for so long that Urbino began to wonder what he should do. Possle's eyes remained closed and his mouth was open. Urbino had a rush of fear that the old man had chosen precisely this moment and this occasion to bid farewell to his long life, but then he detected the slight rising and falling of his chest beneath the silk. Possle was asleep.

Urbino bent down to one of the flowers, a bright red hot-house bloom. What appeared to be dewdrops pearled some of its lush petals. He sniffed the flower. It had no scent. Another pot beside it held a yellowish plant shot through with silver. It looked like something that didn't grow naturally but had been constructed out of a piece of stovepipe. Casting a quick glance at Possle, who was still asleep, he touched the plant, expecting to find that it was artificial. Despite its appearance, it was real.

Urbino turned his attention to the small silver cage hanging from the ceiling behind his chair. He turned so as to be able to get a better view of it. On the floor of the cage was a dead cricket.

Just as Urbino was considering if he should remain silent, make a discreet sound, or get up and leave, Possle's eyes fluttered open.

"You probably think it's an old man's fatigue." Possle shook his head. "It's a condition I've had since I was much younger than you are. How long was I asleep?"

"Only a few minutes."

"Sometimes it's almost an hour. It can happen in the middle of a sentence, I warn you. I apologize."

"I should do the apologizing. I've put a strain on you. My eagerness to meet you has made me forget to count the possible cost."

Urbino, for the first time, was saying something that touched on his own interest in his host.

"You forget, Mr. Macintyre, that I was the one to invite you," Possle retorted. "And as far as any possible cost is concerned, it's too early to reckon that up on either of our parts, don't you think? As Byron said, 'those who would greatly win must deeply venture.' Are you fond of Byron?"

"Yes. That's from *Marino Faliero*."

An ambiguous smile played across Possle's face that once again deepened all his wrinkles on one side, while the smoother side of his face became even more so.

"A sad and tragic Doge. Beheaded, you know."

A vision of the Ca' Pozza's nighttime figure rose before Urbino's eyes. He couldn't shake the feeling that Possle had intended his comment for just that reason.

"You haven't written a biography of Byron," Possle said, as he continued to stare at Urbino through his large, black glasses.

"Perhaps one of these days. I've been looking around for another project. I need something new to turn my hand to."

"You're still young enough to assume you have time for many projects. A marvelous luxury—or a comforting illusion. I've read all your books. I find them diverting. My favorite is Proust."

"It's gratifying to hear that a man of your experience finds my books of interest. If I had known, I would have had my publishers send you a copy of each."

"I'm surprised that you didn't think of that." Possle paused for a beat, then said, "Let me see. I have the Proust book with me somewhere. Ah, here it is."

He retrieved the slim mauve-colored volume from the cushions.

"I've marked a passage. Listen. 'Inevitably, despite Marcel's appreciation of the beauty and secrecy of the city,'" he read in his wavering voice, "'he finds himself somewhat disillusioned, and by the time he is about to leave, Venice is no longer an enchanted labyrinth out of *The Arabian Nights* but something sinister and deceptive that seems to have little to do with Doges and Turners. It doesn't even seem to be Venice any longer, but a mendacious fiction where the palaces are nothing but lifeless marble and the water that makes the city unique only a combination of hydrogen and oxygen.' "

This had been delivered in Possle's thin, sharp voice with its strange intonation and tremulousness. Urbino's own words had sounded somehow different from what he had written, although they were exactly the same.

Possle closed the book. "Is that how you feel now about Venice?"

"I was paraphrasing something Proust said."

"I'm well aware of that. But tell me, do you feel disillusioned now? In this year of your life in Venice?"

"In some ways Venice has become more special than ever," Urbino replied, expressing only a small portion of what was a very personal feeling these days about his adopted city.

"Since your return from Morocco, you mean, with your Moroccan friend." Possle gave a nod of his purple-swathed head. "The enthusiasm of the young can help a jaded appetite, don't you find? I believe he has gone home for a visit. I hope it won't be for too long. You must miss him terribly. Your house must seem emptier than it used to be before he came to stay with you. But I'm becoming distracted, I fear. We were speaking about Venice and Proust. So tell me, my friend, do you also agree with Proust about Venice being sinister and deceptive and—what do you call it?—a mendacious fiction?"

Urbino, who was both uncomfortable and irritated by Possle's references to Habib, responded coolly, "There's something of that."

"Of course there is," Possle replied with a sly smile. "What else would one expect from a person of imagination like yourself, not to mention a person who has your other line of work? As for me, Venice has never disappointed. But our sherry has arrived."

Armando entered with a tray and deposited it on the small

inlaid table in front of the gondola. He poured the pale wine into two cups of translucent Chinese porcelain. He handed one cup to Possle, then the other, with considerably less ceremony, to Urbino.

"Thank you, Armando," Possle said in Italian. "If we need anything else, I'll ring for you."

Armando gave an almost imperceptible bow and left the room.

Possle raised his cup. "To deep ventures and a good death," he said.

As Urbino sipped the dry wine, he was reminded of Poe's story of the man walled up by his enemy in a cellar filled with casks of Amontillado.

"Such a gentle wine for such a troubling story," Possle said, yet again startling Urbino by the echo of what he had himself been thinking. "Ah, stories! One of my sorrows is that my eyes have worsened during the past few years along with my hearing. If only Armando might read to me, but as you've noticed, he's mute, though his hearing is very acute."

"I see. I . . ." Urbino trailed off.

"You thought he was reticent, the ideal servant? He is that. And also once the best gondolier I could have wanted, even better than your Gildo."

First Habib, and now Gildo, Urbino thought. Possle wanted to make a point of showing him how much he knew about him.

"He became mute recently?" Urbino asked, choosing to show as little reaction as possible to Possle's reference to Gildo. "Since you retired your gondola?"

"No, long before I even had the gondola."

"Surely muteness must have been a handicap for a gondolier."

"Armando has no handicaps that I've ever discovered. Don't underestimate him. He could make all the warning cries."

The air in the room began to feel more close and oppressive. Urbino set his cup down.

"Does Armando live here?"

"He's more at home here than I am. He has his little nooks and crannies everywhere. You might have noticed one of them in the entrance hallway. He thinks of himself as my silent Cerberus when he's there. We are well matched, the two of us. He has nowhere to go, and I can go nowhere. Alone together. We are most inseparable."

He ran a hand slowly along the gleaming wood of the gondola. "Armando is part of my daily life," he continued, "my double, my shadow, as someone once said of gondoliers. People either like their gondoliers or they hate them, Mr. Macintyre, and if they like them, they like them very much. Or, I might add, *too* much." Possle looked in the direction of the *sala* with a faraway expression. "I prefer solitude, and so does Armando. We learn how to live from society. But solitude teaches us how to die; it has no flatterers."

In what was by now becoming a puzzling and annoying pattern, Possle's observation about solitude and his earlier one about gondoliers carried a distinctly familiar ring.

"You're looking tired, Mr. Macintyre. Excuse me for drawing attention to it, old man that I am. I never had much patience when the old said I wasn't looking well. There seemed something ghoulish in it. Here. Take this."

He held out his empty cup.

Urbino got up. A pleasant scent struck his nostrils. It was the scent that he had first noticed upon entering the room, but much stronger.

As Urbino reseated himself, Possle reached among the cushions. He held up a large crystal vaporizer. Perhaps the cushions contained an endless supply of items to amuse the old man, which he periodically withdrew like a magician dipping into a deep and voluminous hat.

"It's a combination of ambrosia, Mitcham lavender, sweet

pea, extract of meadow flowers, tuberose, orange blossom, and almond blossom," Possle recited. "That's what you're smelling. It allows me to wander in a constantly changing landscape and all while I'm in my stationary gondola. You can have more Amontillado, if you like. I only allow myself the one. I find I look forward to it much more that way."

"No, thank you."

"I wish I could offer you something more suited to your tastes. I'm inflexible in my routines. And being solitary, or relatively so," he added with a smile, "I'm not accustomed to taking other people into consideration. That's why I hope you'll excuse me if I now put an end to our pleasant little visit."

Urbino was taken completely by surprise and was not a little disappointed. Possle had been giving no signs that the visit was almost over.

Possle pulled a dark purple cord that extended from the wall and whose tasseled end was barely visible among the ubiquitous and encumbered cushions of the gondola.

"You're wondering why I asked you to come, only to dismiss you so abruptly," Possle said. "But all in good time. For the moment you can assume it's only the whim of an old man. I think we've had a successful first visit, though, don't you? When shall I have you here again? Ah, I see from the expression on your face that it pleases you to hear that. But perhaps it would be better not to specify the date. I've always found that when I set up a rendezvous too far in advance, I feel that I should cancel it as the day and the hour draw close. Peculiar, but what else do you expect of a man who makes his voyages in a marooned gondola? Armando will show you out."

Urbino barely had time to express his appreciation to Possle, when Armando appeared in the doorway like an apparition. Urbino threw a last glance back at Possle, lost in the cushions of his unusual divan.

He followed the silent Armando across the *sala* and down

the shadow-filled high staircase. The door to the room where Possle had said Armando kept guard was now closed.

Armando left Urbino to collect his cloak himself and went to the heavy door. A symbol decorated the area above the inner lock, which Armando now turned. There was no bolt or other lock on the door except the one that corresponded to the large keyhole on the outer side.

The symbol consisted of a blue circle. In its center was a red-and-yellow eight-pointed star surrounded by yellow crescents. It had an air of the occult about it and resembled one of the heraldic emblems painted on the stern of the brightly decorated flat-bottomed boats of Chioggia. It struck Urbino as unusual in its combination of elements and even more so, perhaps, in that it adorned the inside of the door rather than the outside. It was as if it were warning the occupants not to venture into the world beyond the door instead of chasing away whatever evil spirits might want to enter.

Armando noted Urbino's interest in the symbol and seemed to give him every opportunity to examine it as he slowly opened the door to release him into the late afternoon shadows.

22

When Urbino got back to the Palazzo Uccello after his encounter with Possle, he was fatigued. Although he had promised to let the Contessa know about everything that had happened during his first visit to the Ca' Pozza, he telephoned her and said that he preferred to wait until tomorrow when he would see her in person. He wanted to think about it all first. Since this was the eve of her first *conversazione*, she didn't press the matter.

Urbino picked at the sandwiches that Natalia had left for him and then went to the library. There he sat thinking for a long time, going over what had happened that afternoon behind the walls of the Ca' Pozza. He spent almost as much time berating himself for what he had failed to communicate to Possle out of caution and reticence as he spent going over what Possle had said—or had seemed to say. He found himself becoming more and more weary and lay down on the sofa to close his eyes for a few minutes. He soon, however, fell asleep, with Serena next to him.

He awakened past midnight.

When he got into bed, he had some trouble falling sleep, but fortunately, when he did, he had no dreams. Yet all the while as he slept he seemed to be lying in wait for the one which had become his dark companion.

23

If you didn't ask him that," the Contessa said to Urbino the next morning as he guided her along the slick pavement behind the Piazza San Marco, "then what *did* you ask him?"

The two friends were making their way from Florian's to the music conservatory, where the Contessa was scheduled to give her first *conversazione*.

The unasked question she was referring to was the one that had been troubling Urbino ever since Armando had delivered Possle's note.

If the Contessa hadn't been the one to secure him the invitation, then who had it been?

"Maybe no one was responsible," Urbino said, "no one but Possle himself. He knows about me, and he knows that I've been trying to contact him, apparently from Armando. As it turns out," Urbino added in a rueful voice, "I didn't end up asking him very much at all."

"Quite unusual for you!"

"There are times when it's better to keep quiet and listen— and observe."

"But why do I get the impression that you're not satisfied with having kept quiet?"

"It shows, does it? I asked a question here and there, and I'd like to think that I didn't press more on him because it would have been premature, or presumptuous, or both. Considering it was my first visit," he added more forcefully.

"And you didn't want to make it your last as well."

He nodded.

"But that's not the whole story," she said.

"No," Urbino admitted with reluctance. "He seemed to be the one asking the questions, when he wasn't revealing what he already knew about me, that is."

"You're a well-known local figure, *caro*, even notorious in your way, not unlike your strange host: The *americano* who lives in an historic palazzo, glides around in his own gondola, and tracks down murderers when he isn't feeding off the dead like a vampire!"

"Thank you for the flattering picture! But that leaves us almost as confused as we were before. Did Possle contact me in my capacity as sleuth or as vampire, as you call me?"

"Perhaps both."

"Or neither." Urbino shook his head. "He gave no clear sign of anything along those lines. I felt as if I were there for his private entertainment."

"That may not be far from the mark. After all, a man in his situation has to import most of his diversions. And years ago he became accustomed to a constant supply of them. It must be rather dull for him these days."

"All alone, it seems, with Armando. What do you know about him?"

"Not anything. I was never in the Ca' Pozza, remember, or in Possle's gondola. And I never knew that Armando was a mute. He was very much in the background, and I certainly don't remember that he looked as—as weird as you say he does now. But he made me feel uncomfortable, as if he was wishing me ill."

"He couldn't have made it more clear that he resented my being there." Then Urbino added, "Or so it seemed."

They came to a stop by a broad pool of water where a flotilla of gondolas was moored.

"At least you can cross him off your list of reasons why Possle might have invited you," the Contessa said, as she searched the gondoliers who waited in their boats for their assignments to various stations around the city.

"Who knows? Possle seemed to be toying with me. Some of the things he said sounded familiar, irritatingly familiar, and I got the impression that he wanted to keep me off balance. Which he succeeded all too well in doing."

"But I'm sure you're going to be your usual patient self and put up with as much of it as possible. For the sake of a greater good."

"If he asks me back."

"Being exposed to you once is not enough," the Contessa said, "if one can judge from my own response. Oh, there's Gildo!"

She waved at the young man. He waved back to them from a gondola at the far edge of the clustered boats. His chiseled countenance showed little of its usual animation. It was one of the days when, according to their agreement, he wasn't in Urbino's service.

"He still looks sad, poor boy," the Contessa said. "Have you found out anything more about his friend?"

"No," Urbino replied, with a twinge of guilt. His interest in Possle was making him neglect other things. He cast a regretful glance back at Gildo. There was an air of isolation about his lithe figure.

Urbino held the Contessa more tightly as compensation for whatever ways he might have been neglecting her as they continued their slow, even stride toward the conservatory. They walked in a companionable silence, broken only by brief greetings given to acquaintances they met along the way. Above them the dark gray sky threatened more rain. The alleys were filled with shoppers and a scattering of tourists. Beneath a narrow, covered passageway, they had to draw to one side as a caravan of young people barged along.

Signs above their heads on the worn stones of the buildings provided direction, but Urbino and the Contessa had no more need of them than they had of any conversation. Each kept to his own thoughts. Urbino's were about his meeting with Samuel Possle the previous day, and the Contessa's, he assumed, were about her *conversazione*.

Thunder sounded as they crossed a square. The Contessa surveyed the leaden sky with a frown.

"Let's go past La Fenice," she suggested.

A few minutes later, under an increasingly darkening sky, they were contemplating the grand old opera house, where they had spent many unforgettable hours together. It was being restored after a disastrous fire had destroyed its jewel-box interior a few years ago.

The Contessa gave a deep sigh. "I'm going to give the biggest celebration ever when it's finished," she said. "But it will never be the same, will it?"

"Of course it will. It's burned down before, and it's risen from its ashes, remember," Urbino consoled her, as they resumed their way, alluding to the name of the theater. La Fenice was Italian for the mythical phoenix bird, which after being consumed by flames, was reborn again from the ashes in its nest.

The thunder became louder and the sky darker. They ducked into the doorway of a shop for a few moments to open their umbrellas.

"I'll take the rain as a good omen," the Contessa said, now stepping across the stones more carefully.

"Your *conversazione* will be a great success. I have no doubt of that."

A worried frown descended on the Contessa's face. The silence they now fell into wasn't an easy one as they continued in the direction of the music conservatory.

An idea started to form in Urbino's mind about the Contessa's *conversazione*, which she had got his pledge not to attend. He entertained the idea privately at first, hardly noticing that the rain had abated and the Contessa had closed her umbrella.

He stopped when they reached the Campo Morosini. At the other side of the square was the Renaissance palazzo of the music conservatory. The Contessa went on a few paces before she stopped as well. She turned around.

"I'm coming to your *conversazione*," he said, shutting his umbrella and giving her the benefit of his recent thoughts. "It's what I should do, and it's what's really best for you."

The Contessa's gray eyes grew large. "Haven't I told you that I absolutely forbid it! Having you there, no matter how well intentioned and supportive you are and how much I love you, will make me a bundle of nerves, a bigger bundle of nerves."

She put her gloved hand on his arm. "Urbino dear, I know you want to put me at my ease so that I'll be calm and silver throated, but the best way to do that is to respect my wishes. I'd rather have you say good-bye and good luck to me in the courtyard. You've heard everything I have to say about those years, and more than once! There are better things for you to be doing. Come. Let me show you something."

They went across to the music conservatory and into the main courtyard. In the large open space beneath tiers of loggias, a group of people were waiting to go into the lecture room. A soprano voice floated down to them:

" 'When e're you pass my tombstone, Oh shed a tear for me love! . . . ' "

It was from the mad scene of *Lucia di Lammermoor*. The woman's voice was uneven but filled with emotion.

The Contessa listened for a few moments with a reminiscent smile on her face, then went over to accept the good wishes of her friends and acquaintances. Among them were Lino Cipri and a woman in a plain black scarf. Cipri introduced the woman leaning on his elbow as his wife. She was bent over, with a heavily wrinkled face, and looked twenty years older than her husband. She stared up at the Contessa from bright blue eyes. They were the youngest thing about her.

"We're looking forward to what you have to share with us, Contessa," Cipri said. "We're almost as interested in music as we are in art."

His wife pulled her arm away from Cipri. "Not only art," his wife rasped in Italian, with the trace of an accent of some kind, "literature, poetry."

"I agree with you, Signora Cipri," the Contessa said, averting her eyes from the woman's. "As it turns out, the relationship between music and poetry at the conservatory will come up during one of my *conversazioni,* but not today. Thank you very much for coming. I hope you'll both find something of interest. If you'll excuse us."

She drew Urbino off into the second courtyard.

"Cipri is going to think it's peculiar that I won't be attending your *conversazione,*" Urbino said.

"Let him think what he wants, but let's hope the signora doesn't keep piercing me with her eyes. They were as cold as ice. But I didn't bring you into this courtyard or to this spot to escape from Signora Cipri. It was because of this other lady. She's what I want to show you."

She indicated the stone figure of a robed and veiled woman a few feet away, standing with one leg bent forward. She clasped a book against her breast and stared ahead, her face visible through the veil in an unusual effect rendered by the sculpture.

"How fortunate that no one has ever discovered her identity," the Contessa said. "The palazzo's little mystery. Don't you dare ever try to unveil her! Oh, I know that you'd like to have your cake and eat it, too—the romance of the mystery and the satisfaction of its solution. But that's impossible. Give your efforts to your Samuel Possle and my disappearing wardrobe. You can leave me now with a clear conscience. Our mysterious lady of the veil will watch over me along with Alvise's spirit and protect me from Signora Cipri's eyes!"

She gave him a kiss on the cheek and left him alone to contemplate the statue.

24

From the music conservatory it was a short walk over the Accademia Bridge to the broad embankment of the Zattere. Urbino headed there after leaving the Contessa, silently sending good wishes her way.

By the time he reached the Zattere, the clouds had started to disperse and sunshine was breaking through. Waiters at the cafés and restaurants were taking advantage of the change in the weather to set up tables on the pavement and on raft terraces that extended out into the wide Giudecca Canal.

The Zattere was an ideal place for a promenade even during winter since it faced south. Even on this less than ideal day, people passed back and forth, pushing baby carriages, carrying the morning's marketing, greeting each other and stopping to chat for a few minutes. Many were elderly Venetians, who could always count on meeting a friend somewhere on the quay. It extended all the way from the Punta della Dogana near the Church of the Salute to the Santa Marta quarter by the maritime station.

Urbino stopped at one of the cafés to have a coffee. He stood outside drinking it and looked across the canal to the Island of the Giudecca. In late July the island was connected to the Zattere by a temporary pontoon bridge in celebration of the Feast of the Redeemer. This floating bridge allowed Venetians to make their annual pilgrimage across the Giudecca Canal to the Palladian Church of the Redeemer, which Venice had built in thanksgiving for having been delivered from the plague in the sixteenth century. The feast was one of fireworks and mulberry eating and bathing on the Lido at dawn. Urbino and Habib had thrown themselves into the festival last summer. They had been able to persuade the Contessa, who usually avoided the celebration like the plague itself, to join them, although she had drawn the line at the early morning rituals on the Lido.

As Urbino drank his coffee, he wasn't thinking of the good times the three of them had had at last year's festival, however, but of Possle. One of the photographs in the slick magazine had captured Possle crossing the bridge of boats in all his vitality. It was hard to reconcile that image with the one that was more firmly engraved in his mind now of the feeble old man in the gondola.

And yet however physically incapacitated Possle might be, he had displayed a sharpness of mind and a sardonic humor that had obviously been honed over the years. If they had impressed Urbino, they had also served to disconcert him, since so much of their force had seemed to be directed at him personally for motives that, at this early point, were obscure. And then there was the unmistakably hungry look in the man's eyes.

Urbino was still upset with himself for not having taken more of an initiative with Possle, but he told himself that there would be time for that, or so he hoped.

He left the café and struck out along the Zattere toward the mouth of the Grand Canal. He stopped to watch a woman with her stool and easel, who was doing an acquatint of the Island of the Giudecca. She was German. Urbino praised her work, and they spent a few moments commenting on the view. Then he set out again.

His steps took him past the salt warehouses, where Biennale exhibitions were mounted, and past the villas of Milanese industrialists and foreigners. This had been a favorite walk of Ezra Pound, who had lived close by with his companion Olga Rudge. Perhaps on occasion Possle had accompanied the controversial poet on one of his promenades.

This thought, with all of its possibilities, was like oil on the fire of Urbino's need to know more about Possle and to be the person who would open light into the unknown recesses of his life.

With his mind a swirl of scenarios and strategies now that he had his foot in the door of the Ca' Pozza, Urbino reached the isolated point where the Giudecca Canal, the Grand Canal, and the lagoon all met. For the moment, he had the spot all to himself. He sat on a bench. A cold wind blew across the waters from the Adriatic, turning the weathervane statue of Fortune on its large golden ball atop the Customs House building.

Urbino gazed out at the swathe of greenish gray water beneath a sky of clouds and patches of blue. He sent some positive thoughts across the distance to the Contessa, who should be fully launched into her *conversazione* by now.

Although the scene before him was one of the most dramatic in Venice, tourists seldom sought it out. On one side the twin columns of the Piazzetta and the Doge's Palace with its Gothic arcades caught the shifting light, while on the other, the Church of San Giorgio regarded the scene with all its cool and beautiful aloofness. Here, with the wind whipping in his face, it was easy to imagine that he was at the prow of a ship, sailing into Venice.

When this pleasant image was immediately replaced by one of Possle on the deck of the ship that had brought him back to the States for his last visit more than four decades ago, as the man had reminded him yesterday, Urbino got up from the bench with both amusement and impatience.

There was very little escape from his monomania, it would seem.

25

Urbino's brisk pace soon had him crossing the small bridge that brought him to the *squero* of San Trovaso, one of the few remaining gondola workshops in Venice and reputedly the best. The Contessa had commissioned his own gondola here.

A man in a beret had his easel set up and was evoking the dark wood buildings that were more Alpine than Venetian. Beneath a long balcony filled with bright geraniums, three of the keel-less boats stood on the canal bank. One was upright, the other two turned over, showing their green-painted flat bottoms. All three were positioned on trestles like the ones holding Possle's gondola. To complete the scene—to the painter's delight, Urbino was sure—was laundry fluttering on a line, a leaning ladder, and two industrious craftsmen or *squerarioli*.

Urbino greeted one of the men. He had struck up an acquaintance with him over the years. Long before the Contessa had given him the gondola, he had been fascinated with their construction and would sometimes come here to this *squero* to watch the men at their work. Making a gondola was an elaborate and time-consuming process that involved cutting and shaping two hundred and eighty pieces of mahogany, cherry, elm, and five other kinds of wood, then bending the long pieces for the sides after they have been heated on open fires.

The walnut *forcole* weren't made in the boatyards but in special workshops elsewhere in the city.

"Is everything all right with the gondola, Signor Urbino?" the *squerariolo* asked him.

"Perfect."

"It had to be. The Contessa was here two or three times a week to check up on us," the man said with a laugh. "I don't know how she kept it a secret from you. We were going to ask her if she wanted a room in the house so she could keep better watch."

The man carried a paint-splattered sawhorse into the enclosed workshop. Urbino let him go about his work for a few minutes, then mentioned that he had just seen a *forcola* that an apprentice had made.

"Even I could spot some flaws, but it was fine nonetheless."

"The young man should keep at it."

This was almost the same thing Urbino had said to Gildo, and now he told the craftsman what Gildo had told him—that his friend, the apprentice, was dead.

The man made commiserating sounds as he brought a pile of lagoon cane, used for the fires, to a corner of the building.

"Do you know an oar and *forcola* maker from the Castello district?" Urbino asked him.

"He's almost ready to retire. We don't get our *forcole* from him, but he's one of the best."

Urbino got the name of the *remero* and his Castello address and let the man go about his work.

26

Shortly after eight the next morning, beneath the clear March sky, Urbino's gondola, maneuvered by the silent and brooding Gildo, swept into the Grand Canal near the palazzo where Wagner died. Crisp air, blown down from the Dolomites, carried the scent of snow. Urbino's reveries, encouraged by the small waterways, dispersed as the gondola, now surrounded by much larger and much more utilitarian vessels, glided between the marble palaces with what seemed to Urbino to be an insolent air.

He gazed at the buildings with some of the precious greenness of the tourist, which, once lost, is so hard to recover.

But his virgin impressions didn't last long. As his eye took in the Church of San Stae, it was difficult to say whether his enjoyment of its baroque facade was increased or diminished by his knowledge that the church's name was a Venetian corruption of Sant'Eustachio. And the same applied to the sumptuous Ca' Pesaro, with its history of the posthumous deception of a duchess, as well as to the mask-fronted Ca' Corner, which had been a plebian pawnshop centuries ago.

But one of the things about knowledge, Urbino reminded himself as the gondola passed the Ca' d'Oro with all of its

Gothic flamboyance, was that once you had it, you couldn't get rid of it, even if you wanted and needed to.

In an indirect but somehow inevitable way, this train of thoughts led him to the Contessa's lost items. At Florian's she had expressed her fear of losing her memory. This was one way that knowledge could be lost, wasn't it, by some perverse shifting of what had once been clear and sharp? But he didn't believe that this was happening to his Contessa.

What exactly this disappearance of her items amounted to, however, he had little idea at the moment, except for his belief that this was no ordinary theft, if it was indeed a theft. The fact that the Contessa's used clothing was missing was more disturbing to him than that the necklace was, even though it had been his gift to her. And he knew that this aspect of it was preying on her mind as well.

He had communicated both his certainty and his ignorance to the Contessa last night after he had called her about her *conversazione*. She had been relieved, for she knew how uncomfortable he was when he was in doubt. He would solve her troubling little mystery, she had reassured them both. She was willing to be patient.

As for her *conversazione*, it appeared that she had charmed everyone. At least this was Urbino's interpretation of her more modest and characteristic "It went swimmingly, swimmingly!" To which she had added, "You were with me, *caro*. Every second. And so was Alvise."

She gave him a brief summary of what she had accomplished and how she and her audience had played off of each other in a way that she said was pure music.

Urbino didn't need to worry about any problems coming at her from this direction, it seemed. And he was determined to do his best to settle the matter of her missing items. He would do it all the more eagerly because it didn't relate to Samuel Possle. It would be not only a welcome service but a welcome distraction as well.

When Urbino looked out the shuttered window as the gondola approached the stone, humpbacked arch of the Rialto Bridge, his eyes sought out a little courtyard washed by the morning sunshine. Because of Gildo, the Campiello del Remer, named as it was after local oarmakers, quickened Urbino's interest more now than it ever had before. He was frequently finding examples like this of how the city could renew itself for him. It was as if it were filled with signs and clues, hints and associations based not on its own past but on the dovetailing of this past with his own present and even future.

For example, how many times had he walked past the Ca' Pozza in the years he had been in Venice without feeling what he now felt about the place? And all that while Possle had been behind its walls, waiting, without knowing that he was waiting, for Urbino to catch up with him.

When was Possle going to invite him back? This question had been Urbino's almost constant companion, and it floated back to him now as Gildo slowed down the gondola. He didn't know whether he had spent more time entertaining this question or trying to chase away its dark twin: *Was Possle going to invite him back to the Ca' Pozza at all?*

Gildo deftly brought the gondola to the Pescheria landing beside the Rialto Bridge, and Urbino disembarked. He arranged for Gildo to meet him at the same place in an hour and headed for the nearby markets set up in the area.

Once or twice a month, more for his own sake than for hers, Urbino relieved Natalia of the errand of going to the Rialto markets. Here people went around buying necessary items. Fruit, vegetables, meat, and fish. It made him feel connected to the natural and essential rhythms of life, although the irony of arriving and departing in the extravagance of his own gondola wasn't lost on him.

He first wandered through the covered fish market in the clear morning sunshine. Behind their stalls the fishermen called and shouted in the Venetian dialect full of what seemed an impossible number of Xs and Zs. Their displays of that morning's catch from the Adriatic in all its variety, colors, and shapes pleased the eye almost as much as they would eventually please the palate. Urbino spent many minutes walking up and down the aisles and standing in front of one table after another, wishing he were a photographer or a painter.

A weather-beaten fisherman joked that if Urbino didn't buy anything they were going to charge him for looking. Urbino decided on *coda di rospo,* and smiled as he remembered Habib's horror at discovering that the name of the delicious fish he had been eating translated unappetizingly as the tail of a toad.

Urbino then strolled into the vegetable market, which was set up in one of the few open places on the whole length of the Canalazzo. He walked past temptingly arranged fruits and vegetables with prices handwritten on cards until he reached the stand presided over by a stout woman named Marta, whom he and Natalia always bought from.

She weighed out and deposited a cornucopia of the local produce into Urbino's two sacks, chatting about the weather and asking after the Contessa and Habib, whom she called his African friend.

Suddenly a voice emitted a stream of execrations. A tall woman in a dark brown coat gesticulated with her yellow scarf at a neighboring vendor. She was in her late forties. Blotches of bright pink marred her pale skin. Her short, brown hair was laced through with gray. Her eyes had a distracted look as they shot around at the staring shoppers and merchants.

Urbino recognized her as the angry woman from the embankment in front of the Ca' Pozza.

"Who is she?" he asked Marta.

"Elvira is her name."

The woman named Elvira stopped shouting as suddenly as she had started off. In apparent bewilderment she gazed around her with a softer expression now in her eyes. She then dashed off into the crowd of shoppers. As they moved aside to let her get through, a dark figure became visible. It looked remarkably like Armando, but the next moment the crowd pulled together again, and the figure was lost to view.

"What else do you know about her?" Urbino asked Marta as he stared into the crowd, searching it to see if his original impression had been correct.

Marta made the universally understood circular motion with one finger beside her temple.

"She's touched, poor thing. Sometimes she's as normal as you or me. She wasn't always like that." Marta's voice dropped into more sympathetic tones as she added, "She's become worse since the death of her son."

"When was that?

"Back in December, before Christmas, poor woman."

"Does she live near here?"

"Not too far. In San Polo. Her son died right in front of her eyes, they say. He fell from a building."

For a few more moments Urbino watched the crowd for any sign of the distracted woman or Possle's valet. Both had vanished.

He still had twenty-five minutes before he had to return to the gondola.

Turning his back on the Grand Canal, he made his way through the shoppers and tourists, burdened with his sacks. The stone steps of the Rialto Bridge rose up on his left with their souvenir and trinket stalls. More stalls lined the street from the foot of the bridge. Beyond them stretched an arcade of jewelry shops.

He joined the flow of people moving deeper into the San Polo district, directing his steps to one of the wine bars in a nearby square. Every once in a while he looked about him for Elvira and a dark figure who resembled Armando, but found only unfamiliar faces. And yet he had a vague feeling that someone, somewhere, was watching him.

Even at this hour the small bar was crowded with fishermen, merchants, local residents, and one lone French tourist with a guidebook. Urbino put his sacks down in a corner where other patrons had deposited bags and cartons. He managed to find an opening at the counter and ordered a glass of white wine.

As he drank his wine and ate some of the *cicchetti* snacks, he kept stretching his head above the crowd to check on his bags.

At first he didn't pay attention to the drift of conversation around him until a boatman started to complain about vandalism on the Rialto and in other parts of San Polo. When he mentioned a forced entry in his neighborhood, Urbino realized that he was referring to an area close to the Ca' Pozza.

"Didn't a young man fall to his death near there?" Urbino asked.

"A thief, he was, signore," the burly boatman responded. "We're better off with one less hoodlum. The streets aren't what they used to be. My wife doesn't like to go out alone in the evening. I pray to God they'll all end up killing themselves one way or another, and as soon as possible!"

His companions nodded and tossed down the rest of their wine.

Urbino consulted his wristwatch. He had just enough time to make his way back to the landing to meet Gildo. He bid the men good day and went to retrieve his sacks.

A white envelope lay on top of one of them among the tomatoes.

His eyes searched the crowded room, then out into the square. Armando was nowhere in sight.

He picked up the envelope. Written on it in purple ink was Raphael Urbino Macintyre. Inside Possle had scrawled, beneath today's date, that he was expected at the Ca' Pozza tomorrow afternoon at four-thirty.

27

A few hours later, after some reflection, Urbino sought out Gildo by the water entrance of the Palazzo Uccello. The young man was industriously but glumly scraping an oar with shards of glass broken from discarded wine bottles. The purpose was to whiten the oar but on this occasion Gildo seemed to have another purpose behind this one, for the oar was already white enough, having recently been scraped, and he was using more energy than usual.

"Excuse me, Gildo."

The gondolier lay down the oar. He turned his frank, handsome face up to Urbino. It was clouded.

"I don't mean to intrude, but I've noticed that you've been sad lately. The Contessa has commented on it, too. Even Silvia is concerned, she thinks."

Gildo showed no reaction to any of this.

"It takes a long time to get over the death of someone you care about. One never does, really," Urbino forged on, wondering what comfort all this might be to the young man. "If you'd like some time off, it would be fine with me. Not that there's anything wrong with your work at all."

"Thank you, Signor Urbino, but it's better for me to continue to work. The water soothes me. It makes me feel close to my friend." Gildo looked away, then added in a more cheerful voice, "I enjoy it even more than you do, even if I'm the one doing all the work." A feeble smile began on his full lips but quickly faded away.

"And you do an excellent job of it, Gildo. As you wish, then, but you can change your mind at any time."

It would have been appropriate at this point to depart and leave Gildo to his work and his musing, but Urbino lingered. He rearranged some of the cloths that Gildo used for polishing and cleaning.

"You say that it makes you feel close to your friend to be on the water. I hope that you're not suggesting that he drowned in a boating accident. In that case, it might not be a good idea to be so eager to return to rowing the gondola."

"No, he didn't drown, Signor Urbino. I just meant because of the *forcola* and because he loved gondolas, too. But I must be strong. It's been three months."

"There are many ways to be strong, Gildo. Give yourself time. If there's anytime that you want to talk about it, I don't want you to hesitate."

Gildo reached for the oar to continue his work. As Urbino was leaving, Gildo called out, "Oh, I forgot something." He took a piece of paper from his jacket pocket. "It's a bill for the new lock. Do you want me to bring him the check?"

Urbino took the bill. "No, I'll take care of it. Thank you."

Urbino went inside the house and telephoned Rebecca. He asked if he could stop by her offices in San Polo that afternoon.

28

Urbino had a deep affection for Rebecca and great respect for her professional expertise. But one thing he couldn't accept about her was her preference for the ultramodern anymore than she could accept his retro taste.

One of the things she often taunted him with was, "You can't build the Ca' d'Oro all over again today! Even your beloved Ruskin knew that," poking fun at his undying love of the Gothic.

Rebecca's offices off the Campo San Tomà seemed designed to slap Urbino in the face with all of its laminated plastic, glass, and chrome. The rooms were punitively illuminated and scattered with hyperpatterned, bright-colored rugs and furniture. Their only redeeming feature, as far as Urbino was concerned, other than one of Habib's paintings in her private office, was that some of the pinnacles and cornices of the Gothic Church of the Frari and a generous slice of its rose window were visible from two of the windows of Rebecca's private office.

Rebecca lay aside a sheaf of papers.

"If you hadn't called me, I would have called you," she said, with a bright smile on her attractive face. "You're here about the Ca' Pozza and Samuel Possle, aren't you?"

"Am I so transparent? How do you know that?"

Rebecca laughed. "I didn't, but I do now. Carla saw you ringing the bell a few days ago." Carla was her assistant. "I put two and two together."

Urbino seated himself on the sofa beneath a painting of Burano by Habib. He picked up a book from the glass table and riffled through it. It was a signed first edition of Daphne du Maurier's *Rebecca* in English. The story and the Hitchcock film of the novel had so impressed Rebecca's mother that she had named her after the haunting title character.

"Why were you going to call me?" Urbino asked, putting down the book.

"You go first. Coffee?"

She poured out two cups from the pot she always kept brewing in a corner of the room.

Urbino wasn't in the mood to go into a lot of detail. He gave Rebecca the essentials, leaving out most of his speculations. He devoted a lot of time, however, to describing what he had seen of the interior of the Ca' Pozza.

"What a strange man and a strange room," Rebecca said when he had finished. "Right up your alley, in some ways, perhaps," she added with a little smile. "Maybe if you become a regular, I can tag along with you some time."

"Listen, Rebecca, you mentioned something about a boy who died in a fall from Benedetta Razzi's building. What else do you know about it?"

"Not much more than I've already told you. I don't know who he was. He seems to have hung around a group of other kids who have been making trouble in the area. As I said, drugs must be involved. There've been break-ins."

"Was he trying to break into Razzi's building?"

"I don't know."

Urbino told her about the woman named Elvira, whose son had fallen from a building to his death in front of her own eyes, it seemed.

"It must be the same kid," she said. "Sad."

"I stopped in one of the *bacari* in the Campo delle Beccarie. Some of the men were talking about the vandalism in San Polo."

"It's become a big problem," Rebecca said. "Fortunately nothing has happened in my neighborhood. But you know how we all console ourselves. Not my street, not my building, not my apartment. Well, not yet anyway."

"Let's hope not."

"As I said when we were in the Campo Santa Margherita, you should be careful yourself during these walks of yours. Someone might think you're carrying around bundles of American dollars. But I thought you wanted to dig up Possle's past. What does this kid have to do with that?"

"Probably nothing."

"Just the old curiosity, eh?" Rebecca asked with a smile.

"Something like that. So what is it that you have to tell me?

"Don't think I haven't noticed how you've changed the subject. I know all your tricks. Just as I know that you're going to like my two juicy tidbits."

"Why didn't you tell me before today?"

"Because I just found out, smart guy. I was having lunch with Luca"—Luca was a friend who worked for one of the banks—"he said that the Ca' Pozza is mortgaged up to the hilt and beyond, and your Possle's already missed a payment or two. He could be out on the street in no time flat along with his gondolier or his caretaker or whatever the man is to him. And don't think the fact that he's an American makes things easier for him. On the contrary."

Urbino absorbed this as he took a sip of coffee.

"And what's your other tidbit?"

"A bit more colorful. Luca also tells me that somebody believes that the Ca' Pozza is haunted."

"Haunted? What are you talking about?"

Urbino immediately thought about the figure at the loggia door of the Ca' Pozza and the laughter and sobs. He had told no one about them yet, but when he might, he certainly wouldn't let anyone get the wrong impression. There was a rational reason that had nothing to do with the building being haunted.

"Ridiculous, isn't it?" Rebecca said. "But what else would you expect of Demetrio Emo?"

"Demetrio Emo the locksmith, Gildo's uncle?"

"Please don't tell me there're two of him! Not someone as big as that! It seems that at a bar near his shop Emo's been talking about the Ca' Pozza being haunted. Luca goes there from time to time. Maybe there's a grain of truth in the rumors about Emo and Black Masses."

"Those are ones I haven't heard."

"Don't take it so hard. Even sleuths are fallible. You owe me. The mortgages and the haunting of the Ca' Pozza. I'll expect at least a dinner."

29

There was something fascinating in seeing so large a man involved with objects as small and slim and secretive as keys. In a corner of Demetrio Emo's shop near the Church of the Madonna dell'Orto an hour after talking with Rebecca, Urbino watched the locksmith cut and polish two keys for an elderly woman. He kept shooting quick glances at Urbino from his flat, dark eyes.

Emo did a thriving business despite his checkered past and his refusal to conceal it. The name of his shop, prominently displayed on a sign above the door and on a plaque behind the counter, was THE KEEPER OF THE KEYS in pointed reference to St. Peter, the keeper of the keys of the church.

When Emo was free, Urbino gave him the check for the new lock and keys.

"You didn't come to pay me," Emo said, as he took the check. "Gildo could have brought it."

His soft, but insistent voice must have been perfected over his years as a priest delivering sermons, giving punishment and counsel in the confessionals, and seducing his parishioners.

"You came about the Ca' Pozza," he said.

When Rebecca had said almost the same thing earlier, Urbino had been amused. Now he was on his guard.

"You're right," he said. "How do you know?"

"No big mystery, Signor Sherlock. Friends have seen you hanging around the building from time to time," Emo explained vaguely.

Urbino wondered if he could be trying to protect Gildo. Perhaps, however, Urbino had been drawing attention in the neighborhood, especially these days when the residents were being more vigilant because of the break-ins.

"I do have an interest in the Ca' Pozza," Urbino admitted, "a professional one. My biographies, I mean," he added, as a smile broadened Emo's already immense face. "The owner of the Ca' Pozza is a connection to the past. He's known a lot of colorful and influential people over the years."

"And his house is just as interesting as these people are, maybe more so."

"Yes, well, someone overheard you talking about the building. You said that it's haunted."

Emo emitted a loud laugh. "Is that what I said? Well, maybe it is. But that doesn't fit into your system of things, does it? Logic and all that?" Emo stared at him with all humor banished from his face now. "My priestly training makes me more susceptible than you. I could tell you stories that would freeze your blood."

He seemed completely serious.

"About the Ca' Pozza?"

"No, not the Ca' Pozza. Not necessarily. Just to give you an idea of what we priests hear, one of our parishioners claimed to see the devil every single night. He had the monsignor convinced, and me, too, almost. But you know how the Church keeps its secrets."

"But why do you say that the Ca' Pozza has a reputation for being haunted?" Urbino asked, returning to the main point.

Emo didn't respond right away. He appeared to be weighing what he was going to say.

"Something I read in one of the old books in the library at

San Gabriele," he eventually said in an almost offhand manner. San Gabriele was the parish church where Emo had been a priest. "You'd be surprised what they have there. A whole shelf of spells and incantations and exorcisms. Just my thing."

"You're interested in the supernatural?" Then, realizing that this was a strange question to ask of someone who had been a former priest, Urbino clarified with, "The occult, I mean?"

"The supernatural, the occult, blood that solidifies and liquefies on command, weeping Madonnas, saints' bodies that never decay, and miraculous cures from slivers of the Cross and crumbs from the Last Supper! It's all the same. Something to occupy my mind with. Kind of an intellectual exercise. Like your own sleuthing, you might say, though in my case I've been trained not to spill the beans."

"And the Ca' Pozza?" Urbino persisted.

"Nothing any more special about that place than about other buildings in Venice. Like the house with the carved angel near the Cardinal Patriarch's residence. The devil possessed the proprietor's pet monkey centuries ago, or so it was rumored. And then there's the Palazzo Mocenigo-Vecchio. People swear that Giordano Bruno's ghost walks through the rooms."

Bruno was a Renaissance philosopher and alchemist who had lived in the palazzo and been burned at the stake.

A customer came in. Emo cut him several keys. When the man left, Emo picked up where he had left off.

"And the Casino degli Spiriti," he said, naming a small, isolated building with a view of the lagoon and the cemetery island a short distance from his shop. It had been the venue of glittering literary and musical parties perhaps not much different from those that the Ca' Pozza had once seen. "Haunted, they say."

Urbino nodded. He was familiar with the legend. "And what about the Ca' Pozza?"

"Maybe not the Ca' Pozza, but the Ca' *Pazza*," Emo

emphasized. "At least that's what one of my books said, Ca' Pazza, the House of the Crazy Woman. Supposedly Ca' Pozza is a corruption of Ca' Pazza."

Urbino hadn't come across anything like that in his own research, but as Emo said, the parish had a special collection of books.

Pazza meant "crazy woman" in Italian. According to the guidebook Urbino had in his own library, however, the Ca' Pozza was named after the *pozza,* or well, that had stood on the spot: the House of Fresh Water, the House of the Well. That was a far cry from what Emo was telling him.

"People used to believe the building was haunted by an insane woman," Emo went on to explain. "She was killed by falling stones during the building's construction in the seventeenth or eighteenth century."

"The seventeenth."

"So you know the story?"

"I know that the building dates back to the seventeenth century."

Inevitably Urbino thought, at this point, about the laughter and sobs he had heard when he was standing outside the Ca' Pozza in the middle of the night. If he were to tell Emo about them, the locksmith would slyly suggest that they were proof of the legend surrounding the house. Of course, now that Urbino knew what he did about Elvira, no matter what the explanations for the past haunting of the Ca' Pozza might be, the explanation for the mad cries and laughter of the past few months was quite reassuringly rational.

Urbino considered giving the ex-priest the benefit of these logical conclusions, but Emo's combination of irreverence and credulousness, both of which showed a vulnerability, deterred him.

Emo was staring at him as if he expected him to say something more about the Ca' Pozza. It only confirmed Urbino's decision to remain silent, at least for the time being.

The telephone rang. Emo answered it and went into a small area behind his shop to talk. Urbino looked around the small shop. Crammed though it was, everything seemed to be in its proper place.

"An emergency," Emo said, coming back into the front of the shop and hanging up the phone. "Someone had his keys stolen and needs me to put in a new lock. Where would I be without house visits?"

Emo started closing up his shop. Urbino lingered a few minutes longer and said, "By the way, I've noticed that Gildo seems sad these days. He tells me that a friend of his died."

Emo looked at him sharply.

"Are you concerned about Gildo, or is this about the Ca' Pozza?"

"What does the Ca' Pozza have to do with Gildo?"

But as he asked the question, the answer came to him before Emo responded. He had a quick vision of Elvira shouting and shaking her fist at the poop of the gondola where Gildo was maneuvering his oar when it had gone by the Ca' Pozza.

"As if you don't know. His friend fell from the building next door to the Ca' Pozza."

30

At nine on Sunday morning, on the day of his next visit to the Ca' Pozza, Urbino climbed up from the attic to the *altana* perched on the rose-colored roof of the Palazzo Uccello. There he found Gildo as Natalia had said he would. The slim young man was gathering the blankets, jackets, and scarves she had put out to air on the wooden terrace in the expectation of a day of sun and gentle breeze. But half an hour ago the day had changed abruptly. Dark clouds, driven in from the sea by a steady wind, were thickening above the city.

"I'll help you," Urbino said.

Together they took down the items. They were already damp and in danger of blowing off the *altana*.

Many of the buildings in Venice had these wooden terraces attached to their roofs. They were as characteristic of the city's architecture as its covered wellheads, inverted bell and obelisk chimneys, and *sottoportici*. Originally they were built on the palazzi for the noble women to sit and bleach their hair in the sun, with the help of a special concoction that included powdered Damascus soap and burned lead. These days, however, they had more mundane functions, unless you were someone like Urbino who would often spend hours on the bench among the geraniums, dreaming and gazing across the roofs of the city.

Gildo was silent as he placed a plaid scarf in the wicker hamper.

"There's something I'd like to mention, Gildo," Urbino began. "I had a talk with your uncle yesterday when I went to give him the check."

Urbino mentioned the check because he didn't want Gildo to think that he had gone to see Emo to get information about him.

Gildo continued to remove the items from the racks. He didn't look at Urbino.

"I hope you know that I'm concerned about you. When I mentioned to your uncle that you were a little depressed lately about your friend, he told me that he died in a fall from the building next door to the Ca' Pozza."

Gildo's head snapped up. There was a wounded look in his generous green eyes.

"Excuse me, Signor Urbino, but we should get everything off the *altana*." His voice, usually slurred in the appealing Venetian manner, sounded stifled and unnatural. "I don't have much time. Remember that today is one of the days when I go to the Bacino Orseolo."

"Of course, Gildo. And Natalia and I are delaying you with this task. We can talk some other time. Here, let me help you with that blanket."

31

In the afternoon, to pass the time before he was expected at the Ca' Pozza, Urbino went to the Accademia Gallery. When he had been there three months ago with Habib he had been distracted, although pleasurably, by playing the role of an indulgent *cicerone* as he so often did with Habib. This afternoon he wanted to have a leisurely, solitary turn through the galleries to soothe his nerves. He expected to be temporarily carried away from the world beyond the walls of the Accademia.

But it didn't work out that way.

Carpaccio's *Dream of St. Ursula*, with the peacefully sleeping saint visited by an angel in her chastely ordered bedroom, a painting that Ruskin had lavished pages of praise on, reminded Urbino by cruel contrast of his very different, troubling dream. He had suffered from it again last night.

As for Giorgione's toothless old woman pointing to the warning words *Col tempo* written on a scroll of paper, it evoked nothing less than the image of Possle's aged face that had changed so much over time.

Another Carpaccio, *The Miracle of the Relic of the Cross*, seemed innocent enough until Urbino fixated on certain details. The old wooden Rialto Bridge carried his thoughts back to Elvira's erratic behavior yesterday morning. The blithe gondolas became superimposed with Possle's stationary one at the Ca' Pozza and, just as he was turning away, also whispered of Gildo's reticence about his friend's death.

Neither was there any relief in Tintoretto's spectral *Theft of the Body of St. Mark from Alexandria*. It wasn't so much that the turbulent sky made Urbino anxious about the storm that was soon to assault the city, but that the repetition of all the arcades and steps with their fleeing, ghostly figures spoke a language of danger and obsession, and all in the service of a supposedly noble intention.

Here in the Accademia he was wandering through a cavern whose decorated walls were looking at him with familiar eyes and emitting confused, but disturbingly appropriate, words and signs. When he found himself trying to search out personal meanings in other paintings, he decided it was time to leave. He still had time for a much needed drink before seeing Possle.

As he was heading for the staircase, someone called out his name jovially. It was Lino Cipri, in a flowing tie and a worn, black velvet jacket. He was copying Lorenzo Lotto's portrait of a brooding gentleman in his study, one of the paintings commissioned by Eugene.

Urbino was surprised to see Cipri since the painter had told him that he was usually home in the afternoon. But perhaps he was eager to finish the Lotto. Urbino looked back and forth between the original and the copy. He nodded in appreciation.

"You've managed to capture the salamander and the fallen rose petals exactly," he said. "Eugene will be pleased with this one as well."

"I hope so." Cipri was visibly delighted with Urbino's praise. "Too bad you didn't stay for the *conversazione*. My wife and I were spellbound. The Contessa had us wanting more. It was like listening to music to hear what she had to say about those days, and there was a lot of participation from the audience."

"It wasn't my choice that I wasn't there. She got my solemn promise to stay away. Stage fright, you know."

"There was no need for her to be afraid. Maybe you'll come next time."

Urbino paid Cipri a few more compliments about the Lotto copy and then left him to his work.

32

Urbino approached the door of the Ca' Pozza. Low, dark clouds raced above the roof of the building with a menacing air. The storm had held off so far, but soon it would unleash itself. He was about to ring the bell when footsteps rushed up behind him. He turned and confronted the face of Elvira.

She grabbed the front of his cloak with both her hands. "Don't go in, signore! Don't go in!" she shouted in rapid Italian. "If you enter, you won't return, not alive. No, you won't return!"

This version of the warning over the portals of Dante's Hell gave Urbino more than a momentary pause. He tried gently to pull away, but the woman's grip was firm.

"You're Signora Elvira," he said, keeping his voice low and soothing. "Don't distress yourself. I'm in no danger."

"You are, I tell you!"

She released him and peered into his face. She was almost the same height as he was. Her eyes glowed with a feverish fire. "You know me?" she asked in a soft voice. "I don't know you."

"Let me take you home, Signora Elvira."

"Home? I have no home. This building destroyed it. It destroys everything. It will destroy you! Don't go inside!"

With this repeated warning she dashed away down the *calle* beside the Ca' Pozza. On the pavement lay the yellow scarf she had been waving at the merchant in the Rialto. It was torn and soiled. Urbino slipped it into the pocket of his jacket.

To Urbino's surprise, the door of the Ca' Pozza stood open. Armando, clad in what was his habitual black, stood aside to let Urbino in. His dark eyes searched the quay with a barely concealed fury touched with fear.

33

T he bone-chilling damp of the Ca' Pozza, more intense than it was outdoors and considerably colder than could be expected of even an old Venetian palazzo, settled down over Urbino again as soon as he stepped over the threshold. His awareness that he was in large part a victim of his own superstition didn't lessen the feeling anymore than it had on his first visit but, instead, seemed to increase it. Reluctantly, he took off his cloak and placed it over one of the gargoyles on the clothes stand.

The grim Armando, giving off his unwashed odor, conducted him across the lower hall, past the closed door of what Possle had called one of the mute's nooks and crannies in the silent house. The high staircase rose at its slightly tilted angle, or so it seemed once again to Urbino.

As they ascended through its heavy shadows, with Armando a few steps above him, the strains of music and a male voice suddenly shattered the silence.

" 'So, we'll go no more a-roving
So late into the night,
Though the heart be ne'er as loving,
And the moon be still as bright.' "

When they reached the long, dark *sala*, Urbino stopped to listen to the rest of the song. It came from the gondola room, whose door was thrown open wide.

" 'For the sword outwears its sheath,
And the soul wears out the breast,
And the heart must pause to breathe,
And love itself have rest.
Though the night was made for loving,
And the day returns too soon,
Yet we'll go no more a-roving
By the light of the moon.' "

Armando, who had continued across the *sala*, stopped at the door of the gondola room and waited for Urbino. His arms, with their scarred hands, were close against his sides. Under his scrutiny, Urbino crossed the *sala* and entered the hot, inert air of the strange chamber.

He took in the scene with a quick glance. The domed ceiling, the shuttered windows, the dark draperies, the rococo mirror, the candles, the pots of exotic flowers, the silver cage with its dead cricket, the orange walls with their portraits and still-life paintings, the improbable gondola under its canopy, and, in it, Possle's reclining figure, dressed in red satins and purple silks.

"An interesting piece of music, don't you think, Mr. Macintyre? Please sit down."

Urbino seated himself in the high-backed armchair close to the gondola, where he had sat on the previous occasion.

"But I'm sure that you found it too loud," Possle went on, after giving a little tug at the purple silk that swathed his head. "You must forgive me, but I refuse to wear a hearing aid."

Considering the man's old-fashioned, if not antiquated air, however, Urbino wouldn't have been surprised if Possle had a hearing trumpet concealed among the orange cushions.

"Armando will bring us our Amontillado."

Armando, who had been hovering in the doorway, nodded and withdrew.

"You know the song?" Possle asked.

His small, dark eyes behind his large, black glasses bore into Urbino.

"It's one of Byron's poems set to music. The refrain comes from an old Scottish song. My grandfather used to sing it to me."

"Indeed? What a coincidence. 'And the soul wears out the breast,' " Possle recited in his tremulous voice. He made no attempt to sing the words. "Byron was barely twenty-nine when he wrote those words. I'm almost three times that."

"Melancholy was in his nature," Urbino observed. "The poem expresses his repentant mood after *carnevale*, I believe," Urbino went on, feeling a little pedantic. Possle was staring at him. "Even the young are susceptible to that," he went on. "Last time you asked me if I liked Byron. It appears that you like him a great deal yourself. Perhaps more than I do."

"Is that what you think? Or *know?*"

Possle's emphasis puzzled Urbino, who remained silent. Possle looked narrowly at him from his recumbent position.

"But you might have a professional interest, Mr. Macintyre." Possle's eyes again searched Urbino's face. "I'm referring to the biography on Byron that you might write one of these days."

He made a longish pause and seemed irritated when Urbino didn't respond.

"And here we both are, you and me," Possle continued, "two lovers of Byron in the middle of Venice, 'the pleasant place of all festivity, The revel of the earth, the masque of Italy.' "

"You're fond of quoting Byron," Urbino ventured.

"But that's an easy one to recognize. Almost everyone knows it."

He fussed around with the cushions for a few moments.

"Your Scottish grandfather, you say? The ancient Celtic clan of Macintyre. 'Son of a Carpenter,' it means, rather a plebeian association for someone like yourself. *Through Difficulties* is your clan's motto. Your crest, a right hand holding aloft a dagger. I believe your ancestor chopped off his own thumb to plug up a hole in the sinking galley of a chieftain. This old head of mine is filled with the most amazing nonsense, Mr. Macintyre."

Possle had obviously done research on him, or Armando had. The question was why.

"I suppose you'd like to be the greatest biographer since Boswell?" Possle now said.

"Hardly."

"More in the line of Lytton Strachey, then? Attacking a life from an unusual angle? Is that what you would like to do with me?"

Possle withdrew the crystal vaporizer from among the cushions and squeezed the bulb once, twice. The aroma of his special potpourri quickly spread through the warm air. Urbino could only distinguish the scent of tuberose and orange blossom but none of the other essences Possle had named.

"You'd be an interesting subject," Urbino said.

"Who knows, Mr. Macintyre? I might be of use to you but perhaps not in the way that you're thinking."

"What do you mean?"

"I'm aware that I'm more of an oddity, an anomaly, call it, than anything else. Some people might think the same of you," Possle added, with a little cough that could have been embarrassment or a cover for amusement.

Urbino had to agree with this, but he did so silently. Despite the theatricality and eccentricity of Possle's gondola, Urbino's negotiation of the canals in his own gondola was certainly not less so in its way. One might even argue that at least

Possle was confined to the privacy of the Ca' Pozza, whereas Urbino was very much in the public eye.

"I'm not Byron." Possle said this with an air of amused regret. "I'm not Peggy Guggenheim. But what I am, Mr. Macintyre, is a source of information about the people who have passed through the Ca' Pozza in its heyday. In *their* heyday. In *mine*," he added, his thin voice dropping lower. "I could be your mirror. Oh, don't look so surprised. I don't mean that you would see yourself in me, but who knows?" he said, with a lifting of his sparse brows. "What I mean is that I could be your filter. The good and the bad, the rich and the famous, the talented and the failures"—his voice grew a little more forceful— "all seen through the eyes of someone who can barely see now, or hear."

At this point Armando entered and deposited the tray next to the carafe of water and the goblets on the small, inlaid table. He poured the pale wine into two porcelain cups. He handed one cup to Possle. This time, the other cup was left for Urbino to reach for.

Armando gave an almost imperceptible bow and left the room.

Urbino had hardly registered the man's coming and going. Possle had just come close to saying that he would be willing to work with Urbino. Could the mystery of why Possle had summoned him be as simple—as wonderfully and unexpectedly simple—as that? Yet even if this were the case, it didn't explain why he had chosen Urbino.

"Is that why you've asked me to come here?" Urbino began, after considering his words carefully. "May I assume that you're making an overture?"

Possle took a sip of the wine.

"An overture, yes, but an overture of what kind?" his host replied. "Perhaps I've been too precipitate in getting your hopes up. I'm a man who likes to proceed slowly and logically, not unlike yourself, but one who will also make a quick leap sometimes to even my own surprise. That's like you, too, I have a feeling."

He scrutinized Urbino with his small, quick eyes, his tongue darting out to moisten his lips in his habitual gesture. If he had reminded Urbino of a preserved saint on the previous occasion, this afternoon there was something almost reptilian about him—frail, yes, but sinuous and with a distinct sense that he might leap and strike.

They sipped their wine in silence. A distant rumble of thunder penetrated the gondola room from beyond the drawn drapes and closed shutters.

Possle kept his cup propped on his stomach. Pressed against his silk shirtfront hung the large, strangely shaped metal talisman on its gold chain, one of whose details was a crescent. Urbino was reminded of the symbol affixed to the inside of the Ca' Pozza's front door. He stared at the talisman, and once he began it became difficult to take his eyes away from it.

When he did, transferring his attention to its owner, Possle's head had dropped on his chest. His eyes were closed. The cup looked as if it might slip from his grasp.

Urbino was about to get up and take it when his eye became caught by something white on the carpet near his feet. It was a piece of paper, the size of a postcard. It appeared to have writing on it. Without thinking, he leaned over and picked it up. He didn't examine it, but thrust it into his pocket, surprising himself with the force of his own impulse.

He had hardly withdrawn his hand from his pocket when Possle's voice gave him a start.

"Tell me, Mr. Macintyre, are you involved in one of your investigations at the moment?"

Possle wasn't looking at Urbino but off in the direction of the rococo mirror on the other side of the room. The cracks of thunder became more pronounced and followed each other at shorter and shorter intervals. Possle, with his weak hearing, seemed to be oblivious to the approaching storm.

"My other line of work, as you called it last time?" Urbino could hear the nervousness in his voice at almost having been discovered. "It's not something I look out for, not like a new subject for one of my books. If something special comes my way, something that touches me personally or someone I know and care about, then I turn my hand to it."

"Your mind, you mean."

Urbino speculated whether Possle could have sought him out, not for his writing skills as he had seemed to hint a little while ago, but for his detecting ones. Possle's next comment gave added weight to this possibility.

"And you're the soul of discretion in your sleuthing."

"I try to be."

"It's in your nature, as you say melancholy was in Byron's."

"And in the nature of what I choose to look into."

"Or what chooses you."

Because of the truth in Possle's emendation and Urbino's sense that it might be a prelude to an offer, he kept silent.

He wasn't disappointed when Possle went on to say, "I suppose you find the Ca' Pozza and myself—along with Armando—something worth looking into. As an intellectual exercise, of course. There's no dead body in the library, and no crime anywhere in sight, except one of taste." Possle made a strangled sound from somewhere in his chest that must have been a chuckle. "I mean this room. Is it to your liking?"

The abrupt shift disoriented and disappointed Urbino. Possle had appeared to be close to making an appeal. But he had seemed to be on the brink of it before with his comments about Urbino's biographies, only to drop the topic. He was doing the same thing again.

Two days ago Urbino had suspected that Possle was toying with him. Now he had less doubt.

The effect of all this was to surprise a response out of Urbino. "You're trying to keep me off balance, Mr. Possle. With what end in mind, I don't know. But to answer your question, let me say that I find your room more than a little strange, as I'm sure you know most people would. And yet it seems familiar to me."

This last comment was drawn out of him almost against his will. He hadn't known he was going to say it until he did. He was about to add that he also found some of the things Possle said familiar, but he let just the one observation serve, at least for the moment.

Possle's half-smile puckered his face. "And well it might look familiar, Mr. Macintyre," he said. "You've been here before."

"I beg your pardon? The first time I entered this room— the first time I even set foot in the Ca' Pozza—was three days ago."

"Nonetheless, you *have* been here before—in your fashion."

Urbino, more and more confused, took refuge again in silence. His recurring dream flashed across his eyes. The room in the dream *was* similar to this one, with its drapes and formal, angular chairs, but surely Possle couldn't know that.

"Perhaps my room looks too much like a wager," Possle said in an insinuating tone, "and you're afraid of being duped by taking it too seriously."

"Whatever game you're playing—" Urbino began with exasperation.

"Or perhaps," Possle interrupted him with his tremulous voice, "you think my room is as monstrous as an orchid. Perhaps you're afraid you'll find me dead in my gondola, shot through the head by my own hand, or dressed in a monk's habit and praying to the Blessed Virgin Mary. Is that what's left for me after all this?" He waved his hand weakly to indicate the room with its unusual details of color, design, and furnishing. "The muzzle of a pistol or the foot of the cross?"

Only then did Urbino, with a sudden rush, understand Possle's puzzling comments.

"Huysmans's *Against Nature*," Urbino said. "Des Esseintes."

Possle nodded, as if a recalcitrant pupil had finally learned his lesson. He drank down the remainder of his Amontillado.

The shock of surprise kept Urbino from saying anything more for a few moments. He leaned back in his chair and let his eye roam around the room. He was now seeing it in a completely different light.

Possle had woven his hints about the room out of comments that Oscar Wilde and others had made about the novel that had played such an important role in Urbino's life. The familiar elements in Possle's room—with the grand exception of the gondola—twinned the décor and architecture of the isolated house where the reclusive character had pursued his eccentricities. This fact would have been unusual in itself.

But the connection to Urbino made it even more peculiar. Here was Possle, an expatriate American like himself, secluded in his palazzo, who had also been influenced by the same decadent French model. And he was also aware of Urbino's own fascination, something not many people knew about.

"I don't mind that you know a great deal about me, Mr. Possle," Urbino said, with more vehemence than sincerity. "What I do mind is the way that you're going about it. If you want to have a meeting of minds, there are much better ways of doing it. Whatever advantage you have over me in this way—or you *think* you have—is worth nothing if you want my cooperation. And have no doubt, Mr. Possle, it's as clear as anything can be that you do want exactly that." Urbino took a deep sip of his Amontillado, waiting for Possle's response.

But this outburst, which made Urbino feel so much better

for having indulged in it, was lost on Possle. The man had dropped off to sleep again.

Light flashed behind the drapes, admitted by the chinks in the closed shutters. Almost immediately afterward a loud crack of thunder broke the silence. Wind rattled the shutters. Possle didn't stir.

Possle's frail chest rose and fell slowly, almost imperceptibly. For the moment, with his purple headscarf, he looked like some aged, dandyish pirate stealing a few moments of rest before going out again on the deck of his ship.

Taking advantage of being left to his own devices for however long or however short Possle's narcoleptic spell lasted, without getting up from his chair Urbino examined the small, squat pots of plants and flowers closest to him. He was careful to avoid the candles. He reached down and touched a petal of one of the exotic flowers. The flower was artificial. So were the dewdrops beading it. A pot next to this flower held the yellowish, artificial-looking plant streaked with gray that evoked a piece of stovepipe. He touched the plant. It was real. These, too, were details from Huysmans. Artificial plants that looked real and real ones that looked artificial.

He also now took the opportunity, still from his seated position, to look more closely at the paintings ranged on the wall across from the gondola. Some were also lifted from the pages of the book. Two of them remarkably resembled ones that Huysmans had described. One was Gustave Moreau's *Salome Dancing Before Herod*. The other was Moreau's *The Apparition*, with its severed head of St. John the Baptist rising from a platter. Urbino had seen it at the Louvre. The *Salome* was in a gallery in the States. The two paintings were copies.

Beside the *Salome* was a portrait of a light-haired young woman in the manner of Sargent. Dressed in a low-cut black dress with a large, pale yellow flower at her bosom, she was seated on a sofa with high, curved sides. Urbino didn't recognize any original for the painting and assumed that it wasn't a copy.

A movement from the gondola caught his attention. Possle was staring at him. "I was off again," he said. "My sessions are becoming more frequent. I hope you were able to entertain yourself."

Urbino sensed that Possle, despite his spell, knew what he had been doing during it and that he was aware of Urbino's little outburst.

"About my own interest in Monsieur Huysmans," Possle continued, showing that he could pick up where he had left off, "be assured on a few points. I don't corrupt street urchins and get them habituated to brothels, and there's no jewel-encrusted tortoise hiding away in a corner of the room."

These were further details from the book, and Possle threw them out with an amused, casual air.

"And even that cage with the cricket, Mr. Macintyre. You probably think now that it's because, like our mutual hero, I want to express my loathing for my childhood by being reminded of the song that accompanied so many of my sad summers, but you are wrong. I like, instead, to be reminded of the old legend of the sibyl who forgot to ask for eternal youth when she was awarded eternal life. She was reduced in her ancient years to hanging in a cage and croaking out, 'I want to die.' You noticed that *my* cricket is dead."

His small eyes strayed toward the silver cage and back to Urbino's face.

"So you see, I don't go as far as I can with my imitations from the yellow book so cherished by Dorian Gray. And as for you, Mr. Macintyre, you haven't gone anywhere near as far as I have. Your Palazzo Uccello has nothing to compare with this, I'm sure. Just the book itself, perhaps different editions, maybe an illustration or two."

This was a good description of what Urbino did have in the

corner of his library dedicated to Huysmans. "As I said last time," he responded, holding back his anger, "you seem to know a great deal about me."

"More than you know about me, you mean? Is that what irritates you? Reflect, Mr. Macintyre. You may not have been as reticent as you think you've been over the years. Venice might be a secretive place, turned in on itself and shut off from the rest of the world, but it's one big stage as well. And in any case, when one has a secret, it encourages others to search it out."

Possle's gaze fell upon the crown of Urbino's head.

"Would you mind coming up the steps to the gondola for a moment?" he asked.

Curious as to what this was about, Urbino got up and approached Possle, with the expectation of being handed something that his host would withdraw from among the cushions or being asked to take the empty porcelain cup lying against them.

But instead, "Bend your head down please," Possle said.

When Urbino leaned closer to him, Possle's hands seized Urbino's head. His fingers groped Urbino's skull from front to back, side to side. Their touch was cold, very cold. Urbino wanted to draw back, but he endured it.

Rain was now beating against the windows of the gondola room, driven by the wind.

Possle held Urbino's head a long time before releasing it. Urbino went back to his seat, meekly perhaps to Possle's eye, but inwardly rebelling against the man's touch and angry with himself for having allowed it, but equally mystified.

"Do you believe in phrenology?" Possle asked.

"No."

"Perhaps you should. I wasn't able to give your head a proper examination, but it reveals a great deal. You have some morbidly developed faculties and some deficient ones. You're strong in philoprogenitiveness, for example, as is displayed in your fondness for your Moroccan friend and your gondolier."

Possle's voice was becoming weaker as he spoke. He took an audible breath and went on.

"If I could get my hands on the Contessa da Capo-Zendrini, I'm sure I'd find that her bump of benevolence is prodigiously developed. I've often wondered if the wealthy puzzle about what to do with all their money."

"The Contessa is a very generous woman."

"And you have been one of her main beneficiaries. But surely all her generosity is a mere pittance of what she has."

Before Urbino might defend the Contessa, Possle forestalled him by saying, "How I would have loved to have a go at Byron's head. He had a fine head on him."

He spoke for two or three minutes about phrenology and Byron, growing increasingly fatigued, and all the while weaving in references—some familiar, some arcane—to the poet, and looking at Urbino covertly and with distinct expectation.

"Might you know if Byron ever had a phrenological reading?" he asked at the end of this monologue. "I suspect that you know more about him than I do."

Urbino had listened to all of what Possle had said in patience, and when Possle finished, quietly took up with the subject that was of more interest to him. "You're strange, Mr. Possle, but maybe not as strange as you want me to believe. You want my cooperation about something. What it is, I don't know, but you're going about it in the wrong way. There's a mystery of some kind surrounding you and your house, as I'm sure you're well aware. But whether it's a real one or only one you're trying to generate—or add to—I have no idea."

"Or one that people have created themselves," Possle supplied, as a further possibility. "Reality is a boring affair. We'll always be outsiders here, Mr. Macintyre, even if I manage to live more years and you live to be as old as I am, which I heartily wish for you."

This latter observation amused him, if Urbino could judge by the same strangled sound that he had made earlier. It came from deep in his chest and grew and grew until his face lost its yellow waxy look and became decidedly red. He was seized with a cough that persisted long enough for Urbino to become alarmed. He arose from his chair and approached the gondola. Possle was now gasping for breath.

"I'll call Armando."

But the mute was already in the room, seeming to have appeared from nowhere. He moved to Possle's assistance, pushing Urbino aside with more force than was necessary. He leaned over Possle, whose eyes were closed as he continued to cough, and threw Urbino a look that said as loudly and severely as any words could that his visit had come to an end.

34

For the first ten minutes after leaving the Ca' Pozza, Urbino
hugged the sides of buildings, waded through ankle-high
water, and suffered the reek of backed up sewers. He cursed
not having brought an umbrella, although with the force of
the wind it would have soon proven as useless as the skeletons
of the ones that littered the alleys.

He found a bar to wait out the storm in and ordered a glass
of wine. He replayed his visit from the moment Elvira had
given him her dire warning before entering the Ca' Pozza until
Possle had been incapacitated by his cough.

Up until a few days ago, a silence had enveloped Possle that
Urbino had been obsessed with penetrating. Now Possle was
directing a barrage of calculated hints, suggestions, and revelations at him, delivered in his tremulous voice from among the
cushions of his gondola. And somewhere among it all he was
concealing his real intentions. Of this Urbino was positive.

He took from his pocket the slip of paper that he had
impulsively and guiltily picked up from the carpet. He
unfolded it. At first it appeared to be a receipt from a dry
cleaner's shop or photographer's studio.

But printed across the top was the name of the Church of
San Gabriele near the Palazzo Uccello. The voucher—for this

was what it was—named the coming Friday, five days from now. A mass for the dead was to be celebrated at seven-thirty in the morning in the memory of someone named Adriana Abdon. The voucher, officially stamped, acknowledged that Armando Abdon had paid the requisite sum. It was signed by the secretary of the Church of San Gabriele, a sister of the Convent of the Charity of Santa Crispina. The convent was associated with the church and located across the square from it.

Urbino now knew Armando's last name, but what was his relationship to the dead Adriana? Had she been his mother, perhaps his wife? His sister? His aunt?

Urbino was disappointed and also upset with himself. He had risked Possle's censure for what? His desire to snatch the paper had been fired by the hope that it would contain some important piece of information about Possle.

He had noticed it right after Armando served the wine. Had it been there before, or had it fallen from his pocket? Could Armando have dropped it for him to find? If he had, what was his motivation?

The rain had stopped. Urbino returned to the Palazzo Uccello, frequently having to reroute himself when the flooded alleys blocked his passage.

35

He's playing with you!" the Contessa cried out over the telephone an hour later, after he had given her some details of his visit.

"My thought exactly. But to what end? I suspect he wants my services, but which of the two might it be?"

He explained how Possle had brought up the topic of his biographies while they were talking about Byron.

"He could be a filter was the way he expressed it," Urbino said. "That's what I've been thinking. When I asked him if he was making me an overture, he got evasive. And a short time later he brought up my sleuthing and my discretion, and suggested that there might be something at the Ca' Pozza for me to look into. But he's sly and slippery. It's difficult to pin him down."

"And we know how many glass cases of butterflies you've collected over the years! I see quite well why Possle annoys you so much, and I wish he wouldn't drag me into the picture. My benevolence indeed! What business is it of his what money I have?"

"It's his knowing tone. Not just about you, but personal things about me and how I think," Urbino went on. "It's as if he's inside my mind or thinks he is, plucking out my secrets.

He's right on target most of the time, I have to admit. And I feel
as if he's saying and doing things that I have myself. It's almost
as if he's—he's appropriating me." He told her about the
unusual coincidence involving Huysmans. "Or maybe it's as if
I've been unconsciously imitating him in some strange way
or—or as if I'm looking at myself distorted in some mirror!"

Urbino was giving the Contessa the benefit of his own
dimly formed but deeply felt suspicions and explanations as he
struggled with the peculiar connection that Possle seemed to
have with him.

"As if, as if, as if," the Contessa mocked him. "Nonsense!
You're getting infected, and after only two visits! What's going
to happen if you spend days and months interviewing him for
a book? Before we know it, you'll be speculating that he's
some kind of vampire, although that would be a more appropriate role for Armando, I suppose!"

"I'll take comfort in the fact that I've seen him in the daytime," Urbino joked, in an attempt to alleviate his darkening
mood.

"Nonetheless, tell Natalia to double the garlic. But seriously, Urbino, maybe what it all comes down to is that you
don't like being around the aged and infirm. *'Memento mori,'*
isn't that what it's called?"

The Contessa knew him well enough to have hit on something sensitive, but he didn't want to pursue it. Instead he
brought up the topic of her next *conversazione,* scheduled for a
week from today.

"I'd really like to come," he said. "It would be a comfort to
me in the midst of all this business with Possle. Cipri seems to
find it strange that I'm not coming, and I'm sure others do as
well."

"As if you care what others think! And as for it being a
comfort to you to come, just think of me, *caro,* worried about
you sitting there and listening to every word! I know you
mean well, but let's leave it the way it is."

It was useless for Urbino to insist.

He hadn't yet told her everything about his last visit. Somewhat embarrassed, he now explained about the receipt from the Church of San Gabriele, and he asked her if the name Adriana Abdon was familiar.

"So it's come to that! Picking up odd scraps of paper at the Ca' Pozza. Leave Armando to his devotions to the dead, whoever this Adriana might have been. Adriana, Adriana. A lovely name. I've never known anyone named Adriana, but with my memory—" She interrupted herself and went on, "As I was saying, leave Armando to his requiems. And try to be more careful. Hold on to that precious logic of yours. Everything you've told me about Possle doesn't tally with my own impressions of him, limited though they were. He was very much the bon vivant, more a person of doing than talking." A sigh carried across the line. "But of course we're speaking of a gulf of forty years. Between the Samuel Possle of then and the cadaverous, housebound man of today."

"He can't have changed all that much. Physically, yes, but not in a basic way."

"If you're thinking of tossing that Proust quotation at me again, the one about a man not changing emotionally after the age of sixteen, don't do it! You're as bad as Possle. And haven't you learned from experience? Too much remembrance of things past can be unhealthy, if not downright dangerous. I have a suggestion. Why don't you come up to Asolo with me on Tuesday? Patricia called me last night." Patricia was her sister in London. "She'd like to stay at the villa in April with some friends. I should see what needs to be done. Some fresh mountain air will be good for us both."

36

Later that evening Urbino roamed around the Ca' Pozza. As he had after his first visit with Possle, he felt fatigued. But he was also restless.

The house seemed particularly silent and empty, even with the knowledge that Gildo was in his little apartment on the *pianoterreno*. Before going to Morocco, Urbino had enjoyed his solitary life in the Palazzo Uccello, but since Habib had been staying with him, much had changed. It wasn't that he still didn't savor his solitude, but that he had come to count on Habib, with all his enthusiasm and his ability to turn the most routine of activities into a celebration, to keep him from being swallowed up by it. Without Habib, solitude felt a little too much like loneliness.

Urbino went into Habib's studio. The poster of Habib's favorite Arab diva stared out at him with her wide-eyed gaze. Habib had neatened up the room before he had left. The paints and brushes were all in their places, the rags were arranged on the rack, the divan was made up, and the cassettes of Arabic music were in neat rows on the shelf. The ingenious storage and drying cupboards that Habib had constructed were closed.

Urbino examined some of Habib's paintings leaning against one wall. Part of a series on the Basilica San Marco, they turned the rich, dark interior into a bazaar of color and movement that evoked an elemental spirituality.

Urbino checked his wristwatch. It was nine o'clock. Perhaps he should call Habib in Fez, but then he decided against it. Habib was sure to detect his melancholy mood. Urbino didn't want to cast any shadow on Habib's visit with his family. He would wait to call him when he himself was in a cheerful mood.

Urbino went into the library. He felt drained. His head ached slightly. He hoped he wasn't coming down with the flu.

Urbino's gaze strayed to the corner of the room that held his editions of Huysmans and illustrations of scenes from the book, one of which was his own. He was puzzled as to how Possle had seemed to know about them and about so many other things as well.

The old guidebook he had consulted two weeks ago was still on the long, wooden table. He sat down and reread the passage about the Ca' Pozza. It now said nothing to him, whereas before it had been filled with promise and suggestion. But since then he had been behind the walls of the building. He had got in, twice.

It made him hungry for more. The Ca' Pozza was turning out to be much stranger and more fascinating than he had anticipated. Possle was an enigma, and one that Urbino couldn't leave alone.

Possle, for his own reasons, couldn't leave Urbino alone either, it seemed. The two of them were bound together on some strange journey together that Urbino anticipated with almost equal thrills of pleasure and fear.

37

The next morning Urbino went to see the widow Benedetta Razzi. She might be able to give him some solid information about Possle and the Ca' Pozza since, as Rebecca had told him, she owned the building next door, the one in which Elvira lived.

At 9:55 the *vaporetto* for Burano was pulling out of the boat landing on the Fondamenta Nuove below Razzi's windows when Urbino sat down in her parlor.

There was just the two of them, and about five hundred dolls.

The dolls were everywhere—on chairs, sofa, tables, shelves, and cabinets, even perched on a wall clock, peeping from open drawers and baskets, and adorning the wooden top of a baroque mirror. Many of them were in regional costumes from Italy and other parts of Europe and the world.

A tiered table was crammed with miniature cups and saucers, tiny porcelain masks, Lilliputian books, and a delicate candelabra with candles no thicker than pencil leads, all for her little ones. Over the years Urbino had learned the advantage of bearing gifts when he visited the old woman. Today it took the form of a tiny fan made out of marbleized paper.

"How lovely." Razzi was a small woman approaching eighty with wispy white hair and faded blue eyes. "My darlings are poor in fans."

She went to the table. She moved some pieces and placed the fan beside a glass swan Urbino had given her on a previous occasion.

"You see, I remember all your gifts," she said.

She lowered herself into a worn love seat, arranging the skirt of her black, sequined dress and straightening up two dolls beside her. One was a Japanese doll with a white porcelain face, slanted eyes, black hair, and an elaborate headdress. The other was a delicate figure in an embroidered pink dress and a pillbox hat draped by a veil.

Urbino seated himself in an overstuffed armchair.

"So what do you want to know this time?" Razzi asked him. She attempted a coy look from beneath long, false eyelashes.

"As it turns out, Signora Razzi, there is some help you might be able to give me and help yourself at the same time as well. It's about one of your properties."

The woman's face lit up. "It would be an honor and a personal pleasure, Signor Macintyre."

Urbino saw the misunderstanding.

"It's not about renting one of your apartments, signora," he said. "It's about the problems in San Polo. I know some people there who are concerned about what's happening to their property. Maybe I could do something to help the situation for them and yourself."

"You've solved many problems, Signor Macintyre, but you don't want to get close to this one. Drugs!"

"Why do you say it's drugs?"

"What else can it be when packs of young people are breaking into houses and stripping them of whatever isn't tied down?" She cast an apprehensive look around the parlor at her dolls.

"Has your building been broken into?"

"Thank God, no, but it's sure to happen one of these days. Then the tenants will blame me and use it as an excuse to try to get money from me!"

"Let's hope not. I believe a young man had an accident in your building about three months ago."

"Suicide!"

"Suicide?"

"Exactly! God only knows what he put into his arms and his nose and down his throat. There are plenty of others like him. None of them want to get old and responsible like you and me; they'd rather kill themselves! Suicide, I call it. They should all get it over with and leave the rest of us alone."

"I see what you mean, signora. This boy lived in your building?"

"Ever since his father died when he was two years old. Marco used to look as innocent as one of my little ones. But almost all of them end up changing, especially these days."

She picked up the doll in the embroidered pink dress and cradled it in her arms.

"His mother is a tall woman, I believe."

"Tall and haughty, that's Elvira Carelli! Well, she's not good for anything anymore except a joke. Completely out of her mind, she is."

"I've seen her acting strangely."

"That's putting it politely! I can imagine what damage she's done to my apartment. And she makes so much noise with her screaming and crying that the other tenants are always calling me up. But what can I do? She'll be there until she dies or until they cart her away to the madhouse."

The laws governing tenants in Italy were strong in their favor. Once someone moved into a building, it was almost impossible to get him or her to leave.

"What happened to Marco?"

"He fell. Two or three months ago. It would have to be from my building!"

"Where did he fall from? A window or a balcony, perhaps the roof?"

She shrugged. "No one knows, unless it's Elvira." She sighed. "She'll be there for years to come if I can't get her out." A shrewd look dropped over her haggard features. "Maybe you could help me, Signor Macintyre. Then one of your friends could move in. We could all come to an understanding about the rent."

Urbino bridled at the thought. "I don't think I'd care to get involved, but I'll see if Signora Carelli is being looked after properly. Her bereavement is recent, after all. With time and good care, she might be able to resume most of her old patterns in her apartment, despite her loss and even if it holds bad memories. That is, if that's what she'd like to do."

Razzi glared back at him.

"By the way, signora," he said, after a few moments of silence, "what's your impression of the owner of the building next door? Samuel Possle?"

She didn't respond right away but sat there taking time to brood over his refusal to be his ally against Elvira Carelli.

"He struck me as a nice man," she eventually said. "Maybe he can help me with Elvira."

"Perhaps. How well do you know him?"

"Hardly at all. I met him once or twice after I bought my building. I've never been the kind of landlady to always be snooping around her own buildings. Some people say he gave noisy parties, but I don't know anything about that."

"What about his employee, Armando Abdon?"

"Is that his name? I've seen him creeping around every once in a while. I wouldn't let him within fifty feet of my little ones."

"Do you know someone named Adriana Abdon?"

"You ask a lot of questions for only one fan," Razzi said, with no attempt to conceal her irritation. "No, I never heard of anyone by that name."

38

At two o'clock the next afternoon, March 12, Urbino and the Contessa were walking through the puzzle maze in the gardens behind her villa in Asolo. They were muffled against the bitterly cold day, Urbino in his cloak and the Contessa in her mother's ocelot coat, which she wore only on the grounds of the villa when she was alone or with Urbino. The blue sky sparkled above them like a jewel, as it often did, winter and summer, in the hills above Venice.

As they made their way through the maze, the Contessa leaned on Urbino's arm, but it was she who was leading him. Despite Urbino's many negotiations of the maze's devious twists and turns and cul de sacs with the Contessa, he had never learned the route.

"Maybe the reason your Samuel Possle is courting you, *caro*, is that he thinks I'll throw some of my benevolence his way," the Contessa said, as she looked straight ahead along the line of neatly clipped yews. "In debt, is he? The way he lived in the old days, I'm not surprised. Maybe you should suggest that he have Demetrio Emo conduct tours or exorcisms of the Ca' Pozza! The House of the Mad Woman! Possle seems as if he'd be receptive to it, what with his phrenology and somnambulism."

"It's not somnambulism. It's called narcolepsy. If anyone's a somnambulist, it would be Armando."

"Does he take care of Possle and the whole house by himself?"

"So it appears. Maximum care of Possle and very minimal care of the house from what I can see."

When they came to a junction along the path, the Contessa turned to the left, then to the left again.

"The poor man can't help the way he looks, can he?" the Contessa observed. "Any more than he can help being a mute. And he does remember his dead. That goes a long way."

"True enough."

"Don't be discouraged. You've solved the mystery of the melancholy gondolier. At least you know why Gildo is so sad. And why that poor woman Elvira is so disturbed. I suppose that makes two mysteries, doesn't it?"

"Sometimes finding answers only opens up more questions."

The Contessa looked up at the viewing tower in the center of the maze. It rose across the top of the hedges less than fifteen feet away but they would have to go much farther than that before they could reach it.

"But all roads lead to Rome, as they say"—the Contessa gave a little smile—"unlike my little maze here."

They reached one of the several spiral junctions of the maze. A covered sign said LIFT IF LOST in three languages. The Contessa ignored it and without hesitation took a path to their right that looked identical to the others.

"Everything leads to the Ca' Pozza, you mean," Urbino said. "It does seem that way. Marco Carelli fell to his death from the building next door to the Ca' Pozza."

"And his poor mother is a mad woman. Of course I know she isn't mad, but that's what everyone seems to believe. Marta. Benedetta Razzi. Cries, sobs, and laughter in the middle of the night. You've heard them yourself. It isn't hard to

understand why the legend of the madwoman of the Ca'
Pozza—or the Ca' Pazza—is alive and well."

"So it seems."

She came to a halt.

"You will have noticed that I haven't mentioned my
clothes. I know that they have a lot of competition for your
attention, but don't forget about them. Don't forget about *me!*"

"How could I do that, Barbara, even if you let me?"

"If I really thought you might, I'd just leave you here and
take away all the signs. Then where would you be?"

"Lost, until you found me."

"Like twenty years ago." She patted his arm affectionately
and they were in motion again. "We're almost there, *caro*. Just
a few more steps and a few more twists and turns."

PART THREE

THEFTS

39

At ten the next morning, a Wednesday, Urbino walked under the shadow of the Ca' Pozza to the building next door. A card on the corroded row of bell buttons indicated that Elvira Carelli lived on the top floor.

He pushed her bell several times, but there was no response. He tried the door. It was open. The lock was rusted and broken. Razzi might complain about the danger to her building from the break-ins, but it seemed she wasn't taking precautions. She should give Demetrio Emo or one of the other locksmiths a call.

He began to climb the flights of worn steps. Nothing broke the unnatural quiet until he reached the third floor. There a woman's low sobs burdened the air. Elvira Carelli, wearing her long brown coat, was standing beyond an open door in a small vestibule. In her hands was a man's shoe.

"Signora Carelli," he said softly.

The woman looked up. Her face showed no trace of tears. Her hair appeared to have been cut unevenly, as if by her own hand. Another sob escaped her.

"You can't have it!" She held the shoe against her chest.

"I'm not here to take anything, signora."

"You're a policeman! You want to turn the house upside and down. There are no drugs! He was a good boy."

She raised the shoe in a menacing manner and spoke in a rapid, garbled flow. The words "My boy" and "Ca' Pozza" and "murdered" fell unmistakably upon Urbino's ears. A look in her eye, something both blank and impassioned at the same time, warned him about attributing too much consistency, or reasonableness, to what she said or did.

He let her diatribe come to an end. She lowered the shoe to a less threatening position. A look of softness descended over what he now saw were refined though ravaged features. Her eyes were clear blue. The height scorned by Benedetta Razzi gave her a regal air as she stared at him.

"Here, Signora Carelli. This is yours."

He drew her yellow scarf from his pocket. She snatched it with her free hand and began to kiss the soiled, tattered piece of cloth.

"Thank you, signore, thank you; but where did you find it? I lost it yesterday afternoon—"

She broke off this rather lucid discourse and stared at him more closely. "You're the signore who was going into the Ca' Pozza. Thank God you weren't harmed! May God always protect you!"

Elvira placed the shoe on the floor beside its mate. Several other pairs were ranged neatly, all of them mens, and all clean and shined.

She placed the scarf around her neck, caressing it.

"Were you on your way out or in, signora?" Elvira returned this with a blank look.

"Perhaps you're about to go on some errands. It would be my pleasure to accompany you and be of whatever assistance I might."

This formal, even stiff offer was nonetheless sincere. From what Razzi had said, Elvira was all alone in the apartment. She

must find it difficult to take care of her needs, given her grieving and her disturbed emotional condition.

"Errands?" the woman repeated. She started to sway.

Urbino caught her arm. "Perhaps you should sit down, signora."

There was no seat in the vestibule. Beyond it opened a
room filled with sunshine. "Here. Let me help you."

He guided her into the room and to the nearest chair. She
sank into it with a little sigh. The room was a parlor, with
worn but clean furniture. An open armoire was full of colorful
dresses and blouses, neatly arranged on hangers. Despite her
difficulties, Elvira was not a lax housekeeper, contrary to what
Razzi had feared.

On a small table in a corner a votive candle flickered in
front of a black-and-white photograph of a young man, whose
features Urbino couldn't make out from a distance.

Urbino was torn between concern for the woman and his
desire to ask her a few questions. He moved aside the curtains
from one of the windows. Directly across from the open shutters were the heavily draped windows of the Ca' Pozza's top
story. The unkempt garden spread below.

Elvira glowered at the Ca' Pozza with rage.

"I'm Signor Urbino Macintyre," he said. "I live in the
Cannaregio. I'm an American, as you've probably realized
from my accent." Elvira seemed to be taking all this in. "I
know Signora Benedetta Razzi, your landlady. And I'm
acquainted with the owner of the Ca' Pozza, Signor Samuel
Possle, another American. I—"

Elvira leaped to her feet and once again gave vent to a
stream of rapid Italian, mixing in the Venetian dialect. Urbino
picked out words and phrases such as "evil old woman" and
"fancy clothes" and "makeup" and "hiding in the house like a
spider." She had as little regard for Benedetta Razzi as Razzi
had for her.

She finished, rushed to the window, and threw open the panes. "Marco!" she cried.

Urbino touched her arm. Elvira returned to the chair and started sobbing. Still, no tears came. A cold draught was coming through the open window. Urbino closed it. He picked up the photograph of the young man from the table. "A handsome boy," he said.

Marco resembled his mother. He was about sixteen or seventeen years old in the photograph. Sitting at a café table, he stared out at the camera with a bright smile. From background details, Urbino identified the Campo San Polo. It was a short but tortuous walk from the apartment.

"And a good boy! Like gold!" Elvira said, a hand pressed against her chest. "My only son. Now I'm all alone."

"I'm sorry for your loss, Signora Carelli."

"Snatched away from me. Right in front of my eyes. He died in my arms. My poor Marco!"

She got up and took the photograph from his hands. She kissed it, then put it back on the table. "Come!" she said. "I will show you."

She went through a door on the other side of the parlor. Urbino followed her and found himself in a small bedroom with a large, unshuttered window without any curtains. Like the parlor the room was neat and clean, but its furniture was new. The bed was freshly made. In a corner were a soccer ball and a pair of sneakers. Elvira was standing in front of the window.

"Look," she said, pointing downward through the window.

Urbino looked over her shoulder. Below was the *calle* that gave access to the entrance of Elvira's building and farther down to the entrance of the Ca' Pozza. It continued to the bridge over the canal. In the other direction it led toward the covered passageway where Urbino had hesitated the night he had thought he heard footsteps pursuing him.

"I was turning into the alley," she said. "I saw him fall. It was because of the spider! Her! Her!"

If Razzi felt she had a lot to blame Elvira for, Marco's mother apparently was even more passionate on her side, and perhaps with just cause. All Razzi cared about when it came to her property was the money that it brought in.

Urbino unlatched the window and opened the panes. He looked down into the *calle*. Marco's bedroom was about twelve feet to the side of the entrance. To the immediate right of the window projected a small stone balcony of the Ca' Pozza's top story. The balcony was a foot lower than the broad sill of the bedroom window. Uneven brickwork and crumbling stone molding marred the wall of Razzi's building beneath the bedroom window. Anyone trying to get a foothold would have a hard time of it. He thought he understood why Elvira was cursing Razzi. She should have been taking much better care of her building.

Urbino turned back into the room. Elvira had thrown herself on her son's bed and was beating her fist against a pillow.

Urbino was feeling more and more like an intruder. He bid the woman good-bye but doubted if she heard him. In the parlor, he extracted a calling card from his wallet and placed it with a generous sum of money on the table holding Marco's photograph and the votive candle.

As he was leaving the parlor, he spied something that brought him up short. On a table cluttered with pens and pencils, elastic bands, scissors, and paperback books was a color photograph torn from a magazine. It was one of the photographs of the Contessa that he had been looking at in his library, the one of her wearing her tea dress and carrying her slouch hat in front of the Palazzo del Cinema on the Lido.

Urbino's eyes slid toward the armoire of clothes a few feet away. What might he find in there if he had the time to go through it? But Elvira's footsteps were approaching. Urbino left the parlor. The door into the hallway was still open, and he closed it behind him.

40

As Urbino proceeded down the stairway of Elvira's building, he knocked at some of the doors. There was no response until he reached the first floor. A dirty-faced little girl with bright red hair opened the door.

A weary-looking woman appeared behind her. Her hair was several shades darker than the little girl's.

"Haven't I told you never to open the door, Maria?" she said.

She put an arm around her daughter and took in Urbino's long, black cloak.

He introduced himself and said that he was concerned about one of her neighbors, Elvira Carelli.

The woman became less wary. A look of sympathy came over her face. "Poor Elvira," she said. "But what is it that you want with me, signore?"

"Do you know if there is anyone to look after her?"

"I check on her from time to time and bring her food or old magazines and newspapers that we've finished with. Sometimes she tells me to go away. Her mind isn't right, and how can you expect anything else? To have her son turn out so bad and then to die the way he did."

"He turned out bad, you say?"

He had to raise his voice as a child started to cry from inside the apartment.

The woman looked apprehensively over her shoulder. When she turned back to Urbino, the suspicious look she had had in her eye earlier had returned. "I thought you said you knew Elvira," she said.

"I do, but it's only been since Marco's death. And she doesn't say anything about the troubles she might have had with him."

"But what do you expect? She's a mother. Or she was, poor thing."

She ran her fingers through her daughter's hair.

"Drugs, ever since he was thirteen. He seemed to have a good heart, but the drugs destroyed everything. Just as his death is doing to her."

"Were you in the building when he fell?"

"Yes. But I didn't see or hear anything until she screamed. No one did. The police spoke to everyone in the building. Elvira was the only person to see him fall."

"How do you think it came about that he fell?"

"You know how young people are these days. Maybe he climbed out of his window just for the fun of it and lost his balance."

Once again the child cried from inside the apartment.

"You'll have to excuse me, signore. I must see to my little one. Don't worry about Elvira. We're doing our best to help her. With the help of God, she'll get through this."

She had her doubts just as Urbino did. He gave her his card.

"Call me if you ever think I might be of help to Elvira. By the way, signora, when was the last time you saw Benedetta Razzi here in the building?"

"Here, signore? That would be strange! She's never stirred more than fifty feet from her apartment in all the time I've known her, and that's going on ten years! It would be like seeing a ghost if she was anywhere near here!"

"What about the building next door? The one on the canal? Do many people come and go?"

The woman stiffened slightly. A cautious look came over her face.

"The Ca' Pozza? The only person I've ever seen come in or out is the strange man, the caretaker of the American gentleman. I've never spoken to him or even seen the American. It's just the two of them in the building."

"Don't they have any help?"

"None that I've ever seen. The caretaker does everything. I see him at the Rialto markets and the shops from time to time. He knows just what he wants. Buys it without wasting a minute. He does the same at my husband's tobacco and newspaper kiosk near San Polo. He comes in two or three times a month and buys a whole pile of newspapers and magazines, all sorts of magazines. It must be to keep the sick American entertained."

"I've seen Elvira in front of the building once or twice. She seemed very disturbed."

The woman nodded. "She curses it sometimes, but she does the same thing to the Church of San Polo. Marco was buried from there. But the next minute she'll be singing. She curses the children and me. I try not to let it bother me. But excuse me, signore, I must go."

41

When Urbino left Razzi's building, he took a long, reflec- tive walk to the Campo San Zanipolo on the other side of the Grand Canal by the lagoon. There in the square he con- templated the large equestrian statue of the fifteenth-century military leader Colleoni.

He always found some inspiration from the sight of the man and his horse in all their virile nobility. But the statue had nothing to say to him today, unless it whispered about the dif- ferences between Colleoni's age and the diminished one that Urbino and Possle lived in. The days of fine, uncomplicated heroics were long past, although Urbino realized that he shouldn't delude himself that he could have or ever would have been a man like Colleoni or even Byron, or would have wanted to be. And yet he turned his back on the statue with a feeling of humility and frustration.

He approached the large Renaissance building behind the statue. It was the municipal hospital. Its facade was heavily decorated with carved cornices, ornate columns and capitals, graceful arches, windows, and lunettes. But these impressive details, no more than the trompe l'oeil sculptures and pedestals adorned with dancing children on either side of the main door, could not dispel the air of gloom that overcame Urbino whenever he entered the building.

The scream of an ambulance siren penetrated the thick walls of the building as Urbino sought out his friend Paola, who coordinated some of the social services associated with the hospital. He described Elvira Carelli's situation to her. She made a few phone calls and learned that Elvira wasn't on any of the city's lists for counseling or house visits. He got her promise that someone would be sent to see her as soon as possible.

Feeling as if he had accomplished more than one meaningful task for the day, he sat at the café across from the hospital with a glass of wine and spent almost an hour in contemplation of the Colleoni statue.

42

"U seless!" Urbino exclaimed to the Contessa the next afternoon as the gondola moved slowly past the palazzi at the mouth of the Grand Canal.

A brightly colored Moroccan blanket with geometrical designs was drawn across their laps. Although the sun had been shining all day in a bright blue sky, only occasionally obstructed by fleecy clouds, the March air carried a penetrating chill.

"What is it, *caro?*"

The Contessa spoke with the dreamy air of someone who was trailing her hand over the side in the water. It would have been an impossible feat on this occasion, however, since the two friends were as snug and sheltered inside the *felze* as two children who had sought out a secret place to shut away the world.

The Contessa gave Urbino a languid glance that would have better suited a hot day in August. "What is it?" she repeated.

"Thomas Mann." Urbino indicated the book in his hand. *"Death in Venice."*

"And how is Herr Mann useless? He's always seemed full of earnest wisdom to me. Keep one's proper balance and all that. Which at the moment," she added, as the gondola rocked from the wake of a motorboat, "seems admirable advice." The gondola soon returned to a gentle cradlelike movement. "Thank God for our melancholy Gildo."

Urbino turned the book to catch the light.

"Listen to this," he said. "*'Leaning back among soft, black cushions, he swayed gently in the wake of the other black-snouted bark to which the strength of his passion chained him . . . The gondolier's cry, half warning, half salute, was answered with singular accord from far within the silence of the labyrinth. They passed little gardens high up the crumbling wall, hung with clustering white and purple flowers that sent down an odor of almonds.'* And there's more."

"Undoubtedly. It doesn't end until the poor man dies on the Lido. But I still don't understand."

"He's done it all before! Mann along with the rest of them! They've used up all the words and images. How can any of us—you, me, or them"—he indicated two tourists with easels set up on the Riva degli Schiavoni—"how can any single one of us be original when it comes to Venice!"

The vehemence and suddenness of this outburst drew a surprised look from the Contessa. She said in quiet and measured contrast, "By making it our own. Isn't that what we've done all these years, *caro?*"

But Urbino hardly heard her. "It leaves us feeling impotent," he said.

"Leaves *you* in that unenviable position," the Contessa came back with a smile. "It doesn't quite suit a woman, does it? Someone else might think you're going through a midlife crisis, but I'd say it has everything to do with Samuel Possle."

"How well you know me."

"How well we know each other. But what I don't know, Urbino dear, is what precisely it *does* have to do with Samuel Possle."

Urbino was in a bit of a muddle over it himself. He attempted to give her the fruits of some recent meditations and in the process', he hoped, reveal something to himself.

"I've told you how it's been striking me that much of what Possle says sounds familiar," he began. "As if he's speaking in code, or trying to test me, or amusing himself at my expense. Sometimes I think that it's just a pedestrian case of déja vu. Maybe all these things together, or alternately, or none of them."

"Poor boy! But that doesn't go far in explaining what Possle has to do with Thomas Mann and impotence and originality."

Urbino threw as desperate a glance in the direction of the Bridge of Sighs as the hapless prisoners used to throw out from its windows at the lagoon as they were led to their cells. He tried again to make himself clear to the Contessa as well as to himself.

"He keeps alluding to books and art and God knows what else that slips by me. But I've been remembering a lot of what he's said and linking it with other things. They're like echoes that keep coming back to me."

"Allusions! Echoes! Links!"

"And it's not just *Against Nature*." At his mention of the book, the Contessa rolled her eyes in mock exaggeration. "He carefully fed me the necessary clues about it so that I couldn't easily miss them. But there are other references he slips in ever so smoothly. I haven't traced them all and I probably can't, but what I do know is that many, maybe even most of them, are related to Byron."

"The song," the Contessa supplied. " 'We'll Go No More a-Roving.' "

"The song and other things. And what this has to do with Mann may be very little after all. It's just that as I've been sitting here reading the book, with Venice all around us, the idea occurred to me that Possle is a kind of thief. He takes the ideas of others. He doesn't just use them, but as you said about us, he makes them his own. And he wants to see if I can find him out. It's a game, but why?"

"He isn't doing anything wrong, is he?"

"It's as if I've discovered what a thief he is," Urbino responded, "but not a conventional one. Maybe not one who's all that different from you and me."

"A thief? Me? It's *my* clothes that have gone missing. They're hanging on someone else's back, possibly an outfit for every day of the week once I figure out what else might be missing!"

Urbino felt uncomfortable. He hadn't told her yet about the magazine clipping in Elvira's apartment or his attempts, unsuccessful so far, of linking the woman to his friend's lost personal items. He needed more time to think about them.

"What Possle is stealing," he said, "are the ideas and words of others."

"I see," the Contessa exclaimed with evident relief. "Like Herr Mann?"

"I haven't come across examples of that, but, yes, like Mann. But as I said, it's Byron I'm more concerned about. Possle keeps coming back to him, and I need to find out why."

"Byron! So now we have another possible motive behind these tête-à-têtes? Not to write his biography and not to look into some crime at the Ca' Pozza, but to spend hours identifying quotations from someone who's been dead for almost two hundred years?"

"Byron has something to do with it," Urbino said, but the conviction ebbed from his voice when he added, "unless that is also a camouflage of some kind."

"Don't you mean a lure?"

"That, too."

Gildo was steering the gondola out of the Basin of San Marco and into the Castello district. If Venice is shaped like a fish, as any map immediately shows, the Castello is its tail. The gondola passed beneath the Ca' di Dio with its many chimney stacks and moved slowly toward the Arsenale.

In the closed cabin of the *felze,* so suited to the two friends when they were together and Urbino when he was alone, each of them dropped into a reflective silence. When the Contessa turned to Urbino a minute or two later, she said with a slight repentant air, "But forgive me, *caro,* I've forgotten about Elvira's son. *We've* forgotten it," she emphasized. "Maybe Possle wants you to look into his death. It can't be pleasant for him to have Elvira shouting like a madwoman outside the Ca' Pozza about Benedetta Razzi having killed her son."

"Possle is a man who's concerned only about what directly touches himself—and Armando," Urbino replied.

The Contessa recognized the ambiguity in his statement and looked at him without saying anything for a few moments.

"But surely you don't think that Razzi is capable of murder. The only killing on her conscience is of someone else's pocketbook. It shows how detached from reality Elvira is to be accusing her. Look at her animosity against the Ca' Pozza, the way she was trying to keep you from going in."

"I wonder, though," Urbino said. "Elvira's lucid enough at other times."

"Benedetta Razzi a murderer! Creeping around in her false eyelashes and a little dagger from her doll collection! Well, if I've learned anything from your—*our*—sleuthing, it's that nothing is what it seems."

"Exactly, or close enough to it."

"Patience." The Contessa took the Mann book from his lap and put it on the carpeted floor where Urbino couldn't easily get it. "Let's wait and see what the next ploy of our thief of San Polo turns out to be. Fortunately, I have my *conversazioni* to distract me." Her next one was on Saturday, the day after tomorrow. "As for you, don't forget your noble quest of my missing clothes."

43

"Why don't we walk from the Arsenale?" Urbino said. He made an effort to shake off the feeling of inertia that had dropped over him as they had discussed Possle and the Ca' Pozza.

The white crenellated walls of the Arsenale rose against the blue, cloud-filled sky. These days the old dockyards, formerly synonymous with the economic and military power of the Venetian Republic, were mainly a ship anchorage. Once a secret area where galleys and weapons were constructed, the Arsenale now was open to the gaze and the cameras of anyone who took the waterbus that passed through its cavernous space twice a day.

"You can pull up here," Urbino called up to Gildo.

Their destination was not the Arsenale, however, but the Naval Museum overlooking the Basin of San Marco a short distance away. When Urbino had picked up the Contessa, she had informed him, rather mysteriously, that Gildo should row them there. "I have my reasons," she had said.

Gildo brought the boat to the landing with more of a kiss than a tap against the stones. Urbino helped the Contessa onto the quay. After arranging with Gildo for a time that they would return to the gondola, Urbino and the Contessa walked across the quiet square. Nearby were the rope works where Habib would be showing his paintings.

As they crossed the bridge to the *fondamenta* opposite, they paused to look up at the Arsenale, with its lion-guarded gateway. No less a figure than Dante had been among those who had mused over the grim ironies of this factory producing floating engines of war for a republic proudly calling itself serene. At the land entrance were a bust of Dante and a plaque inscribed with verses from one of the cantos of *The Inferno,* which found an apt image of the punishments of hell in all the noise, activity, and boiling pitch of the Arsenale.

They proceeded slowly along the long *fondamenta* toward the Naval Museum. A young woman rowing a boat filled with bolts of fabric kept pace with them for a while until her efforts carried her beyond them.

Urbino restrained himself, not without difficulty, from quoting Dante's vivid words about boiling pitch which were written on the plaque. His criticism of the specter of the thief of San Polo, to use the Contessa's epithet for Possle, were too present to him at the moment to indulge in quotations and allusions himself. Yet it angered him to hold back in this way. It revealed how much he felt a victim of Possle's thefts.

Yes, he thought, as they paused at the water bus stop near the Naval Museum, Possle had taken something from him, and certainly more than Urbino had yet taken from the elderly man. The more he considered Possle's effect on him, the more he felt peculiarly violated, appropriated. Urbino held his own secrets close and seldom shared them. This commerce and contact with Possle was an unequal exchange. He wasn't accustomed to it, and it put him on edge as much as it did on guard.

In front of them were the waters of the Basin of San Marco, a deep blue except where the boats frothed them into creamy white. The long line of the Lido stretched in the distance.

"Here we are, *caro*," the Contessa said as they approached an unassuming building with two anchors flanking its doors, "the temple of the Maritime Republic. Have you guessed why we're here?"

"I'm at a loss."

"And you a man of such intelligence and imagination! Come on."

A boisterous group of teenagers were exiting through the glass doors. Inside, Urbino bought their admission tickets, and they passed into a large space where tall windows looked out on the water.

"They're worth the price of admission in themselves," the Contessa said with a mischievous smile. "We can both agree on that."

He followed her gaze to two young men dressed in crisp white naval uniforms with white caps banded with blue. They were the museum attendants and stood with their hands clasped behind their back.

"But let's not linger," the Contessa said. "There are some other exhibits I want us to admire."

They climbed up to the next floor to a large glass case. Resplendent inside was a scale model of a carved and gilded ship decorated with flags and statues of men, women, angels, and lions. It was the Doge's ceremonial barge in which he conducted the city's annual marriage to the sea.

"The last *bucintoro* of Venice," the Contessa pronounced. "I want you to contemplate last things this afternoon. You still don't know why we've come?" she asked slyly. "Up to the top floor then."

Ignoring the other rooms, she guided him to one devoted to gondolas. She walked a little in advance of him with an unmistakable eagerness. They stopped in front of one particular exhibit.

It bore the label, O GONDOLA DA FRESCO, much less romantic in its English translation printed below of SHADOW COOL TYPE.

The extravagant concoction of carved armchairs, a heart-shaped seat, and gilded lions and tridents shone blackly as if it had a life of its own.

Urbino didn't need any more clues from the Contessa to identify it as Peggy Guggenheim's personal gondola. During her controversial years in Venice, it had conveyed her back and forth from her palazzo on the Grand Canal.

As Urbino and the Contessa looked at the gondola, he ran a sobering declension through his mind. Guggenheim's splendid gondola, Possle's fixed one at the Ca' Pozza, and his own. Guggenheim's was the most magnificent of them all by far, but now it was just a reminder of a rich life that had once been lived in the grand style.

"Once it's gone, it's gone," the Contessa said, showing how uncannily she was in tune with his own thoughts. "That's something we all need to remember. This one, *caro,* is the last of the gondolas. The personal gondolas. Not Samuel Possle's. As for yours, let's call it a pale imitation of an original. Yes, my gift is a sad forgery, I'm afraid." She looked into his eyes. "As you said, it's all been done before. It's quite useless to pretend otherwise. You're not an original, and neither am I. The best we can hope for, my dear Urbino, is to be eccentric, but eccentric in as original a way as possible!"

Urbino smiled. "You mean like Samuel Possle?"

"Oh, don't compare me to Possle, if you don't mind! Save that for yourself!"

44

At seven-thirty the next morning, Friday, March 15, Urbino was in the reception area of the Casa Crispina, the pensione run by the Sisters of the Charity of Santa Crispina. It provided a good view of the Church of San Gabriele across the *campo*.

He had come to speak with the church secretary who had signed Armando's receipt for the commemorative mass of the dead, but unfortunately the nun had gone to a convent of the same order in Umbria for several weeks. The nun at the reception desk had no information to give him.

Urbino chatted with her, all the while keeping his eyes fixed on the front doors of the church.

Armando, dressed in his usual black—a color that on this occasion seemed to be particularly appropriate—soon emerged and paused on the top step. An old woman, also dressed in black, appeared behind him. She eased herself down the steps and across the square in the direction of the Calle dell' Arcanzolo. Another woman emerged, older than the first one, and using a cane. She hobbled away from the church.

Armando looked toward the Casa Crispina and seemed to be staring right at Urbino, who drew back from the curtain.

Armando abandoned the church steps and walked slowly and, it seemed to Urbino, sadly, across the *campo* and down the Calle dell'Arcanzolo, his arms close to his sides as was his habit.

As soon as the nun finished her account of two elderly Frenchwomen who had been locked out of the Casa Crispina last night, Urbino bid her a quick farewell.

He walked up the steps of the fifteenth-century Gothic church, many of its stones leprous from damp, age, and chemical corrosion from the mainland. He entered and gazed toward the chapel in the east transept, where a glass coffin stirred up dark memories. The coffin displayed the body of a virgin saint in a white gown, crimson gloves and slippers, and a silver Florentine mask. Venetian merchants had snatched her from her native Sicily hundreds of years ago during one of the serene republic's so-called sacred thefts. Her body had been at the dead center of one of Urbino's most puzzling cases.

The church was deserted. The monsignor and the altar boys must have left by the side exit. The sexton was nowhere in sight.

Urbino left the church and went down the Calle dell' Arcanzolo to a tobacco kiosk where he bought a copy of the day's local newspaper. He moved out of the way of passersby and opened the newspaper to the obituary and commemorative notices. Black-and-white photographs, almost all of elderly men and women, stared back at him. One of them was of a young woman with large, liquid eyes. Beneath the photograph he read:

In beloved memory of my sister Adriana Maria Abdon
Who departed this life seventeen years ago on this day
Eternal Love
From her brother Armando

Urbino studied the photograph. Adriana must have been in her early twenties when it was taken. He could trace some of her brother's features in her face like an angelic version of the grotesque.

45

Half an hour later Urbino was brought up short by a sign on the door of THE KEEPER OF THE KEYS: CHIUSO. The woman tending the newsstand next door called out to say that Emo had been taken sick and gone home. She gave him his address.

Emo's ground-floor apartment was at the end of a narrow alley near the Casa di Tintoretto. The alley stank of cat urine and garbage.

Emo answered Urbino's ring almost immediately.

"It's you," he said. "Another emergency?" The small slice of door that Emo held open revealed that he was wearing something that might have been a bathrobe. Its violet color and vaguely ceremonial cut made it reminiscent of Possle's attire. "Or maybe you're back for more stories about haunted buildings in Venice, is that it?"

"Excuse me for disturbing you, but I need some information about a man named Armando Abdon. You might know him through San Gabriele. He works for Samuel Possle, the owner of the Ca' Pozza."

The locksmith's eyes searched the alley. "Armando, the mute," he said.

"Yes. He has masses said at San Gabriele in memory of

someone named Adriana Abdon. He might have started doing it when you were there."

"He did." A gleam came into Emo's small eyes. "You want information on Armando and Adriana, is that it? For the book you're writing about this man who lives in the Ca' Pozza? Well, it's going to cost you."

"Let me come in and we can talk about it."

"I need to take my medicine and lie down for a while. But there's no reason we can't talk over dinner as long as it's at Harry's Bar. It's way beyond my budget. Is it worth it to you?"

The request didn't strike Urbino as being unreasonable or particularly unusual, if one assumed that Emo's size was a result of his love of good food. Urbino had often ended up paying much more, in one way or another, for information.

"But how do I know that you have anything to tell me?"

"Anything worth the price of a meal at Harry's Bar, you mean? You'll have to find out. But just to whet your appetite, let me do a bit of a calculation. Let me think. Armando and his masses. I'd say he's been having them said now for about sixteen or seventeen years. So is it on for Harry's Bar?"

"Lunch tomorrow?"

"Not tomorrow. Tuesday, if you don't mind. And dinner, not lunch. Get the best table. And do I need to warn you that I have a big appetite? Now, if you'll excuse me, I have to get out of this draft. A current of air can carry you to your grave."

46

Gildo, wearing a cap over his mop of Venetian reddish blond curls, was standing in the sunshine in front of the Palazzo Uccello when Urbino returned after speaking with Demetrio Emo.

"This is for you," the young man said, with a subdued and deferential air before Urbino could say anything.

He handed him a small white envelope.

Urbino's full name was written on it in violet ink and in the script that was now familiar to him.

"Where did you get this?" Urbino asked him.

Gildo's handsome face, usually a clear mirror of his emotions, was closed.

"I found it in the gondola. On one of the seats."

The boat was drawn up to the water steps where Gildo sometimes cleaned, swept, and polished it in the sunshine.

"I went into the house to get a cloth. When I came back, it was there." Then he added in a rush of words, "The man from the Ca' Pozza put it there. The mute. He was going over the bridge when I came out."

"Do you know him?"

"No!" Gildo exclaimed.

Urbino put the envelope in his pocket. Gildo shifted

uneasily from one foot to another. "Signor Urbino, are you investigating something in that building?"

"No, Gildo. Why do you ask?"

The gondolier looked away.

"It's because of your friend, Marco," Urbino answered his own question. "That's his name, isn't it?"

The gondolier nodded.

"Just because Marco died when he fell from the building next door wouldn't be a reason to investigate anything about the Ca' Pozza, would it?"

"But you think that something happened to Marco in the Ca' Pozza," Gildo said in a rush of words. "That's why you go there all the time." Unspoken pain was alive and glowing in his green eyes.

"I didn't even know about your friend when I became interested in the Ca' Pozza," Urbino responded. "Let's go inside. We can explain things to each other better there."

The fact that explanations were necessary appeared to sober the young gondolier even more. He hung his head and followed Urbino into the house.

They went to the parlor. Gildo removed his cap. Urbino left him looking around the room as if seeing it for the first time as he went to fix them coffees. When he returned with them, Gildo was sitting on the sofa and stroking Serena who had settled in his lap.

"The owner of the Ca' Pozza could help me with a book I'd like to write," Urbino began, when he seated himself across from Gildo. "That's why I go there. But I've become interested in your friend Marco for your sake and for his and his mother's. I've come to know her slightly recently. Would you mind telling me how you and Marco became friends?"

Gildo let out a sigh as he continued to stroke the cat. His open and ingenuous face was clouded. "What good will it do, Signor Urbino?"

"It's always good to talk of the dead when they've been so close to us in life."

Gildo's eyes misted. "I guess you're right."

Serena left Gildo's lap and walked out of the room. Gildo ran a hand through his hair. Urbino refrained from saying anything more as he waited. Taking a deep breath and with his liquid voice filled with melancholy, Gildo hurried through an account of how he had known Marco for three years and how Marco had attached himself to Gildo after they had met at the San Trovaso *squero*. They both used to hang around the boat-yard watching the gondolas being constructed and running errands for the *squeralioli*.

"He was five years younger than me, signore. Like a kid brother. I don't have any brothers and sisters, and—and he didn't either."

Urbino nodded with the sympathy of an only child himself.

"He was a good boy, no matter what people tell you about drugs or anything else. He had some friends who were bad, but Marco wasn't like them. He would have been a top *remero*. You saw the *forcola*. You said it was good! His mother sacrificed a lot for him to be an apprentice. That's what got him into trouble. I'm only telling you this, Signor Urbino, because I don't want you to think he was bad. He just wanted to help his mother."

"What do you mean?"

Gildo studied Urbino's face as if to assure himself of something.

"They didn't have much money," he said quietly. "Marco— well, sometimes Marco took things that weren't his. And he sold them, but it was only to give money to his mother."

"Did she know what he was doing?"

Gildo shook his head.

"She thought he was selling some of his woodwork. He never took anything from poor people. Only from people who had a lot."

"And he thought the man who lives in the Ca' Pozza has a lot."

The gondolier shrugged his broad shoulders.

"A week or two before he—he died,' Gildo went on, "he said that he was going inside. I warned him. I always told him he shouldn't be breaking into any buildings, and especially not that one."

"Why not that one in particular?"

"Because of the man who brought the note. He's very strange."

Urbino couldn't disagree with this, but Gildo's response seemed somehow too quick and a bit evasive.

"And I worry about you when you go there, signore," Gildo hurried on. "I could tell that you were interested in it many months ago when you asked me to take the boat that way. It isn't a good place. You're intelligent, but you must be careful. All of your books won't protect you."

"I don't expect them to, Gildo. But as for Marco, he went into the building, right? Is that what you're saying? Did he ever tell you what he saw inside?"

"He broke in somehow, signore, but he promised me he wouldn't. He didn't want me to worry."

"His mother seems to think that he fell from the Ca' Pozza and not from their building, although she's very confused when she speaks."

Gildo nodded. "Did she say anything about me?" he asked.

"We didn't talk about you."

"She doesn't like me. She screams at me whenever she sees me."

"I thought she might be doing that on the afternoon we were passing by the Ca' Pozza."

"You noticed, signore." A blush came over the gondolier's face. "She thought I was a bad influence on Marco because I was older, but it wasn't like that."

"No."

Once again Gildo studied Urbino's face for some kind of reassurance. Perhaps he didn't find it there this time, for he gave an almost inaudible sigh and remained silent. Urbino sensed that he had let the young man down. Gildo seemed to be waiting for him to make up for it, to say or ask something that indicated he really understood.

They sipped their coffees, then Urbino said, "Perhaps someday you and Signora Carelli will be able to be friends. You've both lost Marco, and you both loved him."

Tears brimmed in Gildo's eyes. He didn't try to hide them from Urbino but looked at him directly.

"You're going to the Ca' Pozza to learn more about Marco even though you say you aren't. Sometimes I think something evil happened to him there. Ever since he died, it gives me a bad feeling when I see it. But it's strange, Signor Urbino. Sometimes I—I want to look at it. I can't help myself." He sighed again, then added, almost under his breath, "There are many things I can't help about myself."

"I understand."

Gildo gave him a look of gratitude. "Maybe you'll find out the truth. But if you do, everyone will know that Marco did some bad things. Maybe it's better to forget about it."

They sat in silence. The clock in the hall started to strike ten times. When it finished, Urbino asked him if he knew Benedetta Razzi. He gave a description of the woman.

"No," the gondolier responded. "Do you think Marco took things from her?"

"I don't know. Did he ever show any interest in the Contessa or the Ca' da Capo-Zendrini?"

"No! Is that why you were asking me about Silvia? And he never mentioned this place either. He was a good boy, I tell you!"

Gildo snatched his cap from the sofa and got to his feet.

"Listen, Gildo, I'll make you a promise." Urbino rose. He reached out to touch Gildo's arm. "If I learn anything about

Marco and the Ca' Pozza, or any other place, I'll try to protect his memory. I would never want to hurt either you or Signora Carelli if I can help it."

"But sometimes things can't be helped."

The truth of this stood with them there in the parlor until Urbino broke the silence and said, "I admire your loyalty to your friend. If you remember anything more about him and the Ca' Pozza, no matter what it might be, would you tell me? I can be trusted."

For the third time Gildo gave him the same searching look. "I must go and look after the gondola," he finally said, turning away.

When Urbino was alone, he opened the envelope. Possle was expecting him that afternoon at the usual time.

47

Before going to the Ca' Pozza, Urbino indulged in a long lunch at a restaurant on a quiet canal in the Dorsoduro district. He had asked the Contessa if she would like to join him, but she had regretfully declined, saying that she wanted to stay close to the Ca' da Capo-Zendrini in preparation for her *conversazione* tomorrow.

The *padrona*, in deference to Urbino, who was a regular customer, had set up a table for him in the back beneath the grape arbor, even though this section wouldn't be opened for several weeks yet. His table was dappled with sunshine. The air carried the pleasant scent of orange blossoms from a tree, which, sheltered in a sunny spot in a corner of the garden, had bloomed early.

He took out Byron's *Don Juan* from his pocket, but read only a few stanzas of the first canto. He gave himself up to thinking, or to what the Contessa liked to call brooding. But however you might describe it, it didn't produce anything conclusive about Possle and the Ca' Pozza or the dead Marco and his mother, except for a firmer conviction that his compatriot had a particular interest in Byron, which he was trying to signal to him.

The immediate fruit of this conviction was to direct his

steps after lunch to the former home of another American, now a museum. This was the Palazzo Peggy Guggenheim, a low, rambling building on the Grand Canal that had belonged to the wealthy art collector who had died twenty years ago. Venetians referred to it as the Unfinished Palace—the Palazzo Non Finito—because, according to one explanation, its original owners had run out of money after the first story had been constructed. If it had been completed, it would have been the largest palace on the Canalazzo.

It was now a museum that displayed Guggenheim's farsighted personal collection of modern art.

Once inside the building, however, Urbino made only a quick turn around the rooms with paintings by Picasso, Braque, Dalí, Pollack, and Max Ernst, who had been Guggenheim's husband. It wasn't that Urbino didn't have an appreciation for them, unlike Possle, but he wanted to give his attention to something else at the moment.

This was the bed in Peggy Guggenheim's bedroom in a corner room that looked out on the Grand Canal. The bed wasn't on view because of the woman's well-chronicled love life but because of the silver bedhead. It had been designed and fashioned by Alexander Calder. Urbino stood admiring the whimsical creation with several tourists. Its delicate lines flowed into fishes, a dragonfly, aquatic plants, and other shapes that could only encourage pleasant dreams as the mind slipped into sleep beneath it.

Urbino, who had endured his dream of the fire again last night, was envious of all the untroubled nights Peggy Guggenheim must have spent under its influence. Could any of these nights have been shared with Possle, he wondered? Possle had hinted at a turbulent friendship with her. Had it been intimate as well? This was one more question he wished he could get the answer to. Guggenheim would have been about fifteen years older than Possle. The age discrepancy wouldn't have deterred her anymore than it would have Possle, if he had been so inclined. Byron, whom he so admired, had had an affair with a sixty-year-old Venetian countess when he was barely thirty.

He went out to the terrace with its landing stage and gold-and-white-striped poles. A few people were leaning on the balustrade looking at the Grand Canal and sitting on the stone benches in the sunshine.

Marino Marini's bronze sculpture of a horse and rider commanded the scene. The rider's arms were thrown out as if in ecstasy. The horse's erect penis, which Possle had unscrewed on occasion at Guggenheim's request, was in its proper place.

48

Everything seemed to be as it had been on the two other occasions Urbino had come to the Ca' Pozza. Armando's immediate response to the bell and his silence that somehow went beyond muteness, the pall that dropped over Urbino, and the slow, deliberate procession up the deeply shadowed high staircase and across the *sala* to the waiting door of the gondola room—yes, everything was as it had been before.

Yet something was different. Urbino felt it in his bones.

The difference began to manifest itself when Armando didn't go into the gondola room with him. Instead, he returned to the staircase and descended it, leaving behind him his stale odor. At first Urbino thought he might be headed for his room in the entrance hall. But then the front door opened and closed. Urbino went to one of the loggia doors and looked out. Armando was crossing over the bridge.

Urbino entered the gondola room. Everything here was as it had been before, too. The curtains were drawn. The scent of flowers lay on the warm, heavy air. The candles were lit. A fire burned in the fireplace. Possle was lying in the gondola.

But he was asleep.

Urbino had to make a quick decision. Should he seat himself in his accustomed armchair and wait for Possle to awaken? Or should he make better use of whatever time alone he might have, with Armando out and Possle in one of his spells?

He could have no idea how long Armando would be away from the building or Possle would stay asleep. Hadn't he told Urbino that sometimes it could be as long as an hour? On the other hand, as Urbino had experienced last time, it could be as short as a minute or two.

Into his computations Urbino placed Armando's errand, brief though it might be. It might give him enough time to do what he now realized he wanted to do. He wanted to see more of the Ca' Pozza.

Casting one last glance at the sleeping Possle, he went into the *sala* and across the floor, aware that his footfall was far from as quiet and stealthy as Armando's. Even if he had only a few minutes, he might learn something. At the very least he could tell himself that he was, after all, taking an initiative of some kind, after having been so passive within the walls of the Ca' Pozza. He stifled the thought that he might be risking any possibility of writing Possle's biography, at least with the man's cooperation.

He opened the door on the other side of the large room through which Armando habitually passed. He closed it behind him. He found himself in a long, dark hall. At the far end a servants' staircase rose up to the next floor and beyond it, presumably, to the attic. To his left were heavily draped and shuttered windows.

Three closed doors ranged themselves on his right. After putting his ear to each door and hearing nothing, he tried the doorknobs in turn. The first two doors were locked. The third opened to his touch with hardly a sound. He went through the door and closed it behind him.

The room was darker than the hall and burdened with stale and slightly foul air. A large mahogany bed with a canopy, so different from Guggenheim's bed and vaguely reminiscent of Possle's gondola, dominated the space. This must be Possle's bedroom.

The room wasn't so much small as overcrowded with furniture, items of clothing, books, and—on a table beside the bed—what was close to a pharmacy of small bottles, pillboxes, packets, and tubes of various medications.

A window had its shutters open slightly behind the dark drapes, but not enough to rid the room of its unpleasant odor. The branches of the tree in the garden shuddered in the wind that had started gusting through the alleys during Urbino's walk from the Guggenheim Museum.

A copy of Byron's *Don Juan* was splayed open on the bed.

A commode was angled into a corner. Urbino had discovered the source of the unpleasant odor. The pot of the closestool must not have been emptied and cleaned.

A painting hung beside the door. It depicted St. Sebastian in his customary loincloth and with the requisite arrows piercing his body. In this version of the young Roman martyr, though, the artist had shown remarkable restraint in the number of arrows, there being a mere two. Urbino had no trouble identifying the artist or rather the original artist, for this was a detail copied from Giovanni Bellini's *Sacra Conversazione* altarpiece at the Church of San Giobbe in the Cannaregio.

A bookcase against one wall was crammed with books. Many were in old bindings. Near the bookcase was a Vernis Martin writing desk. He went over to it. Its surface was littered with pens, pencils, rings, tie bars, keys, postcards, and several twisted nests of rubber bands.

He examined one of the postcards. It was a black-and-white photograph of a gondola floating in the lagoon. On the reverse there was no address and no stamp or postmark, but only the words in English in bright blue ink: "From my gondola to yours. *Tante grazie!* Peggy." Urbino replaced the postcard.

More than a dozen keys were among the pile. One of them caught his eye. He picked it up. It looked remarkably like the key to the Contessa's main door. His own copy of her key was back at the Palazzo Uccello, making it impossible for him to compare the two of them here in Possle's bedroom.

Less impulsively than he had taken the receipt from the floor of the gondola room, but just as guiltily, he slipped the key into his pocket. For better or worse, this time was easier, and not only because no one was in the room with him. If he was lucky, neither Possle nor Armando would notice it missing among all the others. He might have a chance to return it at a later date. A flicker of apprehension, however, coursed through him, not enough to make him replace the key, but making him decide it might be a good idea to leave.

But then he saw a door on the opposite side of the room. He went over and tried the handle. The door opened inward. He stepped into another room, smaller than the bedroom. It seemed to have no particular function except as a lumber room of odds and ends, mostly small pieces of furniture, crates, and piles of newspapers and magazines. There was a door to his left. According to his calculations, it must be one of the doors he had tried a few minutes ago and thus must lead back into the hallway.

This realization made him look for another door on the assumption that he was in a suite of three rooms. There it was opposite him, partially blocked by an ornately carved dressing screen. Over it a red robe with embroidered stars and crescents in yellow had been thrown. He was reminded of the symbol on the inside of the entrance door, and on Emo's robe.

He slipped behind the screen and tried the door.

It opened into a small, empty room. Pale squares and rectangles on the walls were like ghosts of the paintings and furniture that had once been there. A damp draught blew against his flushed face from a single window with its shutters thrown open. Beyond the window on the other side of the garden Elvira Carelli's building looked back at him through the dying light.

Having reached this final room in the suite, Urbino was struck, not only with what he had seen so far, but also with what he hadn't. Nowhere was there a wheelchair. Not in the gondola room or the *sala* either, not today or the other times. Was one kept somewhere out of sight? Or did Possle have another means of getting around? But perhaps his assumption, however, that Possle couldn't get around easily on his own was all wrong.

Suddenly, low moaning floated through the open window, then turned into deep, convulsive sobs. His eyes moved to Elvira's building, searching out her windows. The sobs ended abruptly. He spent a few moments thinking about Elvira, with her grief and her view of the garden and Possle's private chambers.

With one last glance around the empty room, he returned through the storeroom to the bedroom. He closed the door behind him as he had the others.

Urbino turned. A dark-faced, bald-headed man stood against the far wall. It fetched Urbino up as if he had been punched over the heart. He took a few steps backward and knocked his shins against a stool.

The man, who was in profile and little more than five feet tall, didn't move an inch.

"Who are you?" Urbino exclaimed, immediately regretting the loudness of his words and their absurdity, considering that he was the intruder.

But the man didn't speak or move.

In a sudden flash of relief, followed by anger at himself, Urbino recognized his error. He had been victimized by his own nerves and distorted impressions. The ominous profile was nothing more than a wooden representation of a man's head that stood on a chest of drawers. It was a model used to illustrate phrenology.

But why he hadn't noticed it before was peculiar. Surely it

had been there earlier. This seemed more probable and far less disturbing than that someone had placed the wooden head there while Urbino had been in the other rooms.

As he approached the door to the hall, he was seized with a more comforting thought in reference to the head. For it seemed that one of the mysteries of the Ca' Pozza had been solved, and it turned out to be a mundane one. Obviously the person he had seen in the window—the person he assumed had been Armando—hadn't been cradling anything as unbelievable as a severed head.

He hoped that the other mysteries of the Ca' Pozza could be explained away so comfortably, the way they were in a novel by Ann Radcliffe.

His hand was on the doorknob when what sounded like footsteps tapped above his head. He gazed at the ceiling, with its broken chandelier and peeling paint. The sound, whether footsteps or something else, didn't come again. Perhaps Armando had returned and ascended to the floor above. Or perhaps a branch of the tree had been scraping against the building. In any case he felt an urgency to get back to the gondola room.

Urbino checked his wristwatch. He had been gone for five minutes. When he opened the door, the dark hallway was empty. He stepped out, closing the door behind him.

The private stairway that led to the upper stories was too much of a temptation to resist. It seemed to beckon him. He had reached the first step before he had fully considered the further risk he was taking. The staircase was dark, much darker than the one in the entrance hall, and rose at a rather steep angle. It was made of wood, and the steps were partly covered in cloth. Careful though he was, his weight soon produced a creak, which he was sure reverberated through the entire house. He stopped and peered into the darkness above him. Then, whether his own anxious state made him hear

imagined sounds or he heard real ones, Urbino thought footsteps were descending toward him, or if not footsteps exactly,
then something like a rustling sound.

As his eyes became accustomed to the darkness, he made
out something light-colored, thin, and elongated lying on one
of the upper stairs. It was slightly twisted and curved, and part
of one end, even in the dark, glistened. It didn't move, but he
felt that it just had or was about to. It gave every appearance of
being a partly coiled snake with a slightly mottled skin and
with eyes that were catching whatever dim light penetrated
the darkness. Slowly, cautiously, Urbino moved up another
step. The shape remained strangely still. As he now stared at it,
its various details assumed a different form, and he realized,
not without relief, that it was a belt. What had caught the light
was the delicate buckle and tongue. It was a slender belt and
might even have been of snakeskin.

He couldn't linger any longer. He left the belt where it was.
He descended the staircase and regained the hallway. Pressing
his ear against the door into the *sala*, he listened for any sound
in the room beyond. He opened the door slowly, then went
through it, closing it behind him with barely a sound.

The chairs and paintings ranged against the two sides of
the large room were silent witnesses to his hurried passage
across the cold, empty space. He reached the open door of the
gondola room.

Footsteps began to ascend the staircase from the hall
below. Urbino wasted no time. He slipped into the gondola
room, his heart beating quickly. A fearful glance assured him
that Possle was asleep among all the orange cushions and
black-painted wood.

But the next moment, as soon as Urbino had settled himself in the armchair and as if a spell had been broken, the
reclining figure opened its eyes like a doll and said, "Please
excuse me, Mr. Macintyre. I fear I've been far away. It's most
inhospitable."

The footsteps approached the door. Armando appeared. His hair was more matted than usual. His face was slick with sweat.

"There you are," Possle said in Italian. "You know what we usually have, the two of us."

Armando gave Urbino a severe look from his dark eyes. He held Urbino's gaze for longer than he ever had before. Urbino, to his chagrin, was the first to look away.

It might have been his guilty conscience or his intuition that was so seldom wrong, but he could swear that Armando's bold, unflinching stare revealed that he had been found out and that he wanted Urbino to know it.

What Armando might do with the knowledge remained to be seen. Urbino had now relinquished even more power within the walls of the Ca' Pozza and perhaps even outside of it.

The mute went off to get the Amontillado, indulging in what seemed to be a cruel, self-satisfied smile on his thin lips as he passed Urbino.

49

Urbino figured that the best way to recover from the strong suspicion that Armando was in possession of his secret was to sit back and listen to his host for a while.

And Possle seemed inclined to be particularly garrulous this afternoon, at least at first. He began by indulging in a series of insinuations and calculated confessions. As usual, they were sprinkled with quotations and paraphrases of someone else's thoughts, a good proportion of them related to Byron. He seemed gripped by a nervous agitation, tugging more than usual at his turbanlike headscarf, and he soon started to move from one observation to another with an incoherence and inconsistency that he tried to cover up. When he paused, he did so with an uneasy glance at Urbino from his small eyes behind the large glasses. He seemed afraid that Urbino might take the opportunity to interrupt him and ask an unwanted question or make a disturbing comment.

But Urbino remained silent, except for the sounds that encouraged Possle to go on. Possle's manner this afternoon suited Urbino and got him through the crucial ten minutes during which Armando served the Amontillado and left. All the while he felt the full weight of the key in his pocket and the advantage that Armando now seemed to have over him.

His uneasiness gradually dissipated, however, though surely to come back again. Taking its place now was the resolve that had been growing in him during the past few days to get at some answers.

When Possle made one of his pauses, Urbino straightened himself in his chair from his slump and said, "I find your reminiscences quite interesting, Mr. Possle. But I'd be misleading you if I continued to sit here and listen to them. We'd be misleading each other in fact. It would be a good idea to bring some things out in the open." Urbino said this latter with a renewed twinge of guilt over what he himself was concealing and what Armando might soon reveal to Possle. "I appreciate your hospitality. But forgive me if I say that I'm a little suspicious of it. I'd like to keep coming back, and I think that you want me to, but if that's going to happen I'll need to have some questions answered. I said last time that there's a mystery of some kind surrounding the Ca' Pozza."

"And you want to add some feathers to that stalker's cap of yours, is that it?"

"Before I rang your bell last time," Urbino went on, not to be distracted, "a woman warned me not to go in."

"Obviously your curiosity was stronger than your confidence in her. I believe I know this woman—or who she is. Her mind has been turned."

"Because of the death of her son. He died in a fall."

" 'In Adam's fall, we sinned all,' " he recited. "A sad accident."

"His name was Marco Carelli," Urbino persisted.

"You're making progress in this little mystery, whatever it is. His fall was an accident."

"His mother seems to have some resentment against your building."

Urbino had chosen these words very carefully.

Possle's tongue darted out to moisten his lips.

"Didn't we agree that she's disturbed in her thinking?"

He looked at the fire crackling in the grate on the other side of the room, adding the faint trace of burning wood to the scent of the potpourri in the air.

"Did you know her son?" Urbino asked him, intentionally risking the man's anger by pursuing the topic. "Was he ever here in your building?"

"Now what are you accusing me of? Luring young boys into my den? I told you last time that I draw the line at such things despite my love—our *mutual* love—for Huysmans. You're barking up the wrong tree, Mr. Macintyre. But perhaps you don't believe me. I think it would be a good idea to get Armando's opinion."

Possle pulled on the rope. Armando's long, lean figure soon appeared in the doorway without a sound, his scarred hands held tensely by his side. His sharp, dark eyes sought out Possle's in a few quick moments of silent communication.

"Signor Macintyre has asked me a question," Possle said in Italian, "a question that I can't answer myself. He wants to know about a young man named Marco Carelli. That's the name, isn't it, Mr. Macintyre? This Marco Carelli seems to have been the young man who fell to his death a few months ago. Tell us, Armando, was this young man ever in our building?"

It was impossible to envision a look of more suspicion and dislike than the one that Armando shot at Urbino.

"When you've been around Armando as long as I have," Possle said in English, "you'll know the difference between one of his silences and another. He said no, most emphatically. Armando, would you take this cup please?"

The mute climbed the steps. As he reached for the cup, Possle touched his cheek.

"Don't be upset, Armando. Our guest is an inquisitive person. He earns a living and amuses himself by poking around in people's lives."

Urbino felt uncomfortable. He felt even more so when,

this time, Armando made a point of not looking at him. Instead he exchanged another glance with Possle. It left Urbino with the peculiar sense that somehow Possle already knew about his search through his rooms.

Urbino appeared as unconcerned as he could manage, but he was afraid that his smile of nonchalance was too evidently pasted. Armando left the room with his head held higher than usual, as if he had just scored a victory.

"As you see, we know nothing about this unfortunate young man. Is there anything else you'd like to know?"

Urbino intended to press on. He was motivated not only by the desire for an answer but also by a curiosity to see how far he might be able to go. He asked if Possle was acquainted with someone named Demetrio Emo. "He's a locksmith in the Cannaregio," Urbino explained.

"Such unusual questions this afternoon. Grieving mothers and locksmiths. No, the name's not familiar to me. Whenever we might need a locksmith, I don't send Armando so far afield."

"Emo seems to have some interest in the Ca' Pozza."

"And so do many other people, yourself included."

"So you're saying that Emo has never done any work for you?"

"And I'm also saying that I never heard the name before. Why are you being so persistent? Are you yourself today? I fail to see what all this is about. When you said you had some questions about the Ca' Pozza, I thought that they'd be much different ones. I don't know whether I should be relieved or annoyed."

"You see," Urbino went on, "Demetrio Emo is the uncle of my gondolier, Gildo, and Gildo and Marco were good friends."

"Very interesting to you perhaps, but I don't see what it signifies."

Neither did Urbino, but nonetheless he had learned something if it was only that Possle was slightly distressed to find that Urbino had been thinking about him and the

Ca' Pozza in ways that he hadn't expected and perhaps didn't want.

"And before you ask," Possle went on, as Urbino considered what to say next, "I only know your Gildo by reputation, thanks to Armando. He's my eyes and legs, and I—well, I'm his tongue. No, Gildo has never been here. But perhaps we can ask Armando about Gildo. Would you like me to call him back? No? That's wise. He doesn't like to be disturbed too often."

Urbino stared back at Possle with a face that he hoped showed none of the uneasiness he was feeling.

"Let's lay our cards on the table, Mr. Possle. You wouldn't keep asking me here unless you wanted something from me, and I wouldn't continue to come unless I wanted something from you."

"How cynical! Here we are, two expatriate Americans with so much in common. We're just getting to know each other."

"If what you'd like me to do is to write your biography," Urbino said as if Possle hadn't interposed, "that's something that we can discuss, but if I agree to do it, you'll have no success in manipulating me and you would in no way have final approval of what I might write. You would have to give me free rein or as close to it as possible and try to answer whatever questions I'd need to ask. You could answer them or not, as you wish, of course. I'd also expect you to provide access to your correspondence and to inform your friends and family that they should share whatever letters they have from you— all within reason, of course," he finished, in what had turned out to be a greater rush of words than he had intended.

"Ah yes, Mr. Macintyre, all within good reason. That's always been your dominant trait, hasn't it? But you speak of my friends and family. I'm afraid that very few of them are left alive."

"There's Armando."

"Armando, of course. He'd be a treasure house of information."

"But not forthcoming, even taking into consideration his muteness. And there's another thing. If you want my services as a biographer, I'd need to have a look at the memoirs that it's rumored you've been writing."

"Ah yes, my memoirs. There used to be a lot of talk about them."

"Do they exist?"

"The last time I looked in my desk"—he paused here and regarded Urbino with his small dark eyes—"I believe they were there, however many—or few—pages there might be."

Once again Urbino had the odd feeling that Possle already knew about his foray into his rooms, but it only made him all the more determined to finish saying what he wanted to.

"But despite what I've been saying, Mr. Possle, I don't think that you have any interest in my skills as a biographer. Or let me say, no interest in my skills as a biographer of your life, even though it was my main interest before I met you. You might have heard, through Armando, I would assume, that I've been making inquiries about you and trying to find a way to meet you. You . . ."

Urbino trailed off. Possle's eyes were closed. To Urbino's irritation, he had apparently dropped off to sleep again, and at such a crucial moment. But his breathing seemed less deep and regular than usual, and his eyelids were not quite closed.

Urbino decided to behave as if he were in fact asleep. He had already risked a great deal because of his curiosity today, but surely he would be expected now to take a closer look at some of the objects in the room. To do otherwise would be to reveal too much of his own suspicions about the man.

Urbino picked up one of the small candles ranged on the floor and brought it over to the copy of Moreau's *The Apparition,* with its severed head of John the Baptist. Having seen the original painting at the Louvre, Urbino was impressed by the copyist's success. There was no signature. He wondered whether the same painter had made the copies of the other

Moreau in the gondola room and of the St. Sebastian detail in the bedroom.

He looked for a signature on the less impressive copy of Moreau's *Dance of Salome* next to *The Apparition*. There was none.

Possle was still asleep, or giving a fairly good semblance of it. Urbino went over to the portrait of the light-haired young woman. He brought the candle nearer. The woman looked out at him with her refined features, her blue eyes mirroring the celestial blue of the ceiling's oval. She was beautiful and elegant in her low-cut black dress and totally unfamiliar to Urbino.

In the lower right-hand corner of the painting, written in black, was the painter's name: Lino Cipri.

" 'That's my last Duchess painted on the wall' " came Possle's voice.

" 'Looking as if she were alive'?" Urbino completed the quotation from Robert Browning.

"The last I heard, she was very much so. Do you like Browning?"

Urbino replaced the candle on the floor. "I do," he replied, dropping back into the armchair.

"And the painting? You think it's good?"

"Very good. And the copies as well."

Urbino was tempted to bring up Lino Cipri, but he would wait. There was something more important he wanted to talk about now.

"But it's Byron I'm interested in."

Possle nodded. "So now we've come to it," he said. "I salute you."

"You've enticed me here—"

"A peculiar choice of words," Possle broke in. "You've been practically besieging the battlements of this rather dilapidated castle, as you said yourself."

"Fair enough," Urbino conceded. "Let me say then that you've been kind enough to invite me here because of something to do with Byron. I've become as certain of it as I could possibly be without confirmation from you."

"Intuition, a professional hunch?"

"So what is it that you have?" Urbino went on. "Letters? The memoir of some Venetian woman who saw him swim from the Lido to the Canalazzo?"

Possle smiled.

"Nothing as pedestrian as that. Something much better. Something that might even interest the Contessa."

Possle gave a longish pause. It could only have been for the sake of suspense. "I have poems. Unpublished poems. Seven of them, in Byron's own handwriting, and in excellent condition."

Urbino tried to conceal his excitement. "Are you sure they're Byron's?"

"I always speak from a position of strength, despite this," and Possle glanced down at his body against the orange cushions.

"How do you come to have them?"

Provenance was the crucial issue after authenticity. And about this latter point, Urbino wasn't prepared to accept Possle's flat assurance.

"All in good time. You've been racing ahead like your Contessa's motorboat. I prefer the more sedate pace of a gondola. All things considered, we've accomplished a great deal this afternoon. I think it would be better if we put off any further discussion until the next time."

Urbino, surprised at this abrupt dismissal, especially on this occasion, wondered what might be behind it. Did Possle want to gain time? If so, for what? Or did he want to keep Urbino off balance? Perhaps even punish him, in some way, for having been the one to broach the topic of Byron?

Whatever it was, Urbino would have to comply. This was Possle's domain, and he had to play by his rules, but yet he'd do his best to subvert them. Despite Possle's air of unconcern,

Urbino had disturbed him, and this gave Urbino some satisfaction.

"To show you my good will, Mr. Macintyre," Possle was now saying, "I'm not going to keep you wondering this time when we'll have the pleasure of seeing each other again. Shall we make it for Thursday at our accustomed hour?" That was six days away, longer than Urbino expected. "And now if we can get Armando to show you out."

But as he reached for the bell rope, a shadow fell into the room.

"Always anticipating my needs, aren't you, Armando?" Possle said in his precise Italian. "It's time for our guest to bid us good-bye. Shall we shake hands on our parting this time, Mr. Macintyre?"

Urbino, feeling Armando's eyes boring into his back, went over to the gondola. He reached out to take Possle's hand. He was surprised at the strength with which it grasped his, and with its coldness. It was more like the hand of a dead than a living man. It felt even colder than it had been when it had groped his skull.

Before Urbino reached the door, he stopped. "Your last Duchess, as you called her," he said. He indicated the portrait. "She's by Lino Cipri."

"You know him?"

"A friend of mine commissioned some work from him. Copies. Do you know him well?"

"Not these days, if I ever did." Possle gave a hollow laugh. "There's no one I seem to know these days. You're in very select company."

"Did Cipri make the copies of the Moreau paintings?"

"Such interest in Lino Cipri! Yes, he did. I'm sure he's got as much money from your friend as he could. He doesn't believe in art for art's sake. And in the case of the portrait here, he got the original."

Urbino looked at the beautiful woman and then back at

Possle.

"Just my little joke, Mr. Macintyre. By the way, I would suggest that you get more rest. You're looking a bit haggard. Until the next time."

Armando conducted Urbino across the *sala* and down the staircase. He stood in the hall without any expression on his hard-featured face, watching Urbino put on his cloak. But as he was closing the heavy door on Urbino, he did it with a smile full of malignancy and satisfaction.

On his walk back to the Palazzo Uccello, Urbino couldn't quite shake the chill that he always had when he was in the Ca' Pozza. The chill on this occasion had been intensified by the touch of Possle's hand and Armando's smile of farewell. Once again he felt the fatigue settling in that he now came to expect after these encounters at the Ca' Pozza.

As soon as he got back home, he compared the key he had taken from Possle's bedroom with the key to the front door of the Ca' da Capo-Zendrini.

He didn't know if he was disappointed or relieved to find that the two didn't match. He realized now how much he had expected them to.

He spent a long time thinking about what he had seen in Possle's rooms and even more of his experience on the back staircase. It was inevitable that he associate the belt with the Contessa's lost items, although she hadn't said anything about missing a belt. It might only be a coincidence. He wasn't even sure if the belt was a man's or a woman's.

A key, a belt, and Possle's revelations about Byron.

In one way or another, Urbino had come away from the Ca' Pozza today with each of these things. He couldn't assume that they were connected or that they weren't. Each of them might be nothing more than what the detective novels called a red herring. But on the other hand, one or all of them might lead him to some of the answers he was seeking inside Possle's dark house and the world outside it.

50

Urbino spent most of Saturday morning, while the Contessa was giving her second *conversazione*, arranging for Cipri's copies of the Longhis to be shipped to Eugene in New Orleans. It was a time-consuming affair, and he occupied himself during all the waiting by pondering over the copyist's former relationship with Possle.

When his task was finished, he had lunch at a favorite restaurant on the San Marco side of the Rialto Bridge that was bustling at this time of the day. He ate at the bar, hoping that all the conversation and activity around him would help draw him out of his thoughts about Possle and the Ca' Pozza, about the key he had taken, the belt he had seen on the staircase, and the recluse's provocative remarks about Byron. But he only ended up feeling more solitary.

As soon as he stepped into the *calle* after lunch, he decided to seek out some of the locales associated with Byron as a way of concretizing some of his thoughts. The poet had spent several years in the city where, according to his own estimate, he had been the lover of two hundred women as well as a few men.

The possible existence of unpublished Byron poems, perhaps written during his notorious residency in the city, was even affecting Urbino's dream now. Last night a new element had entered. As the Contessa approached the thronelike chairs, the young Possle slipped a hand beneath the veil of the woman wearing the Contessa's silver cascade, withdrew a sheaf of papers, and waved them in the air. They were covered with florid handwriting in purple ink. When the Contessa reached Possle, the fire broke out as he knew it would, but instead of the drapes catching fire, the papers did.

As always, Urbino had awakened when the flames started to engulf the room.

The dream was still very much on his mind as he walked in the general direction of the Piazza San Marco on this gray, overcast day. The sun kept trying to break through but succeeded for only a few scattered moments. Traces of fog curled above the waters of the Grand Canal and crept across the squares and alleys like something alive.

Packs of boisterous students interrupted Urbino's progress and reflections. Their easy camaraderie and enthusiasm could not have been more of a contrast to his meditative mood.

Urbino needed to be skeptical about Possle's possible possession of unpublished poems by Byron. It wasn't that such things didn't happen or that people like Urbino didn't unearth them. He was aware of several instances. In fact, he knew a woman who had stumbled on previously unknown letters by Henry James, which had shed light on his sexual identity.

But for every genuine discovery, a thousand hoaxes confounded the public; and if ever there was a person who would perpetrate such a hoax, that person was certainly Samuel Possle, the thief of San Polo, as Urbino was more and more coming to think of him. Everything about him, from his clothes and his Amontillado to his allusions and his choice of décor and music, was calculated, and nothing more so than his bizarre divan.

And yet Urbino couldn't discount the possibility that unpublished poems by Byron were hidden somewhere in the

Ca' Pozza, waiting to be exposed to the light. If they were, how long had they been there, and how had they come into Possle's hands? Possle had said that there was no doubt of Byron's authorship. Did this mean that someone had authenticated them? All of them? And what were they about? Were they a sequence? Isolated poems? First draughts of poems that had already been published?

Urbino had a sinking feeling as he formulated this latter question. It made him realize how much he was already hoping, so soon after Possle had made his revelation, that he indeed did have authentic poems and ones that had never seen the light of day. They might not provide the answer to the riddle of the universe, but they would certainly shake the lesser world of Byron studies and help make the reputation of whoever found them. They were just what Urbino needed at this time. Much better than a biography of Possle would be.

The idea of the poems remained temptingly before his eyes as he plunged through the tortuous alleys. If Possle had them, Urbino would do whatever he could to get possession of them, do anything, that is, within reason. This amendment he almost voiced aloud as if to assure himself of an inviolable personal principle. It was also one that Possle had ironically drawn attention to yesterday.

Urbino threaded his way through the alleys until he reached a *calle* that led toward the Grand Canal. Fog from the waterway was brushing against the brick and stucco.

He came to a halt at a building on his right. It was the Palazzo Benzon, the first stop on what he had decided would be his contemplative little itinerary in honor of Byron. This wasn't the best way to view the building, for like most of the palazzi on the Grand Canal, it turned its back to the pedestrian world and showed its full splendor only by water.

But his imagination had little trouble investing it with some of its past glory when the Contessa Marina Querini-Benzon had conducted a literary salon in one of its sumptuous apartments. She was none other than the blonde woman named in the Venetian love song "La biondina in gondoleta" that gondoliers still serenaded their customers with. Byron, who had begun as a luminary of the sixty-year-old contessa's salon, had ended up her lover, as Urbino had been speculating about yesterday in the presence of Peggy Guggenheim's bed.

He retraced his steps down the *calle* and bent them toward the four Palazzi Mocenigo, which stood at the *volta* of the Canalazzo where it made its sharpest turn. The fog was thicker here. It obscured first one part of the scene, then another, as it stole along.

The Palazzo Mocenigo-Vecchio was the one that Demetrio Emo had described as being haunted by the ghost of the alchemist Giordano Bruno.

But Urbino was drawn to the Palazzo Mocenigo-Nero, for it had been here that Byron, from 1818 to 1819, with a dog, monkey, fox, and wolf to keep him company, had created the romantic aura of his Venetian years. He had pursued his mistresses, swum the length of the Grand Canal, ridden horses on the Lido, and argued incessantly with his friend Shelley, who disapproved of Byron's sexual obsession that had gondoliers soliciting lovers for him on the streets and canals. And in its rooms he had carried on his notorious affair with a woman known as La Fornarina, the baker's wife, who had attacked him with a knife during a quarrel and then jumped into the Grand Canal from the balcony of his rooms.

Here in the Palazzo Mocenigo-Nero, Byron had made his decision to study the Armenian language on the island of San Lazzaro degli Armeni in the lagoon and had written the first two cantos of *Don Juan*. Perhaps he had also written the poems that Possle had mentioned.

A young man and a woman, speaking French, came down the *calle* and stood beside Urbino to read the plaque honoring Byron. The man carried a recently published biography about the homosexual component of the poet's libertinage. When the woman consulted her map, Urbino realized that they needed to get to the Accademia Bridge. He walked a short distance with them to show them the way and then sought out the thickening flow of people. Eventually he entered the fashionable street of shops that ended near the Piazza. He turned down an alley and stopped when he reached a secluded courtyard.

A middle-aged nun in a blue dress and white scarf was sweeping the pavement of her order's retirement home. Urbino wondered what the good sisters lying in their beds after a lifetime of faithful service would think if they knew that Byron had met and fallen in love with a beautiful married woman in a house in this same courtyard. But perhaps one of the sisters, after decades of devotion to her heavenly bridegroom, was at that very moment reading, through thick glasses, about how Byron had become the married woman's *cavaliere servente,* an ambiguous but socially accepted role in the morally lax city, and how they had settled down into a domestic relationship. The enthralled sister might even wet her dry cheek when she came to Byron's death from fever in Greece at the age of thirty-six and close the book with the consolation that she had read nothing more than a moral tale.

Urbino abandoned these thoughts and turned out of the courtyard. There was one more stop on his itinerary. A few minutes later he was standing in a busy street behind the Piazza San Marco and gazing up at yet another building. Here Byron had first lodged in Venice, shadowed by rumors of incest after he had left England. Soon after moving into his rooms, he was thick in an affair with the landlord's wife.

Perhaps Byron had written the poems that Possle claimed to have to this woman, whose dark eyes had mesmerized him. Perhaps they had somehow found their way from the heart of San Marco across the Grand Canal to Possle's isolated palazzo in San Polo. The point of all this walking and all this intense contemplation of some of the stones of Venice was to make him even more hungry for whatever poems Possle might have.

Urbino, buffeted by passersby, pulled himself out of his speculations and headed for Harry's Bar a short distance away. The small, unpretentious front room, however, was smoke filled and crowded with tourists, most of them drinking their obligatory Bellinis. He left after having a quick glass of wine and making a dinner reservation for next Tuesday for Emo and himself.

The number one *vaporetto* was about to leave from the landing in front of the bar. The boat attendant held the gate open until Urbino squeezed through, and then the boat set off up the Grand Canal through the fog. Urbino sat outside in the stern away from the wind and contemplated the view as the palaces and churches unrolled themselves. He mulled over the various notions that had been a counterpoint to his walk this afternoon.

On his way to the Palazzo Uccello from the boat landing, he stopped at a locksmith's, but not Demetrio Emo's. To go to THE KEEPER OF THE KEYS might have been a mistake.

The locksmith made a copy of the key Urbino had taken from Possle's bedroom. He had to search through a box of old key patterns before he was able to find a suitable one to use.

Back at the Palazzo Uccello, Urbino first telephoned the Contessa to ask her how her *conversazione* had gone. Although she was modest in what she said, he could tell that it had been another success. She promised him that she would give him more details when she saw him in person in a few more days. She had to go to Asolo again early tomorrow morning to attend to some problems at the villa in preparation for the visit of her sister and her family.

After speaking with the Contessa, he opened a bottle of Corvo and took it to the library. For the rest of the afternoon and evening, sustained by the wine and a plate of *tramezzini* sandwiches Natalia had left for him, he immersed himself in Byron's poetry and correspondence and in biographical accounts of his life.

Nothing he read gave him a clue about any unpublished Byron poems. Yet almost everything he read increased his hunger to lay his hands on them if they indeed existed, stashed away somewhere in the dark Ca' Pozza—to lay his hands on them by fair means, of course, he quickly amended as he turned off the lights of the library.

51

The next afternoon at two o'clock Urbino boarded the
motonave for the Lido near the Doge's Palace. Sun and a
pale blue sky had succeeded yesterday's fog and damp.

The boat was crowded with people taking advantage of the
fair weather for an outing to the Lido. Gentle waves rocked
the buoys and rippled the blue-green waters of the lagoon,
scattered with *vaporetti*, delivery boats, and pleasure craft.

The curve of the Riva degli Schiavoni with its broad pavement, balconied buildings, little bridges, and moored boats and
ships slid past. They were soon passing the Naval Museum,
with its memories of the day the Contessa had provided the
epithet that Urbino kept returning to: the thief of San Polo.

Farther along spread the area that was being prepared for
the art exposition. Urbino would soon be swept up with Habib
in the parties, photographic shoots, and stream of friends and
family coming through Venice. Was it too much to expect that
by the time of the opening in June he would be in possession
of the poems, if they existed, and that his mysterious business
with Possle would be at an end?

As the boat swung away from the tail of Venice, the small
monastery island of San Lazzaro degli Armeni, with its
cypresses and onion shaped cupola, became visible.

A warm sea breeze was blowing down the main street of the narrow strip of land when Urbino disembarked on the Lido. Some of the passengers who had come over on the boat were renting bicycles from the shop near the landing. One couple was already pedaling away in a tandem in the direction of the open sea.

Urbino went into a bar and, under the influence of the large sign that dominated the boat landing, ordered a Campari. As he drank the bitter red liquid, he asked the bartender for directions to Lino Cipri's apartment on the assumption that the dapper painter was known in the neighborhood. He was. The bartender named a street a short distance away.

Urbino strolled in the sunshine down the broad avenue toward the sea past the shops, restaurants, hotels, and villas.

Despite his love for Venice, Urbino was sometimes glad to escape it for a few hours on the Lido, although never in the height of summer. At this time of the year, even on a Sunday like today, with more visitors than usual, it was a pleasant change from the claustrophobia of Venice. This was close to what Byron must have felt when he left Venice's society and intrigue to come horseback riding on what were, in his day, the barren strands of the Lido.

Urbino angled back toward the boat landing and soon reached the street where the Cipris lived. It was closed to traffic and bordered by one of the Lido's few canals. Small boats were moored alongside the brick walls of the quay.

He went up the cracked front steps of one of the least well-kept buildings and pushed the bell.

52

Cipri was in good spirits and seemed pleased to see Urbino. All pink and shining as if recently shaved and showered, he was dressed in a beige suit with a flowing blue cravat. He guided Urbino to a chair in the parlor across from the one in which his wife sat with a stern expression on her face. Cipri lowered the volume of Liszt's *Todtentanz* that was playing on a record player and slipped into the kitchen.

Signora Cipri wore a faded housedress. Her head was bare today. Urbino was dismayed to see that she had only a few wisps of gray hair.

The small room was crowded with worn furniture. Books were crammed into a bookcase and scattered in piles across the carpet and on tables and chairs. Unframed paintings were stacked against the wall behind the sofa.

Signora Cipri's armchair, with its floral fabric, provided a view of the entrance hall and the kitchen. A small table overflowed at her elbow with bottles of medication. She kept glancing in the direction of the kitchen as if she was impatient for her husband's return. When her sharp blue eyes rested on Urbino, they didn't move away at once but stared with an almost insolent air. He tried to engage her in conversation, but she remained silent. Taking it as a sign that she preferred Liszt's *danse macabre* to anything he might have to say, he leaned back and listened to the paraphrase of the *Dies Irae* with her.

Fortunately, Cipri soon emerged with it. On the tray were a pot of espresso, cups, an anisette bottle, and a small plate of biscuits. He fixed an espresso for his wife first, pouring in a generous portion of the anisette and a sliver of lemon, and gave her a biscuit.

Urbino mentioned that he had sent off the paintings and said, once again, that Eugene was sure to be pleased with them.

"I hope so," Cipri said, as he seated himself in an armchair across from Urbino.

"Although I shouldn't speak for him, Eugene might want more Longhis. He had a hard time choosing which ones he wanted you to copy."

"I'm at his service," he said, "and yours, too, although I know that you're not interested in copies."

"But perhaps you could do a portrait of someone," Urbino said casually. "My friend Rebecca Mondador, the architect. I'd like to give it to her as a gift. That is, if she has time to sit for you, and if you have the time to do it."

"Oh, I have the time!"

"Let me speak with her first. The portrait should be nothing like the style of the one you did for my fellow countryman, Samuel Possle. The one of his wife, his ex-wife now. I've been a recent visitor to the Ca' Pozza."

Cipri threw a glance at his wife. Her keen blue eyes beneath their black brows, the eyes that had so disconcerted the Contessa at the music conservatory, flashed with some emotion Urbino couldn't identify.

"I've seen the portrait on two occasions. Along with two other of your paintings. Copies of Moreau. But the portrait—"

"Ah, yes, the Moreau copies," Cipri interrupted nervously. "Can you believe that Signor Possle sent me all the way to

Paris to do one of them, *The Apparition*? I even had an expense account. He was very generous. The other copy, the one of Salome, I had to do from reproductions. It's not as good. Do you like Moreau, Signor Urbino?"

"Yes. But about the portrait, unfortunately it's hung in a rather dark room. But what I could see of it impressed me. It's very good. And Mrs. Possle is extremely beautiful, or she was."

Cipri was growing increasingly uncomfortable. His wife uttered a few words that Urbino couldn't make out.

"Of course I don't know how long ago you painted the portrait."

"Thirty-eight years ago."

"That *is* a long time, but even so, true beauty always leaves its traces, haven't you found?"

Cipri made no response.

Urbino drank down the remainder of his espresso. Without asking, Cipri poured anisette into the cup as well as into his own.

"Tell me, Signor Cipri, how well did you know Mrs. Possle?"

"How well did I know her? But—"

He looked at his wife again. Urbino now knew, too late, what Possle meant when he had said that Cipri had got the original of the portrait. Mrs. Cipri's eyes were closed. She was swaying slightly.

"Excuse me," Cipri said.

He helped Signora Cipri out of her chair and guided her across the parlor and through a door. He returned a few minutes later, closing the door behind him. He shut off the *Todtentanz*.

"I'm sorry. I had no idea."

"She'll be all right. She's changed so much since then."

"I only realized a few moments ago that she was Samuel Possle's wife."

Cipri nodded.

"Hilda. I married her eight years after I painted the portrait."

"I've only become acquainted with Possle recently, you see," Urbino explained. "I know he was married to a German woman, a poet, but other than that . . ." He trailed off.

"Hardly anyone knows that Hilda was married to Possle. We keep it to ourselves. It wasn't because of me that they divorced. And, yes, she's a poet. She still writes in German under her maiden name, Hilda Krippe. Some of her poems have been published recently. People come from Germany and Austria to see her."

He reseated himself, poured more anisette, and took a sip.

"Don't be embarrassed," he went on, "but she's sensitive. She's a very intelligent woman. Her mind hasn't dimmed at all. But the body . . ."

He shook his head and looked in the direction of the closed door.

"She's been feeling more poorly than usual. She was fine the day you saw us at the music conservatory, but she's had a relapse since then."

Urbino considered what would now be appropriate. He could thank Cipri for his hospitality, apologize again, and take his leave, promising to let him know about the portrait commission.

But instead, after sipping his anisette, he said, "If things work out, I might write something about Possle. One reason for coming here was to ask you for your impressions of him. I had no idea of your wife's former relationship to him."

"But now you'd like to ask her some questions, too."

Cipri stated it so simply that Urbino was relieved that he could be more direct than he otherwise would have been. But he still needed to let Cipri believe that the main thrust of his questions was a biography of Possle.

"Considering her reputation as a poet," Urbino said, "she

might like to have her say in anything I write about him. I'd respect whatever privacy either of you might ask."

"My wife will have to decide for herself. I'll mention it to her when she's feeling better." Cipri glanced at the bedroom door, then leaned back in his chair. "As for me, I don't have much to tell. I only went to the Ca' Pozza for Hilda's sittings and the unveiling and to discuss business. I haven't seen Possle in over thirty years. He was kind and generous in his dealings with me."

Urbino was puzzled as to how he should take Cipri's praise. Kindness and generosity didn't seem to be among Possle's strongest traits, but as Cipri said, he was speaking of the Possle of three decades ago. One would expect someone in Cipri's position, married as he was to Possle's ex-wife, to have less good to say about the man. In fact, any information, positive or negative, needed to be taken with a grain of salt, considering the animosity that might exist between them.

"Possle never remarried," Urbino prompted.

"Marriage doesn't suit some men. Not that it's their fault," he added, perhaps because of Urbino's own bachelorhood. "Or the fault of women like Hilda either. He never had any cause to complain about her."

"I'm sure he didn't," responded Urbino, somewhat mystified but immensely interested.

He decided to approach things from a different angle.

"I'd like to interview his former gondolier, Armando Abdon. He's still with him, but it could prove to be difficult with his handicap."

"There's no reason he couldn't write things down, but I'm not sure how much he'd be willing to tell you. He was devoted to Possle in those days, very devoted, according to Hilda."

He held Urbino's eye for several beats, then looked away.

"He still is," Urbino said.

"That doesn't surprise me. But let me give you some

advice. Go carefully with him. He's easily offended. He never did anything to Hilda or me, you understand, but I know as well as I know my copying that he's not someone you want to have angry with you."

Cipri's words reawakened Urbino's uneasiness about the man and the advantage that he might have over him since the last visit.

"I'll keep that in mind. Did you know his sister, Adriana?"

"Slightly. She used to hang around the Ca' Pozza. She had a crush on Possle, Hilda said. Maybe she had hoped to marry him before Hilda did."

"When did Hilda marry Possle?"

"In the late fifties. But it seems that Adriana was sticking close to Possle five or six years before then."

This places the time close to when the Contessa was briefly acquainted with Possle, Urbino thought.

"Adriana was lovely," Cipri continued, "and with a beautiful voice, but she flew into rages over nothing. You wouldn't want to cross her anymore than her brother." Cipri appeared to have more to say about Adriana than he had implied a few minutes before. "She seemed emotionally unbalanced, but maybe I'm not the best judge. I'm not one of your wild, raging artists. I've always liked to do my work with a tranquil mind and heart."

"Did Hilda have any problems with her? Because of Adriana's feelings for Possle, I mean?"

"We've never talked about her. I was probably wrong about the crush," Cipri retreated.

He looked at the bedroom door. It seemed now to be open a crack.

"Do you know how she died?"

"She drowned," Cipri said, in an even lower voice than he had been speaking in so far. "Right here off the Lido when she went out sailing with Possle and her brother. Maybe there was someone else with them. I don't know."

Urbino finished his anisette and got up.

"I'll tell Hilda that you'd like to speak with her," Cipri said, as he accompanied Urbino out of the parlor and into the foyer.

They stopped by a table. Its surface was littered with sheets torn out of a sketch pad, an Italian-German dictionary, keys, an old palette knife, and an assortment of pens and pencils.

Urbino indicated the sheets. "May I?" he asked Cipri.

Cipri nodded.

Urbino picked them up. Each contained an ink portrait of a woman. Because of the portrait in the gondola room, he recognized her as Hilda, but a Hilda much younger and healthier, with a beatific smile. Clouds of hair framed her face.

"They're lovely. When did you do them?"

"A few weeks ago."

Urbino looked up at Cipri.

"It's the way she sees herself," the artist said, "and the way I see her."

Urbino replaced the portraits on the table.

"She still writes poetry, you say. Is there a copy of one of her books that she might let me borrow? I have a passable understanding of German."

"Let me see."

Cipri bent down by a nearby bookshelf and after a few moments extracted a slim paperbound book. He handed it to Urbino. "It's one of her old collections," he said. "You can have it."

"Thank you, and thank your wife for me."

On the book's gray cover in black German Gothic script was printed *"Byronic Inspirations* by Hilda Krippe, privately printed in Munich, 1967."

"Lord Byron," Urbino said.

"Hilda has always loved Byron ever since she was a young woman. Before I met her, the only thing I knew about Byron was the Byron Cup," he said with a little laugh. He was referring to the annual boat race along the length of the Lido in memory of the poet.

Urbino thanked Cipri and slipped the book into his pocket.

"Did Possle share Hilda's love of Byron?" he asked Possle.

"It was one of the things they had in common. He had a foreign friend who loved Byron, too. A tall man with a beard. He would sometimes read Hilda a Byron poem when she was sitting for me."

"Do you remember what the man's name was?"

"A strange name, but I can't remember it. He was Armenian. Like the fathers on San Lazzaro degli Armeni."

53

Urbino didn't return directly to the boat landing. Instead he walked down to the beach to the shuttered Grand Hotel des Bains, closed until April. He seated himself on the stone steps of the verandah.

Ghostlike ships drifted slowly along the horizon. A small plane droned over the water toward the low line of the Euganean Hills in the far distance. Bicycles and tandems passed in the road, and a mother posed behind a stroller while her husband took a picture of her and the baby. Two young couples were walking hand in hand on the hotel's private strip of beach.

Usually when he came to the Grand Hotel des Bains, his thoughts were full of Thomas Mann, for it was here that Aschenbach had fallen desperately in love with his Polish boy and had died in the snare of his obsession. But today Byron dominated his thoughts, Byron who had ridden along this same stretch of beach long before it became a bathing resort. Byron who may have written unpublished poems that were in Possle's possession. And the same Byron who fascinated Hilda.

He riffled through Hilda's volume of poetry. The pages had already been cut. Ten poems, most no longer than twenty lines, haunted the pages in their Gothic script. He began to read. The German didn't give him too much difficulty, although some words and phrases were unfamiliar.

Not only did Byron inspire all of them, as the title said, but they also had a Venetian theme, taking as their subject some place or activity associated with Byron's Venice years. The Bridge of Sighs figured prominently, as did his swim from the Lido up the Grand Canal and his love affair with La Fornarina.

Hilda's talent had the ability to create vivid, if derivative, word pictures, clouded by rich, suggestive allusions that made Urbino feel as if he were looking through a smoky glass into a more vital and meaningful past. A current of emotion, albeit muted and therefore all the more powerful in his opinion, ran from one poem to another.

He sat there reading them, part of his mind searching for some connection between Hilda, the poems, and the strange events at the Ca' Pozza, another part caught up in their spell regardless of their relevance to his present case.

54

Back at the Palazzo Uccello, Urbino called his friend Corrado Scarpa, who was a contact at the Venice Questura. He needed a copy of a report about a Lido boat accident that had ended in the death of someone named Adriana Abdon. He gave the approximate date. Scarpa would do his best and get back to him.

Urbino then gave Rebecca a call and invited her to stop by that evening.

"I'll break out a bottle of the Henri Jayer," he promised. "Consider it belated payment for the help you've given me about Possle."

"And a retainer for future help?"

"Perhaps."

But once Rebecca had come and was seated in the parlor across from him, Urbino didn't ply her with any more questions about the former renovations of the Ca' Pozza. Instead he told her that Possle had invited him back for two more visits.

"Good for you. So tell me, did I put you onto a good thing? Do you think it's haunted?"

She smiled at him over the rim of her wineglass.

"Not in the way that's usually meant perhaps, but there are plenty of ghosts that need to be laid to rest."

"That's your job, isn't it? Or I should say, it's part of both your jobs. Don't worry, I'm not going to pump you. I know when you're pulling down the shutters."

"Not all the way." Urbino gave her an affectionate smile. Then, far less lightly, he told her that the boy who had fallen to his death had been Gildo's friend.

Rebecca absorbed this in silence for several moments.

"That brings everything closer to home, doesn't it?" was her eventual response.

"I suppose it does. But I don't know quite what to make of it yet. Do you know if there've been any recent break-ins in San Polo?"

"Things seemed to have calmed down."

Rebecca's attractive face was full of questions.

"You know how I like to speculate and turn things over in my mind," Urbino said, as she continued to scrutinize him.

"Do I ever!"

"And you also know that I'm grateful for all you've done for Habib and me," he said, in an abrupt, but tactical shift. "That's why I've decided to have your portrait done. For you to have, not me. And no, not by Habib, but Lino Cipri."

It was Urbino's way of making his lie to Cipri true.

"A portrait? By Cipri? You've got something up your sleeve, my dear, but once again I'm not asking. The ego of even a thoroughly modern woman like me can take only so many rebuffs, and I've had more than enough from you over the years."

55

I t's irises today," the Contessa said.
It was Monday morning, March 18, and the two friends
were on San Michele, the island of the dead in the lagoon.

A small bouquet of violet irises stood on the austere grave
of Serge Diaghilev, the impresario of the Ballets Russes. Next
to the bouquet was one of the worn, moldy ballet slippers that
always seemed to adorn the tombstone.

The Contessa gave a shiver that the chill in the air couldn't
completely account for.

"Irises die so quickly," she said. "These will be gone by
tomorrow. Let's go."

Under the gray sky, they turned down a path toward the
main part of the cemetery. Graves with Russian names, most
of them women and some of them princesses, conjured up the
ghosts of characters out of Tolstoy. The Contessa, dressed
against the weather in a thick, gray wool coat, faux fur hat,
and matching muff, looked very much in the Slavic spirit of
the place.

"Since one must be buried somewhere," Urbino said, as
they passed through the gate and left the Orthodox section,
"Venice is as good a place for it as any, don't you think?"

"And what about Possle?" the Contessa asked. "I would

guess that the two of you are of the same mind as far as that's concerned."

"It's not something that I care to ask him."

"You've been rather timid about asking him anything, it seems to me."

"You wouldn't say that if you knew about our last meeting."

Except for an account of his visit to the Cipris and his conversation with Gildo about Marco, Urbino hadn't yet filled her in about other things. During most of the time Gildo rowed them across to San Michele, snug in the cabin beneath their blankets, she had described her *conversazione* on Saturday in more detail than she had done over the telephone.

Now, as they entered an area with tiers of burial niches for the ashes of the dead, he began to tell her about his last visit to the Ca' Pozza. He described his search through Possle's rooms, but he didn't tell her about taking the key. He was embarrassed, and he also wanted to figure out first what he might do with the key and with the copy he had made, or so he told himself. He did tell her, however, about the serpentine belt on the back staircase and about everything that Possle had revealed about the poems by Byron.

He was coming to the end of his account as they drew near the Da Capo-Zendrini mausoleum with its statues of weeping angels. They halted.

"I'm glad that Alvise isn't here to see all the intrigues you've pulled me into over the years," the Contessa said.

"Or the ones you've pulled *me* into."

It was a particularly pointed reference, since one of Urbino's cases directly involving the Contessa had come to a violent conclusion in front of the mausoleum a few years ago.

"*Touché!* But this time around, it's only some clothes and one lovely necklace that I've enlisted your help over. No blood will be shed over them, surely. Not unless belts prove to be snakes after all."

A pensive look came over her face. Urbino didn't interrupt her thoughts.

"You aren't even sure if the belt was a man's or a woman's," she said after a few moments. "I do have several snakeskin belts, but as far as I know, none of them is missing. I'll check. But should I hope to find one missing or not? That's the difficult question for me at the moment. I just can't conceive of how a belt of mine, or anything else, might end up on the back stairs of Possle's house!"

"Neither can I. And as you just reminded me, it might have been a man's belt."

"Exactly. You may be seeing what you want to see and not seeing what you should."

"That's always a possibility."

"In any case, as I said a little while ago, there's no blood on the scene anywhere," the Contessa emphasized. "We're lucky for that."

"There's Marco Carelli."

"A boy who fell to his death when he was on drugs?"

"There could be more to that situation than meets the eye."

"That's what you think of everything!"

"Don't forget the Byron connection."

"So what are you suggesting? That Possle is like a spider enticing the fly—or maybe I should say the flies—and that he's using these Byron poems as bait?"

She didn't wait for an answer if, in fact, she expected one. She went to the steps of the mausoleum and moved an urn of fresh white chrysanthemums a fraction of an inch to one side and then back again.

"At any rate," she continued, "I'm glad you're being more aggressive with Possle. You need to find out more about these

Byron poems he claims to have; but whatever you do, don't go stalking around the house anymore. Wait a minute!" she said, straightening up and looking at him. "You're not thinking that this Marco broke in to get the Byron poems, are you?"

"It's a possibility."

The Contessa, framed in the closed doorway of the mausoleum, shot Urbino an accusing look.

"There are more possibilities and speculations about the Ca' Pozza than there are graves on San Michele, it seems. And I wish the man wouldn't keep mentioning me. Why should I find the Byron poems of particular interest?"

Urbino remained silent.

The Contessa took a handkerchief from her coat pocket and started to rub the door handle with an air of industry.

"I'm well aware that you're not telling me everything. And I know that my clothes aren't your top priority, especially not now that you're salivating over the prospect of laying your hands on these Byron poems, *if* they exist. But I hope you haven't forgotten about me completely."

"As a matter of fact, you and your clothes have been very much on my mind."

The Contessa gave one more unnecessary swipe at the door handle, then returned the handkerchief to her pocket. She bowed her head for a few moments in silent prayer.

"And now, *caro*, let's get the rest of this visit over with."

56

The Contessa gave Urbino her arm, and they walked slowly along the path toward fields planted with rows of small wooden crosses.

When they had arrived on the island, Urbino had inquired at the cemetery office about two particular graves, one recent and the other almost two decades old. The friar had been able to locate only one. Now, with a map, Urbino and the Contessa sought it out.

But first they had to traverse an area of graves that were being exhumed to make way for the newly dead. The requisite twelve years of the former tenants had passed, and the remains from these graves would be deposited in a common grave or in an ossuary.

The Contessa averted her eyes from the piles of dirt, shattered pieces of concrete, plastic flowers, and broken wooden crosses. This sight was particularly disturbing to Urbino as well. He preferred his graves to be romantically unkempt or well tended, with the bereaved making their pilgrimages and leaving their tokens.

This was why he was moved by the otherwise stony and vicious-looking Armando's devotion for seventeen years to the memory of his dead sister. Urbino firmly believed that people could be most contradictory and inconsistent.

His impression of Possle, for example, didn't mesh with either Razzi's or Cipri's opinions. In their way, they had both praised him. Could Razzi and Cipri have some reason for misleading him about their true feelings?

They both apparently disliked Armando, however, and they had felt as uncomfortable around him in the past as Urbino did now. Yet Armando was capable of at least the one good act of remembering his dead. It redeemed a great deal.

And hadn't Marco been inconsistent as well, if he were to believe Gildo? Elvira's son might have hung around with a rough crowd and broken into houses, but his motivations hadn't been the worst.

"I wonder where Adriana is buried?" Urbino asked, when they had almost reached the last of the disinterred graves.

The cemetery office had no record of any grave for Adriana on San Michele.

"It could have been in one of these areas," the Contessa observed, still averting her eyes. "It's been much more than twelve years."

"But the friar searched the records all the way back to the year she died. He found nothing that indicated she had been disinterred."

"You've lived here for all these years, and you're putting your faith in the Italian bureaucracy? Even if it's the version the good friars have here? And you saw how slow and confused the man was, not to mention the thickness of his glasses. Adriana Abdon's name could have been written in capital letters and in red ink and he would have had trouble making it out."

"But a man who puts obituary notices in the paper," he pointed out, "and who has commemorative masses said every year, isn't the kind to have allowed his sister's body to be dug up."

"Perpetual care costs perpetual money. But surely it's the

living Adriana who interests you, isn't it?" The Contessa waited. "Well, aren't you going to answer me?"

"You're exactly right," he conceded.

"Thank God for that. I was beginning to think you had some theory that she didn't die accidentally." She continued to look at him for a few moments and then said, "Maybe I'll play my cards close to my chest, too, when it comes to this Adriana."

It was Urbino's turn to give her a sharp, inquisitive look. "What do you mean?"

"My *conversazioni* have stirred my memory. And when you mentioned something that Cipri said about Adriana, I got an extra nudge. Her voice. A girl about five years younger than me used to hang around the conservatory. Beautiful, with coal black hair and pale skin. But it's her voice I remember best. She would sing her heart out in the courtyard by the veiled lady until they chased her away. She had no money to study there. We're probably talking about the same girl. It's not just the voice, of course. It's the name, too. Remember how I thought it was familiar? I think that's why. I must have heard someone call her that."

Urbino took a piece of paper from his pocket and handed it to her.

"It's her. It's Adriana," she said, gazing down at it. "But how—oh, but of course, it's the obituary photograph Armando put in the newspaper."

He nodded.

"Did you ever see her in Possle's entourage?"

"No, but my contacts with him were limited." She handed the clipping back to Urbino.

"There's something I haven't told you yet," he said. "I didn't want to get your hopes up."

"It's about my clothes!" she cried jubilantly.

"As a matter of fact it is."

He explained about the photograph he had found in Elvira

Carelli's apartment, the one of the Contessa taken at the film festival.

"But why would Elvira Carelli have a photograph of me?"

Urbino didn't respond. He wanted her to think it out on her own. She gripped his arm and they came to a halt.

"My tea dress! My hat!"

He nodded.

"You see the implications," he said.

"Marco broke into the house somehow. Nothing has been taken since he died." The friar at the cemetery office had given the date of Marco's burial as three days before Christmas. It confirmed what the woman at the Rialto market had told Urbino.

"But there's still a three-week period between when he died and when you realized everything was missing," he pointed out.

She shook her head.

"*He* took them. For *her*. What was it that Gildo said? Marco only took things from the rich and gave them to the poor? But why would she want *my* clothes?"

"I just don't know. We can't even be sure that's what happened."

"I just don't understand," the Contessa said in a dispirited tone.

They resumed walking. Urbino was about to consult the map when he realized he didn't need it anymore. All they had to do was direct their steps to the tall, bareheaded woman standing in one of the long rows of small crosses in the burial field ahead. She was singing a song that floated through the air.

"It's Elvira Carelli," Urbino said.

"Speak of the devil!"

Dressed in her brown coat and yellow scarf, she was oblivious to their approach. Urbino and the Contessa stopped a short distance from her.

She was singing an Italian lullaby. Her voice was full of feeling. As she sang, she stared down at one of the crosses, the sunlight making the gray in her hair gleam.

The lullaby came to an end.

"She has a lovely voice," the Contessa said. "Untrained, but lovely."

"Like Adriana's."

The Contessa looked at Urbino questioningly, as if she expected him to say something more, but he turned away and started to approach Elvira.

The woman looked up. Her eyes widened. "You!" she shouted.

"Excuse me, Signora Carelli," Urbino said, "we didn't mean to—"

"You!" she repeated, interrupting him.

But it wasn't Urbino she was staring at, it was the Contessa.

"You killed my son! You killed my Marco! How dare you come here! You with all your fancy clothes!"

"Excuse me, signora," the Contessa began, but she didn't have a chance to say anything else.

Elvira rushed up and snatched the muff from the Contessa's hands. She waved it in her startled face, then raced across the field with it and down the path toward the cemetery exit.

57

"Another mystery solved," the Contessa said as the two friends sat in the closed cabin of the gondola fifteen minutes later. The island of the dead was receding behind them, thanks to Gildo's strong, smooth movements of the oar. The young man had a more abstracted air than he had had when he had rowed them out. Urbino wondered whether he had had an encounter the Elvira.

"Another?"

"Have you forgotten? The severed head. No decapitations at the Ca' Pozza, and next door perhaps a closetful of my clothes, including a newly acquired muff."

"You're taking this lightly."

"But don't you see? No one in the house is involved, and I'm *not* going out of my mind. Not that I ever really thought I was, of course," she quickly added. "Elvira had her son take my things. Now we have to get them back, but without making trouble for the poor woman, of course. I'm counting on you for that. Then you'll be free and clear to give all your attention to the dark mysteries of the Ca' Pozza. And you can forget all this nonsense about one of my belts poised to bite you on its back staircase."

The Contessa looked over at Urbino as he gazed off toward

the Fondamenta Nuove where Benedetta Razzi lived with all her dolls.

"You're not saying much," she said. "Thinking?"

"Always thinking. You know me."

They spoke in lowered voices although, with the noise of the water traffic in the lagoon, Gildo had little chance of hearing them from the poop behind the cabin.

Urbino turned to the Contessa. "Why do you think she says you killed Marco?" he asked her.

"You're asking *me?* That's for you to figure out, but we shouldn't expect the poor woman to make much logical sense. Don't forget that she originally said it was Benedetta Razzi."

"That's what I thought she was saying at the time. You're right. We can't put too much faith in what she says."

"Obviously not, considering that she thinks I'm a murderess!"

The gondola rocked and dipped. Gildo managed to restore it to a smoother course as it continued across the gray waters of the lagoon.

"There's another thing," Urbino said. "One could understand, in a twisted way, why she would want your clothes if she believes that you were somehow responsible for Marco's death, but why would she have wanted them *before* his death? He had to be alive to take them, unless we're going to believe that Elvira's the thief."

"I can't see that."

"Neither can I."

But the Contessa was not now paying attention to him. "Look," she said in a quiet voice, "you don't see many of these anymore."

She was referring to a funeral cortège making its somber way across the gray waters toward San Michele. In advance was the funeral gondola, a bargelike vessel larger than a regular gondola, adorned with the figures of a grieving angel and a lion and with an ornate double garland around the hull, all the details carved and gilded. Near the stern, in the place of the *felze* on Urbino's gondola, was the casket on a canopied and gilded platform with black curtains. A pair of black-clad rowers was positioned immediately before and behind the casket. Behind the funeral barque were three gondolas with fur-clad women and men in dark suits.

Gildo slowed their gondola as the cortège passed.

"It *is* unusual," Urbino said. He had seen very few processions like these since he had been living in Venice. It wasn't the way that even the well-to-do Venetians usually conveyed their dead to San Michele these days, let alone someone like Elvira or Armando.

The sad and impressive sight drove the two friends into their own reflections as their gondola moved farther and farther away from the island of the dead.

Gildo, possibly under the influence of the cortège, was still rowing them at a slower rate than usual, and it seemed to take a long time before they left the lagoon and entered the Misericordia Canal. On their right was the Casino degli Spiriti, one of the Venetian locales with a reputation for being haunted, as Demetrio Emo had reminded Urbino.

Urbino contemplated it now, hoping to chase away the dark mood that had descended on him in the last few minutes. He thought about the legend of the madwoman associated with Possle's building, a legend that could be said to have a contemporary equivalent in the person of Elvira, with her singing, laughter, and curses that seemed to come from within the walls of the Ca' Pozza.

Possle's hearing was too weak to allow him to hear Elvira, but if he could have, he might have been reminded of Adriana and her voice. But would it have been a welcome reminder?

The same could apply to Armando. Urbino assumed that he often did hear Elvira singing from next door, but it wouldn't necessarily make him feel positively disposed toward her. Although his commemorative masses for Adriana indicated that he hadn't forgotten her, it was logical that he would want to remember her on his own terms. Elvira's voice, so close to him all the time, could even be a form of torment.

Urbino had become so lost in his thoughts that he didn't realize that the Contessa had been staring at him. She had a distressed look on her face. "It's not over yet, *caro*, is it?"

"I'm afraid not."

The Contessa drew the blanket more securely over her knees and shivered as she had on the island of the dead.

PART FOUR

WE'LL GO NO MORE A-ROVING

58

At ten-thirty the next morning, Tuesday, March 19, Urbino was on San Lazzaro degli Armeni off the Lido. To his silent exasperation, the old bearded monk seemed determined to tell him everything about the island, including the specific dimensions of its onion-shaped cupola and the names of most of the fifty relics in the reliquary given to the Armenian fathers by the Patriarch of Venice.

Under other circumstances Urbino would have been more fascinated, for when he had visited the monastery island in the past, he had been a member of the island's guided tour. This morning Father Nazar was conducting him around privately and giving him access to areas and collections usually unavailable to the public.

He owed this special treatment to the Contessa, who was a generous benefactor to the Armenian monks. She had made phone calls as soon as they had returned from San Michele after he had told her he needed to make a visit.

Father Nazar was taking his mission seriously. He had already run through an entire history of the island from its days as a leper colony to the establishment of the monastery by the abbot Mechitar in 1715. And then he had described the events of all the years since then, not only in loving detail, but also in a bravado of five languages with hardly a breath between. The Mechitarist fathers were famous for their multi-lingualism and not a little proud of it, as Urbino's enthusiastic guide could not quite conceal.

Urbino dutifully read the plaque to Byron in the court-yard, admired the Tiepolo ceiling, viewed the illuminated manuscripts, Coptic Korans, and Armenian Bibles, com-mented on the nobility of Mechitar's bust, and asked questions about scraps of medieval tapestries, carved wooden chairs, and Buddhist papyrus inscriptions. He poked into every nook and cranny of the Byron Room with its paintings and memorabilia, all under the proud eye of Father Nazar who kept up a run-ning commentary on the poet's habits and program of study.

If all this wasn't enough, he also peered at an Egyptian mummy in its sarcophagus and feigned curiosity about a col-lection of scientific instruments. Then he spent a good half hour examining the printing and typesetting hall. There he paged through a book on Armenian national costume, plate after plate of women with embroidered and ornamented dresses, silver belts, and headdresses.

Having shown such remarkable patience, Urbino hoped that Father Nazar, when they were out in the cloister, forgave him when he didn't ask about the old cedar of Lebanon tree looking so noble against the gray sky, but instead broke out with, "I meant to ask you earlier, Father. Has the monastery ever heard about any unpublished poems by Byron?"

A look of interest sharpened the monk's face.

"Wouldn't that be a find?" he responded in colloquial En-glish, holding his hands against the skirt of his black cassock, which was blowing in the wind. "But it's strange that you should ask," he continued, now in excellent, though accented Italian. "Years ago there was talk of unpublished Byron poems. As many as half a dozen, maybe more."

"When was this?"

"Twenty, twenty-five years ago."

"What kind of rumor?"

Father Nazar gave Urbino a narrow, glinting glance.

"I call it a rumor even though a man swore to me up and down that he had poems written by our Lord Byron."

"Did you examine them?" Urbino asked, suppressing a smile at Father Nazar's use of the title and the pronoun to refer to the poet.

"I never saw them, if there were any to see," he responded in English, which he continued to use for the rest of their conversation. "Although one day when I came into the library, this man was sitting at a table with sheets of paper. They had handwriting on them and looked old. He put them away quickly. I wasn't close enough to see the language, but it wasn't Armenian. The writing wasn't like what you'd find in a letter or a story, but in a poem. Maybe *they* were the Byron poems he was always talking about. All the monks know about your books, Signor Macintyre. We have copies in our library. Is that your interest in these poems?"

"Call it curiosity. Tell me, Father, who was this man?"

"His name was Mechitar."

"Mechitar?" Urbino repeated. "The same name as your founder?"

"The same. Mechitar Dilsizian. Dilsizian means the son of the tongueless one. Many years ago an ancestor must have had his tongue cut out by the Turks for speaking Armenian."

Urbino couldn't help but think of Armando who was unable to speak, he assumed, for less gruesome reasons.

"Was he from Venice?" he asked.

"Vienna. There are many Armenians there."

Urbino waited for Father Nazar to give him more details. The monk stroked his beard and looked thoughtful, gazing off toward the Roman statue on the far wall of the cloister.

"His son Zakariya was one of our students."

San Lazzaro had about a dozen students in addition to the same number of seminarians.

"His father wanted him to study Armenian culture."

"He could have done it in Vienna."

"True, but his father had a love for Venice. And Lord Byron. And for Armenian poetry, too. He had a good memory. Always quoting lines of poetry."

"What was his son like?"

"An intelligent boy and an excellent pianist. But he was worldly. He had a passion for cardplaying that he got from his father. Mechitar was a real gambler. He lost a lot of money. Zakariya was headed in the same direction, I could see. Well, it all came to a bad end, may God have mercy on their souls."

Urbino's interest quickened even more.

"What happened?"

"About twenty years ago, maybe a little less, they drowned in a boating accident off the Lido—a young Italian woman did, too—during a pleasure trip arranged by one of your countrymen. Such a sad funeral at Santa Croce. Two coffins, father and son. It was the end of that branch of the Dilsizians."

59

The wind whipped the gondola and Gildo's lithe figure on the poop as Gildo rowed it past the island of San Servolo, once the site of a psychiatric hospital. Soon the gondola was moving parallel to the broad embankment that eventually became the Riva degli Schiavoni. Everything around them was suffused with cold color, except for the rosy bricks of San Giorgio Maggiore and the Doge's Palace, which captured the gray light and somehow transformed it into something almost phosphorescent.

Sheltered in the cabin, Urbino went over what he had learned from Father Nazar. It had been more than he had expected. Now he had the task of trying to make sense of it.

On an impulse, as they were approaching the Church of La Pietà, its doors closed to preserve the warmth for the evening concert, Urbino asked Gildo to make a detour. He wanted to see the old street of the Armenians had.

Gildo steered the black craft out of the lagoon and away from the mouth of the Canalazzo into a small waterway. The temperature dropped several degrees as they passed through the shadows of buildings and under the vaults of bridges that threw back the plash of their movement and the strokes of the oar. Soon Gildo was bringing them to a gentle stop at a little square behind the Piazza San Marco.

Urbino got out.

He crossed over a bridge and entered the first *calle* on his right. Narrow, dark, and short, this was the Calle degli Armeni. It had once been busy with Armenians who had established the first foreign community in Venice and had built the small church under the *sottoportico* ahead.

In the covered passageway he stopped in front of the unassuming church wedged in among the other buildings. A simple cross marked the door. Mechitar and Zakariya had been buried from the church. Nowadays it was closed indefinitely.

He continued to the end of the *calle* and retraced his steps back to the larger street. No sooner did he do this, however, then he turned around and went back again, pausing as he had a few moments before in front of the church.

He encountered perhaps half a dozen people, some of them advanced in age. He was tempted to stop two or three of them who had a distinctly non-Venetian look and ask if they were Armenian and, if they were, whether they had ever heard of a man named Mechitar Dilsizian and his son, Zakariya.

But he kept his distance, having already drawn attention as he paced up and down the small street. He leaned against one of the buildings, wondering how often Mechitar and Zakariya might have passed this way and if they might not have even stayed in one of the houses. He imagined Mechitar sitting in a room above all the street activity, taking out the Byron poems, and reading them over and over again.

That is, if he had indeed *had* any Byron poems.

Father Nazar said that Mechitar had never shown any of the poems to him or the other monks. This could be because they didn't exist or because Mechitar might have been afraid that his precious poems were vulnerable. He had shuffled sheets of handwritten poetry out of sight in the library as soon as Father Nazar had come in.

But Mechitar no longer had the poems. He was dead, and so was his son. And Possle said that he was in possession of them. Possle had been on the boat off the Lido when Mechitar and his son had drowned, and along with them, Adriana Abdon, if Urbino were to make the obvious connection between what he had learned from Cipri and from the monk.

Urbino headed back to where Gildo was waiting with the gondola. He was preoccupied with thoughts of Mechitar and Zakariya, Samuel Possle and Adriana, Hilda and Armando, and of the connection that each of them had, in life or in death, with the poems that might be hidden away in the Ca' Pozza. Three of them were still alive; three were long dead.

Perhaps he would learn something about Armando and Adriana this evening from Demetrio Emo at Harry's Bar that might shed light on the question of the Byron poems and how they had come into Possle's hands.

60

When Urbino came through the swinging doors of Harry's Bar that evening at eight-fifteen, he almost expected to find Emo running up a tab but the locksmith was nowhere in the crowded, smoke-filled room. Urbino ordered a drink and started to read the copy of today's *International Herald Tribune*, which someone had left at the bar.

He kept glancing at the entrance and the large round clock over the bar. When half an hour had passed and Emo hadn't come, Urbino went upstairs to the dining room. Almost all the tables were taken. Urbino was glad he had made reservations. The maitre d' escorted Urbino to a table by the windows with a splendid nighttime view of the Basin of San Marco and the Island of San Giorgio Maggiore.

Urbino ordered another drink and a plate of antipasti as he waited for Emo to arrive. When another half hour had passed, Urbino assumed he was being stood up. Although he didn't have much of an appetite, he couldn't very well leave after having reserved a table at such a busy time. He ordered several items and did his best to enjoy them, all the while trying to figure out what Emo's absence might mean.

As he stared absently out at the evening scene beyond the window, his mind wandered without focus over his last visit to Possle and the prospect of his visit tomorrow. He knew that his meeting with Possle tomorrow would be crucial, and he tried to work out the strategy he would use. But he kept glancing at the door for Emo and becoming more and more distracted.

"Excuse me, signore," the waiter said, after Urbino had managed to get through a plate of pasta and a chicken dish. Under any other circumstances it would have been delicious. "There's a young man downstairs who's asking for you. I asked him to come up, but he prefers to stay in the bar."

Urbino went downstairs.

Gildo was standing by the entrance, his cap in his hands, his tousled head of curls bowed.

"What's the matter?" Urbino asked him.

The gondolier's handsome face was tense. "My Uncle Demetrio had an accident. He was attacked in San Polo. He was hit on the head and knocked to the ground."

"How terrible. Is he in the hospital?"

"At home. He wasn't hurt badly, thank God."

"Are you sure?"

"He'll be all right. He wants you to make another reservation."

Urbino was disturbed by this turn of affairs, but he didn't want to show it any more than he already had. He asked Gildo if he would like some dinner.

"No thank you," he said quickly.

"Very well. I'll be back in a few minutes."

Urbino went upstairs and settled the bill. When he returned to the ground floor, Gildo was outside in the Calle Vallaresso. They boarded the *vaporetto*.

On their way up the Grand Canal, Gildo assured Urbino that his uncle was fine despite bruises. When Urbino asked why Emo had been in San Polo, Gildo said that he had gone there to change a lock.

Urbino regretted that his talk with Emo was delayed and

hoped that what had happened to him in San Polo had nothing to do with the Ca' Pozza. It seemed a feeble hope.

Gildo was withdrawn. He kept looking through the window at the passing scene. When he spied some friends walking along the Rialto embankment when the *vaporetto* was about to pull away, he said a hurried good-bye to Urbino and jumped off to join them. As he threw his arm around one of his companions, he cast a quick glance back at Urbino.

61

Early the next morning, Urbino crossed the long, wooden bridge that led to the island of San Pietro di Castello in the eastern part of the city.

On the other side of the canal a man in a boat repair yard was applying bright green paint to a *sandalo*. Nets were stretched out in the sun under the blue sky. Near the boatyard was a row of simple houses with chimney pots. The gleaming white campanile of the church, leaning at a precarious angle, beckoned Urbino, for on this small island he might fill in some gaps in the story of Marco Carelli.

Consulting the address provided by the gondola maker at the *square* in San Trovaso, he went to one of the quaint houses on the canal where a man and a woman were sitting in chairs in the sunshine. When he asked them where he could find Carlo the *remero*, the man smiled and said that he was Carlo. He was a thin, friendly faced man in his late sixties. The stout, bespectacled woman, who was embroidering a handkerchief, was his wife.

Urbino explained that his gondolier had been Marco Carelli's friend. "He has the *forcola* that Marco worked on."

"So you're the American gentleman with the gondola!" the wife exclaimed, looking more closely at Urbino now.

"Did you know Marco?" the *remero* asked.

"No. Gildo has told me about him. He treasures the *forcola*. It's good."

"Marco made some mistakes. He was still learning. I gave it to his friend to comfort him after the accident." His eyes filled with tears. "He was one of my best apprentices. He could have had his own workshop some day. Maybe this one. I'll be retiring in a few years; we have no children."

His wife busied herself with her needle, glancing at Urbino from time to time.

"I'd like to make a gift on Marco's behalf," he said. "For the *forcola*."

"That's not necessary," Carlo began, evidently surprised. "We—"

"How kind of you, signore," his wife interrupted him.

Urbino took out his checkbook and started to write a check for a sum that he believed would more than satisfy them.

"Marco was generous, like you, signore," Carlo's wife said. "Sometimes he gave us extra money. He knew we had our difficulties. We still do."

Urbino gave Carlo the check. He thanked Urbino and handed it to his wife. She looked at the amount written on it and smiled.

"Thank you, signore," she said. She folded it and put it in her pocket.

Urbino described Armando and asked if they had seen him around the quarter or anyone else who had asked them about Marco.

"No," Carlo said. His wife shook her head. "Maybe you're asking because someone spoke against him. A neighbor said something about drugs and a wild crowd in San Polo, but he was an angel from what we could see."

"And even if it were true, signore," his wife added, "we wouldn't have cared. How he behaved somewhere else wasn't our business."

62

That evening Urbino, the Contessa, and Rebecca went out to dinner together at a trattoria in the Santa Croce district. It had everything a trattoria should have. A roaring fire, simple, delicious food, an acceptable house wine, good company, and a family that did all the cooking and serving. There was even a group of men in a corner playing cards amicably.

As if by a common agreement, no one brought up Possle and the Ca' Pozza. Urbino appreciated this brief respite from something that he had been living and sleeping with for many weeks now. Whenever it intruded on his thoughts in the course of the evening, as it inevitably did, especially since his next visit to the Ca' Pozza was tomorrow, he pushed it away.

Rebecca shared her impressions of the newly restored Giotto frescoes at the Scrovegni Chapel in Padua. The Contessa discussed the music program she was putting together for the Contessa's last *conversazione*. Both Rebecca and Urbino would be attending, he having received her carte blanche to be there on this occasion.

For his part, Urbino, who had called Habib the previous evening after returning from Harry's Bar, told them about the young man's recent activities in Morocco. They included the sale of some of his paintings to a Barcelona dealer and an outing to Marrakesh in the Deux Chevaux Urbino had bought for his own use when he was in the country and left for the family.

Urbino had them laughing when he described how Habib had put, not only his mother on the line, but also each of his six sisters and two brothers.

All in all, the only disappointment of their evening was that their bill wasn't toted up with chalk on a slate to make the spell complete. Urbino got home feeling less fatigued than energized for tomorrow's visit to the Ca' Pozza.

But as it turned out the evening, or rather the night, was not to be without its far less pleasant side, for the dream of Possle and the fire was more vivid and disturbing than ever.

63

The next day was Thursday, March 21. Urbino had his rendezvous with Possle at four-thirty.

Before he left the Palazzo Uccello, he called Corrado Scarpa about the boat accident report. Scarpa was having trouble locating it, he said. He would keep trying.

Urbino then telephoned his friend Paola, who coordinated social services at the municipal hospital. It had been a week since he had asked her to have someone at her office make a visit to Elvira Carelli to see what might be done for her. Paola said that she had arranged to have her assistant stop by Elvira's apartment a few days ago. Elvira had allowed her in, and they had had a brief conversation. Elvira had ended up crying and screaming about Marco and had made incoherent comments about the neighboring building.

The assistant's observations confirmed Urbino's impression on his own visit. Despite her emotional problems, Elvira kept the apartment in fairly good order. The refrigerator and pantry had been well stocked and a pot of food had been cooking on the stove. The social service worker had given Elvira her phone number and had said that she would stop by again. Elvira hadn't given any indication that this would be unwelcome to her.

This was the most that Paola's services could do for Elvira at this point. She would let him know when her assistant made another visit.

As he was leaving the Palazzo Uccello, Gildo was coming in. Urbino asked him how his uncle was doing and learned that he had returned to work yesterday, the day after the attack.

64

Armando's sharp eyes, his loud silence, his cold smile, and even his unhurried passage up the staircase of the Ca' Pozza, although all no different than usual, were nothing less than accusations. Urbino was amazed at how much the man communicated without words, unless what he should have been amazed at, as well as warned by, was his own facility for reading meanings where there might not be any. But this was surely a circumstance in which it was better to think and believe the worst.

But as soon as he saw the old man buried among the cushions of his calculated divan, Urbino instinctively knew he was safe. This didn't mean that Armando hadn't informed Possle about Urbino's tour of the house, but that, if he had, Possle was going to do all he could to give no sign of it.

If Urbino had wanted to seek comfort by confessing after being accused, he wasn't going to find it here. No, everything about the recluse that Urbino absorbed in the first few moments of being in the gondola room told him that if Possle knew anything, he would utter at most, an almost diabolical, "I accuse you, I accuse you of nothing!"

Urbino's feelings as he seated himself were further complicated by his host's physical appearance on this occasion.

Although he was decked out in his customary red satins and purple silks, his face beneath the purple headscarf looked more pinched and drawn than usual. One hand trembled slightly but all too evidently. Urbino hoped that all these signs didn't presage an attack that would snatch Possle away before he might get the information he needed.

Perhaps this fear and the realization that he was safe from Possle if not from Armando emboldened Urbino to seize the moment and try to gain the advantage. He sat patiently until Armando came with the Amontillado and left, all the while listening to Possle's long anecdote, delivered in his tremulous voice, about how one of Peggy Guggenheim's dogs had once become lost in the Ca' Pozza.

When Possle finished, Urbino leaned forward in his armchair and said, "Do you really think we need to go through the motions today? We both know what's on our minds—the Byron poems. Why pretend? Once you've shown your hand, there's no use in covering it up again."

"An even more apt metaphor than you think."

All the wrinkles broke out on one side of Possle's face as he gave his half smile. The other half, by contrast, remained disconcertingly smooth.

He had been fingering his crystal atomizer. The scent of the special potpourri hung heavy in the air. He thrust the atomizer back among the cushions.

"Very well," he said. "I'm sure you've given some thought to my revelation."

"Not only thought"—Urbino aimed for as neutral a tone as he could manage—"but also some action."

"And what might that have been?"

"Let me say that I know about an Armenian named Mechitar Dilsizian."

"You've gone to San Lazzaro degli Armeni, just as I thought you would," Possle said, with a self-satisfied air. "Good for you."

Urbino was annoyed. Once again, Possle spoke as if Urbino had no secrets from him, almost as if he somehow had an insidious influence over what Urbino did or didn't do.

"I know that this Dilsizian had Byron poems in his possession twenty years ago"—Urbino drew out the words—"or poems he claimed were written by Byron."

"Oh, they were. They are! And you have little doubt yourself. Why else would you be so excited? You're trying to conceal it, but it's clear to me."

"I know that Dilsizian and his son died in a boating accident off the Lido," Urbino went on, controlling his rising irritation. "You were on the boat and so was Armando and his sister, Adriana. She drowned along with them."

Urbino was sweating. The room seemed hotter this afternoon.

"You must be careful that Armando never hears you speaking about his sister," Possle said. "Her memory is sacred to him. I hardly mention her, and especially not at this time of the year."

Urbino looked in the direction of the *sala*.

"So Armando makes you uneasy," Possle said. "Yes, he could be standing right outside the room. Such a quiet man, Armando. Would you take this, please?"

He held out his porcelain cup. Urbino got up and took it, using the opportunity to take a closer look at Possle's face. It was yellow and waxen. His eyes glittered feverishly behind their large glasses.

Urbino reseated himself and put the cup down on the table.

"I know what you're thinking about all this," Possle said. "Mechitar Dilsizian had the Byron poems, and now I have them. Mechitar and his son drowned, and so did Adriana," he added, whispering the woman's name, his eyes sliding toward the open door. He took a long pause during which he seemed to collect his energy from an increasingly depleted reservoir. "Only Armando and I survived," he went on. "And now I have the poems. Do you think such things are worth killing for? Mere words on paper, even if they're Byron's?"

In Urbino's experience people sometimes killed for far less. And the fact that Possle had been the one to bring up murder alerted him. He could be trying to put him off the scent.

"So the poems you say you have—"

"The poems I *have*," Possle interrupted with quiet emphasis.

"So these poems are the ones Dilsizian had in his possession before he died?"

"Not right before he died or even *when* he died. The way you phrase your question makes a link between my having the poems and his accident. I'm no fool. They were in my possession before that sad event."

"And how did that come about?"

"You sound skeptical. Are you a gambling man? Roulette? Baccarat? Poker?" One of Possle's eyes started to twitch. He pressed a finger against it. "I don't think so, but I am. I had a gaming room in this house in those days. Mechitar Dilsizian was an obsessive gambler."

Father Nazar had said the same thing.

"Do you see now why your comment about having showed you my hand amused me?"

"Are you telling me that Dilsizian lost the poems to you in a gambling game?"

"Don't look surprised. Fortunes and dukedoms used to change hands in the Ridotto in the old days." Possle was referring to the former gaming house near the Piazza San Marco. "Dilsizian considered himself luckier at baccarat than he was. In the end all he had left to bet were the poems."

Urbino wasn't prepared to accept this convenient explanation.

"If you're wondering if there was a witness to the affair," Possle said, regarding him with a crooked little smile, "I give you my Armando."

"I'm wondering a great many things. Like how the poems came into Dilsizian's hands to begin with."

"A most interesting story. They were passed down from generation to generation in his family. Byron had many Armenian friends, and at least one Armenian lover. Dilsizian claimed that this woman, very beautiful, who lived in the Calle degli Armeni and is now mere dust, as we all must come to, was the original owner of the poems."

"Are they love poems?"

"*Pazienza!* Don't ruin everything now."

"Do you have copies of the poems? Photocopies?"

"Only the poems themselves. And they're in very good condition."

Possle fell silent. His breathing became shallower. He closed his eyes but after ten or fifteen seconds they fluttered open.

"Was I asleep?"

"If you were, it was only for a few moments."

"Moments can seem like an eternity, and an hour can seem like a moment or two, when I drop off like this." He had a perplexed look on his face. "Sometimes when I close my eyes I see so many people from the past, as clear as you are to me now. Sometimes I even see them when my eyes are open. They seem to be staring at me. I'm speaking of the dead, of course. And they don't always look as young as they were when they died, but old, very, very old."

His eyes traveled to the mirror on the other side of the room. He couldn't see himself in it from where he was, but he stared at it as if he could.

"The dying man looks into the mirror someone holds in front of him and he says, 'Farewell. We won't be seeing each other any more.' That's not from Byron, Mr. Macintyre, if you're trying to figure it out. But I can't remember who said it. Someone I knew a long, long time ago, I think."

Urbino was trying to think of what to say to bring Possle

back to the poems when Possle gave a sigh and resumed, in a less tired and resigned voice, "I have a statement from Mechitar, Mr. Macintyre, a statement that swears the poems are mine beyond any question or dispute. Properly signed by two witnesses. Armando and"—he glanced toward the door and lowered his voice—"Adriana."

Very convenient, Urbino thought, trying to keep his expression impassive: a mute, dedicated employee and his dead sister.

"What do you want of me?" he asked Possle.

"I know what you want of *me,* Mr. Macintyre. You want the poems. If I had a more suspicious nature, I'd say that you've wanted them from the time you started besieging the Ca' Pozza with flowers."

"I had no idea—"

"Perhaps. But you wanted something from me nonetheless, and now I have something to offer."

"To offer?"

"To sell. I give you the first option. Isn't that what it's called? I give it to you and the Contessa da Capo-Zendrini."

"The Contessa?"

"I'm aware that you don't have the kind of money that such a treasure would cost. However, the Contessa's wealth is almost legendary, as is her generosity, especially when it comes to you."

"She'd never agree."

"Are you sure? Not for your sake? Not to see your career advanced?" Possle raised his hand to his chest and pressed it against the red silk of his shirt. "You could shake off quite a bit of the reputation of the dilettante that you've accumulated over the years. Urbino Macintyre, the man who discovers unpublished poems by one of the world's greatest writers. The man who writes a brilliant scholarly introduction. Don't be overly scrupulous. The rewards are all yours, and you won't have to turn over a cent."

These remarks seemed to take whatever reserve of energy

Possle had left. He dropped back against the cushions of the gondola. He had said what he wanted to say. Everything was out in the open now. The poems were Urbino's for a price, and the price was one that only someone like the Contessa could afford. It was all so simple, so neat.

Suddenly, in the silence that had fallen between them, a woman's shrill laughter, muffled but unmistakable, seemed to emanate from beyond the drapes and closed shutters of the room. The laughter stopped. A few moments later the woman broke out into a song that was at first indistinguishable. Then he recognized it as the Countess Almaviva's aria, *"Pour, O love,"* from *The Marriage of Figaro,* as the countess prays for the restoration of her husband's love. Even more feeling suffused the voice than when Elvira had sung the lullaby in the cemetery, and the choice of an aria indicated a range and interest that Urbino would never have associated with the grieving woman.

The aria came to an abrupt end. Laughter broke out again, then there was silence.

Possle was staring at him. It appeared that he hadn't heard anything.

"You have nothing to say, Mr. Macintyre? Is it because you're already contemplating what's going to come your way?" Possle's tongue darted out and ran over his lips. "It would be a suitable arrangement for all of us. The Contessa would do a good deed for her good friend, you would get the poems, and I would get the money. I've never paid much attention to money. There always seemed to be so much— until recently. I've left affairs like that in Armando's hands. But the coffers must be replenished. The poems mean nothing to me, but the money they'll bring me—bring *us*—means a great deal. Would you mind giving me some water?"

Urbino poured water from the carafe into one of the goblets. He got up and handed it to Possle.

Possle drank down a large portion of the water. Some of it

dribbled from his mouth and spattered against his silk shirt-front. He handed the goblet back to Urbino.

"If I've been silent," Urbino said, after reseating himself, "it's because I'm surprised that you'd think the Contessa would involve herself with something, poems or whatever, that came into your hands in such a way. Something that might not even be yours to legally sell."

"Are you so sure of that? And do you have such a low opinion of your place in her heart, not to mention of your ability to persuade her of things she might not be completely eager to do? As I said, Mr. Macintyre, this is not the time for scruples. I—I—"

He put a hand to his chest and coughed. His face looked more yellow than before. "Could you give me a little more water please?"

Urbino poured some more water into the goblet, got up, and gave it to Possle, who drank it and handed the goblet back.

Urbino remained standing. He had a better view of Possle amid his cushions, the cushions that might very well conceal the poems.

"That's a little better." Possle wiped his mouth. "As I was saying, consider my offer. Speak to the Contessa. "I—"

He stopped and gave another cough. "I prefer that the poems end up in your hands, Mr. Macintyre. I have a fondness for you, believe it or not. We're not all that different. And we're neither fish nor fowl, living away from our own countries. But have no illusions. If the Contessa won't buy the poems, I'll find someone who will, and they'll be out of your hands forever. Speak to her. I'll give you until the first of April. That's eleven days from now. I've always been lucky on April Fool's Day. Perhaps we both will. Have the Contessa come here with you at the usual hour. It will be a pleasure to have her inside these walls for the first time."

Possle seemed to gauge the effect of all this on Urbino, who tried to keep his face from registering any interest.

"So speak with her. Make her understand how important it is to you—to both of us. She's a woman of sense as well as sensibility. I believe you do her an injustice in assuming she wouldn't jump at the chance of helping you." Possle's words were coming more slowly. "And it will gladden my heart when I see her come through that door with you. But if she doesn't, you will be coming for your last visit."

"If you could just let me see them." Urbino struggled to banish the eagerness from his voice and, distressed by his own behavior, nonetheless could not refrain from looking down into the cushions. "It would—"

He broke off. He smelled something burning and felt heat against his lower leg. The next second he was slapping against his pants leg that had started to smolder from being too close to the flame of one of the candles placed on the floor beside the gondola.

"My God, Mr. Macintyre, please be careful!" Possle was visibly alarmed, but he tried to make a joke: "I don't want something happening to you just when we're so close to getting our prizes."

"I'd advise you to be careful, Mr. Possle," Urbino said, with a touch of irritation. "These candles might be atmospheric but they're dangerous, as you see."

"You're right, of course, but I—I find some things difficult to give up. I'm sure you understand." He put a hand to his chest as he had before. "I—I've become so accustomed to them, you see, and—"

He broke off and threw both his hands up in the air in an almost violent gesture. He was seized with a spasm of coughing. His body thrust itself up from the cushions. Urbino had a vision of his prize slipping away from him.

One of Possle's hands was wildly searching for the purple

cord. Urbino grabbed it and gave it a sharp tug. More quickly than seemed possible, Armando entered the room but without any appearance of haste, his arms with their scarred hands close to his sides.

The cadaverous man went over to Possle, who was still coughing. As he bent over him, he threw Urbino a malevolent glance. It also held, on this occasion, a trace of uneasiness.

Urbino mumbled a quick farewell. When he looked back over his shoulder, Armando was lifting Possle out of the gondola like a doll.

65

That evening after returning to the Palazzo Uccello, Urbino felt his usual malaise after these encounters with Possle, but it soon intensified. He had an onslaught of chills and fever and an intense headache. The slight burn to his leg, which he salved with a cream, increased his discomfort. When the doctor came, he diagnosed the flu.

Urbino spent the next few days sleeping as much as possible. He missed Habib and his therapeutic *tisanes* brewed from herbs brought from Morocco. The Contessa wanted to stop by, but he insisted that she stay away. Her final *conversazione* was next Thursday, less than a week away, and he didn't want to risk her getting ill herself.

He couldn't keep himself, however, from thinking about Possle and Byron, about Armando and what he knew or didn't know about his own intrusion into Possle's quarters, and about what he might or might not have told Possle about it.

Urbino realized how things had changed since he had first dreamed of getting into the Ca' Pozza. Back then—had it been only as recently as a few weeks ago?—he had been fired with a desire to hear the man's anecdotes. Now he had more pressing concerns. He wanted to gain possession of the Byron poems. That they existed he no longer had any doubt. Possle was showing Urbino a way for him to get his hands on them, but he feared that the price demanded, and not necessarily one of money, would prove much too high to pay.

Despite the doctor's firm diagnosis, it was only natural that Urbino linked his illness with Possle and the Ca' Pozza, since he always felt strangely drained after his visits.

It also occurred to him that there could be something in the Ca' Pozza itself that made him ill. He retreated from this somewhat superstitious thought into a more disturbing one about the Amontillado. It wouldn't be difficult for Armando to put something into his portion. What he would accomplish by this was perhaps what Urbino was enduring now, a period of confinement to the house and the inability to make another foray into parts of the Ca' Pozza.

When he was almost well again, he made another reservation at Harry's Bar for the next day, Wednesday, March 27. He informed Emo through Gildo.

One merciful aspect of Urbino's convalescence was that he wasn't once visited by his dream of Possle and the fire, a circumstance unusual in itself.

66

Still weak the next evening, Urbino took the *vaporetto* to Harry's Bar for his rendezvous with Demetrio Emo. This time Emo, dressed in a sober black suit that might have been left over from his days as a priest, was waiting for Urbino at one of the tables against the wall on the ground floor. He had a Bellini in front of him. From the flushed look on his large face, Urbino could tell that it wasn't his first.

Emo still showed evidence of his recent attack in San Polo in the form of a fading bruise on his cheek.

"Where did it happen?" Urbino asked.

"Not near the Ca' Pozza, if that's what you're thinking," Emo snapped back. "Two boys pushed me from behind and grabbed my case. All they got was a lot of keys. I gave a description to the police. Is that enough for you, Sherlock Macintyre? We're not eating down here. That's not part of the deal. Should I take this with me?"

He held up his Bellini, but before Urbino could say anything he downed it in one gulp.

The dining room was full. The maitre d' led them to one of the round tables and removed the RISERVATO sign. Urbino and Emo seated themselves. The boats, the churches, the expanse of the inner lagoon, and the mouth of the Grand Canal were like a stage set beyond their window.

But Emo seemed uninterested in contemplating the scene. He immediately gave all his attention to the menu after ordering a whiskey sour. Urbino, sipping his Martini, sat back while Emo commanded an entire banquet for himself. In a surprisingly short time he ploughed through one dish after another, beginning with the Carpaccio, the tuna tartare, and dried salt cod from Vicenza, and then moved on to the minestrone, pasta with wild mushrooms, chicken risotto, and scampi. He finished, without any evidence of flagging appetite, with Zabaglione and flambéed crepes. All of this was washed down with glass after glass of Dom Perignon. Urbino did all he could to stretch out his caviar and ravioli with artichokes.

Emo, who didn't seem to see the sense of mixing eating with talking, rebuffed Urbino's attempts to ask him anything about Armando and Adriana. Urbino was afraid that when the locksmith finished his second dessert, he would stand up and bid Urbino a hearty and somewhat tipsy *buona sera*.

But as it turned out the former priest had a sense of fairness, if he didn't have one of moderation. While he sipped from a generous portion of Benedictine, he started to sing for his already consumed supper.

"So you want to know about Armando and Adriana Abdon," he said in his low voice. "You say that it's for some book you're writing. I'll believe that if you'll believe that I have no reason for telling you anything but the truth." He laughed and took out a small cigar. He eyed Urbino, who made no protest. But Emo put the cigar back in his pocket. "The three of us grew up together, more or less."

Urbino made a quick calculation. Yes, Emo and Armando must be about the same age, somewhere in their early sixties.

"In the Ghetto. Their father and mine were both deliverymen. Armando and Adriana were the only twins I knew even existed in those days."

"They were twins?"

"Not that they looked like each other. Not the way two twin brothers or sisters can. But they couldn't have concealed it if they had tried. It was as if they were the same person. They hardly left the house without each other. They liked to play tricks on people. Sometimes girls would get telephone calls and think it was Adriana, and say personal things, but it was Armando. He could speak in those days, and he was a good mimic."

"When did Armando lose his voice?" Urbino asked.

"It was after the fire," Emo replied, with a little smile. "I'll get to it."

He sipped his Benedictine and regarded Urbino with his small, shrewd eyes.

"It was when we were fifteen. Armando and Adriana were wild. Their mother and father couldn't control them. And when they locked them in the house, they'd always find a way to get out. They were clever, those two. I admired them, the way kids will. They'd slip into houses when no one was home, rearrange the furniture, take something and put it in another apartment. Adriana urged Armando on, as if he was under her control. One day she dared him to jump into the Canalazzo. He did. He almost drowned, until she jumped in and saved him."

"Armando almost drowned?"

"You mean because Adriana drowned years later. So you know more about them than you've let on. But do you know that Adriana was a sick girl? And I don't mean in her body. She was beautiful and as healthy as a horse. It was her head." Emo tapped his own massive one. "She'd fly into rages, then be walking around like a zombie. She'd laugh one minute and cry the next."

"I understand she had a lovely voice."

"Yes, she had a gift. But I still haven't told you about the fire," Emo said, with an awareness of his story despite his inebriation. "It broke out one night in December. Their father seems to have fallen asleep with a cigarette. The bedroom went up like a tinderbox. Armando and Adriana escaped. He never spoke again after the fire. His hands were burned, but there wasn't a mark on Adriana."

The vision of Armando's scarred hands swam before Urbino's eyes.

"There was some talk that Adriana had started it, maybe the two of them together, to kill their mother and father. Who knows? My parents made me keep my distance after that, and soon I went into the seminary. Well, we both see how that turned out for me."

Emo shook his head slowly and drank down the rest of his Benedictine. Once again, as Urbino frequently did, he wondered what Emo's personal life was like now that he was out of the priesthood. Whereas the rumors about his sexual exploits with parishioners had been thick in the air during his years at San Gabriele, now it was almost as if he were a celibate, if one were to judge by the silence that surrounded him. Urbino recalled the morning he had stopped by Emo's apartment. Although Emo had said he was ill, Urbino had had the impression that he was expecting someone, perhaps a neighbor's wife or daughter. Strange as it might seem, maybe he needed to be more cautious now that he wasn't a priest.

"After the fire their aunt moved in," Emo continued. "She had no success with them either. She died six years later when she hit her head in a fall. No one saw much of Adriana after that. Armando took care of everything. That's when he started working as a gondolier for the Ca' Pozza. Rumor had it that Adriana was interested in marrying the man who owned the building and that Armando encouraged it, but it came to nothing. He married someone else."

He waved in the air to attract the attention of the waiter.

"From what I heard from my family and some friends I kept in touch with," he went on, as the waiter made his way to their table, "Adriana still lived in the Ghetto, but she used to hang around the Ca' Pozza. When the American divorced, she thought she had one last chance to marry him, I guess, and when it didn't work out . . ." Emo shrugged his big shoulders. "That's when Armando had to hide her away in some clinic outside of Florence. Not permanently, but for three or four months at a time. We all lost track of what was going on. She could have been locked up longer than that. And no one knew where he got the money. The last time she was out of the clinic, she drowned, but you know that part."

The waiter came over. Emo ordered another Benedictine.

"Do you know the name of the clinic?"

"The Villa Serena. Not hard to remember here in the serene city. And Gildo tells me you have a cat named Serena."

So far Emo had provided a great deal of information, perhaps suspiciously so. Urbino warned himself that he shouldn't be too quick to believe everything.

The waiter brought Emo's Benedictine.

"Did either Armando or Adriana ever show an interest in the Contessa da Capo-Zendrini?"

"None of us even knew who she was back then."

He drank half the Benedictine.

"What about the commemorative masses for Adriana? You said that Armando's been doing it for a long time."

"That's right. From the first anniversary of Adriana's death, seventeen years ago. I was at San Gabriele by then. Didn't get very far, did I? I took care of it for him, for old time's sake, but he acted like a stranger. He came every year until I left. I guess he still goes. He'd have the information written on a piece of paper."

"Do you ever see him these days?"

"I come across him every once in a while. Actually I've been seeing him around more often than usual. I say hello, but it's as if he's never seen me before. He looks depressed, maybe anxious, like something's on his mind. I've known him for a long time. I'd notice the difference."

Urbino reached into his pocket and took out the key from Possle's bedroom. Not the copy the other locksmith had made, but the original.

"By the way I found this key among a lot of other ones," Urbino said, silently thanking the Jesuit fathers who had taught him how to lie while also telling the truth.

"That's an abrupt change of topic."

Emo took the key, squinted at it, and held it up to the light. He raised his fat hand with the key in his palm as if he was weighing it.

"Does it belong to my old lock? The one on the front door?" Urbino asked. "There are so many locks for the different doors of the house, most of which I never use. I've never really sorted through them all."

"It doesn't belong to that old lock." Demetrio handed the key back to Urbino. "And not to any of the other doors in your place, not even the water entrance, I'd say. But it's an old key, as you can see. It might be for the front door lock before the one that Natalia just broke."

"Maybe that's it."

Urbino put the key back in his pocket.

"By the way," he said, "did you ever make any keys for Gildo's friend Marco?"

Emo finished his Benedictine.

"All this sudden interest in keys! Why do you ask that?"

"I'm worried about his mother. Something could happen to her while she's in one of her states. If you cut a key for Marco, maybe it was their house key. You might have an extra copy. The Contessa, you see, would like to give the key to one of Elvira Carelli's neighbors, someone she knows is extremely trustworthy."

Urbino was going into the kind of detail that always alerted him that someone was lying. Emo stared back at him with his flat, dark eyes.

"You should ask whoever owns the building. They might

have a key. As for the boy, he never asked me to cut a key of *any* kind for him. By the way, since you don't need that key, why not give it to me? I collect old ones."

"I'd rather keep it. It might fit one of my doors after all."

"You never know. Or someone else's door."

Emo stood up. "I'll be outside," he said. "Be sure you leave a good tip. We want the waiter to remember us when we come back next time."

67

A few hours later Urbino threw on his clothes and his cloak and slipped his pencil flashlight into his pocket along with the copy of the key he had taken from Possle's bedroom. Within minutes he was crossing the bridge in front of the Palazzo Uccello. The night dropped down silently around him.

He had awakened from his dream of Possle and the veiled woman and the Contessa in a room that blazed into flames. The dream and Demetrio Emo's words about the key and someone else's door had driven him out into the cold, damp night.

The silence was at first comforting, but by the time he reached the other side of the Rialto Bridge, it had become oppressive. It made him feel as if he couldn't breathe. He stopped on a deserted quay. Almost out of desperation he strained his ears to catch the lap of water against stone or the unmistakable scratch and splash of one of the city's legions of water rats.

Nothing.

It wasn't the hour for bells. Even if it had been, he feared that they would be swallowed by this strange night as profoundly as his own footsteps. Where the city usually played its deceptive game of echoes and ventriloquism, tonight it seemed determined to be withdrawing from him and leaving him to his own devices, watching and listening to *him*.

Even the stones beneath his feet seemed to give him only the minimal resistance to allow him to turn down the next alley, go over two bridges, slip beneath a covered passageway, and gain Elvira Carelli's building. No light illuminated it. Above, a sprinkling of stars was visible before the clouds covered them again.

He withdrew the key from his pocket. He unwrapped it from the chamois cloth. It was slick with the olive oil he had rubbed over it before leaving the Palazzo Uccello. He put it to the eye of the old lock and tried to slide it in. It wouldn't fit.

Closing his hand protectively over the key, he walked farther down the *calle,* his footsteps still eerily silent. The bridge, where he had so often paused to contemplate the Ca' Pozza, was a black hump among the shadows. He gazed up at the old building. Its dark frown reproached him. He was the enemy. He hadn't come with good intentions.

His heart was beating against his chest as he went up to the door. A perverse urge grabbed him to reach out and push the bell. Instead he raised the key to the lock and slowly, carefully he slid it in. He hoped that Possle was as lax about security as the Contessa was. If he wasn't, an alarm could start sounding at any second. But there was only silence, except for the sounds he was making himself, which were magnified in his ears.

The key went all the way in with barely a sound, but what sound there was screamed through Urbino's head. He twisted the key and felt the tumblers starting to turn. Then the door clicked open with the loudest possible sound. It echoed from the buildings opposite and, surely, all the way up the inner stone staircase.

After peering into the dark hallway, he slipped in, leaving the door open. The familiar and peculiar cold of the building invaded his body. The house rose silently around him. He took his pencil flashlight from his pocket and moved toward the closed door beside the stairway. The iron knob felt as if it was made of ice. He turned it and the door opened inward. He stepped inside.

Urbino was going on the assumption that Armando didn't spend his nights in the room, but on one of the upper floors. A quick survey proved him correct.

He switched on his flashlight and played it around the room. It was small, but furnished with the essentials. A worn divan stood against the opposite wall. A large pillow and blanket thrown on it indicated that it served as a bed on occasion. A pitcher and a wash basin were evidence of whatever ablutions Armando might indulge in during the time he spent in the room.

A low table in front of the divan held a messy scattering of magazines. Most of them seemed to be women's magazines. On the top of the pile was an oblong of paper not much larger than a postcard. It seemed to be a color photograph of someone.

Urbino picked it up.

It was a clipping from a magazine. The flashlight revealed the Contessa in her Fortuny dress. From the background Urbino recognized the occasion. It had been taken when the two of them had attended a chamber concert at the Palazzo Labia in January. In the original photograph Urbino had stood next to her but someone had scissored his image out and had circled the Contessa's dress in red ink.

Despite the bone-chilling cold, beads of sweat stood out on his forehead.

He returned the clipping to the pile. If he looked through it, he believed he might find more clippings of the Contessa, perhaps even one of her wearing a snakeskin belt. But he couldn't stay any longer. He shut off the flashlight and left the room, closing the door quietly behind him.

He threw an apprehensive glance in the direction of the staircase. Its dark shadows were impenetrable.

He went back out into the night, carefully pulling the heavy door closed behind him, and relocking it. He slid out the key and thrust it into his pocket. He retreated up the alley past Elvira Carelli's building. Every step he took, one after another, resounded as if to compensate for their former stillness and to accuse him. It was time to return home. He had learned enough for one night. And he had risked far too much.

When he entered the *sottoportico* that ran alongside the narrow canal with the two bridges, footsteps sounded behind him. They were quiet and cautious, but persistent. They stopped when he did.

He looked down the length of the dark, covered passageway. It was possible that, given the city's deceptive tricks of stone and water, the footsteps had come from ahead of him, from a *calle* on the other side of the canal or one of the alleys opening into the covered passageway.

But Urbino couldn't easily shake the feeling that someone was pursuing him and had halted when he had.

To test this, he started to walk farther into the passageway. The footsteps sounded again. He was almost at exactly the same spot he had been a month ago on the night he had also heard footsteps and the laughter and sobs.

His nerves were on edge because of his second violation of the Ca' Pozza's secrets. Could Armando have been on the staircase and be pursuing him now? Or perhaps it was the person or persons who had attacked Demetrio Emo. In either case, he didn't want to be a victim.

He had to make a quick decision. Should he continue through the passageway and over the crooked bridge or turn around and take the other bridge? He decided on the latter. Even though he would be moving in the direction that the footsteps seemed to be coming from, he might confuse the person and gain an advantage. And he would more quickly reach a large open space where there was a fair chance of there being other people.

Urbino turned around abruptly and rushed across the slick stones to the beginning of the passageway. His own rapid steps echoing in the *sottoportico* made it impossible for him to hear any other sounds. He slid once and felt himself losing his balance. He steadied himself by grabbing the crumbling stone of a building. He barely prevented himself from tumbling into the canal.

Urbino threw a quick look up the *calle* that led to the Ca' Pozza and Elvira's building. A tall figure stood pressed against the wall of a building about twenty feet away.

Urbino dashed over the bridge and into the *calle* on its opposite side. It was better lit than the area he had just abandoned. He rushed to the end of the *calle* and turned right over another bridge. In a few moments he was in the Campo San Polo. He went to the church on the other side and was greeted by some men who slowly walked by.

He looked back across the wide square. No one emerged from the alley he had just deserted. He continued to look in its direction for several minutes.

Even this far away from the Ca' Pozza, he felt it exerting its influence. Nothing was what it seemed in the old building. Of this he was sure.

Urbino was a rational person. Any explanation, if he ever found one, would surely be logical and it would probably be rooted in the past. Whatever bleeding portraits there might be in the Ca' Pozza, figuratively speaking of course, would be explained as reasonably as the mystery of the severed head and the disembodied laughter and cries.

Encouraged by these thoughts and by the clipping that he had just discovered of the Contessa in her Fortuny dress, disturbing though it was in its implications, Urbino quit the square and started for home, alert for any unusual sound.

68

Half an hour later, when Urbino was crossing the bridge in front of the Palazzo Uccello, a shadow detached itself from the building near the water steps. Urbino was brought up short. But then he recognized that it was Gildo, capless and dressed in dark clothing, and he advanced.

Gildo's face, covered with a thin film of sweat, gleamed under the bulb affixed to the side of the Palazzo Uccello. He was breathing heavily. He ran a hand through his hair.

"Is something the matter, Gildo?"

"I couldn't sleep."

"I couldn't either."

Gildo made a nervous gesture of looking at his wristwatch.

"Are you going for a walk?" Urbino asked. "Or perhaps you just came back from one. I took one myself."

Gildo stared at Urbino with an appeal in his green eyes. "Be careful, signore," he said. "It isn't safe to walk around in the city in the middle of the night."

"I try to be careful. I know the city well, just as well as you do."

"Perhaps, signore, but you shouldn't even go near that bad house. Not at night. It's dangerous."

"How do you know I've been to San Polo?"

Gildo looked away. "I guessed."

"Where you there tonight?"

"No!" His denial echoed across the narrow canal.

"Are you on your way in or out?" Urbino asked.

"I'm going in now, signore. I—I just came out for a few minutes, but now I think it's best to try to get to sleep. Good night."

He returned to his apartment through his separate entrance by the water steps before Urbino might ask him anything else.

69

The Contessa, all liquid fingers and rapt expression, was giving Urbino just what he needed the next week in the concert room of the conservatory.

Under the spell of her grace and spontaneity, he felt bathed in order and harmony as she approached the end of the *allegro assai* of Mozart's F major sonata. The fatigue and headache after his almost sleepless night receded.

Today the Contessa was allowing her talent at the piano to speak for her, and her only words were the briefest of introductions before each piece. Whereas Urbino's presence at her lectures would have risked tying her tongue, it now was only freedom and inspiration for her fingers.

Hardly had the final cadences of the movement started to fade away than the applause broke out. Urbino and Rebecca, who was sitting next to him, joined in with the others. They were a small group, though more obviously select than embarrassingly spare.

Lino Cipri, but not his wife, was there. Urbino hoped that she had recovered from the shock of his visit. Before the Contessa began her next piece, Urbino caught Cipri looking at him and Rebecca. Urbino returned a smile and gave his attention to the Contessa, who was beginning to say a few words about the Chopin *ballade* she was about to play.

It was one of Urbino's favorite pieces, and he often asked the Contessa to play it for him when they were alone together. He closed his eyes now as he listened to it, feeling himself healing with almost every note. He was disappointed on her behalf when the audience received it warmly but less enthusiastically than the Mozart.

The final piece on the program was *I Quattro Rusteghi* by Wolf-Ferrari. It was a particularly appropriate piece, not only since Wolf-Ferrari had once been the conservatory director, but also for more personal reasons.

The barcarolle intermezzo, which captures in its notes the movement of a gondola, had drawn the Conte's attention to her when he had heard her practicing it at the conservatory many years ago. It had been the beginning of their long and happy relationship.

Before playing the piece, she related this anecdote in a shy and touching manner and dedicated her rendition to the Conte. It had a sympathetic effect on the audience. Cipri had a pleasant smile on his smooth, pink face.

Urbino had heard the Contessa play *I Quattro Rusteghi* many times, and always with passion and sensitivity, but this afternoon she outdid herself. Her interpretation was pure genius. The audience was spellbound.

When she came to the end to thunderous applause, the Contessa exchanged a quick, brilliant glance with Urbino. He smiled back and cried out *"Brava!"* It was soon echoed around him.

The Contessa got a standing ovation.

After embracing the Contessa with two kisses on each cheek, Urbino left her to enjoy the praise of the group gathered around her. He would wait for her outside for their celebratory circuit of the city in the gondola. Rebecca had to dash off to an appointment.

As Urbino left the concert room, he looked around for Cipri. He had already left. Urbino went out to the courtyard to the statue of the veiled lady. Cipri was nowhere in sight.

Standing by the statue of the Veiled Lady, the euphoria induced by the Contessa's performance started to ebb as the statue inevitably reminded him of the figure in his dream of fire.

"How fortunate that no one has ever discovered her identity," the Contessa had said to him here in the courtyard before her first *conversazione*. "Don't you ever try to unveil her! Give your efforts to your Samuel Possle and my disappearing wardrobe."

It had seemed to make good sense at the time, before he had learned what he had since then. Now, as he waited for the Contessa by the mysterious statue, he wasn't so sure.

Different worlds and separate problems were starting to converge, or they seemed to be in his still confused perceptions. At his elbow was the ghost of Adriana Abdon, singing her heart out beside this same statue as the Contessa took her lessons in one of the rooms above.

Ghosts here at the conservatory and ghosts, in one form or another, behind the walls of the Ca' Pozza.

And even the dream of the fire, in the light of day, now seemed to be the ghost of something that had already happened or a premonition of what was about to.

70

For the first fifteen minutes of their gondola ride, as the black barque slipped down the Grand Canal and then into the labyrinth of smaller waterways, it was as if Urbino and the Contessa were floating to their own private barcarolle. The air was warm, and the light, that had been rosy in the morning, was now turning the stones golden and burnishing the metal work of the gondola. Companionable and pregnant silence was their only conversation as they drifted between the sea and sky in the closed cabin, sipping the Prosecco that Gildo had kept chilled for them. The Contessa had a relaxed expression on her attractive face as she absently contemplated the scene.

For his part, Urbino was pursuing the train of thought that had begun as he had waited for the Contessa by the statue of the veiled lady.

The gondola was now passing behind the Scuola Grande di San Rocco, where the Tintorettos kept all their glory and mystery.

The Contessa turned away from the external scene and looked at Urbino. "You're obviously holding yourself back, *caro*," she said. "It's been in your face, your voice, your every gesture."

Urbino nodded. Between his illness and her preparations for the last *conversazione,* he hadn't told her anything that had happened since the morning of his trip to San Lazzaro degli Armeni more than a week ago.

His next rendezvous with Possle was in four days, on Monday. He would be expecting an answer to his offer. If the Contessa didn't come with Urbino, it would probably be his last visit.

"I'm all yours again, and I'm all ears," the Contessa prompted.

As they drank the Prosecco, Urbino told her in a lowered voice everything that she didn't already know, everything, that is, except about his second violation of the Ca' Pozza and what he had found in Armando's little room. He would save these for a little later.

The cabin, closed like a confessional, and the slow movement and cradlelike rocking of the gondola were conducive to his detailed account.

The Contessa allowed him to give it without any interruption, although he was in little doubt of her reactions throughout from her facial expressions and the pressure, sometimes firm, sometimes gentle, with which she held his hand or touched his arm.

When he finished, he looked through the shutters as the gondola passed under first one bridge, then another. The Contessa broke her silence with considerable force.

"If your fellow American thinks I'm going to give him a lira or a pence for something that he stole and might even have murdered for, he can go right back where he came from!"

"My fellow American? It sounds as if you're blaming me."

"Not blaming you, but you *have* encouraged him. If you had given your attentions only to my poor lost clothes! You should get these Byron poems out of your mind completely, at least insofar as they might have anything to do with me! And don't give me that little boy wounded look, either, because you had another look on your face a few seconds ago. It was disappointment!"

The Contessa was right. Although Urbino didn't want her to get involved in what was undoubtedly a suspicious and perhaps even dangerous situation, his heart sank at the prospect of losing the poems completely. Perhaps there was some other way. Perhaps she—

"Forget about the poems, I tell you," she interrupted his reverie. "I know how important they'd be to you, especially now that you've been adrift in your work for a while. But stay away from them, with or without my help! Be content with your usual rewards. There's a mystery here of some kind. Solve it and walk away with no spoils except the intellectual ones!"

"Good advice, Barbara. But there might be a way to get the poems without paying *any* price," he added, "after we figure out whatever has been going on at the Ca' Pozza, and still might be."

"You're determined, aren't you?" She shook her head in concern and disapproval. "You mean Elvira, because of her fear of the building?"

"Elvira, yes, and maybe Hilda Cipri, too."

"What you're saying is that you want to have your cake and eat it, too. Didn't I tell you when we were standing by the veiled lady and thinking about *her* mystery, that it was impossible? If you solve her mystery, you'll lose a perpetual source of fascination. And if and when you solve the mystery of the dark and brooding Ca' Pozza, you'll surely lose the poems forever."

"You think so?"

"And so do you! I can tell from the tone of your voice, not to mention the look on your face that you yourself can't see! You'll find out that those poems have blood on them in one way or another; and even if they don't, they're most probably not Possle's free and clear. If I buy anything, even for *you*, I need to be sure that the seller really owns it to begin with. And what would it mean if you became associated with something like that? Is that what you want? A form of fame that's not much different from notoriety? *You'll* bear some moral burden, and don't think you won't."

Urbino made no response. In any case, the Contessa was far from finished.

"So find some way to put back the key you stole—yes, stole!" she went on, doing all she could to keep her voice down. "Find some way to put it back where it belongs and throw the copy into the Canalazzo. I'll do it for you. What do they call it? Incriminating evidence?"

It was now that he told her how he had put the key to use late last night and how he had discovered the clipping of her in her Fortuny dress.

The Contessa merely stared for a few moments, and then said, "But I don't understand. What does it mean?"

"It's what I've been trying to sort out."

"Perhaps Elvira gave Armando that clipping and other ones," the Contessa ventured. "Unless . . ."

She trailed off.

"Unless what?"

"Unless Armando was giving them to *her*. But why, *caro?* Why in either case?"

"I don't know. And we shouldn't be too quick to assume that those are the only two possibilities. Have you checked to see if you're missing one of your snakeskin belts?"

"They all seem to be there. But I didn't do as thorough a search as I could have. Now that I'm finished with my *conversazioni,* I'll go through everything again very carefully, if only to know what we'll have to get back from Elvira. You still do think she has everything, don't you?"

"Be sure that you have all your snakeskin belts. And what about your Fortuny dress?"

"Of course I have my Fortuny! I just saw it in the closet this morning. But you're not answering my question."

"Because I can't answer it without having some doubt in my own mind, one way or another. Maybe with a few more pieces of information and after reconsidering what we already know, things will be different."

"I hope so. But really, *caro*! Whatever have you been thinking of with these late-night forays? Be careful! Someone was following you last night, you say. Well, maybe it was Gildo looking out for you," she said, lowering her voice even more. "Maybe it was a mugger and maybe not! Maybe it was Armando, who wants to discourage your snooping! Maybe Possle himself. For all we know, Possle might be as spry as you are, and Armando could sing the role of Figaro without taking a breath!"

Despite her exaggeration, much of what the Contessa was saying was true. And yet if she came to the Ca' Pozza with him, she might be able to do something with Possle that he couldn't. He feared that he was coming close to losing much of his treasured objectivity when it came to Possle. The Contessa might be able to prevail upon Possle to be more honest about the poems, to tell the whole story about them. It was a wild shot.

"In case you have any doubts remaining," the Contessa said, showing that she still hadn't finished, "I have no intention of compromising either of us for those poems. And I'll be pleased to tell your Samuel Possle the way I feel in person!"

Urbino turned toward her.

"So you'll come? Not to make him an offer—"

"But not to say that I won't either, is that what you're thinking?" she broke in, throwing him a defiant look before glancing out. "For a clever person you're transparent. But our discussion might be moot, *caro*. Considering Possle's seizure, or whatever it was, he might not be in a position to hear anything from you or me on April Fool's Day or any other day. Yes, Possle could—"

The Contessa stopped speaking. Her eyes were looking at an upward angle. He followed the direction of her gaze. Up above them was the Ca' Pozza. The old building loomed against the dusky sky as they drifted past its unused water entrance. No light showed behind any of the windows. Most of them were shuttered, except for a small square one on the attic story.

Urbino had not said anything to Gildo about avoiding the Ca' Pozza. Given the gondolier's warnings to Urbino, however, he wondered why the young man had taken a route that passed by it. But hadn't Gildo also expressed, albeit indirectly, a wish that Urbino might get to the bottom of whatever role, if any, the Ca' Pozza had played in Marco's death? The young man might very well be as conflicted as Urbino was himself.

"No sooner does one speak of the devil, or rather the devil's house," the Contessa amended, "than it appears. Gildo!" she called out. "Draw up by the embankment, please."

"What are you doing?" Urbino asked her in a hoarse whisper.

"I'm getting out and I'm going to ring the bell. What your Samuel Possle needs is a little bit of spontaneity!"

Gildo had hardly brought the gondola to the water steps beside the bridge than the Contessa, with Urbino's help and under Gildo's silent, nervous stare, was stepping onto the embankment.

She went up to the large grim door of the building and pushed the bell. She waited, then pushed it again. When there was still no response, she stepped away from the building and looked at its upper stories.

Urbino did, too. The building looked back.

"Did you see that?" she called down to Urbino.

"See what?"

"I can swear there was someone at the attic window. It was just a flash."

She came back to the gondola. She was shivering. When she had seated herself again in the *felze*, Urbino arranged a blanket around her shoulders, another around her knees. Her face was pale.

"Are you all right, Barbara?"

"Did you see anything?" she asked in a weak voice.

"No. Did you?"

"No," she said after a few moments.

"Are you all right?"

"Yes, but I'd like to go home. I feel tired—tired and old."

As Gildo pushed and then rowed the gondola away from the Ca' Pozza, the Contessa continued to look back at the building until it passed from view.

71

W hen they reached the Ca' da Capo-Zendrini, Vitale informed the Contessa that the Conte's cousin Clementina had suffered a relapse and that her daughter would appreciate it if the Contessa could come as soon as possible. She made arrangements for Pasquale to have the Bentley ready to take her to Bologna early the next morning.

"I'm going upstairs," she told Urbino. "I'll just have Silvia bring me something to eat. But stay as long as you want. They can fix you dinner. I want to get a good night's rest before I leave tomorrow."

She avoided his eyes and hurried upstairs.

Urbino went to the library where he poured himself a drink. He sat in an armchair that gave a view of one of Habib's paintings of Morocco. The Contessa had honored it by hanging it in the corner devoted to her collection of travel books, some of them dating back to the seventeenth century. The painting showed an alley in the Fez Medina, re-created last winter from Habib's nostalgic imagination. Its swirl of primary colors, movement, and emotion made no distinction between the human figures and the cafés, shops, and houses that seemed alive themselves. Urbino sat staring at it, considering the way it erased any line between the public and the private and how different this was from Possle and the Ca' Pozza or, for that matter, from Urbino himself and his own Palazzo Uccello.

He then went over what had just happened in front of the Ca' Pozza. The Contessa had been shaken. He wished he had told her that he had seen something, but he had only seen the empty windows staring back at him. If he had lied to her, she would feel better now. He drank the rest of his drink and left the library.

He climbed the broad staircase to the next floor and knocked on the door of the Contessa's boudoir. "Barbara," he called out quietly. "Are you there?"

"Yes, what is it?"

Her voice sounded very far away.

"Would you like some tea?"

"No thank you. I'll need to rest if I'm going to be any use at Clementina's. The performance took everything out of me."

"I think you saw something in one of the windows. What was it?"

The silence was so long that he thought that she wasn't going to respond. When she did, it was in a firmer voice. "I wish I had seen something, *caro*, that's the problem. I didn't see a single solitary thing. And you didn't either. I don't want to talk about it anymore. Not tonight. Never. Excuse me, *caro*. I want to get as much rest as I can before I go to Bologna tomorrow. Good night."

72

A t two o'clock the next afternoon, a Friday, Urbino rang the Cipris' doorbell on the Lido.

The artist appeared, his thick white hair in disarray, but otherwise looking as dapper as usual in a bright blue cravat and tweed sport jacket. He couldn't conceal his surprise at seeing Urbino.

"It's you, Signor Urbino. It was a pleasure to see you yesterday at the Contessa's concert. Brilliant, it was! Most brilliant!"

"Yes, it was," Urbino agreed.

He looked over the painter's shoulder into the parlor. Hilda's chair was empty.

"I'm sorry to disturb you. I had some business today on the Lido. I thought I'd stop by and ask your wife to autograph her book. The poems are very good, and I'm sure that if my German were better, I'd be even more impressed. She carried me back to the time of Byron in Venice."

He took Hilda's collection of Byron-inspired poems from his pocket.

"I had it with me at the concert yesterday, but she wasn't there. I do hope she is all right."

"She was feeling poorly."

"I'm sorry. Perhaps I'll come back some other time. Give her my good wishes."

Urbino started to put the book back into his pocket. He sensed that Cipri was aware that Hilda's autograph was only a pretext for his visit.

"No, it's all right," the painter said. "I'll take it to her. She's resting but I'm sure she wouldn't mind being disturbed for a second. Would—would you like to come in?"

"That's kind of you, but I don't want to intrude. If you're sure it wouldn't trouble your wife, I'll be gratified to have her autograph, and then I'll leave and not take up anymore of your time."

"As you wish. She'll regret not being able to see you today. Perhaps some other time when she's feeling up to it. Please make yourself comfortable."

Cipri indicated a chair beside the door and left.

As soon as Cipri was out of sight, Urbino went over to the table where he had noticed the sketches of Hilda. They were still there, as well as the pens and pencils and the Italian-German dictionary. The keys, however, were nowhere in sight. Urbino wondered how significant it might be that the table held everything that it had held not much more than a week ago, everything except the keys.

He seated himself in the chair by the door.

Cipri returned a few minutes later with Hilda's book. The painter opened it. *Hilda Krippe* was written in bright blue ink on the title page.

"She was most pleased," Cipri said.

Urbino thanked him and put the book in his pocket. What he probably had was an excellent forgery of Hilda's signature.

"By the way," Urbino said, as he was about to leave, "since my last visit I've become interested in someone you mentioned. It's the foreign gentleman who used to stay at the Ca' Pozza. He was Armenian. There's an interesting relationship between Venice and Armenia. I thought I might write a short book about it."

"I see. I suppose that would be interesting."

Cipri's smooth, pink face became impassive.

"Did you know that he drowned with his son in the same accident that Adriana drowned in?"

"He did? I didn't know. I never had much to do with him except for the few times I saw him at the Ca' Pozza."

Urbino would have expected Cipri to show more shock and surprise at learning about Dilsizian's death in the same accident that had killed Adriana.

"That's too bad. But when you did see him there, did you notice what kind of relationship he had with Armando? Were they friendly?"

"As I said last time, Armando is devoted only to Possle."

"And the memory of his sister."

"If you say so. I wouldn't know. I never see him."

73

After leaving the Cipris' apartment, Urbino hired a water taxi to take him the short distance to San Lazzaro degli Armeni. He hadn't set up an appointment with Father Nazar or any of the other friars, and there was no scheduled tour today.

As he climbed on to the pier of the monastery island, where the driver would wait for his return, the stillness around him was comforting. He went down the empty path and across the silent courtyard in front of the low, brick buildings. Not even the cry of one of the island's peacocks broke the quiet.

The friar who answered the door was very accommodating. He recognized Urbino's name and spent a few moments praising his book on the Minolfis, a family of restorers. Urbino explained that he needed one of the books printed by the monks for his research and hoped he might buy it at the bookstore even if it might be closed. The friar conducted him past the printing and typesetting hall, inactive at this hour, to the bookstore. Father Nazar was nowhere in sight.

The friar tried to interest Urbino in some large, colored photographs of the Ca' Zenobio degli Armeni that he said he had taken himself many years ago. The building had formerly been the seat of the Armenian College and was now used for commercial and private functions. To please the man, Urbino selected three of the photographs, and then searched for the book on Armenian national costumes that he had glanced through on his last visit.

"I'll take this, too," he said, when he found it.

"An excellent choice."

Ten minutes later as the motorboat was taking him across the lagoon to the quay in front of the Piazza San Marco, Urbino paged through the book until he found the color plate he was interested in. It was a photograph of a pretty woman in an embroidered and ornamented dress, silver belt, and head-dress and veil.

Urbino stopped in at Florian's. As he had a drink at the bar, he tried to put together the pieces of the puzzle that were Samuel Possle, Mechitar Dilsizian, and Lord Byron. He didn't have much success. He then telephoned Corrado Scarpa. There was no help from him either. He had not yet been able to locate the boating accident report. If and when he did, he would have it delivered to Urbino immediately.

74

Why, thank you, Signor Urbino," Benedetta Razzi said at ten-fifteen the next morning. She took the tiny fan of marbleized pink paper. "It's even nicer than the one you brought last time. My little ones will love it."

"You said that they didn't have many fans. When I passed the shop, I knew what I had to do."

Razzi continued to examine the fan.

"I'll put it right by my *senorita*," she said. "Senoritas love fans."

"They do. But perhaps it would be more suitable with this other doll."

He indicated the refined figure in an embroidered pink dress displayed on one of the tables. When he had been here before it had been beside her on the love seat. A pillbox hat draped by a white veil gave it an exotic look.

"Of course," Razzi agreed. "The colors of the fan and the dress go together perfectly." She placed the fan next to the doll. "There!"

As she eased herself into the sagging love seat, she gave him an amused look from beneath her false eyelashes. She was wearing the same black dress with black sequins, but today she had added a necklace of pearls.

"I think you have a soft spot in your heart for that little lady. I'm jealous. You brought the fan especially for her."

Urbino seated himself in the armchair across from her. "You've discovered my secret, signora. I must admit that I find that doll intriguing. Her costume, I mean. It's Armenian, isn't it?"

"How clever! Armenian, yes. I had to look up the country on a map. I had never heard of it before. It's near Turkey."

He waited.

"A gentleman gave it to me, a kind gentleman just like yourself. He came from Armenia."

"Really? How interesting."

"He was my tenant in the San Polo building. Oh, that was many years ago. He had a strange name. I can't remember it. Ah, but his face, Signor Urbino! His face! I'll never forget it. And even if I did, I have a photograph."

"You do?"

"Bring me that album from the table over in the corner."

Urbino fetched the large, worn book.

Razzi started to turn the pages slowly. She alternately smiled and frowned as she looked at the photographs. After a minute or two, she stabbed at one photograph with her finger. "Here he is, and here's me, too, all those years ago."

She sighed and handed him the album.

A color photograph, poor in quality, of three people, was on the page.

Razzi, who appeared to be in her forties, was dressed in a brown fur coat and matching fur hat. She was recognizable for her large, expressive eyes. Next to her was a tall and sharp-featured man in a moustache and pointed beard.

On the other side of Mechitar Dilsizian was an attractive young woman in a gray dress and small black apron. She was almost as tall as the Armenian. On her head was a gray cap. She looked vaguely familiar.

"You see how hard his face was, but he had a kind heart.

He gave me the doll a few days after this picture was taken. He moved away and went to Switzerland or Austria or someplace like that. I don't know what happened to him."

Urbino was tempted to tell her about Dilsizian's fate, but if he did, it would reveal his deception to the woman. Instead he asked who had taken the photograph.

"His son. He was sweet, too. The face of an angel!"

"You've always been elegant, signora. Who is the girl with you?"

Razzi took the album back and closed it. "That's crazy Elvira. She wasn't crazy then. She wasn't even married."

"She seems to be dressed in a uniform of some kind."

"In those days she was a maid—for Signor Possle and some other people. Maybe she took the apartment after her husband died to be close to him. She seemed to have a crush on him, so much older though he was."

Urbino absorbed this in silence. Then he asked her what Elvira's relationship with Dilsizian had been.

"Who knows? I wouldn't put anything past her, then or now. She's a schemer. She managed to get into *my* building, didn't she? And she'll be there for life—*her* life, I mean—unless I can get her out some other way!"

75

A gentleman left this for you, Signor Urbino," Natalia said, when he returned to the Palazzo Uccello after speaking with Razzi.

She handed him a large manila envelope. Urbino immediately knew what it was. Corrado Scarpa had found the accident report.

He took it to the library, where he poured a glass of wine, then seated himself in the old leather armchair.

The envelope contained several photocopied sheets covered with script and typewriting, signatures, and official stamps. He read through them once quickly, then a second time more carefully.

Possle, Armando, Adriana, and the Dilsizians had gone out in a sailboat they had rented in Burano. The sailboat was a *topo*, a type of vessel originally designed as a fishing boat but now used by the Buranelli, with a motor, as a cargo transport. Their *topo*, however, didn't have a motor but only a sail.

The unusually mild weather for mid-March must have encouraged the group. Mechitar had been in control of the boat.

When they were near Chioggia, a short distance from Venice, violent gusts had started blowing from the north. They had decided to head back to Burano.

But when they had been off the Lido and within sight of the Lungomare Marconi, the weather had turned even worse. Mechitar had lost control of the boat. According to Possle's and Armando's affidavits—the mute had written his own account in response to questioning—the whole party had been tossed into the sea. The only witness among the five about what happened from this point on was Armando. Possle was knocked unconscious when the boat hit him in the head. Armando managed to secure him to the capsized boat. Armando then looked for the others. Mechitar was trying to save his son as they thrashed around in the water. They both disappeared beneath the waves. Adriana was nowhere in sight. Armando swam a short distance from Possle and the boat in search of her. He didn't find her.

The report also contained the testimonies of a middle-aged couple who were on the Lido bird-watching. While the woman ran to call an emergency number, the man witnessed the drama through his binoculars. From what he could see, everything had unfolded just as Armando had described, except that he added one detail. He had seen Adriana slip beneath the waves as the capsized *topo* had passed over her.

The bodies of Mechitar and Zakariya had been found three hours later, washed up on the shore of the Lido.

Adriana's body had never been found.

It was time to make a trip to the Villa Serena in Florence. Urbino made some telephone calls and managed to get an appointment to meet the director the next afternoon.

76

After dinner Urbino telephoned the Contessa in Bologna to see how she was doing. She spoke in a calm and almost emotionless voice, and spent most of the time telling him about Clementina, who was fortunately out of danger. He told her that he hoped she was taking care of herself as well, and left it at that for now. Although he had no intention of keeping silent about her strange behavior after sounding the bell of the Ca' Pozza, as she had vehemently told him he should, he didn't want to speak about it over the telephone.

"I'll be back late tomorrow night," she said, "but there's no need to call, *caro*. I'll be going straight to bed. We'll all be losing an hour of sleep."

Tomorrow was March 31 when the clocks were turned ahead one hour for summertime.

"I won't bother you. Give Clementina my love, and have a safe return." But he couldn't say good-bye without adding, "Possle is expecting us on Monday."

"I haven't forgotten."

77

At ten o'clock that night Urbino, wrapped in his cloak, took a walk, but he was determined to keep his steps away from the Ca' Pozza. He would rather contemplate it tonight in its absence. It would be more real and palpable this way and less able to exert its baleful influence.

Fog had made a stealthy invasion of the city during the past few hours. It transformed the few people he met into mysterious, faceless figures who reminded him of the silhouette he had seen against the window of the Ca' Pozza more than a month ago.

He crossed the iron bridge into the Ghetto and wandered beneath the tall buildings, his mood darkened by the sad associations of the place. Invariably it had this effect on him even on a warm, sunny day, let alone on a night like this. The stones seemed to bleed from the wrongs of the centuries, and he could easily imagine the generations obliged to wear their bright-colored but far from gay hats and confined behind walls and locked gates.

But tonight the story of the Abdons temporarily displaced this long, tragic history in Urbino's thoughts. He considered the series of premature, violent deaths that had begun with those of the mother and father in the fire and that might not yet have come to an end.

He turned away from the sad, empty streets in the direction of the Grand Canal, where the fog was thicker. Walking past the closed shops and kiosks and beneath shuttered windows, Urbino unrolled Demetrio Emo's story about the Abdon family. He added what he had learned on his own. It was a tale of sudden death and madness—or if not madness, then certainly severe emotional disturbance.

Was there any apparent explanation for Adriana's condition as there was for Armando's muteness? Urbino could understand if she had suffered a breakdown after the deaths of her mother and father, but according to Emo it hadn't been that way. She had been ill before then. And yet Urbino believed that there was a close connection between her illness and the fire that had killed her mother and father, and had almost claimed the life of her brother and possibly hers as well.

Emotional imbalance was often a mystery. There wasn't always a convenient cause to make one feel more comfortable about it. Sometimes madness just dropped down over a person, it seemed. Perhaps this had been poor Adriana's fate, but, one way or another, Urbino didn't think he would ever know.

But other things he was sure he would know, and soon, to flesh out what he strongly suspected. When he went to the Ca' Pozza in a few days, with or without the Contessa, he would find out whether he was right or not.

In the long, narrow Campo Morosini he ducked into a bar for a quick glass of wine before heading across the square toward the Accademia Bridge. He stopped to look up at the music conservatory. He turned his thoughts to something that was at the heart of the dark mystery of the Ca' Pozza.

It was Armando's devotion to his sister that had begun in their childhood, that had extended into their adulthood, and that was still far from dead. His arrangements for her commitment to the Villa Serena, the mass celebrated every year in her memory, the obituary notice on the date of the boat accident—they all testified to his love and loyalty, or seemed to.

And what he had learned from Benedetta Razzi about Elvira Carelli complicated the picture even more. Elvira not only lived next door to the Ca' Pozza and considered it a blight on her life, but years ago she had also worked as Possle's maid and had been romantically attracted to him, if Razzi could be believed. Possle had indicated that he only knew her as a neighbor. What might he be concealing about his relationship with her?

And to implicate Elvira even more in the secrets of the palazzo, she had been acquainted with Dilsizian and his son. What the extent of this acquaintance might have been, especially with the father, was shrouded in the silence of the past. Razzi, not even with all her ill will for Elvira and her interest in gossip, had been able to lift one small edge of the veil.

Urbino was still staring up at the music conservatory. A lone window was illuminated. Perhaps a privileged young student like the Contessa so many years ago was practicing a Mozart sonata. Perhaps somewhere in the shadows where Urbino couldn't see her was a less privileged young woman who was looking up with envy and anger at the lighted window.

Urbino climbed the wooden steps of the fog-wreathed bridge and paused in the middle. The night air blew across his face like an astringent.

Slow, hesitant footsteps approached from the Dorsoduro side where the fog was thick. As he peered into the fog for someone to appear, the footsteps stopped suddenly. The fog revealed nothing. He waited for the footsteps to sound again. All he could hear was the *put-put* of a boat that soon faded away farther up the Grand Canal. Then, after what seemed a long time but which was probably scarcely more than ten or fifteen seconds, the footsteps broke the stillness of the night again.

Almost as soon as they did, two gray figures gradually

became visible like prints in a photographic tray and climbed the last few steps of the bridge.

It was an elderly couple. The woman, muffled against the unseasonable cold in a fur coat similar to the one that Razzi wore in the photograph with Dilsizian and Elvira, held a muzzled cocker spaniel against her chest. They bid Urbino good evening in Italian, walked slowly down the opposite steps, and vanished in the fog.

Urbino gazed down at the Grand Canal. The fog crept over the surface of the waterway. It made some buildings disappear but isolated others as if they stood alone.

One of these latter was the Palazzo Guggenheim farther down the Grand Canal, the former home of a woman who had bestowed some of her glamour and notoriety on Possle's gatherings. From its water steps had floated what had surely been the last private gondola in Venice as such legendary matters were reckoned. It hadn't been Possle's and it certainly wasn't Urbino's.

Possle was a thief of one kind or another, and Guggenheim's distinction of having had the last gondola was one of his appropriations. Maybe Urbino wasn't too far behind him. Wasn't he more than a little proud of his own gondola, proud of the figure he cut in it? And didn't he sometimes fantasize, for long, self-indulgent moments, that he was one of the last of the passionate pilgrims who had descended on the city in the grip of what Henry James had called their palazzo madness?

But too much had been lost since those long-ago days. Nothing could bring them back.

Possle had dreamed that dream, and look what had become of him.

Casting a last glance down at the Canalazzo, this time in the opposite direction, toward the bend of the waterway where fog swirled around the Byron-haunted Palazzi Mocenigo, Urbino descended the bridge into the Dorsoduro. He searched out the square to catch any sign of another person in the shadows or the fog, but the area, with its shuttered kiosk and boat landing, was empty. The booth for boat tickets was closed.

Several minutes later Urbino found himself on a quay where fruit and vegetable barges were covered with tarpaulin for the night. To his right was a bridge on which a traditional bloody fistfight used to take place centuries ago between rival factions whose aim was to throw their opponents into the canal as violently as possible. Footprints, embedded in the bridge in white marble, gleamed in the dark and marked the spots where the rivals had confronted each other.

Urbino had always shied away from outward shows of aggression. Yet since moving to Venice he had become involved in devious and bloodstained forms of it. The mystery of the Ca' Pozza might be yet another example of this, except that in this instance he was directly responsible for having put himself in the heart of it.

As he continued along the deserted quay, his thoughts turned to the Byron poems. Possle had won them in a card game with Dilsizian, he claimed. He had a document to prove it. And Dilsizian had drowned on a pleasure trip in the lagoon.

Possle didn't seem to have ever been the type for fistfights any more than Urbino was, but appearances were nothing if they weren't deceiving. The young Possle could have brutally struck out to get what he wanted or to keep what he already had, just as he still might do. His current infirm condition didn't mean that he had been robbed of every power at his disposal. For there was the silent, cadaverous Armando, with his loyalty to Possle. Was the mute nothing more than a spectator, like the men and women who had gathered to see the fistfights on the bridge? Had this been his role over the many years of their relationship?

Or had it been something else entirely, a role more malevolent that was still unfolding? Had it been set in motion during the days of Possle's life of high publicity and might not end even with Possle's own death. And how might the clipping of the Contessa in Armando's little room, with Urbino's figure cut out of it, fit into the picture? Along with the belt, which he was now almost completely convinced was a woman's, that he had seen on the back staircase of the Ca' Pozza?

The questions unfolded out of each other like black flowers. Before he had proceeded much further he was in possession of a whole dark bouquet of them.

Their scent was as difficult to describe as the aroma that emanated from Possle's crystal vaporizer and as rank as the odor that Armando gave off. Only then, as he mentally clutched his perverse little blooms, did he realize where his footsteps were now taking him and where they had inevitably been taking him for the past hour.

No, not to the Ca' Pozza. He was strong enough to keep to the resolve that he had made upon quitting the Palazzo Uccello. Tonight it was the Ca' Zenobio degli Armeni. The building was only a short distance down the quayside and over another of the city's ubiquitous bridges.

He was soon standing on the bridge that provided a view of the silent, unilluminated palazzo on the other side of the canal. Wisps of fog drifted against its white-painted baroque face. A small boat was moored by its water steps. One of the photographs of the palazzo that Urbino had bought from the friar on San Lazzaro degli Armeni had been taken from this same spot.

Last year Urbino and Habib had escorted the Contessa to a ball in the palazzo's sumptuous Sala degli Specchi with its waves of white-and-gold stuccoes, Dorigni and Tiepolo frescoes, and extravagance of ornate mirrors that gave the room its name.

But now its much more sinister association with the drowned Dilsizian and his Byron poems eclipsed the memories of that magical evening. Surely the Armenian had visited the palazzo as he had San Lazzaro degli Armeni. He might even have spoken about the poems to someone there, as he had to Father Nazar.

If Possle were to be believed, those same poems were now in his exclusive possession. They would be somewhere in the Ca' Pozza. Possle wouldn't be inclined to have them far from him, but somewhere in his bedroom or the gondola room. Perhaps they were buried among the cushions of the gondola. It somehow seemed the thing that Possle would do with his spoils.

On the Accademia Bridge, Urbino had reminded himself that Possle was a thief, the thief of San Polo, as the Contessa had dubbed him the day of their outing to the Naval Museum. Thefts came in many different forms. At first Possle's had seemed innocuous enough, being versions of the ideas and words of those who had gone before him. In a manner of thinking such pilferings weren't even thefts at all but instead clever, even artistic, manipulations, rearrangements, recreations. There could be no doubt that Possle, over the many decades of his life, had, in a sense, cobbled and created himself. Now that same self was trapped and decaying in the Ca' Pozza.

If only Urbino could find out whether the Byron poems had come Possle's way without any form of violence or deception. According to the report of the boating accident, it didn't appear that Mechitar had died through foul play, but Urbino had a temperamental and professional suspicion of appearances.

He had already stolen a key and broken into the Ca' Pozza like a thief. It was proof of how far he would go when it came to acquisition of the poems. Urbino wanted them, and he wanted them for the reasons Possle had named and for others he hadn't. It was a measure of Urbino's peculiar form of greed that, when he turned his back on the Ca' Zenobio and started to make his way toward home, he almost believed that with the Contessa's help he might succeed in laying his hands on them if they had indeed come Possle's way through a card game with Mechitar Dilsizian.

But then reality set in as he broke into his elastic stride. He had temporarily and conveniently forgotten about Armando, about Armando and his devotion to his twin sister, and about what might very well be the darker secret of the Ca' Pozza.

These thoughts made him more wary of the night and the fog than he had been when he had set out earlier from the Palazzo Uccello.

78

The next morning Urbino took the earliest train to Florence. He passed the time before his rendezvous at the Villa Serena wandering through the streets and in and out of some of the churches and galleries.

As he stood in the tiny Chapel of the Magi at the Palazzo Medici and in front of the Fra Filippo Lippi *tondo* of the Madonna at the Palazzo Pitti, his mind was far away from their charms: it was filled with thoughts of Samuel Possle and Dilsizian, Elvira and Hilda, Armando and Adriana, Gildo and Marco.

He was therefore glad when the taxi was climbing into the hills above the rose-colored roofs and domes of the city. The Villa Serena wasn't far from Bernard Berenson's former home, the Villa I Tatti. An *allée* of cypresses led to the entrance of a large Renaissance building. Other buildings, much smaller and of newer, but discreet, construction were nestled in gardens behind the main building.

Urbino wondered how Armando had been able to scrape together enough money for even a week at the clinic for Adriana, let alone the many months that Demetrio Emo had mentioned.

The director was a cheerful, efficient woman in her late

fifties who lived on the grounds. Although it was a Sunday, she had agreed to see him when he had mentioned Adriana Abdon's name yesterday afternoon. She didn't have to consult her files to give him some of the information he needed.

"A beautiful woman with an exquisite voice. She first stayed with us twenty years ago. For five months. Two years later she spent a few more months here. The third time was much, much longer. Almost ten years. We discharged her into her brother's care."

"Ten years? Are you sure?"

"Yes." A reminiscent smile crossed her face. "The day she left she wore a dress that was an exact copy of one that I had bought myself a few years before for my fiftieth birthday. She always said she loved it and had many photographs of the two of us with me wearing it. Her brother must have arranged for it to be made."

79

At nine the next morning, the first of April, Urbino tele-phoned the Venice Questura. After being on hold for what seemed hours, he was put through to Commissario Francesco Gemelli.

Over the years of his sleuthing, Urbino had developed a fragile relationship with the commissioner of police, since they both had need of each other and since Urbino had, on more than one occasion, allowed Gemelli to take all the credit for the solution of some crimes.

But the Sicilian was prickly and almost always hard to deal with. He listened to what Urbino had to say without interrupt-ing him. It all sounded rather far-fetched even to Urbino's own ears, but he plunged on. When he was finished, there was silence from the other end of the line for what seemed a long time.

"And on the basis of these wild ideas, you expect me to make a fool of myself as well?" Gemelli finally said. "You haven't given me one shred of evidence that there's anything criminal here at all. The muggings in the area are another thing, of course."

"I'm only asking you to put a few men in the area in case I need them."

"The Venice Questura doesn't exist for your personal and private protection, Macintyre. Hire a bodyguard!"

Urbino remained silent. He was fairly confident that Gemelli would see that this could be a matter of his own self-interest.

Urbino wasn't proven wrong when the commissario said, "All right, Macintyre. All this sounds like infighting between you and this other American, but you haven't burned me, not yet anyway. But let me warn you, my men will have to have a good reason for going in—a very good reason."

"I hope they won't have one."

"In which case you'll be proven wrong."

"I wouldn't mind that at all."

80

Urbino was about to go downstairs to seek out Gildo in his quarters when the telephone rang. To his surprise it was the Contessa.

"I was going to call you a little later," he said. "I wanted you to get as much rest as possible."

"I feel a lot better. On the trip back from Bologna I did some thinking. And being away for a few days helped to clear my mind. As soon as I got back to the house, I went through all my clothes again, without Silvia. You'll never guess what I found."

"You mean what you didn't find. One of your snakeskin belts."

"Exactly! It's one I bought in Bologna years ago. Being in Bologna stirred up the memory. My belt on the stairs of the Ca' Pozza. What does it mean?"

"I prefer not to go into it over the phone."

"Come here at two. I have some things I want to tell you, too. The appointment with Possle is at four-thirty, isn't it?"

"You're coming?"

"It's one of the things I want to talk about."

81

Y ou look tired, Signor Urbino," Gildo said half an hour later. He had been about to go out. He removed his cap and put it on the table in the middle of his crowded parlor.

"I didn't sleep well," Urbino said. After his walk last night, he had spent two hours in the library, running various scenarios through his mind. And then, when he had finally gone to sleep, the same dream of Possle, the veiled lady, and the fire had tormented him, except now beneath the veil had been the face of Adriana. "I need your help, Gildo. May I sit down?"

Gildo cleared a pile of nautical magazines from a chair. Urbino seated himself. Gildo remained standing, his slim body tense, his open face clouded with uneasiness.

Urbino started to explain what he wanted Gildo to do that afternoon if necessary. He was taking Gemelli's suggestion of a bodyguard seriously. He wanted to reduce as many risks as possible. He knew that dangers remained, however, and yet he couldn't stop himself from going ahead. He had begun something, and he needed to see it to the end.

As Urbino spoke, the boy's expressive green eyes grew wider and his gaze moved from Urbino's face to the *forcola*. It stood there with them like a silent witness and reminder.

"That building frightens me, signore. I told you that."

Gildo's voice had an uncharacteristic fragility and tremulousness.

"Do you mean that you can't help me?"

The youth lifted his head a little higher. "I'll do as you wish. Maybe we'll find out what happened to Marco, as you say. And the Contessa is a good lady. I wouldn't want anything bad to happen to her if she's with you."

"Between the two of us, we'll be sure that it doesn't. And the police won't be far away if we need them. Take this."

Urbino handed Gildo the copy of the key to the front door of the Ca' Pozza.

"And your cell phone is in good working order?"

Gildo took it from his pocket.

"Yes, signore."

"And so is mine. Now to be certain that we both understand each other, why don't you repeat what I told you that you might have to do."

"Very well, signore. I take you to the Ca' Pozza in the gondola. I moor the boat. You get out and ring the bell of the house. If you go in, I leave the gondola and stand by the door. I don't do anything unless I get the signal from your phone to mine. I don't even try to see where the police are waiting. If I get your signal, I waste not a second. I push the code for the police. They will know what it means. Then I take the key and I open the door. I must be sure to leave it open. I—I go inside and up the stone staircase. On the other side of the *sala* there's a room with a wide door, wider than the others. I go into the room."

Gildo said this in a voice that became increasingly stronger. When he finished, he stared back at Urbino, a muscle quivering at his jaw.

"Right. And if you see the man who dresses in black—or anyone else? What do you do?"

"Oh, Signor Urbino, I hope I don't see him! But—but if I do, I tell him that I must find you, you and the Contessa, if she comes with you."

"And if we aren't in the room with the big door?"

"I push the button to call the police again."

"And then?"

"Then—then I go outside and wait for them if they haven't arrived yet. But, signore, I could not leave you and the Contessa in the house if you need help! I must stay."

"It would be best for you to go outside. That's how you could help us if it comes to that. Maybe none of this will be necessary. Maybe you'll never have to go inside the Ca' Pozza."

"I hope not, for the sake of all of us!"

Urbino got up. He threw his arm around the young man to reassure him, but it was also for his own sake.

82

I t's impossible!" the Contessa cried out at three thirty that afternoon. Casting a nervous glance at the closed door of her *salotto blu,* she added in a lower voice, "And yet, considering what I can now admit I saw the other day, it's completely possible!"

She had denied seeing any figure in the attic window of the Ca' Pozza, she had explained earlier, because she feared she had imagined it, as Urbino had suspected. She was particularly susceptible because of all the worries she had been going through— and still was, she had emphasized—about her lost items.

"Probable is more like it," Urbino said. "I don't know all the details. I can only speculate about many of them, and that's what I've just done with you as I did with Gemelli. But I needed to tell you everything to—"

"To make me want to lock all the doors," she interrupted, but still in a quiet voice. "To make me want to pull the bed covers over my head even more than I wanted to before! Is that it?"

"To make you decide whether you still want to come with me. If you do, it could be unpleasant. I don't believe you'll be in any real danger though, not with the arrangements I made with Gemelli and Gildo."

"Remember that you tend to trust too easily."

"You mean Gildo? Believe me, Barbara, I'm not making a mistake with him."

"Let's hope neither of us turns out to be a fool today. Let's hope a lot of good things." She took a sip of tea. "So tell me, *caro,* how did you figure it out? It couldn't have just been because you suspected that I saw someone in the attic window."

"No, but that took its place. The clipping of you in your Fortuny dress in Armando's room played a large role. Not just in itself but along with the belt. The more I thought about that belt, the more I became convinced that it was a woman's. Even before you told me earlier that you're missing a snakeskin belt, I realized that the belt in the Ca' Pozza had to be yours. It all fitted together so well. And then, of course, there were all the sounds. Possle couldn't have been making them. I heard them sometimes when we were together. Admittedly, Armando was a possibility though until I ruled him out."

"The mute who might have cried and laughed like a woman?"

Urbino shrugged.

"Emo told me he was a good mimic. But Elvira was the logical explanation, if you threw in the city's strange acoustics, but none of that ever satisfied me. And then there was what Elvira said about some evil old woman in fancy clothes and makeup who hid in her house like a spider. What better description of Benedetta Razzi could she have given, I thought at the time, unless she had mentioned the dolls, too. And I thought of what happened on San Michele with Elvira. And then I went to the Villa Serena."

The Contessa looked at him steadily for a few moments.

"You can't outfox a fox," she said. "Possle's already taken enough advantage of you. All you can see in front of your eyes are those Byron poems. They're coloring everything else. I don't think I need your protection at the Ca' Pozza. If I'm going with you, it's because you may need mine!"

She drained the last of her tea and stood up. With his eyes on her embroidered vest, whose sequins were sparkling in the light, Urbino finished his flame red Campari.

83

The first thing that was strange about the Ca' Pozza on this visit was that Armando was nowhere in sight.

A few moments after Urbino rang the bell, a buzzer sounded to release the lock on the door. Urbino clasped the handle and opened the door. He checked to see if the lock was the same. It seemed to be. It was rusted and showed no sign of recent repair or replacement.

He looked back at the Contessa. She was staring up at the building. "Do you see anything?" he asked her. She shook her head. "It's the first time I've ever been let in this way."

Urbino peered into the darkened recesses of the foyer.

"Who pushed the buzzer? Armando or Possle?" the Contessa asked.

"I have no idea. Possle could have one within reach from his gondola."

They passed into the foyer.

"It's chilly in here," the Contessa said, pulling the collar of her coat against her neck.

"It's warmer in the gondola room."

As Urbino closed the door behind them, Gildo was approaching the building from the bridge where he had secured the gondola. They exchanged a quick look.

Urbino placed the Contessa's coat, along with his cloak, on the gargoyle clothes stand. Her eyes moved with a silent question toward the door to Armando's little room. He nodded. They ascended the broad, stone staircase.

They paused for a few moments in the large empty *sala*. Late afternoon light gleamed through chinks in the closed shutters. The door of the gondola room was open. The smaller door at the far end of the room that connected with Possle's suite and the back staircase was ajar. The door had always been completely closed before.

A few minutes ago Armando's absence had disconcerted Urbino, but now he hoped that the man might stay away long enough for him to say what he wanted to say to Possle. It would be easier without Armando lurking in the background.

Urbino tried to remember whether Possle had mentioned the precise date of their next appointment in Armando's presence. He didn't think so.

They were about to proceed, when his heart sank. Footsteps, slow, stealthy, sounded from beyond the partly open door at the far side of the room.

The Contessa turned her head in that direction. She, too, had heard the footsteps, which now came to an abrupt halt.

Urbino sensed the Contessa's nervousness. As they advanced toward the gondola room, he touched her hand.

The floor and the walls around and beyond the open door squirmed with the shadows thrown from within by the candles and the fire.

They entered, the Contessa's step more hesitant than his own. A wave of hot, stale air struck them. Possle looked more dwarfed by the mass of the gondola than usual, as if he had shrunk since Urbino had last seen Armando lift him up in his arms. He was dressed, as he invariably was, in his rich purple silk and red satin, but he wasn't wearing his glasses. The past days following his seizure appeared to have taken a severe toll.

His eyes were more sunken in his skull, and the less wrinkled side of his face was turned down ever so slightly. His head covering was loose and had crept farther down on his brow.

Sheets of paper, many of them cracked, flaking, and browned with age, were spread on the cushions around him and across his chest. The great majority were newspaper clippings, but other sheets appeared to be letters and official documents of some kind. None, however, resembled the sheets of paper that Father Nazar had described to Urbino.

The carafe and the goblets stood on the small, inlaid table. One of the goblets was half filled with water.

The candles, the small ones at the base of the gondola and the two stately ones flanking it, were lit. Possle's eyes reflected their flickering light, but something else burned in them, distantly but hungrily.

"You've brought the divine Contessa." He wriggled weakly up against the cushions. "I've sent Armando away from the house on an errand—to allow us to be alone. I released the lock." He indicated a button on the wall behind the gondola that Urbino hadn't noticed on his previous visits.

Urbino was pierced with sharp anxiety. Armando would return and find Gildo by the door. It was an unforeseen development. But if he and the Contessa were lucky, they might be able to accomplish what they had planned before he returned.

Possle was staring at Urbino. Urbino had the impression, not for the first time in his contact with the man, that Possle knew what he was thinking. But when Possle spoke again, it was not to him but to the Contessa.

"Welcome, dear Contessa!" he said. "The last time we met so many years ago, you were la signorina Barbara Spencer. Ah, time! But surely you know how little you've changed. If only the same could be said of me." Possle's voice sounded more fragile than usual and it had a slightly slurred quality.

"Thank you for inviting me," she replied simply and smoothly, mastering whatever shock she felt at his appalling appearance.

"And thank you for coming. Please make yourselves comfortable."

They seated themselves in the two high-backed armchairs drawn up in front of the gondola. The Contessa looked apprehensively at the candles gathered on the floor a few feet away.

"I'd like to make one thing clear at the start, Mr. Possle," she said, turning her attention to his wizened form. "I've come here out of courtesy to you and Mr. Macintyre. I thought it best to tell you in person that I have no intention of buying a collection of poems by Byron, even if they are authentic. He informs me that you've been kind enough to offer them to me before anyone else."

"To have them in your hands and thus in those of your good friend Mr. Macintyre would be a great pleasure to me," Possle responded. He was making an effort to keep the tremor out of his voice and to inject as much firmness into it as he could. "But as he certainly must have told you, I'm ready to consider other—what shall I call them?—other *interested* parties. It will be some trouble to me, but I know what the end will be. I'll have my money and someone else, not you and your dear friend, will have the poems."

"We're prepared to accept that," the Contessa replied. "We wish you good luck in finding a suitable buyer."

Urbino had let the Contessa take the lead so far as they had arranged. Possle turned his head toward Urbino expectantly and with a condescending smile on his gaunt face.

"But perhaps you will reconsider selling them at all," Urbino said.

"What do you mean?"

"Perhaps you would be willing to give them to a Byron

collection. I could recommend the library at San Lazzaro degli Armeni."

"But that wouldn't be as convenient for you, would it? San Lazzaro, might be only a short boat ride away—gondola ride," he corrected, "but you would be competing with other scholars and with the good monks themselves, who would certainly want to publish them. The poems wouldn't be your exclusive possession. That arrangement would be a sad second best."

Urbino couldn't disagree. It was proving hard to give up the idea of having the poems for his own private and professional use. But at this thought, he had a twinge of conscience. He had to beware of his own form of greed. If not, any real distinction between Possle and himself would collapse, wouldn't it?

"But let me ask you this, Mr. Macintyre. If you believe that these poems are tainted, do they lose their taint if I give them away and get no money for them? Do your own hands remain clean if you take advantage of them under those circumstances? If you make it known, as you surely would, that you have been instrumental in bringing them out into the light? What difference does money make in that respect? It's a mere formality. You're both being overly scrupulous or should I call it hypocritical?"

The uneven quality of his voice, its combination of tremulousness and faintness and indistinct pronunciation, made it necessary for Urbino and the Contessa to strain to catch all his words.

When he finished, there was a moment of silence until the Contessa, after exchanging a look with Urbino, said with spirit, "I beg your pardon, Mr. Possle, I find that quite inappropriate."

"Inappropriate, you call it? And all the while some perfectly lovely and fascinating poems are waiting to be given life."

A self-satisfied expression settled on his sallow face. But Urbino's next question chased it away. "Do you know whether Adriana Abdon had an interest in Byron?"

Possle's face was now marked by puzzlement. It gave way to wariness and even fear. "Adriana Abdon?" Possle repeated in a low voice.

His eyes shot in the direction of the *sala*. No shadows except the ones cast from the candles and the fire were visible beyond the door. The large room beyond emitted no sound.

"Why do you bring her up?" Possle said. "And haven't I told you that Armando doesn't like to hear her name mentioned?"

"But Armando isn't in the house, is he?"

As soon as Urbino said this, he thought he detected a soft, stealthy tap against the floor of the *sala*. The Contessa didn't seem to have heard anything.

"But it's best not to fall into a dangerous habit."

"Why dangerous?" Urbino asked.

Possle gave a rictus of a grin. It had little, if any, humor in it. "Armando can become angry if he suspects that anyone is too free with her name or her memory. And in my position— well, it's best for me if he doesn't get angry, you see."

His eyes met Urbino's. In them Urbino read vulnerability and loneliness and great sadness. Urbino, uncomfortable and embarrassed and suddenly very sad himself, looked away. It was almost enough to make him reconsider what he was going to say next.

But burying the sympathy welling up within him, he pressed on. "You've said you never go down, Mr. Possle, but do you ever go up?"

"Up?"

The Contessa shifted uneasily in her seat and didn't look at either Urbino or Possle but at the candles arranged so precariously on the floor.

"Yes, to the upper floors? Especially the attic?"

Possle seemed genuinely puzzled. "What a strange question. You see my condition. And what concern is it of yours whether I go upstairs?"

"Not as much a concern of mine perhaps as it is of the Contessa."

Possle turned his small eyes on the Contessa.

"What does he mean?" he asked her.

She lifted her gaze from the floor. "I prefer that Mr. Macintyre explain."

"I prefer that *you* do."

The Contessa made no response.

"I'm referring to Adriana Abdon," Urbino said.

He inclined his head slightly toward the *sala*. Once again he thought he heard a stealthy step approach the door.

"I'm not sure whether you know or not," Urbino went on. "I believe you don't, but maybe you've suspected. Maybe some of those papers you have there are related to the boating accident. What they can say in all truth is that Mechitar and Zakariya Dilsizian drowned that day. Their bodies were found. But Adriana's body never was." He paused. "Adriana didn't drown that day off the Lido. And for the past five years she's been right with you in this building. Upstairs."

"Whatever are you talking about? Are you mad? Adriana here? Adriana alive? But Armando—but he couldn't—"

Possle pressed his hand against his chest. A violent cough shook his body. Alarmed, the Contessa jumped to her feet, grabbed the goblet of water, and rushed to the gondola. She leaned over Possle, who was jerking and shaking. Urbino approached the gondola. Possle's hands thrashed upward and knocked the goblet from the Contessa's grasp. It went flying and crashed against the iron *ferro*. Fragments of glass scattered in all directions. Possle seized the Contessa's shoulders.

Urbino fumbled for the cell phone and pressed the number to alert Gildo.

Footsteps, now rapid and loud on the bare floor of the *sala*, rushed toward the gondola room. Urbino and the Contessa, who was trying to disengage Possle's hands from her shoulders, turned in the direction of the footsteps.

A moment later a figure appeared at the threshold like a specter. The Contessa gasped. It was a woman. She was tall and emaciated, with long, black hair thickly streaked with gray and snaking out of a cloche hat with flowers. Her face was lined and wrinkled. The Contessa's lost tea dress, ripped and soiled, hung loosely from her frame. One end of the Regency scarf was tied around her neck like a noose. The cascade necklace shimmered against her shrunken chest.

Her eyes were red. They seemed to be rolling, until they fixed themselves on the Contessa, who had her hands on Possle's arms. Urbino started to put his body between the woman and the Contessa, but with a sudden lunge the woman sidestepped him and rushed to the gondola.

She pulled the Contessa violently away from Possle's grasp. The two women fell to the floor. Possle, who had suddenly stopped coughing as if shocked out of his fit, now lay frozen against the cushions, staring at the crazed woman as she seized the Contessa's throat. His mouth formed the word Adriana soundlessly.

Urbino grabbed Adriana by the shoulders. He strained to pull her away from the Contessa. She had the strength of a man. She finally released her grip and sprawled on the floor.

She scrambled to her four limbs. The dangling edge of the scarf brushed a candle flame. It caught fire. As she sprang up with a scream, she knocked against one of the tall candles. It tipped and fell into the gondola.

Within a few seconds the newspapers were ablaze. Possle beat his hands against the flames, but he only succeeded in spreading the fire to the sleeves of his jacket.

What happened next was a blur in Urbino's mind. His only concern was for the Contessa. He didn't see or hear Gildo enter the gondola room, but suddenly he was by Urbino's side. Urbino registered a pale, stricken face with eyes looking wildly around the room, then a pair of strong arms helping him to pick up the half-conscious Contessa.

Armando rushed past them toward the gondola. He moved more quickly than Urbino had ever seen him do. His lips were drawn back in a grimace of fear and rage.

Urbino and Gildo carried the Contessa out of the room, into the *sala,* and toward the stairs.

Urbino risked a look behind him. The doorway framed the fiery scene.

Possle was engulfed in flames, screaming. The woman reeled against the drapes, her hair on fire. The drapes burst into red and orange.

Armando stood between Possle and his sister. He threw back his head. An animal-like howl rose above the noise of the crackling flames and Possle's screams. Only Adriana, now a torch, was silent.

The gondola room became a crackling inferno.

Smoke and the odor of burning flesh filled Urbino's nostrils. His throat closed. His eyes watered. The heat was intense.

Urbino and Gildo, carrying their precious burden, made their way down the staircase and out into the blessedly cool, fresh air.

EPILOGUE
The Spoils of Florian's

"All those years," the Contessa said to Urbino as the two friends gazed out into the Piazza San Marco from their seats in the Chinese salon.

On this April afternoon the large space was more theatrical than sociable. Almost everyone seemed to have come either to be the center of someone else's attention or to indulge in calculated displays of enjoyment as they thronged beneath the arcades and milled around on the stones beneath a bright blue sky. Even the orchestra made its contribution in the form of a relentless stream of tunes and classics that were the popular fare of movie theaters and concert halls in almost every capital and province.

The scene was a far cry from its more serene state in February when the two friends had been troubled by the problems that had so strangely resolved themselves within the fiery walls of the Ca' Pozza.

The Contessa turned her eyes to Urbino, who was still staring into the Piazza. He had been abstracted ever since they had kept their rendezvous at their favorite perch.

"Did you hear me, *caro?*" the Contessa asked. "I was saying that it was such a long time for Adriana to be living up in the attic."

After taking a sip of sherry, he said, "My guess is that he committed her to a much less expensive rest home after the Villa Serena. For her to have lived for seven years in the attic without having been detected would have been quite a feat."

"Jane Eyre's Mr. Rochester managed to get away with it for longer than that, I think."

Urbino smiled. "I suppose he did. But I don't see that as having happened at the Ca' Pozza. Armando must have taken her somewhere else. Probably she wasn't there for very long."

"But how long is not very long? Something for you to find out?"

"I don't think so."

"But what about filling in all the gaps and answering all the questions?"

Urbino looked around the crowded, cozy room before responding with a shrug of his shoulders. "That's never been possible, not completely. And this time we're going to be left with more unanswered questions than usual. But I don't want to mislead you," he went on. "I've been trying to sort out a lot of things. Some of them might seem of little importance, but not to me."

The Contessa's silence was an encouragement for him to continue.

"Yes," he said, "I've got some black-and-white answers in one particular area. You know how much of what Possle said sounded suspiciously familiar. I made a list of all the suspects. I've found the source of most of them. He was a thief, but not all that more devious than the rest of us when it comes to originality." He paused. "But his thefts *were* original in a way. He made them his own." Urbino smiled ruefully. "That's what you said we did with Venice."

The Contessa, who had been trying unsuccessfully to pinpoint his mood this afternoon, asked with an air of concern, "How does it make you feel, though, not being able to fill in all the gaps?"

"Not as bad as I once thought it might. It's only a comfortable illusion anyway."

"What is?"

"That things can be tied up in a neat package with a pretty bow on it. Life's not that way."

"More the pity."

"Yes, well, it isn't, and I'm not sure we'd want it to be."

The Contessa considered for a moment. "Maybe you're thinking of what I said about the veiled lady," she came out with. "Having the cake of the mystery but eating the—the"—she struggled to complete the metaphor—"the solution, too, I suppose it would be," she finished.

The power of association, perhaps, rather than hunger, drew the Contessa to the plate of petits fours on the table. She selected a delicate oblong. Its mauve icing matched one of the colors in her multicolored Fortuny dress that had provided Urbino with one of his essential clues.

"But how do you feel about losing the poems?" she continued. "Not getting all the answers is one thing. Not getting the poems is another—if they existed."

"They existed. I have no doubts about that. Possle had them, and now they're gone, along with Possle, Armando, Adriana, and almost everything else in the Ca' Pozza."

The conflagration had spread rapidly and consumed most of the old building. It was the worst fire the city had seen since the one that had destroyed La Fenice. Nothing could be done to save Possle, Armando, or his sister after the fireboats had arrived. Urbino and the Contessa had been lucky to escape with Gildo's help.

"If only things had worked out differently," the Contessa said.

"It wasn't meant to be."

"I see Habib's influence on you more and more. Fate! There's a great deal to be said about accepting the inevitable instead of fighting against it." After a few moments she added, "Sickness, age, death."

She gave a soft pat to her hair. It had become a habitual gesture during the past week. After the singeing her hair had received in the fire, it had been cut and restyled into something shorter and sleeker than she usually wore. It became her.

"One minute Possle is scheming over how he's going to get enough money from the poems to keep him and Armando going for a while longer," Urbino said, extending the implications of the Contessa's comment, "and the next minute they have no more worries in this world."

"Nor in the one after, let's hope. Possle and Armando didn't murder anyone, did they?"

"No. The reports make it clear beyond any doubt that Mechitar and Zakariya drowned accidentally. Armando saved Possle, and Adriana saved herself. She was a good swimmer, according to what Demetrio Emo told me, much better than Armando. But it must have been a horror for him until he found out that she hadn't drowned. He seems to have made a choice between saving her and Possle."

He was spared the same decision at the Ca' Pozza last week. There was never any chance that he could have saved either of them, but only himself. Urbino would never forget the frantic look on the man's face and his guttural cry as he took in the situation and remained in the gondola room to share the doom of the others.

"But why didn't he tell Possle about Adriana?" the Contessa asked. "Not only that she hadn't drowned, but that she had gone back to the Villa Serena?"

"Yet another one of the questions," Urbino replied. "I'd say that it was something he wanted to do for his sister all by himself—look after her. Remember that Possle seems to have rejected Adriana's overtures before his marriage to Hilda and after their divorce. Armando must have assumed that

Possle wouldn't have been inclined to help. As it was, he was probably siphoning off money from the house for Adriana's expenses. Possle said that the money had been disappearing quickly. If he had only known why."

Urbino took a sip of his sherry before adding, "And then there's jealousy."

"Jealousy?"

"Possle's bond with Armando was very close. Cipri implied that Hilda had a story to tell there. I wish I had got it, but now . . ." He trailed off and gave a little shrug. "Possle would have resented the attention Armando was giving to Adriana. He needed almost all of it himself when his own world was becoming diminished. Yes, there were many reasons why Armando decided it might be best to keep it all a secret."

"But what was he thinking? Keep it a secret forever?"

"He did a pretty good job of it, didn't he?"

"Until you came along. Until *we* came along."

"Right. If neither of us had gone anywhere near the Ca' Pozza, she'd still be Armando's precious—and dangerous—secret. And still be alive."

"We can't think of that. And Possle set it in motion himself by asking you to come to see him," the Contessa pointed out. "Now you know why Armando felt animosity toward you from the beginning. You were endangering everything. Snooping around after Marco's death. He must have thought that was your main motivation. Thank God he didn't try to prevent you from coming, by doing something violent, I mean."

"He probably saw the good sense of not trying. If I had thought that anyone was trying to scare me or put me out of commission, it would have made me even more suspicious. And it would only have drawn attention to the house, given my reputation as a sleuth. He was relieved that Marco's death hadn't revealed his secret, but he was nervous about Elvira. I once thought that with her lovely voice she reminded him of his sister, but actually she was a danger and a constant reminder of what his sister had done to Marco. And if he had known that I had seen the belt and had discovered the clipping of you in his room—an illustrated item in Adriana's shopping list of your clothes, let's call it—he might have realized he had little to lose by going after me.

"We can be more clear about Adriana's responsibility for Marco's death, though," he continued. "With a madwoman's strength, she pushed him when he was trying to get in or out of the Ca' Pozza. Elvira might even have seen her do it. Everyone else but Armando thought Marco had fallen from Razzi's building. All of Elvira's hatred of the Ca' Pozza was because of Adriana, although she didn't know who she was."

"She thought Adriana was me," the Contessa said. "I'll never forget the look in her eye when she saw me in the cemetery."

"You understand now why she reacted the way she did. There you were, standing right over her son's grave. Up until then she had only caught glimpses of Adriana in the windows. Armando must have had some arrangement, some provision, to try to keep Adriana from drawing attention to herself in that way. She may have been showing herself more boldly than usual during the past few months. Possle said that he was seeing the faces of the dead, but faces looking very old. She could have been wandering around the house at will at times."

"And when Elvira saw her during the past few months, she was wearing my clothes. Such a brother, such a sister," the Contessa observed. "And twins, no less. Don't they say there's always a good and an evil twin?"

"I give no credence to that. And you know how I feel about categorizing people as good or evil."

"Despite the Jesuits who taught you so well?"

"Despite them, yes. Armando and Adriana were both emotionally disturbed, she more so than he, obviously."

"But it does seem as if the women are the ones to go mad, or *more* mad, not just Adriana but poor Elvira."

"She's been torn apart by grief. Once she fully grasps that you weren't responsible for Marco's death, but that it was Adriana, who's had a grisly form of justice, she should start to heal with the proper care. We have to do what we can to help her. And speaking of the fate of women, remember that there's a woman who's a survivor in all this—Hilda."

"The survivor of her beauty," the Contessa replied.

"But a woman who still creates," he pointed out. "That counts for a great deal."

"Of course it does," the Contessa agreed. "And she was wise to divorce Possle for whatever reason."

"Most likely all the frenetic activity and intrigues at the Ca' Pozza in those days took their toll on their intimacy and her need for quiet. And then there was Armando and his devotion to Possle. As I said, Cipri seemed to be insinuating a great deal when he observed that marriage doesn't suit all men. Hilda must have decided that it was better to cut herself loose from Possle and the Ca' Pozza. Eventually she retreated into her work and her life with Cipri on the Lido. She probably knew about the boating accident, of course, but not that Adriana had survived it."

"As for Adriana, evil or not," the Contessa said after a few moments of reflection, "she was the only one who brought blood to this case. She must have set the fire that killed their parents. Armando knew that she had done it, don't you think?"

"Yes, and their aunt's death seems suspicious as well."

Urbino looked at his wristwatch and then out into the square beyond the tables set up under the arcades.

"I still don't understand why she wanted my clothes," the Contessa said. "Why she wore them."

"You're wearing your Fortuny dress today, aren't you, the dress that seems to have been next on Adriana's list?"

"Yes, but . . ."

She looked down at the dress that had once belonged to the actress Eleonora Duse.

"Haven't you always said that there's something talismanic in it?" he went on. "That it can lift your spirits? Chase away clouds? And I think it's always ended up doing that in one way or another, hasn't it?"

The Contessa nodded in agreement.

"It's a form of superstition," he went on. "Adriana seems to have had it, too. The director of the Villa Serena mentioned how Armando brought Adriana a dress to wear when she left the clinic, a replica of one the director favored. Having your clothes could have made Adriana feel as if she had some power or victory over you, or maybe some of the power and influence you had. She wore your clothes, and she absorbed your energy."

"So now we're talking about vampires?"

"Remember, Barbara, that she must have resented that you studied at the conservatory when she couldn't. And you were on the scene when she first was hoping to marry Possle. Years pass and she sees you come up to the Ca' Pozza and ring the bell. And then you turn up inside the house in the gondola room with Possle. Within her madness, it was all logical."

"But why did she suddenly decide that she wanted my clothes?"

"There had been all those photographs of you in the local papers. We know Armando bought magazines and newspapers for the Ca' Pozza, obviously for her as much as for himself and Possle. Adriana saw the photographs and resented your visibility. She cut them out and told Armando to get the different pieces of clothing and jewelry."

Since the fire at the Ca' Pozza, the Contessa had discovered that she was missing a coral necklace, a blouse, and a pair of shoes that she had worn at a garden party late last summer. A group photograph of the occasion had appeared in the local Sunday supplement. The Contessa had also worn a snakeskin belt in the photograph. It wasn't, however, the one that she had discovered was missing. It would appear that Armando had become confused by the other belts and taken the wrong one.

"But why did she cut you out of the Palazzo Labia photograph?" the Contessa asked.

"There's no way of knowing if she did it or Armando. It could have been just a way of emphasizing what he had to steal or—who knows?—his way of taking out his resentment against me, if he was the one to scissor me out."

"Well, if he was, thank God that's as far as he went."

"And one more thing about all the publicity you've been getting. The photographs caught even Elvira's attention, and she recognized your tea dress. Adriana was wearing it when Elvira saw her in the attic window."

"To think that I was upset with you for neglecting my problem when all the while you were taking care of it behind the walls of the Ca' Pozza. Your obsession—well, that's what it was!—turns out to have been my own. What did we say when we were here in February? All for one and one for all? And being so inseparable?"

"Not just you and me, but Possle and Armando, and Armando and Adriana, up until the very end."

"And don't forget yourself and Possle! You can't fool me, *caro*. Part of your fascination was because he was similar to you. Or should I say it was part of, not only your fascination, but your fear as well?"

Urbino looked away. The Contessa didn't press the point. Instead she told him that she had decided to put in a full security system at the Ca' da Capo-Zendrini.

"Long overdue, I'm aware, and like locking the barn after the horses have got out. I can't shake the thought that Armando got in somehow, maybe more than once, and went creeping around my rooms and taking things for his sister! I should have faced it all before, but it didn't seem real, not the way it has since last week." She sighed.

"Ca' Pozza, Ca' Pazza," she recited. "It was the house of the madwoman all along."

Urbino consulted his watch again.

"Are you expecting someone?" the Contessa asked.

"Habib might drop by."

Habib had returned yesterday. The Contessa hadn't seen him yet.

She joined him in looking out into the square in search of the young Moroccan. The orchestra was playing the overture from Offenbach's *Orpheus in the Underworld*. Three blonde women, cheered on by friends and onlookers, were dancing the can-can to the familiar strains of the tune. The quiet days in Venice were over until the autumn.

"I'm starting to think of Asolo already," the Contessa said, showing how in tune she was with his own thoughts. "Far away from it all up in the hills."

"Soon enough," Urbino said.

The Contessa indulged in another petit four.

"So tell me, *caro,* are you going to write a book about Samuel Possle? You might not have learned much about the good old days of his expatriate life, but think of what you *did* learn! And you have a great ending. You could put together something different than usual."

"I'll let this one go, Barbara."

Yet his sigh betrayed that it wouldn't be easy.

"So you've come out with hardly any spoils at all. Not the poems and not a full picture of what happened. And now you say you're throwing away the idea of even writing about it?"

"But I've come away with a lot. Much more than you might think."

The Contessa stared. "Like knowing that some things are not worth going after? Like having seen the face in the mirror?

Like having confronted the ghost of the person you might have become?" she summed up, drawing together many of the threads of their conversation.

"All those things, and more."

"I'm not going to ask you to name them. I have a good idea of what they are. But what I am going to ask you is this," she added, with an amused look in her gray eyes. "If you ever have any more dreams with me in them, will you let me know? All I'll need to hear is the first sentence, whether it's 'Last night I dreamt of Manderley again' or whatever it might be," she said referring to the Du Maurier novel and the Hitchcock film that Urbino had recently been reminded of in Rebecca's office. "When I hear it, I'll promptly run as far away from you as possible. Who knows what we could avoid!"

"Nothing," he responded dryly.

He had barely got this out when the Contessa cried, "Habib!"

At first Urbino thought that her cry was in response to his fatalistic philosophy, reinforced by his relationship with the superstitious Habib. But the Contessa's excited exclamation had been provoked by the young man's entrance into the Chinese salon. The North African sun had darkened Habib's face in the weeks he had been away. He gave them his radiant smile.

In his hands was a small box wrapped in paper with an arabesque design and tied with a green ribbon and bow.

He seated himself beside Urbino.

"This is for you," he said to the Contessa.

"Aren't you a sweet boy! It seems I *am* getting my neatly wrapped package after all." She threw an amused glance at Urbino. "May I open it now?"

"You must!"

"Well, since it's a question of must . . ."

As she carefully removed the ribbon and paper, Habib said, "I collected it from customs an hour ago. They unwrapped it and I had to do it all over again. That's why I'm late."

"All good things are worth waiting for," the Contessa said, "and I mean you and not the—oh my, look at this!"

She held up a necklace of cascading silver ovals. Murmurs of admiration came from a nearby table.

"It's my necklace! Its twin! Its double! Aren't you a clever boy, Habib! Thank you so much. Let me give you a kiss."

She leaned over and kissed Habib on each cheek.

"May God protect you when you wear it," Habib said.

The Contessa was already putting it on. It suited her Fortuny dress.

"Only when I wear it?" she teased.

Habib looked in confusion at Urbino for clarification as he so often did.

"She loves it," Urbino said.

Habib smiled.

"And I love you, both of you!" the Contessa said. "May God protect us all."

She caught the attention of the waiter.

"*Cosa desidera?*" he asked when he came over.

"What I would like is a Coppa Fornarina for our young friend here." As the waiter was moving away, she said, "Excuse me, on second thought, bring us three."

As they waited for the concoctions of maroon-and-cherry-garnished *gelato* named after Byron's lover, the Contessa said, "It's a much safer way to indulge one's interest in Lord Byron."

Once again Habib looked at Urbino for help.

"She's joking again," Urbino said, "but as usual her joke is full of truth."

He began to explain, all the while exchanging a warm, conspiratorial smile with the Contessa.